Praise for *Midnight on the Celestial*

"I devoured *Midnight on the Celestial* like a five-star buffet on a haunted cruise ship. Never have I read anything like this glittering, gothic debut. Alexandra threads silk and horror into every scene, spinning a decadent critique of wealth, power, and the consequences of spectacle. I couldn't look away." —Mikayla Bridge, author of *Of Flame and Fury*

"Vivid and captivating! Exquisite horror haunts the halls of the *Celestial* cruise ship, where nothing is as it seems. Alexandra enchants with dark secrets and a simmering mystery that kept me gasping all the way to the last page." —Leslie Vedder, bestselling author of the Bone Spindle trilogy

"Darkly magnetic and twisty, *Midnight on the Celestial* sweeps you onboard its titular ship and won't set you free. Alexandra exquisitely weaves mystery, class prejudice, found family, and romance into her compelling heroine's unraveling of a dangerous secret. A propulsive debut that will have readers turning the pages long past midnight." —Shalini Abeysekara, *Sunday Times* bestselling author of *This Monster of Mine*

"Welcome aboard the most deliciously immersive ride you'll never want to end. *Midnight on the Celestial* has everything you could want. Dazzling magic, swoony romance, tension-filled mystery, and hints of horror. Julia Alexandra has crafted an enchanting debut." —Dana Swift, author of *Cast in Firelight*

"An imaginative tale about the difference between having power and hoarding it, *Midnight on the Celestial* combines a spirited heroine, a spooky ship, and a skilled found family into an immersive and unique debut adventure you need on your shelves." —Kamilah Cole, Lodestar Award finalist and bestselling author of the Divine Traitors duology

MIDNIGHT ON THE CELESTIAL

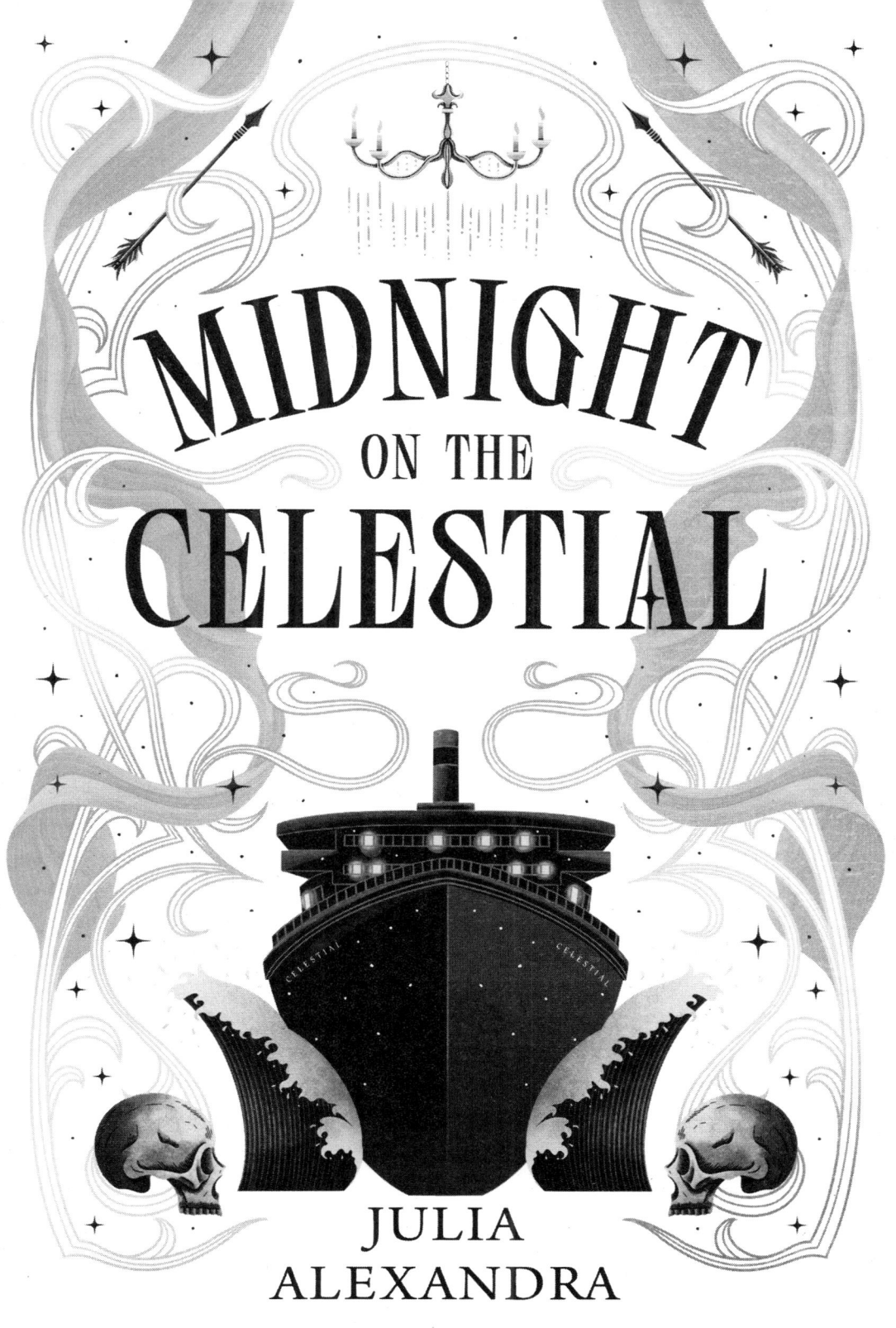

First published 2026 in the US by Wednesday Books

First published 2026 in the UK by First Ink,
an imprint of Pan Macmillan
The Smithson, 6 Briset Street, London EC1M 5NR
EU representative: Macmillan Publishers Ireland Ltd, 1st Floor,
The Liffey Trust Centre, 117–126 Sheriff Street Upper, Dublin 1 D01 YC43
Associated companies throughout the world

ISBN 978-1-0350-7112-8

Copyright © Julia Alexandra 2026

The right of Julia Alexandra to be identified as the author of this work has been asserted in accordance with the Copyright, Designs and Patents Act 1988.

All rights reserved. No part of this publication may be reproduced, stored in a retrieval system, or transmitted, in any form, or by any means (including, without limitation, electronic, mechanical, photocopying, recording or otherwise) without the prior written permission of the publisher.

Pan Macmillan does not have any control over, or any responsibility for, any author or third-party websites (including, without limitation, URLs, emails and QR codes) referred to in or on this book.

1 3 5 7 9 8 6 4 2

A CIP catalogue record for this book is available from the British Library.

Printed and bound in the UK using 100% Renewable Electricity by CPI Group (UK) Ltd
Designed by Jen Edwards

This book is sold subject to the condition that it shall not, by way of trade or otherwise, be lent, hired out, or otherwise circulated without the publisher's prior consent in any form of binding or cover other than that in which it is published and without a similar condition including this condition being imposed on the subsequent purchaser.
The publisher does not authorize the use or reproduction of any part of this book in any manner for the purpose of training artificial intelligence technologies or systems.
The publisher expressly reserves this book from the Text and Data Mining exception in accordance with Article 4(3) of the European Union Digital Single Market Directive 2019/790.

Visit **www.panmacmillan.com** to read more about all our books and to buy them.

For Caitlyn

No one has longed for magic more than the two of us. We found it in the pages of books, and now, because of you, someone will find it in the pages of mine.

This book has always belonged to the both of us.

PRELUDE

We are swept into a sea of dancers, the desperation and terror that has become our daily uniform buried in the tide of one night of freedom. The faces of the people I've come to know, to care and fight for, warm me like the rush of my magic.

"How can you dance when everyone's watching?" he says, bending down to my ear.

An unbidden wave of heat prickles along my skin at how close his mouth is to my cheek. *So the performer gets stage fright offstage.* "Pretend you're onstage. You can criticize my foot placement to make it feel more real for you."

"Very funny."

I twirl myself under his arm, pressing close to his chest. He may be all sure of himself with the guests, but around me, he's shy. There's something frustratingly attractive about that. The truth is, once he finds the courage to dance with me, he's much better than he knows. The muscles of his arms and the effortless flexibility of his legs and spine outpace my stiffer movements I learned from formal dancing at our estate's balls. He whirls me around the dance floor and makes it feel like we're flying.

For a moment, I swear we are.

Until I hear the screams.

CHAPTER 1

Father hosts a yearly soiree where I summon every dead person in the province.

The festivities flood the ballroom of Father's grand estate, and I'm the party trick. Even now, as I stare out from the dais over the mass of guests in their finery, I wonder how many more spirits I have left to bring back. Twenty, maybe thirty, if some of our guests expect both grandparents. I look forward to this all year, but I'm also starving.

Father's servants have pulled out all the stops, as they often do. The rich mahogany floors of Damarcus Estate gleam like a mirror's surface. Gold chandeliers hang from the arched wooden rafters, lighting the banquet table. A maroon tablecloth stretches under the weight of platters of roast chicken, decanters of wine I'm not allowed to drink when Mother's looking, and towering trays of chocolate truffles filled with raspberry sauce.

Those are my favorites, though I doubt I'll get any before midnight. The line to the dais is almost out the door. I crane my neck, surveying the guests crammed in front. A forced smile tugs at my lips, and I smooth the front of my dress to mask twitching fingers. I wasn't expecting this many people.

Mother places her hand on my arm, digging gold nails into my skin. "Rosaline, take Lady Sandralyn's hand."

My lips purse at Mother's clipped tone and her insistence on using my full name for the evening. But one look from Father's scrutinizing brown eyes and lowering bushy brows assures me now is not the time to argue with her.

It's an important night for the Damarcus family. I know that better than anyone.

Lady Sandralyn stands on the step below me and reaches out to grasp my hand. My insides writhe when I think of her clammy palm in mine, but the momentary repulsion is necessary. I close my eyes, arm steady as our fingers clasp. The electric spark of her life flows from her veins to mine. Her hand trembles with the fear and awe trapped beneath her skin. The dizzying exhilaration of summoning takes over me. Heat builds in my fingertips and races up my arms. The comforting warmth gathers in my chest, expanding with each breath I take.

Nothing feels better than this.

"Who do you want to see?" My words come out soft, but sudden nerves flutter in my stomach like caged fireflies. Where is this coming from? I'm never nervous. Then again, this could be my last Resurrection Ball. Pushing the thought as far down as it will go, I open my eyes to look at Lady Sandralyn. Father tells me this puts non-Morphics at ease. *Let them look in your eyes and see that you appear human before showing them you're not*, he often says.

"I want to see my father," Lady Sandralyn murmurs, a whispered secret between the two of us. "He . . . he died last year." She swallows hard. "I'm sorry. I've never done this before. Should I tell you what he looks like?"

"No need." The bonds between family are stronger than with any other deceased spirits. Without warning, my eyes drift to the family portrait on the far wall across from the dais. It stretches from ceiling to floor. My gaze lingers there.

Easy to bring back family members as long as they're not mine.

My palm heats, itching with the energy of Lady Sandralyn's life force. I dig deeper and search through every particle for the bright connection to her father. I cannot afford any mistakes tonight. Panic claws up my throat as I reach for him, but I force myself to stay calm. Relief eases the tension in my shoulders as the familiar pull of the spirit beckons me. There he is. A hot bubble of fire in her cool energy.

A floating sensation makes it feel like I'm lifting off the ground, but I'm still standing in uncomfortable four-inch heels. Wisps of glowing white light burst from my clasped hand, and a body takes shape.

The spirit of a man stands beside Lady Sandralyn, but he appears solid and lifelike.

Lady Sandralyn sucks in a sharp breath, and her eyes brim with tears. The crowd gasps and erupts into applause upon seeing the emergence of yet another spirit. Father beams, eyes shining with pride. I bask in this moment, letting the warm tingle of admiration wash over me. It's not only the adrenaline pumping through my limbs or the warm gaze of my father that makes me look forward to this all year. It's the way I control this moment. The power I wield on this night fills me with more satisfaction than any drink or delectable truffle ever could.

But I watch closely. When resurrected spirits stay for too long, their solid forms begin to rot. Their bodies stink, and they take on the wounds of their last moments of life. That tends to scare the guests, so I cut the interactions before they get to that point.

"Thank you, Lady Roe. Thank you," Lady Sandralyn says, relieved.

The spirit of her father places his hands on his hips. "What happened with my estate?" He narrows his eyes at his daughter. "You better not have let your husband make those renovations."

Good, this spirit feels like talking. Sometimes they don't.

After a few minutes, Mother clinks her nails against the green hourglass on the small table beside us. "Time's up," she says. Lady Sandralyn won't see her father again until next year. I roll my shoulders back and lift my chin as Lady Sandralyn leaves. There *will* be a next year. I force myself to think it. I've proved myself thus far tonight.

Father places his hand on my shoulder. He smiles, laugh lines crinkling around his eyes. Not everyone gets to see this side of Lord Cyrion Damarcus. He's one of those people who saves his smiles for those who earn them. "You're doing beautifully, Roe." He hands me a round glass bottle with indigo liquid inside. My cheeks heat, but I snag it from him, hoping our guests won't notice. I've been taking this concoction each night at dinner to steady my nerves and focus while summoning, but it's embarrassing to need it.

My father's gift as an alchemer allows him to create potions that aid with a variety of ailments. Before Father found the right mix of ingredients, I became overwhelmed and unable to stop unwanted spirits from bursting forth and following me throughout the day. This was a nuisance at home and rather disturbing in public—spirits don't always look pleasant.

I swallow the indigo potion and relish the familiar taste of warm cinnamon and the tingling in my nostrils as it sizzles down my throat. My nerves from this evening give it a bitter aftertaste. "You've been up here long enough." Father takes my empty glass and kisses my cheek. He waves his arm over the line of guests and indicates the crowded dance floor. "Take a break."

"Thank you." I curtsy to the long line of strangers and acquaintances. Anytime I bring back a whole host of spirits, I pay with deathmares. I definitely won't sleep tonight. That's the way it is with Morphia. Every power has a price.

Our guests do their best not to groan, but they've waited over an hour. Let them wait.

I descend the dais, careful of my heavy maroon skirt, and do all I can not to race to the refreshment table. The best I manage is a fast walk across the dance floor. I stop at the table and drink two glasses of sparkling berry punch and grab a handful of truffles before I realize who I'm standing beside.

I curse internally but plaster a wide smile on my face. "Having a good time, Eliza?"

"Yes," she answers as she folds her hands over her lilac bodice. Her light brown hair bobs as she nods. I've always been jealous of her perfect brown ringlets and light blue eyes, but that sneer she's got on her face is all Mother. She can keep that. Sparkling sapphire jewels decorate her long, sheer sleeves. With my gold beaded bodice reflecting the light of the chandelier, the two of us must look like a constellation of stars. Neither of us hold back on fancy occasions.

And tonight is more than a fancy occasion. Tonight, Father reminds everyone why he is Lord of Damarcus Estate and a member of the High Council. Tonight, we celebrate my eighteenth year of life and the impending trial that comes with it.

I swallow hard and shove the fear as far down as it will go, grateful for the potion helping me focus. Eliza won't get to see me shatter.

"I hope you're having a good time, dear sister," she says. "After all, it may be your last."

Her choker is tied so tight it threatens to sever her windpipe. If only. My fingers pulverize the small napkin in my hand, but I won't let her ruin this for me. Annoyance contorts my words into a sharp-edged hiss. "Let's not do this now. Come stand on the dais with me."

Eliza scoffs and pops a dark chocolate–coated strawberry into her mouth. The rosy undertones of her pale cheeks flush bright red. "Please. They don't care about non-Morphics. You're the one they want."

I don't say the words burning like fire in my mouth. She could've been like me. She could heal broken bones and cure sickness with her tears, but she gave up her life as a mender. Voluntarily.

She peers down at me. She may be a lady, but she's got the intensity of a hurricane and she turns it on me. "I'm surprised you're acting so calm about all this. You have two days left until your trial. Less than that, really. Aren't you worried?"

Her voice lifts on the last word. She's loving this. Usually, she can't get to me, but she knows I care about my gift. If I fail my trial, the High Council will strip the Morphia from my body. I'll never resurrect again . . .

A spike of fear cuts through the buffer of contentment the soiree creates for me. I long to plunge into the sea of dancing bodies, allow the expensive silks to sweep me up as the protective cocoon of tonight forms around me.

I grab a chicken drumstick with silver tongs and ignore her. The servants would give me looks if I grabbed it with my hands. I sigh, feigning indifference. "All I have to do is prove to the judges my Morphia isn't dangerous. It's not too hard."

Eliza crosses her arms over her chest, reveling in the crack in my enjoyment. She leans in so close I can smell her wisteria perfume. "Reginald's coming over to dance with you. Enjoy the rest of your night."

This time, I curse aloud. Reginald's the son of a gem miner and *very* proud of it. I'm proud of my father too. He's the only Morphic on the council, but I try not to work it into every conversation.

Reginald bows low before me, fluffy hair bouncing as he inclines his head. He holds out his hand, gemstone rings gleaming in the candlelight. "My father said I should ask you for a dance. As he's an incredibly intelligent man, I'd be a fool not to listen to him. As would you, Rosaline Damarcus." He clears his throat and adjusts the buttons of his crushed blue velvet coat.

I struggle to keep my lip from curling in disgust and take his hand to silence him. "Thank you, Sir De'Lacy. I'd be honored." The words come out half choked and taste bitter in my mouth.

"Take my handkerchief before we go. You have chocolate on your face." He pets my arm with fingers greasy from eating roast chicken. "If people see you dancing with me, you'll want to look your best."

The waxed mahogany dance floor creaks with the weight of a hundred dancers. People come from all over our province for this ball, traveling for days in over-packed carriages for a single night of resurrection. With my trial looming, Father says my gift has even attracted wealthy families from the northernmost provinces of Tamarynth. Most of them are on the dance floor now, red-faced and laughing. They're drunk on the thrill of seeing their dead come back to life.

It's all wondrously normal for me. Like breathing or blinking, I don't think about it. Except when it doesn't work. My eyes drift back to the family painting on the wall.

"You stepped on my foot."

"Sorry," I mutter. Reginald smells of garlic and grease, and I breathe to the side. I drag him to the right side of the dance floor, where there are vast glass windows. Being closer to the starlight and sweeping green hills of the front lawn gives me my breath back.

Reginald's hand moves down the bare skin of my shoulder blades and settles on the small of my back. "Imagine my powerful family name at the end of yours."

I shrink away from his touch. The soft chords of violin music envelop us. Damn. It's a slow song. I'll be lucky to make it out of here without a unity proposal.

Through the windows, I glimpse a spirit outside until I realize the apparition is me.

Thick, dark auburn hair hangs down my back, swinging with each turn. Pale skin glows back at me, corpse-like in the window. When I look down at my real body, the ghostly illusion shatters with the constellation of freckles dotting my arms.

Picture-perfect, but there's a gaping hole in my chest. Even as I try to enjoy myself, a hollow pit threatens to consume me. Is this my life if I fail my trial? Dancing with men and women, trying to decide whose ornament I'd like to become?

Easy for Eliza. She's always wanted to teach at a boarding school like Mother did before she moved on to summer semesters at the University of Credence. Their goals are different from mine. Much different. And—

When did Reginald put his hand on my ass? With ladylike grace, I squeeze his shoulder until he has no choice but to raise his hand or lose the arm. I'm torn between wanting to run from the dance floor or smack him in the face. Both are equally appealing.

My eyes sweep the room, settling on a tall young man wearing a deep emerald-green coat at the edge of the dance floor. He bobs along with the music; a tattoo of a spider is etched into the warm brown skin of his neck. A gold pin of a hawk in flight fastened to his lapel marks him as a member of the esteemed Morphic hunters.

Jasper cranes his neck to lock eyes with me, but his lopsided smile slips when my eyes widen in a silent urge for him to hurry.

He shoves through the crowd to get to me, treading on toes and jostling men of high standing.

"Roe," he says, pushing Reginald aside and holding his hand out to me, "I'd love a dance if you're game." I allow him to pull me away from a disgruntled Reginald. Jasper swings me in a lavish twirl. "Thought you needed rescuing, kid."

Jasper will always call me kid, even when I'm fifty. He's twenty-five now. The same age Leith should be. His soft eyes remind me so much of my brother that I want to cry. I force myself to look over Jasper's shoulder and focus on the family portrait. There he is. Forever eighteen.

Leith had blue eyes like a sky after a storm and dark brown hair cut short. He stood as tall as Father and had the long eyelashes and sly smile of his mother. We may have been half siblings, but Leith was never half anything. A golden pin in the portrait marks him as a member of the Hawks, just like Jasper.

As a Hawk, he hunted and imprisoned rogue, dangerous Morphics. Morphics who escaped their failed trials and fled. Morphics who hurt other people with their abilities. He always said he did it for Eliza and me. The two people he loved more than anything. *I don't want anyone to be afraid of you*, he'd say to me. *That's why we take the bad ones. You're not like them.*

But I've never been able to resurrect him, to talk to him again. Leith doesn't come to me like the other spirits do.

Jasper pokes me in the ribs. "Quit daydreaming." He looks over his shoulder and follows my gaze. "I know he'd want you to relax a little. He always said your gift was beautiful."

"Not just beautiful." I lift my chin, emboldened by my successes in summoning this evening. "I could be useful. I'd bring back victims the dangerous Morphics killed, talk to them. They can help us track rogue Morphics."

Jasper spins me around and dips me, incorporating some fancy footwork as a few girls watch us. "Not this again." He stops and pulls me to the side. I set my jaw, preparing for another warning. "Joining the Hawks is dangerous. You know that better than anyone. Besides, it's not me you have to convince. It's your dad."

I'm about to roll my eyes hard enough for Mother to sense it across the room when a hand lands on my shoulder. "It's time," Father says to me.

With one last stomp on Jasper's foot, I follow Father back to the dais. The people in line, who've been talking quietly and sipping drinks, straighten when they see me coming. I ascend the steps, wishing I'd eaten more than a few truffles. My legs quiver beneath me, and the dryness in my mouth makes it difficult to swallow. The usual pride I feel from summoning is replaced with the unfamiliar urge to tear from the room without looking back.

Father places his arm over my shoulders and squeezes, addressing the crowd. The music putters to a stop. I straighten my spine. "As always, thank you for coming. This is a very special time for our family, and I'm so grateful you all get to be a part of it. We have some guests from all nine provinces of Tamarynth tonight, but I know the residents of my province of Credence are especially excited for Roe to pass her trial. I'm certain she will take her place on the High Council one day."

Cheers erupt, and I should smile, but a wave of dizziness makes me unsteady. Father's words regarding the importance of tonight echo in my skull, thundering so loud that the applause fades to a dull buzz. As a man approaches me, I grab his hand but can't focus on his energy. I'm distracted by the nauseating texture of a callus by his thumb. Perhaps I should have taken a second dose of Father's potion. I know this man but can't think of his name. He's asking to see his late wife.

Jumbled thoughts cram my brain, making me sweat. It's hard to breathe. Why is it so hot up here? The small, cruel voice comes back, sounding too much like Eliza. I could fail my trial, and if I do, they might take my Morphia. Or worse: They might send me to the *Celestial*—a place more dangerous than prison for Morphics.

Wisps of silver light shoot from my palm in blinding rays. I can't control it. My chest heaves with the strain of trying to hold back. I've *never* lost control like this before. It's as if my nerves from this evening have finally broken free, a wild energy eager to escape my tenuous grasp. The body of a dead woman stands before us, not solid and rosy-cheeked the way she should be.

Rotting flesh clings to the protruding bones of the woman's shoulders, and her cracked yellow teeth part as she opens her mouth. Oozing black goop drips from her eyes onto her stained nightgown. Translucent skin stretches over her arms, but chunks of flesh are missing from her neck and collarbone.

The scent of decomposing corpse hits the room, and people slap handkerchiefs over their noses. Guests run for the doors.

The dead woman trembles, clutching frail arms to her bleeding chest.

She yells at her husband, slimy spittle running down her chin. "I was sleeping, Derrick! You woke me up, and now it hurts again." She moans as blood blooms on the front of her nightgown.

People scream. She can't hurt anyone. She's not solid, but none of our guests consider that. I freeze, unable to make myself move. With my mouth as dry and brittle as her exposed bone, I can't form the reassuring words racing through my head. *She can't hurt you. She can't touch you.* My chest is so tight I can't take a breath. I can't make the magic stop no matter how much I want to.

I'm not used to seeing the guests' unbridled horror, and the fear of what they think of me immobilizes my mind and body.

Father pinches my arm. "Stop this. It's going to be okay, but you have to stop."

Eliza's smirking face peers back at me from the crowd. I close my eyes and sever the connection, like cutting a string. But it's too late.

The faces staring back at me are wide-eyed and gagging behind handkerchiefs. They're all thinking it, just as I am. I've never believed it until now.

My trial is in two days, and I could fail.

CHAPTER 2

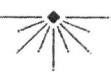

Most children who ruin celebratory balls might be punished with a day of answering their father's letters from disgruntled Tamarynth residents or sorting their mother's twenty-pound Morphic history books.

My father offers me a hunt.

My rain-sodden cloak hangs like a leaden weight across my shoulders. The moist smell of damp earth mingling with wet horsehair tingles in my nostrils. I relish the sensations of the forest. Although I wish I'd gotten the chance to braid my hair and eat breakfast, I don't complain about the early hour.

This is the first time Father has let me ride with the Hawks. Although he's made it clear he expects me to spend the next few years learning from him about what it takes to sit on the council, he's starting to come around to the idea that I may have a future with the Hawks. Letting me go on this hunt is his way of saying he *might* agree to my joining in a few years. I just have to figure out a way to convince him I'm ready now.

His words from this morning come back to me and replace my initial surge of excitement with a stone sinking in my gut. *This is not a punishment, nor is it a reward. What happened last night cannot happen again. This hunt will show me and the Hawks you're ready to start training with them.*

Even if Father lets me train, I'll be lucky to spend one evening a week with the Hawks. If he gets his way, I'll spend the majority of my days shadowing him in his council duties and the rest, attending university. Although I've tried to argue that Leith started training seven days a week when he was sixteen and became a full-fledged Hawk at eighteen, Father reminds me Leith didn't make it through his first year. As if I need that reminder.

Grayson leads our group of hunters atop his broad gray stallion. He hasn't looked at me once since we rode out before dawn. No longer all lanky limbs and shy grins, twenty-five-year-old Grayson Caddel has filled out with muscle. His hair glistens dark gold, and his pale skin has splotches of pink from the cold rain. I catch a flash of his green eyes as he throws a glance over his shoulder, a gaze that reminds me of the sensitive eighteen-year-old boy I used to see in Leith's company every day.

"No Morphia on this hunt. I mean it, Roe."

Gray may have been my brother's former lover, but that doesn't mean he plans on giving me special treatment. It's been seven years since Leith died, and Gray's lost the carefree smile he used to have when he and my brother would steal away into the barn together. His warning chips away at my confidence, frigid as the icy rain pelting the back of my neck.

I incline my head in a stiff acknowledgment but turn my attention back to the forest. I ride a dark bay Thoroughbred with one hand on the reins and the other on the arrows in my quiver. At the slightest sound, I prepare to draw one. I don't care that all the Hawks snicker at me.

"Careful," Jasper croons, letting go of the reins to wave his arms. "There could be an attack at any moment."

If he were closer, I'd knock him off his horse, but some of the Hawks are less accustomed to me than Gray and Jasper. After my brother died, many of his friends took me under their wing, but not every hunter appreciates their powerful boss's teenaged daughter coming along on a mission. They'll need to start seeing me as one of them. No better time than under a cloudy gray sky with rain plastering our hair to our faces.

Several of the Hawks sneak nervous glances in my direction. Many were in attendance last night and witnessed my disastrous performance. I fight the sag of my shoulders under the weight of their suspicion. I can't let them see their doubt bothers me.

A piercing scream sounds a few paces ahead of me, yanking me from my thoughts. Although the sharp shriek makes my hair stand on end, none of the Hawks stir. My heart threatens to stop beating as I fight to stay calm. My horse shifts beneath me and exhales a nervous snort. The scream comes from a woman riding on horseback ahead of us. She's lost control of the reins and narrowly misses colliding with a tree.

The girl locks eyes with me, and the fear in her ice-blue gaze is almost enough for me to gallop forward to help her. But before I can react, the horse missteps and the girl tumbles onto the ground. Her shout of surprise is followed by the wet smack of her skull colliding with a rock. Blood seeps into the dirt as the horse sprints away. When no one else reacts, I slowly realize this is nothing more than a waking deathmare. I take deep breaths to remind myself it's not real.

The worst part of the deathmare closes in at the end. Spirits reach out to me, smothering me with their hands as they try to use me to visit the mortal world. I cannot move, and I'm grateful my horse keeps pace with the other Hawks while I try to calm myself. It's been fourteen years of deathmares, and I still can't stand the feeling of skin against mine.

When I use my Morphia and summon spirits, I pay in waking deathmares or horrific deathmare dreams while I'm asleep. The worst part is, sometimes I can't tell if they're real.

This time, a dark thought seizes hold of my mind and won't let go. I don't want to see a stranger die in the forest that stole my brother from me. The bitter sting of disappointment lingers. It's like a cruel joke to see another person's death in these woods. As if the forest is sending me a reminder that no matter how much I want it to, it will never show me Leith.

"So, what do we know about this Morphic?" I ask, desperate to redirect my thoughts from the woman's glassy stare and slack-jawed mouth.

One of the young women smirks. She urges her horse forward. "We know he's destined for a nice, long stay in Malachite Prison."

The Hawks break into a trot. We weave between tall trees with glistening green leaves and spiderwebs dappled with raindrops. Mud and rocks squelch underfoot. I suppress my shudder and try to pass it off as a reaction to the cold.

Malachite is the prison for Morphics who run from their trials or commit crimes. I've never been, but Father tells me it's a frightening place. Since he works closely with the Hawks, our estate isn't far from the prison. Mother talks about how unsafe it is every other night at dinner. *I don't care how thick the forest is, Cyrion. It would take those prisoners less than an hour to get to us. Think of the children*, she'd say through gritted teeth.

I clear my throat. "I meant, what's he done?"

Gray holds up a closed fist, indicating for us to stop. He swings his leg over his horse, patting its flank as he dismounts. He crouches, examining a pair of footprints embedded in the mud. "A mender," he answers, standing and swinging back up onto his horse. "He's been luring families with false promises. Takes their money but doesn't heal anyone."

Frustration tightens in my gut. Morphia magic is sacred to me, and I can't stand when someone uses it to hurt others. It's Morphics like him who make people afraid of us. All menders should technically complete two years of service in their province's infirmaries, which I'm guessing he skipped too.

"Don't worry," Jasper says to me. "We've got him now."

As if on cue, Gray brings his fist down fast. The Hawks draw bows and arrows, galloping forward with only the strength of their knees to keep them from falling. Morphic crafters enchant their arrows to fly as fast as the bullets from a pistol. They can enhance weapons, but their magic fades. Father wishes the Hawks would carry pistols, but the council thinks there's some sort of justice in having rogue Morphics taken down by their own weapons.

I urge my horse into a gallop and pull an arrow back on my bowstring. My blood pumps with adrenaline.

A man wearing a deep green cloak and torn trousers weaves among the trees on foot. The labored gasps of his breathing and the snap of twigs are the only sounds he makes as he runs. Gray raises his voice and orders the man to stop.

He doesn't.

We're gaining on him, but he has a major head start. Another sound floods my ears. A sound I don't think Gray recognizes for what it is. The crash of a large body of water slamming into rocks. We're close to the divide between Credence and Windmere Provinces, which means he's heading for . . .

"Damn," Jasper yells. "He's heading for Windmere Falls."

The woman scoffs and releases her bow to clutch the reins. "He wouldn't jump, would he?"

The man runs in a straight line toward the sound of water. Gray holds out his hand as we ride hard to catch him, but the undergrowth's thicker and the rocks more slippery. "Don't shoot! We catch him unharmed unless we have no other choice."

Jasper coughs. "I think we're coming up on no other choice."

Without waiting for Gray's signal, a Hawk to my right releases an arrow. It's a narrow miss. Another arrow from somewhere behind me grazes the man's leg. I grimace at the spatter of blood and the way it reminds me of the deathmare woman's cracked skull.

Before I can stop to think, my body heats. The chill from the rain leaves me as my arms tingle with white-hot energy. I catch a swift shake of Gray's head as he realizes what I'm about to do, but he can't stop me. This is what I'm good at—made for, even. I close my eyes, allowing my horse to guide me. The blues and grays of the realm beyond life call to me, and I reach for a spirit.

Sorry, Gray, but you'll thank me later. Wispy silver threads of light spring from my fingertips and shoot through the trees. Concentrating, I pull the spirit with me and throw it down in the fugitive mender's path.

A vast oak tree falls from the sky, landing with an echoing boom in front of the mender. The dead oak slams into the ground, and I hold on to the image. I focus on the rough brown bark and the sticky sap embedded in its grooves. I'm not limited to human life energies.

Please don't turn into a corpse tree. It needs to look real.

The Hawks scream in surprise, and the man skids to a stop. He doesn't realize it's not solid. He stops long enough for our horses to reach him. Gray jumps from his mount and clasps crafter-made bindings around his wrists.

My first prisoner.

The man begs the Hawks to free him. The sound sends a sharp pang through my navel. He may have been swindling people, but who knows what they'll do to him at Malachite Prison. I send up a prayer to the Riveners that they'll watch over him. Riveners guide spirits across the divide between this world and the after, but they also watch over us in life. I have to hope they'll spare some mercy for this man. At Malachite, prison guards could siphon the Morphia out of him against his will and lock the jars of his magic away on the *Celestial* cruise ship. It's what could happen to me if I fail my trial.

A feeling like cold skeletal hands wrapping around my throat holds my voice captive. I throw up a prayer for myself too. With any luck, the Riveners will take pity on a girl who also bridges the gap between the living and the dead.

I leap from my horse and follow Gray toward the prisoner. Gray mutters harsh words under his breath, avoiding my eyes. Jasper prods the man in the back until he seats himself atop Jasper's horse. The man's eyes shine with unshed tears.

An urge to grab his hand overtakes me. It's an odd sensation as I'm usually uncomfortable with physical touch from resurrection, but his misery seeps from him in tangible waves. The pressure in my navel spreads to my chest.

Tomorrow, this could be me. The thought propels me to take one step closer to the man atop Jasper's horse. "How could you do this?" he spits, his tears hardening to anger. "To your own kind?" He knows the tree was mine. The bark has started to decay into crumbling gray flakes and smells of acrid rot.

The man lunges forward, revealing a knife tucked away in his boot. I gasp as the glint of silver cuts toward my chest. He wields it with two hands, catching the edge of my cloak. The Hawks around me notch arrows, but only one flies.

I stumble backward as an arrow pierces the man's upper arm. A woman with long black hair unbound rides toward us on the back of a massive chestnut mare. She lowers a large bow. The prisoner slumps, the arrow sticking out of his shoulder.

Lysandra Jamison pulls back on the reins and skids to a stop beside us. "Careful there, wild girl."

"Are you okay?" Gray asks. Any anger he harbored toward me for disobeying him dissolves. When I nod without speaking, he looks to Lysandra. "She's not coming with us to the prison. Will you see her home safe?"

The knot in my stomach tightens. There's no way he's leaving me behind, but I can't find the words. What's gotten into me? I've dreamed of hunting with the Hawks since Leith left on his first mission, but maybe I'm not cut out for this.

All the Hawks in my province are non-Morphic. I can understand why most Morphics aren't eager to hunt their own kind, but I'd never had any qualms about it. Like Leith, I believed capturing the dangerous ones would make people less afraid. But then why did seeing that man in cuffs rattle me?

All I know is I don't want to take this man to prison. Even if the Hawks don't go inside, it's still eerie getting close. But it's better they think almost getting stabbed is what makes me hesitant. I'd rather be seen as scared than sympathetic toward a prisoner.

Lysandra's blue eyes linger on Gray. He hasn't had much to say to her since her son, Leith, died. She nods. "Of course."

"I'm fine," I say, knowing Gray won't leave unless he hears it. For a moment, his eyes soften as he looks at me. He's the boy who made me wildflower crowns, and I'm the girl who chased bullies with rat spirits as he and Leith egged me on. He nods to me, looking like he wants to say something, but thinks better of it. He checks the man for additional weapons before swinging back up onto his horse.

"Come on," Lysandra says. "I'll take you home."

The Hawks ride off together. Unease raises the hairs on the back of my neck, and I can't shake the feeling that I should have joined them.

Windowless, with dark maroon walls and a thick rug stretching over wood floors, Father's study is more a cave than a room. Many centuries ago, before society evolved and learned the intricacies of Morphia, the non-Morphics used to call us witches. Despite it being an ancient, often condescending term, Father reclaimed it and ran with witchcraft as inspiration for his interior design.

The moment Lysandra and I step inside, the simmering heat of a bubbling potion kisses my skin. Father stirs the cauldron with a bare hand. As an alchemer, Father's gift of potion mixing makes him valuable to the council. Two decades ago, he designed a potion that sears through rock for efficient access to gem deposits with minimal damage to the environment. This saved the council many angry letters and made my father famous throughout Tamarynth. Just last year, he brewed the cure for the Breathless Blight that spread through Kalenar and crowded the infirmaries for weeks. While this cure earned him respect and continued to prove his usefulness, it also ignited further questions about Father's power. If he could cure a blight, could he cause one too?

Alchemy earned my father his place on the council that makes decisions for the realm, but one wrong move could jeopardize his standing. Even though my father's proved his usefulness, some of the council members still worry that his magic is dangerous. Alchemers are the only class of Morphics who pay no price for the magic they create. Not to mention, there are some potions Father and his alchemer ancestors have been banned from experimenting with. Potions that lengthen life, erase memories, and act as poisons.

Father was once asked by a man visiting from the province of Laverne what was to stop him from making a potion that controlled people's minds. Father didn't deign to answer but told me later it is the same thing that stops a man from killing his brother. He is not a bad person.

I can't imagine conjuring spirits without paying dearly with the deathmares I've come to know so well both when I'm asleep and awake. Sometimes I'm jealous of Father tinkering with new potion recipes for hours on end with no consequences. Although he's quick to remind me even alchemers have limits. His father showed him the basics before he died—potions for cleaning, simple medicines, and those to briefly increase strength or speed. But it takes lots of experimentation and failed attempts to make complex concoctions.

When Father finally notices me, he yanks his hand from the potion and steps out from behind his desk. He wipes his hand on a cloth and wraps me in a tight embrace, resting his chin on the top of my head. "I shouldn't have let you go," he whispers.

"I'm fine," I manage, but tears prickle at the corners of my eyes.

Lysandra stands back from us. Her eyes settle on the potion on Father's desk. Even after Father dissolved their union and married my mother, he maintained respect for Lysandra and above all, his son.

Leith should have been an alchemer. The gift of alchemy passes from father to son, but Leith was born non-Morphic. This wouldn't be unusual as Morphia runs through families randomly, but alchemers are different. Father and Lysandra were shocked, but I never heard them complain. If anything, Father almost seemed grateful Leith was not burdened with the task of producing potions for the realm. Lysandra swallows hard, blinking back tears. Seeing Gray and the potions in one day must bring the memories back to her.

I avert my eyes from her before our gazes meet. The guilt I feel around Lysandra clings to me like the pungent stench of death. She'll never see Leith again. Never get the closure of speaking to him because I can't bring him back. I've tried time and time again, grasping her hand so hard my knuckles turn bone white. Nothing happens. It's like I'm up against a block. I fail her every time.

I pull away from Father. His brows pinch as he adjusts his waistcoat. Something stern in his expression makes me take a step back. Whoever brought him the news of the fugitive mender's attack must have also shared that I used Morphia during the hunt.

"You must do well tomorrow," he rumbles. "There is no alternative."

Yet there is. My gaze wanders to the oil painting hanging over the mantel.

A grand black cruise ship drifts in calm aquamarine waters with a glowing lavender mist around the bow.

The *Celestial* was created as a vessel to contain the Morphia magic extracted from dangerous Morphics who fail their trials. The cruise ship was not only a place for wealthy patrons to experience the wonders of Morphia magic at low risk but also a way to give Morphics one last chance to keep their abilities.

Father's eyes follow mine, and his mouth tightens. "The guests hold the staff to impossible standards. It is a punishment, a dangerous one not to be taken lightly." He returns to his potion and drops an eagle talon in the liquid bubbling a pale green color. "Promise me if something happens, you won't board the ship."

Lysandra places a hand on my shoulder as I bristle, but I tear free of her grip. "You're saying I should let them suck the Morphia out of my body and leave me—"

"Like your mother and sister . . . and brother, I might add," Father finishes calmly. "Non-Morphic."

Lysandra freezes at the mention of Leith, but I run blazing hot. How dare he use my brother to influence me. Mother's always been non-Morphic and wanted Eliza and me to give up our abilities. Eliza was only too eager, not wanting to be used and employed only for her healing, but Father understood what it meant to me. Resurrecting the dead makes me feel the most alive.

I thought he cared as much as I did.

The pit in my stomach grows, weighing me down. He does care, but the realization settles like a physical barrier between us. If I had to go to the *Celestial*, it would embarrass Father.

It's not going to happen. He's only telling me this because I panicked yesterday. It's my own fault if I lose control during my trial. If I am dangerous, they *should* take it from me.

Still, I can't deny the impact his words have on me. Doubt is a weed. It adapts to my excuses and grows as he waters the roots I'm desperate to rip from the ground. Even if he's right, I can't look at him.

With as much calm as I can muster, I leave Father's study before he can see his words have shaken me.

Lysandra follows on my heels. We emerge outside together on the raised porch overlooking the sprawling gardens and green grass of my family's estate. I breathe in the earthy smell of mushrooms and fragrant herbs Father uses for his potions. The caw of ravens and crunch of carriage wheels turning over gravel meld in a harmony of sound as I close my eyes. I know the creak in every floorboard of this estate, and I've grown so used to the smell of sage that it's strange when I enter a home without it, but I can't imagine any of this without my magic.

"I want to give you something," Lysandra says.

She reaches into her woven bag and pulls out a homemade book. "A gift before your trial." I take the book from her, then flip gingerly through the pages. Sketches of Leith and me. She must have been watching the two of us, and I never realized she was there. Leith and me plunging our hands into icy streams for fish. Leith helping me learn to ride. The two of us sitting under a tree as he read aloud from a book.

"You'll do well tomorrow," she says. "I know it."

I blink hard to clear my lashes of rain droplets and tears. My eyes shut as I fight to swallow the spiked lump in my throat until Lysandra grips my arm tight and squeezes.

A carriage marked with the official Tamarynth seal, pulled by large black horses, groans as it bumps along the stony path to Damarcus Estate. My mouth dries, and Lysandra's hand on my arm is the only thing that stops me from running back inside.

They're here.

The judges for my trial have arrived a day early. And they're sleeping under my roof tonight. One thought holds me hostage as I watch them.

The trial is tomorrow. The trial is tomorrow. The trial is tomorrow.

CHAPTER 3

The ballroom could belong to a stranger's estate today. Cherrywood walls stretch from ceiling to floor, bare and imposing. The paintings of Damarcus family ancestors have been removed from their usual spots. A long table rests at the far end of the room. Four glasses of water sit in front of four solemn judges in iron-framed chairs.

I used to love dancing and singing in this room because of its echoing vastness. Today, the expanse of space is intimidating.

My hands tremble, but I clutch the fabric of my skirts tight to steady them. My hair is pulled into an elaborate spectacle of braids and forced ringlets. My lips are painted red while my hazel eyes are outlined with black paint. I pull my shoulders back far enough that my shoulder blades might actually touch.

My dress gleams with the colors of autumn—gold, burnt orange, and deep scarlet. With a voluminous skirt and large teardrop earrings, I feel more like a dessert than a warrior preparing for battle. But that's what today feels like. A battle to keep my Morphia.

With each step, my heels click against the polished wood. Each step draws me closer to the judges' table. Their scrutinizing gazes make my stomach flip. They scribble with quills into thick, leather-bound books.

I force my gaze from the table and focus on the three rows of chairs on the left side of the room. Father, Mother, and Eliza sit in the front row. Mother flicks a hand nervously through her tawny brown hair.

Who am I kidding? She's more nervous that I'll trip than she is about the trial.

There's an empty chair next to my father—a gap between him and Lysandra. She gives me a small wave and a white-toothed grin. In the second row, a few of Father's friends from the council sit with their hands in their laps, their faces grim. Most of them have probably never attended a Morphic trial before. Trials are usually private in wealthy families to lessen the shame of potential failure, but with Father, everything is a public affair.

Few of the prominent members in our province have Morphics in their close family. The lords and ladies of Credence are mostly made up of ancient families whose properties sat atop lucrative gem mines long ago, or those who founded the first hospitals and schools. Others in the high class are primarily non-Morphic families responsible for the innovation and construction that built the cruise ship years ago. Father contests that we have Morphic crafters to thank for most innovation in construction. But Father is rare. Morphics don't often gain titles, even for exemplary service.

When I glimpse the third row, a heavy breath escapes my lips. Most of Leith's friends from the Hawks are here. Gray and Jasper are among them. Jasper sticks his tongue out at me and reaches forward to tug one of Eliza's ringlets. She bats his hand away with practiced swats.

For a fleeting moment, it's almost like having Leith here. Father turns over his shoulder and gives Gray a look. Although Gray sits ramrod straight with his face arranged in solemn interest, he slaps Jasper on the forearm.

I can't help smiling as I approach the table. Now that I'm here, wearing my heavy dress and wondering what banquet food's waiting in the dining hall, I can't believe I was so nervous. My body relaxes, and I hold my head high. I will not be afraid of my power in my own home.

One of the judges, a woman with medium beige skin and black ink tattoos on her arms, glances up from her writing. "Name?" she asks.

With a slow, steadying breath, I answer. "Rosaline Damarcus."

All four of the judges scribble into their journals, and the woman speaks again. "Morphic ability?"

Another easy one. "Resurrection."

More scribbling. More tense silence. It doesn't unnerve me this time. It all feels mildly absurd. Like a performance where I need to remember my lines, but no one gave me any to memorize. The judges aren't anyone to fear. Most judges for Morphic trials belong to the Morphia Watch Program, a respected division of Morphics and non-Morphics dedicated to exposing problems created by Morphia within the realm.

I wonder how many other Morphics will have a trial this year. Other trials across the nine provinces often take place in barns or fields in case the Morphia gets out of control. Rarely do they happen in the grand halls of an estate. Another woman clears her throat and taps her quill to the end of her jutting chin. Her red hair hangs short, tucked behind pink-toned ears. She leans forward. The others follow.

Here we go.

"As you know, the Morphic trials were created to prevent dangerous Morphics from ruining the prosperity of Tamarynth. We owe the Damarcus family a great debt for this simple test that keeps us safe." The woman turns her head so she's looking at my father and not me. "You have Spokesman Malyk's and the High Council's deepest gratitude."

Ah, yes. The age-old Damarcus family bedtime story: How a Damarcus Saved the Realm. Hundreds of years ago, Morphics roamed Tamarynth freely, unregulated. Morphics, desiring more power, rebelled in a war against the non-Morphic council. Family members turned on one another as the realm divided into Morphic and non-Morphic armies.

Father's too-many-greats-to-remember grandfather petitioned the past council with an idea to keep the peace. He devised the trials meant to prevent dangerous Morphics from keeping their magic, but that wasn't all. Great-Grandfather Damarcus knew Morphia made us all better and that people still wanted to experience it. So he came up with the idea for the *Celestial*. As the inventor, he owned a majority stake in the ship and oversaw its development. He maintained that the ship would lock up the dangerous Morphics but highlight the beauty of Morphia at the same time.

I scrounge up memories of family voyages aboard the cruise ship. Seeing as it's an expensive family heirloom, we got free stays every year.

It was always magical. I hardly thought about what it was like for the Morphics working there.

Dangerous Morphics. They were serving time until they got a retrial—*if* they got a retrial.

Father inclines his head with a stiffness I seldom see. There's a note of bitterness in the curved lines of his tight smile. The judges may be thanking him for our family's past contributions, but Father tells me there's always a higher rung to climb.

The woman continues with her introduction without acknowledging the tension in Father's shoulders. "Morphics channel their magic into something useful, but once it leaves the body, it's unpredictable. If that raw magic were released, the realm would see vicious creatures roaming the forests and objects transforming in unpredictable ways. The *Celestial* keeps extracted Morphia contained aboard and out of Tamarynth."

I think of Mr. Barrington, who sells clothing in one of Credence's markets. Father tells me he used to be a crafter, but during his trial, the clothing he created to morph to each judge's shape strangled and burned them. Even when they yelled at him to stop, he'd kept going.

After time aboard the *Celestial*, now he sits in front of his shabby stall, muttering. He never earned a retrial and had his Morphia extracted. But he still mumbles about haunted hallways "trying to kill him" and bosses who left him with two fewer fingers. As a child, I was both frightened and intrigued by him, unsure if I believed the rumors about the ship. I'm still not sure what I believe.

The woman's voice jolts me from my thoughts. "This trial date has been set since the day of your fourth birthday to be completed between the ages of eighteen and nineteen. Those who try to hide their Morphia and escape trial face dire consequences." She presses her lips together.

Blood roars in my ears. Every time I think I'm over the nerves, they come racing back. The woman taps her chin with a long finger decorated with rings. "This trial will force you into a high-stress situation to examine your reaction. If you fail, you will have two choices." She holds up one finger. "One, have your Morphia extracted from your body. Your magic will be sent to the *Celestial* cruise ship for containment, and you can rejoin society as a non-Morphic." She holds up another finger. "Two, you may choose to serve a punishment sentence on the *Celestial*. There, you will donate your Morphia in increments to help power the ship and earn a chance to win your retrial."

That's the part nobody likes to talk about. If you're sent to work on the *Celestial*, what does the punishment look like? When I attended as a guest, I never noticed staff looking particularly miserable. Then again, I was seven or eight, and I know what Mr. Barrington looks like now.

I can picture extraction. Morphics drink a potion of my great-grandfather's making, and they cry tears into a jar—tears of their magic. I've seen the jars of raw Morphia carted from extractions to the ship. Technically, anyone could steal a jar and use raw Morphia the way a Morphic would, but it's very dangerous for non-Morphics. They become physically ill if they use it enough. Those jars are only meant to be stored on board the ship.

The thought makes me sick now that it's my Morphia on the line.

A man with brown skin and glasses coughs. "Rosaline? We asked you a question."

Shit. I have no clue what he asked. The man sighs and pushes his glasses up his nose. "Do you understand?"

I smile, ready to get this over with. Ready to show them what I can do. "Yes."

The first woman with the tattoos picks up her quill again. A tinge of sadness swims in her dark irises. "We're going to give you a minute to prepare yourself."

I take a deep breath in through my nose and out through my mouth. Breathe in for four seconds, hold for four seconds, and breathe out for four.

Then a judge with shaggy black hair shuts his journal with a thunk that reverberates throughout the room. Even the Hawks are silent, holding their breath.

The man rubs his hands together and looks at the table as he speaks. "Before we begin, you need to understand. What I'm about to say may be distressing for you to hear, but I'm afraid it must be done."

My blood freezes in my veins. Every muscle tenses. Why can't he look at me?

"Unfortunately, we have come to the decision, with approval from Spokesman Malyk, that you will not be having your trial today." The man holds up a scroll bound with Spokesman Malyk's house seal.

Father leaps from his chair, and the chair legs screech across the floor. Mother puts a hand on his arm, but his eyes blaze. "What's the meaning of this? My daughter—"

"I'm sorry. Let me explain." The man holds up his hands, a feverish red hue rising in his cheeks. My own skin tingles all over, and I feel like I've fallen off a steep cliff and am waiting to hit the ground, grateful for the impact just so the dizziness will stop.

"Resurrectors are too dangerous. They offer no real benefit to society and suffer very little consequences for their use." As he speaks, the red-haired woman reaches into a case beside the table. "We cannot allow your daughter to continue. If she'd been an alchemer, of course she would be permitted to stand trial. But resurrectors . . ."

The tingling stops, and I'm numb. I wonder why they let me prepare for so long if they were going to take it from me. But I know why. They were afraid of how I'd react. How my father might react.

The woman now holds a potion bottle in her clenched hand. Cloudy gray liquid.

An extraction potion.

The judge murmurs, "We're so sorry." Strands of black hair fall in his eyes as he tries not to look at me or my father.

Gray, usually calm and collected, jumps to his feet. "You can't do this. There must be a mistake."

Mother clings to Father's sleeve to keep him from lunging forward, but her pursed lips tell me everything I need to know. She never wanted me to keep my Morphia. All her children are now safe and normal.

The thought makes me want to scream. The ice in my veins melts. My hands shake, not from nerves, but from anger. Stomach clenching and heartbeat thumping hard in my chest, I force myself to breathe.

The judges repeat their apologies. The woman holding the potion uncorks it, her eyes cast downward. Black spots seep into the edges of my vision, and I press a clenched fist to my chest. People are talking, but I can't tell what they're saying. Someone grabs me from behind and secures me in place. I don't struggle. Gray clamps silver crafter-made bindings around my wrists, the same kind he used on the prisoner yesterday. He does it fast for someone who protested only moments ago. Tears sting my eyes, but I don't let them fall. My chest aches with the thought that Leith would never tie me up. Even if the judges had a knife to his throat.

He believed in me, and now it's all over.

The woman with the potion walks forward and holds the bottle out to me. If I drink it, the Morphia will come out through my tears. I'll cry until there's none left. Nothing of me left. Voices clamor in my ears, but they may as well be in a different language. They're afraid of me. Terrified to look at my face, to get too close.

Good. They should be.

Something snaps inside me. A tornado of anger, anxiety, and fear forms in my stomach. The tips of my fingers throb, vibrating with the energy pumping through my body. I reach for the spirits waiting in the spiritual plane. They itch to escape and run with my rage.

I call on the spirits of two black wolves. Their bodies turn solid, and they gnash frothing, fanged jaws at the judges. With powerful muscles in their broad hindquarters, both wolves lunge forward, talons clinking against the wooden floor.

Mother screams and Eliza ducks behind her chair as the wolves crash into the judges' table. The table clatters to the floor with an echoing bang. I've never done this before. The spirits I conjure look solid, but they've never been able to do any real damage.

One of the wolves circles back and lashes out at the judge holding the potion. Its muscular front legs leap from the ground, and its wide jaws clamp around the woman's arm. She screeches and drops the bottle. Blood drips down her arm in thick streams of hot scarlet. The wolf won't let go and snarls as her flesh tears in its mouth.

These spirits are real. Solid. They're hurting people.

With a start, I realize Father's shaking my shoulders. "Roe, stop! Stop!"

I let out a gasping breath and cut the cord of energy between me and the wolves. The connection severs, and the bodies dissolve. They decay and then disappear in a fine, silvery mist.

That's not the only thing to disappear. The scene dissolves too.

I stand in the center of the room with my hands at my sides. My family, our guests, and the Hawks are seated, their faces tight and colorless. Father's still in his seat, but he holds a hand to his mouth.

Three judges sit in their seats, but the table's toppled over. The red-haired woman clutches her bleeding arm, but the smashed potion bottle's gone. Maybe it was never there.

The tattooed woman slumps in her chair. She's lost energy. She must be an illusive. Someone who can manipulate the mind. Illusives lose energy for a time comparable to the amount of Morphia used.

The truth slams into me with all the force of a crashing waterfall.

None of it was real. She made me hear and see lies.

I did get my trial. The judges did give me a chance to prove my Morphia is worth keeping.

But I failed.

CHAPTER 4

A judge slips silver cuffs over my wrists. The cool metal engraved with symbols digs into my skin. These cuffs neutralize Morphic abilities. I'm defenseless. I should have known it was an illusion when the bindings from my vision didn't restrain my Morphia.

Tears threaten at the corners of my eyes, but I hold them back. Today's been humiliating enough. I won't let them see me cry.

Father approaches the woman with the bleeding gash in her arm. He bends his head to speak with her. "I'm sorry," he says in a shaky voice. "Jasper can take you to our physician."

Jasper stands from his chair, moving slow like his legs are stuck in tree sap. He takes the woman's uninjured arm and guides her from the ceremony room. He throws a glance over his shoulder, but I look away.

Maybe this is all a bad dream. A deathmare of mine. I'll wake up, and the judges will arrive in a carriage, and they'll file into the ceremony room and wait for my trial to begin. *Please, Riveners, tell me it hasn't happened yet. Tell me this is all a nightmare.*

Father speaks to the judges seated behind the overturned table in a low voice. The judges ask if they can administer the potion to take my Morphia. Father inhales a long breath through his nose and lets it out.

"Yes . . . of course." The words wobble out of him, weak and afraid.

My heart sinks. I don't know why a part of me thought he'd protest.

Father's mind is always working, and he doesn't let anyone influence him. The wild outrage he showed in the illusion no longer exists.

But I don't recognize this man either.

Mother presses a hand to her chest and grips Eliza's fingers tightly in her own. But she's not upset. She wanted me to be like her. Mother approves of Father's Morphia because of what it's gotten him. Wealth, power, prestige.

But it's not about any of that for me. Resurrection is a part of myself I can't cut out as if it were diseased. My knees quake, and my bottom lip quivers. I take a tentative step forward, but the judges shrink back in their seats. The man with glasses leaps back from me like he's been burned. Just like the crowd at the ball.

My voice is a strangled choke. "Don't do this," I croak. "It was an accident." It's like I'm watching myself speak from the outside.

Without a word, the illusive with the tattoos removes the real potion from her case and sets it on the table. I look to my father, and the tears fall despite how hard I tried to hold them back. The lump in my throat makes it hard to swallow. Hard to talk. When he says nothing, my shoulders heave with sobs. I'm not dangerous. "Please."

But I remember the rage coursing through my body. I remember the way it felt to tear into a human's flesh. The wolf was solid, with teeth capable of shredding skin. For the first time, my spirits were capable of real destruction.

The slosh of liquid in the potion bottle makes my stomach churn. The judge removes the stopper from the bottle. Sickening fear drenches my clammy skin in sweat.

"Wait!" I yell, not caring how my voice echoes off the bare walls. "What about— What about the *Celestial*?"

The remaining judges exchange a glance and clear their throats without looking at my father. I glimpse the left side of the room in time to catch the shake of Mother's head. Her pale blue dress crinkles as she rises to her feet. "That ship is not the vacation you remember, Roe. Not for Morphics." Her fingers curl around the fabric of her skirts. "It's a punishment."

"What choice do I have?" I whirl around to look at her. The tears dry on my cheeks, and the hot wave of anger returns. "It's that or . . ." I can't finish.

Lysandra's voice makes my throat even tighter. "Maybe your mother's right."

Eliza smirks. She crosses her arms over her chest and leans back in her chair with eyebrows raised. No help there. I look to my father, but his eyes are on the floor. When he finally does look at me, my tiny speck of defiance shrivels up and dies.

It's shameful. A Damarcus child going to the very place his family built to keep Morphia contained—to keep dangerous Morphics from destroying Tamarynth—is unthinkable.

Father clears his throat and adjusts the pocket watch on his waistcoat. He looks up and faces the judges with his usual rolled-back shoulders and lifted chin. He presses his hands together and smiles. It's a forced, tight smile, but the judges relax when they see it. "Out of respect for my family, would you be good enough to give us a couple of hours to decide?"

As judges, these three may hold higher positions in the Morphia Watch Program, but Father still outranks them. The judges exchange another weighted glance but plaster on their own fake smiles. "Of course," the man says.

A judge unclasps the cuffs from my wrists, but I feel no less a prisoner. Father thanks him with a deep bow of his head and grabs me by my shoulders. The pinch of his brows and the emptiness in his dark eyes sends fear down my spine. This isn't the man who drizzled honey on my toast in the morning. This is the man who locks away dangerous Morphics and mixes intricate potions for the apothecaries.

We exit the ceremony room and walk to the long hallway with dark walls and iron lanterns that leads to the bedrooms. Portraits of our ancestors hang on the walls, watching me as I pass. Father's too-tight grip on my shoulders makes me want to scream. The pressure of his touch is too reminiscent of the forced skin contact required to summon family members. Something I might not feel again.

The fast click of heels assures me Mother's close behind us, but my mind whirs too fast to care. I'm working on a plan. A speech that will somehow convince my family to let me go. If I can't convince them, the judges will attend to Father's wishes over mine. They respect him enough to override my choice.

I can picture it now. Mother locking me in my room and refusing to let me anywhere near the port in Windmere Province until the ship is long gone on a charter.

Father opens the heavy wooden door to my suite and pushes me inside. He shuts the door and locks it before my mother and sister have a chance to follow. A vast four-poster bed with emerald-green blankets and a sheer black canopy rests against the wall. I long to sink into it, but Father steers me to the chairs beside the windows.

An arrow snaps under his shoe. I sit in the chair across from him and focus on a pile of academic books on the floor. A few weeks ago, I'd been wondering if I should agree to Father's request for me to pursue university. After seven painstaking years in boarding school, I'd finally had the option to move on to studying whatever I wanted at the University of Credence. I could spend years researching the history of resurrectors uncovered from Illoryan holy texts or completing projects about the annual crafter fair in Kalenar. I could train with the Hawks in the evenings and on school breaks if Father agreed to it. Now the thought of any of those goals feels like a hollow dream.

"Roe." Father's voice is low and gravelly, chafing at the edges of my frayed nerves. "Maybe . . . maybe it's time to think about what life could look like without Morphia." I open my mouth, but he shakes his head to silence me. "I know. I'm the last person you want to hear this from, but we can't break the very laws my family helped to create."

He's referring to his position on the High Council. Council members are appointed by lords and ladies of each province every three years to settle disputes between provinces, regulate trade, and vote on laws affecting both Morphics and non-Morphics. Although anyone can be appointed, the members only come from respected families, and the appointments tend to stay in those families. If Father were to fall out of favor, it would mean a council without a single Morphic left.

"Then don't break them." My words come out in a fierce whisper. "Let me serve on the *Celestial*."

Father pauses and looks away from me. "Do you know why we call it Morphia?" he asks, changing the subject. "It's the magic of altering—of transformation. We manipulate and build upon matter or feelings that are already there. You draw upon the realm beyond life."

I blink at him, wringing my hands. "Maybe we just need to alter your plans a little." Father smiles, eyes crinkling with crow's-feet. "You will begin studying council duties with me—you can still achieve an appointment to the High Council one day without Morphia. You'll still fight for Morphic causes." Father sighs and rubs the bridge of his nose. "And I'll talk to Gray about letting you start training with the Hawks. Two evenings a week. I'll expect you to attend university too."

Father stands and brushes invisible specks of dust off his pant legs. Silence stretches between us. Painful. Heavy.

That's it. He wants me to give up. He's so ashamed of his only Morphic child being reduced to a delinquent staff member in need of rehabilitation that he's giving up on me.

I've heard of some upper-class families pressuring their children to give up their Morphia, but my father has always been vocal about the benefits of our gifts. He's always supported me until now. My mouth tastes dry and bitter. I couldn't speak if I wanted to. When I say nothing, he crosses to the door. "Take some time alone. I'll come back in an hour. We'll go back together. I'll . . ." His voice cracks. "I'll stay with you when they take it."

He wrenches the door closed behind him. My breath catches in my throat, and I struggle to get a good inhale. Hot, salty tears fall from my eyes. I try to rub them away with the back of my hand, but they keep coming.

Father didn't want me to fail. This isn't what he spent years envisioning, but now he's doing damage control. He's trying to pick up the broken pieces of my life without asking me how I want to put them back together.

For a moment, I wonder what it's like to live in the closest neighboring realms beyond Tamarynth. The ones without trials. In Correndra, they still burn witches at the stake. No Morphics live freely there. Father has been urging the council to provide aid, but he can't push too hard if he wants to keep favor with the other members. On the island of Gryndar, rogue Morphics aren't controlled. Power changes hands every couple of years, and people constantly flee its lawlessness.

Even losing Morphia is better than living in Gryndar. I should be grateful I live here, where people are protected.

Protected from people like me.

My fingers trail downward to the corset of my dress. I claw at the fabric, ripping it from my skin. The sharp tear is satisfying. I slash at the gown until I'm sitting in my shift with my knees pulled to my chest.

I sit motionless until my limbs are stiff. The sun's peeking through the heavy green curtains, highlighting the freckles on my legs and arms. I stand and walk gingerly to the windows, throwing open the drapes. I've got a nice view of the stables from my room. Lysandra gifted me a white stallion, Specter, for my fourteenth birthday. He's the fastest steed in our stables. The inkling of an idea takes root.

The *Celestial*'s port is just a two-day ride south of Credence.

I don't need anyone's permission to try for a retrial on the *Celestial*. Not technically now that I'm of age. As long as I can slip away from Mother and Father, they won't be around to overrule my decision. The judges won't have to worry about ignoring the wishes of Lord Damarcus in favor of his teenaged daughter. I'd still have to sneak out of the house. But it wouldn't technically be against the law because I wouldn't be running from my trial. I'd be running to the only legal option left to me.

And if I take Specter, I'll outrun anyone who's chasing me.

Father gave me an hour. Forty minutes left.

I leap to my wardrobe and toss on a pair of brown riding pants, a tunic, and a dark green riding cloak. After shoving my feet into riding boots, I grab my comb and tease out the forced ringlets in my hair. Once I'm dressed, I snatch up a burlap sack and my treasured white bow and arrows. I pack a journal, quill, and purse of gemstones for payment, though I have no idea what to expect.

I fasten the cloak around my neck and ease my bedroom door open. It creaks, and I stop short. No one's coming.

I throw one more glance over my shoulder. It may be a while before I'm allowed to come back. If I can come back. My gaze locks on the small book of sketches from Lysandra nestled beside my bed, but I turn away.

No time to rethink. I swallow the lump in my throat and make my way down the hall past Eliza's room. The floor groans under my feet, and I hold my breath. No footsteps.

I follow the hallway to the entry room and sneak past the grand staircase. I dart behind a large marble sculpture of a dragon bursting from a flower and wait for two servants with a tea cart to pass. I thank the Riveners Mother and I share a love for large, elegant statues of dangerous creatures.

When they're gone, I run on tiptoes to the kitchen, sliding open the pantry door. With all the excitement from my trial, the area's deserted. I seize a few apples, a block of cheese, and a bread loaf. As I'm filling my canteen with water from the spigot, the door groans open.

I whirl around, not sure if I should duck behind one of the wine barrels or string an arrow. My throat constricts.

Eliza stands in the doorway—and my only way out—with her arms crossed over the bodice of her aquamarine dress. "I thought I heard someone trying to sneak past my door." She gestures to the knapsack slung over my shoulder. "Going somewhere?"

The words catch in my throat, and for a fleeting second, I want to seize my bow and shoot an arrow through her leg. But she's my sister, and no matter how much we fight, Leith always said we should take care of each other.

So I do the next best thing.

I lunge forward and plow into her. Taking advantage of the couple of inches of height I have on her, I reach over her head and slide the door the rest of the way open. Weighed down by her heavy dress, Eliza struggles to a sitting position. I crawl over her and push to my feet, but she catches my ankle. She clings to my leg and screams for help. "She's trying to run!"

Panic seizes me, and I kick hard with my riding boot. I hit her face with my heel, cracking her nose. Blood spatters the floor, and I'm free of her grip. Guilt urges me to pause, but desperation wins out, and I don't look back.

I bolt through the entry room, pushing open the doors of the estate. Servants shout behind me, and I hear Hawks yelling for me to stop, but I don't. Even if they pursue me, I still have to run. I have to try.

I make a beeline for the stables, kicking up stones as I run along the path. Father's voice is louder than the rest. "Roe, don't do this!"

The solemn voice of the bespectacled judge reaches my ears. "We'll have to send your hunters after her."

My heart sinks, but I still have a chance. I won't have time for Specter's saddle. Just the bit and a blanket. I'll—

Someone's waiting for me in the barn.

Lysandra leans against Specter's stall, clutching reins in her hand. The roaring of blood in my ears makes her words sound like distant echoes.

"I don't think this is a good idea, but it's your choice." She leads the great white stallion out of his stall. He's fully saddled and wearing his ceremonial bridle. "Thought I'd at least give you a chance."

There's no time to thank her, but the sting behind my eyes says it all. She gives me a leg up and dips into a low curtsy. "My lady," she says, nudging Specter's hindquarters. He takes off.

I don't look back. I don't want to see Father's shame, Mother's disapproval, or the legion of Hawks chasing after me. We fly over the hills of Damarcus Estate like spirits passing to the next world. A world still within my reach.

Guilt makes my shoulders heavy, but Lysandra is right. This is my choice, and no one else should get to make it for me. I ride hard for Carodmoor Forest, the pounding hooves of hunters in pursuit behind me. The adrenaline makes it easy for me to dip into the well of power in the spirit world. Wispy silver spirits fly out behind me, obscuring the Hawks' view as I weave between trees.

My breaths come in fast, anxious gasps. I can't ride like this all the way to the port. They'll catch me. If they catch me, this will have been for nothing.

As we breach the trees and are no longer visible from the estate, a strong, calm voice sounds behind me. At first I think he's shouting for me to stop like the others, but then I hear him.

"Let her go." Gray must pull back on the reins because hooves squelch in the dirt as a horse skids to a stop. "Let her go," he repeats. "She's heading for the port, anyway."

I turn over my shoulder to look at him, but I can't make out his expression. The Hawks have all stopped at his command, but they're sweaty and panting.

"She's a fugitive, Gray!" one yells.

"No," Gray answers as I turn back around to face the path ahead of me. "She's a prisoner of the *Celestial* now."

CHAPTER 5

My ass aches something fierce by the time I reach Windmere Port.

Riding for two days through dense forest and villages in Credence and across the main trade route in Windmere Province has left me exhausted and hungry. Even worse than the time I followed a spirit through Credence's busiest market and ended up lost for hours until Leith found me. There are twigs in my hair and dirt smudged on my face. The last of my bread and cheese ran out this morning. I dig in my bag and extract the small purse of gemstones. I ran away without much thought to what was coming, but now the reality's set in: I've left my family behind for a ship full of strangers and an uncertain chance at a retrial. As foolish as my plan sounds, I like to think Leith would have supported this bold move to save my magic. But we always were the impulsive ones.

Windmere Port is crowded with luxury carriages and upper-class travelers in vibrant jewel-tone dresses and waistcoats. A man with tawny skin and smooth black hair kneels to straighten his son's collar while a pale woman flushed from the heat directs a staff member to her towering pile of luggage. A woman with umber skin and dark curls descends from her carriage in a heavy dress made of expensive silk crafted in Kalenar. Servants unload heaps of luggage and formalwear bags. The carriages struggle to reach the docks through the crowd. A vague memory tickles the back of my mind. I was eight years old and wanted to carry my own luggage onto the *Celestial*. Mother clung tight to Eliza's hand, but I ran ahead to get a better look at our famous destination. Leith put me on his shoulders to see over the crowd.

I don't need to be on anyone's shoulders to see it now.

The *Celestial* eclipses the port, its black, glossy exterior gleaming in the afternoon sun. The ship is majestic and immense, stretching twelve decks high, and wide enough that it blocks out the horizon. Rows upon rows of windows dapple the lower part of the ship, while grand balconies adorn the upper levels. The cruise ship, with shimmering silver stars painted across the bow and stern, lives up to its name. At night, the black exterior shifts to a bright, ethereal silver.

The first guests, who had seen Tamarynth on the brink of a magical war two hundred years ago, had been hesitant to board a ship full of Morphia. My great-grandfather assured them his ship would be like sailing through the cosmos, where glowing jars of Morphia were wishing-stars that made impossible things happen. While future generations forgot the initial fear surrounding the ship, the otherworldly theming and name stuck. The ship, resting in a mist of violet-hued fog, looks as if it has come out of a dream.

A carpeted gangway protrudes from the side and connects to the docks below. Staff members roll luggage up and check guests in with wide smiles and foreheads beading with sweat. They wear black vests with a vertical line of silver buttons down the front over a tunic shirt paired with beige or navy pants and short brown boots. In their uniforms, the staff all look the same. When I think of my vibrant wardrobe back home, the staff's lack of individuality is unsettling.

I run fingers through my tangled hair and pour water from my canteen into my hand, furiously rubbing my face to clear the dirt. I'd hoped to arrive earlier than what appears to be right before departure.

Specter snorts and paws the ground as if to tell me we'd better get a move on. I should be happy I made it before the cruise left for its voyage. The shortest cruise is a week, which means I would have been holed up in some dinky inn waiting on the ship to return to port for the next guests. But I'm frozen in place.

Carriages and people on horseback pass me by with disgruntled looks. "If you're just going to sit there, get off the road!" one carriage driver shouts.

I can't make myself move. I've only ever been a treasured guest aboard. Not a dangerous resurrector sent to serve her time.

Most don't talk about their time aboard out of embarrassment, but memories of some former ship staff members, people now working in our household or neighbors I'd met elsewhere in Credence, come back to me now. The scars embedded in their skin, their murmurings of shadows on the ship's walls, and strange happenings aboard. Mother would tell me to ignore them because they had been deemed violent enough to serve on the ship in the first place, but it still makes me wary.

Come to think of it, I've never served anyone before. Not to mention upper-class guests who expect everything done right the first time. My fingertips tingle with nerves, but I lift my chin and urge Specter forward through the crowd. This is my one chance to earn a retrial. I'll do all it takes to prove myself.

Navigating the guests isn't too hard since they leap out of the way to avoid the dirty, windswept girl who hasn't bathed in days. A woman narrows her eyes in my direction as she turns her child's gaze away from me. I try to ignore her, but it's hard not to wonder if she's right to fear me.

I glimpse a tall wooden sign on the right side of the gangway that reads: MORPHIC ENROLLMENT. A smaller sign beneath it with cheerful silver lettering reads: PUT YOUR MAGIC TO BETTER USE! MAKE MAGIC FOR GUESTS! Beside it, soldiers dressed in uniforms with silver wolf pins fastened to their chests escort Morphics into line. Large carriages with a similar wolf insignia painted on the side screech to a stop, providing transportation for Morphics to the ship. The wolf is a symbol of Tamarynth's army due to the large wolf populations in the forests of Aryndar Province, where the army trains. The soldiers look less than pleased to be here. They don't trust Morphics who failed their trials to travel here on their own. Not the way I did.

With a heavy sense that I don't belong, I swing down from my saddle and lead Specter to the sign. I wait in line behind young people with duffel bags slung over their shoulders. Their nervous expressions and drab clothing don't match the electric excitement and opulent fabrics on the other side. As I stand behind them, I wonder what Morphic abilities they possess. While many of the families who live in nearby estates didn't have Morphic children, I met others at boarding school. I marveled at the way they used their gifts, even if they didn't appreciate mine.

I run through the known Morphic gifts in my mind, forcing myself to stay calm as another person is called forward in line. Enhancers manipulate the properties of foods and drinks to transform them into fantastical flavors. Menders alter the body, healing in ways physicians cannot. Time winders change the passage of time, while crafters manipulate matter in unusual ways. Shifters transform their own bodies, while illusives influence the mind. Emotives can enhance or diminish feelings.

Most of these gifts could make someone popular with guests, but I have no idea how mine will help me here.

Bored from standing in line, I gaze out over the throng of people and at the Rivenwind Sea twinkling in the afternoon sunlight. There's a small group of men crowded around a young boy near the docks. Although I can't see the boy well from here, he appears to be yelling and kicking.

I squint to see him better as one of the men lunges forward and grabs him around the abdomen, hauling him over his shoulder. The boy kicks and hits with curled fists at the man's back. I stiffen and wait for someone else to notice. The boy's hollering now, although I can't make out what he's saying. I clap a hand over my mouth as one of the other men holds a knife to the boy's throat to silence him. Staff members from the *Celestial* pass by the docks, but none of them look up from their work. My stomach leaps into my throat as the men toss the boy into the water. I yell, but it's nothing compared to the gurgling scream of the boy who knows he's about to die.

As the other Morphics standing in line give me concerned looks, I know it's happening again. I squeeze my eyes shut and wait for the deathmare to pass. By the time I open them, the docks are back to normal.

The woman checking us in finally beckons me forward, and I'm grateful for it. It's good timing, as Specter's begun nibbling the back of my head. I wipe the sweat from my brow and incline my head to the woman with graying hair and wrinkles lining her face. "Name?" she asks sharply.

"Roe Damarcus," I answer, still shaken.

The woman runs her finger through the pages of a crafter-made registry book that magically adds the names of Morphics who fail their trials. She stops her finger on the *D*'s. "There you are." She grabs my bag and dumps the contents on the table.

She pushes the gemstone purse to the side along with my remaining apples. She leaves the journal and quill inside but extends her hands again. "The weapon," she clarifies.

With reluctance, I hand it to her. She examines the white bow frame and quiver of arrows with pinched brows and a tight mouth. Finally, she hands me back my knapsack with only the journal and quill inside. "You'll get these back at the end of your stay."

My chest tightens, and I open my mouth to argue. I'm a lady of Credence. I've had that bow for most of my life. And that's all the money I managed to sneak out of the house. But the withering look she gives me assures me I am no lady here.

I stay silent but snatch the bag from her and throw it over my shoulder. The woman smiles, but it doesn't reach her eyes. "Ms. Damarcus, you will serve on the *Celestial* for as long as it takes to achieve your retrial, or you may age out of the process before that happens. You have four years to earn a retrial."

No part of me wants to be aboard for four years. "Okay—"

"I'm not done." The woman continues reading from a list of rules. "Retrials take place four times a year, and they accept three applicants each time."

My stomach lurches, and I grab hold of Specter's saddle to steady myself. My eyes pass over the hundreds of staff members loading luggage. There's got to be hundreds more already aboard, preparing the ship for its next departure. I swipe my tongue over dry lips and force my mouth to move. "How is that fair?"

The woman pats the list. "I don't make the rules, darling."

My head's spinning, and I really wish there was somewhere to sit. If there are hundreds aboard—maybe even a thousand—and three get to do a retrial each quarter, then that means twelve Morphics get a retrial a year. Twelve. Father never mentioned this. I never bothered to ask anyone who'd been a staff member before me. I'm starting to wonder what else he forgot to tell me about this place.

Unaware or unconcerned by my disbelief, the woman hands me a small slip of paper with the name of another staff member and a room number. "You're here to work, not to enjoy the ship," she reminds me. "You'll serve the guests to the best of your ability and hopefully earn a retrial within four years. If not, we'll extract your Morphia in the port when you disembark for the final time. While aboard, you will donate your Morphia to the ship's stores. Daily donations from staff help power the magic on the ship, as well as keep it strong enough to contain the Morphia from extractions." She raises her arm to indicate the massive cruise ship. "We have this ship to thank for keeping dangerous Morphia contained and distanced to minimize the risk of harm to our cities and residents."

Not to mention, keeping *Morphics* out of their lands. With my mind tossing and turning like a stormy sea, it occurs to me she hasn't mentioned how to earn a retrial. "How—"

"Ivander will explain everything else to you." She cuts me off again. I look down at the crumpled slip in my hand. Ivander. The staff member I'm assigned to for the day. Great. No last name. I'm sure that will make them easy to find.

I catch a whiff of sweat and soiled clothes and realize the smell's coming from me. The thought of the men and women boarding in their elegant, perfumed clothes makes my ears burn. "Is there somewhere I can make myself more presentable?"

She laughs. "You'll be out in the sun a bit longer, anyway. No use getting clean. Besides, there's no time. You start work immediately."

Anger clenches in my gut, but I push it down. This woman's doing her job, and I've spent days riding without washing before. I just didn't expect to board the freaking *Celestial* with my armpits stinking like one of my corpses.

With a false smile of my own, one I learned from Mother, I pat Specter's flank. "Is there somewhere I can have him boarded while he waits for me to get back?"

The woman's face falls, and a somber twinge darkens her eyes. "Oh dear, you still think you're coming home soon." She pulls from a stack of rectangular wooden cards beside her chair. "Made by crafters," she says. "Write where you want to send him on the surface of the card and slip it in his saddle. He'll find his way home."

She hands me a quill, and I write *Lysandra Jamison's farm* on the surface, although the quill makes no mark as I write. I brush Specter's broad white face and slip the card into his saddle. The stallion snorts and nudges his nose against my cheek. The gesture makes my throat tight. With a short whinny, Specter shifts his weight and turns back in the direction we came.

I try not to envy him for getting to leave. As I watch his long tail swishing as he retreats, I wish I could talk to Lysandra. She'd give me the no-nonsense advice I need to hold my head up in this place.

The woman clicks her tongue. "Get a move on, girl. You're holding up the line."

I step out of the way and run a finger over the paper in my hand. STAFF MEMBER: IVANDER. STAFF BUNK: ROOM 306.

I hold my hand over my eyes to block out the sun and squint at the staff scurrying like ants. They direct guests over the elegant gangway and haul luggage and port supplies over a separate wooden gangway at the back of the ship.

With a heavy sigh, I start walking up and down the lines of staff members. As I elbow between them and dodge passing carriages, I call out for Ivander every few minutes. Each staff member I approach either gives me a hard stare and looks away, or smirks when they hear the name and says, "Good luck."

Surly or friendly, it doesn't matter. Not a single person stops long enough to help me. Finally, with sweat dripping down my back and wisps of hair sticking to my face, I pause to catch my breath, leaning against a barrel of what I assume is wine.

"You going to help or are you just going to sit?" A smooth voice startles me, and I whirl over my left shoulder to look at the young man whose raised brows suggest I better start helping.

Droplets of sweat cling to his deep brown skin as his eyes—like crackling wood over a fire, brown with flecks of gold—sweep up and down my rumpled clothes. Although he wears the same uniform as the others, his vest has elegant silver swirls that move over the fabric like water, forming new patterns the longer I stare.

"I'm looking for someone," I snap, the exhaustion from the two-day ride catching up with me.

He crosses muscular arms over his chest, jostling a bag slung over his right shoulder. The sharp angles of his face catch the light of the beaming sun. "Doesn't seem like you're looking. Seems like you're taking a break."

His mouth turns up at the edges like he finds it funny. I step away from the barrel, standing up straight. Something about his clothes looking pristine while mine smell like actual death sets my teeth on edge. "Excuse me? I don't know who you think you are, but you have no right to tell me what I should be doing."

"Do I not?" He reaches down and grabs a bag, hauling it into a pile nearby. "I've been here longer than you. Maybe I'm someone you should listen to."

Now he's trying to scare me. It's the same heckling I got on the first few nights of boarding school. Eliza warned me the older kids would try to frighten me with tales of what happens to new students on their first nights, but they were wrong to try to intimidate a Morphic who can raise the dead. "Fine," I huff. "I've been cooking in this sun looking for the same person for over an hour with no help from anyone. If you really want to help me—"

"When did I say I wanted to help you?" He drops another bag in the pile as his lips pull into a grimace. "You think you're the only one out here sweating? Don't blame the others for not stopping their work. Everyone tries to stand out on the first day of a new charter."

I bite my tongue to keep from snapping back at him. Maybe I shouldn't have let the stress of the day rule me, but now he's going out of his way to be unhelpful.

He turns from me and angles a barrel labeled POTATOES on its side. He rolls it over to the supply pile across from the luggage, narrowly missing my toes. "As it happens, I'm looking for someone too. A new recruit. Some arrogant girl with a rich family who's hoping to steal our spots. Couldn't be you, could it?"

Shoulders slumping, I resist the urge to turn and run. This isn't the start I had in mind. "You're Ivander?" Of course he is. "Glad to meet you."

He nods. "Ivander Harpyrian." He points out over the mass of staff members. "I'm going to tell you something. Every single one of them is looking to earn a spot for a retrial. Most of us are. And the odds don't look as good for *us*. We don't all have famous names to hide behind."

My stomach drops into my toes at his icy tone. He thinks I'll get special treatment because of my family name and be on my way back home in a few weeks. Bold assumption to make. My father didn't even want me to come here. My Morphia would be gone already if it were up to my family. Before I can arrange a coherent argument, Ivander moves on.

He reaches with painted-black fingernails into the bag over his shoulder. "Here's your uniform. I'll be helping you until you get a guest assignment." I wrinkle my nose at the word "helping." He glances up from beneath dark lashes as I take the uniform. I stay a few paces back so he doesn't smell the mixture of sweat and anxiety wafting from me. "I'm a shifter. I work with the performers. Aerial arts," he clarifies.

So that's why his clothes look better than mine. He can change aspects of his appearance. I notice a bandage laced around his hand and another peeking out from beneath his pant leg. Like all shifters, he pays a price of physical injury for shifting. I'm a little distracted by the idea of him swinging on a hanging curtain of silk, muscles rippling in the stage lights. I get the sense I'm supposed to respond. "Resurrector. Roe Damarcus."

"I know who you are." Ivander raps his nails against a barrel ready to be loaded onto the gangway. "Famous father couldn't save you, huh?"

The hairs on the back of my neck bristle. My father couldn't save me from my trial, and he can't save me from this either. When I don't say anything, his voice lowers, and he waves a hand to indicate the staff members around us. "First thing to remember. They're not bad people. They're just here."

His words seep into my skin and dull the ache in my chest. Since I left home, I've been feeling like a prisoner headed to the gallows. Like a girl who murdered someone in her sleep and can't remember why she's being punished. I thought I could control the spirits until two days ago. His words give me permission to forgive myself, if only a little.

Ivander gestures elegantly at the ship, wasting no time in overwhelming me with rules. "You've got to remember that's a prison, not a playhouse. Not for us. For the guests, this is their chance to experience real magic." He places a hand on his chest. "But we're prisoners here. Whether we're right or wrong. Good or bad."

Most of the staff members look disheveled and exhausted, but not Ivander. Definitely not Ivander. I look away before I can get stuck on the defined angle of his jaw. I must look more like the others. The thought terrifies me. Now I'm one of the desperate staff members Mother would be nervous to approach. But like it or not, I did fail my trial, just like everyone here. Staff might be treated like prisoners here, but those are the rules I'll have to follow to make it through this. I don't want to live among the dangerous Morphics like they do in Gryndar.

I don't say any of that, though, and instead ask the question that's been on my mind since check-in. "How do I earn a retrial?"

Ivander holds up a finger and the tip of his painted nail extends into a talon. He wags it in my face, a little too close to my nose. I shrink back to avoid the sharp point. "I'm not done. There are rules." He ticks them off on each taloned finger. "Don't piss off the bosses. Don't piss off the guests. And don't forget to donate your Morphia when asked." He must see my lip curl because he continues. "They don't bleed you dry or anything. Just take enough to power the ship and help keep the Morphia aboard contained."

"Easy as that?" I ask with an edge. None of this sounds easy at all.

He ignores me and claps his hands together. "Right, then. You're going to help me with the luggage." With that, he heads in the direction of the gangway where guests board.

I scurry after him. As we approach the guests handing over luggage, their noses wrinkle as they look at me. My cheeks burn. Ivander, however, flashes a wide smile I've never seen before. Clearly, he saves the charm for the guests. We stand to the right side, greet the guests, and collect their luggage before they board the gangway.

"Let me take that for you, Madam Karmyne," Ivander says with a relaxed smoothness I long to steal. It's as if he's trying to exaggerate my incompetence. He takes an immense rectangular suitcase from the woman's servant. The woman, wearing a heavy sapphire dress and a wide-brimmed traveling hat, smiles.

"Are you here for a week or a month this time?" Ivander asks.

The woman touches his arm with a gloved hand. "Sadly, just a week," she says. "But we'll make the most of it."

"You better come visit me at the theater," he says.

She turns to me. "You're lucky to learn from Ivander. He's always our favorite staff member. I've been saying it since last year."

I force a smile. Last year. Ivander's the best, and he's already been here at least a year. Panic and dizziness come together to make my legs heavy and my vision spotty.

Ivander continues placing bags in a neat pile for other staff members to take to the luggage plank. His pleasant chitchat sounds like the far-off buzz of insect wings. My lips go numb, and my head swims when he says my name. He must be introducing me to one of the guests. I have no idea. The world's spinning, and I hold out my arms vaguely when he tells me to. "Roe will take your bags, Lord Benefor. She'll be careful with them."

Before I can tell him it's a bad idea, Lord Benefor plops a heavy trunk in my outstretched arms. As my knees buckle and arms give way, the trunk plummets to the ground, smashing in an earsplitting cacophony of antique glass shattering and a lord yelling.

Well, shit.

CHAPTER 6

Ivander swoops over me, blocking the sun with his body. I dare to hope he's helping me up, but he leans over me to brush broken glass back into the trunk. My knees sting from hitting the ground. Sweat drips down my face, and I swallow hard to keep from puking.

"She's new, my lord." Ivander lifts the trunk and sets it in the luggage pile. He gives the lid an affectionate pat and sticks a slip of parchment to the top. "I'll have this sent straight to the crafters. Your dinnerware will be good as new by the time you arrive in your room."

The man jabs a quivering finger at me. "But I'll know they've been broken. Those are a family heirloom."

Ivander steps between me and the lord. His smile stays, but his voice lowers an octave. "It's her first day, Lord Benefor. If you hold it against anyone, hold it against me."

Although my head's still foggy, I release a short exhale. I didn't expect him to defend me, especially at his own expense.

"I don't care if she's new. I'll make sure no one gives her their vote. I swear it." Lord Benefor grits his teeth, puts his arm around his wife, and ushers his children onto the gangway.

Ivander's shoulders droop. He drops to his knee beside me when the lord and his family board the ship. The nausea abates, and I peer up at him through the sweaty strings of my hair. "Who brings antique plates onto a cruise ship?"

"Rich men. Only the best for our dear guests." A flicker of a grin dashes across his lips before he smothers it. His eyes narrow as he stands and looks down at me, brown eyes ablaze. "Don't expect anyone else to cover for you again. If you're not going to be more careful for your own sake, at least think about the others who've worked years for their retrials."

Anger prickles beneath my skin. He's acting like I did this on purpose. I wick beads of sweat from my brow with a furious swipe. It's only then I notice other staff members watching us in tense silence. It dawns on me that this situation could have been worse. Much worse. Who knows what that guest might have done if Ivander hadn't stepped in? He might be obnoxious, but he's right.

"Come on. We have plenty of bags left."

I spend the rest of the scorching afternoon lugging heavy bags and trunks to the pile. Despite the sweat rolling down my back and the ache in my joints, I smile at each of the guests as Ivander does. I try to remember their names, although I forget most of them the minute they disappear into the atrium.

Finally, when the sun's dropped beneath the horizon, Ivander stretches his arms over his head and yawns. He runs a hand over the tight curls of his dark brown hair and wipes a bead of sweat from his brow. The port's clear, and all the carriages have left for the day. The luggage and port supplies have been loaded onto the ship, and now only a few staff members check for remaining personal belongings.

"That's everyone." Ivander extends an arm to the gangway. "After you, my lady." He sinks into a mocking bow, and I debate stomping on his foot. Seeing as I don't want to make a worse impression, I go for a grimace instead.

"Here, it doesn't matter who I am." I motion to my muddy riding pants and tunic shirt.

"Now you're getting it." He looks up at the full moon in the sky. "Better get a move on. Guests aren't supposed to be out of their rooms after dark, and neither are we."

I remember something about that rule. Even as a child, I'd been warned not to leave the suite when the stars were awake. Mother always seemed scared at night, even when Father assured her all was well. Eliza hid under the covers, but I stayed awake most nights, peering through the peephole and hoping I'd get a look at whatever monster they wanted us to believe roamed the hallways.

"That's just a trick to keep the guests in their rooms, right?"

Ivander cocks his head. Outlined by the last light of dusk, he could be a spirit himself. "No. That rule's deadly serious."

He gives me a funny look but steps onto the gangway without another word. I follow him, but my feet drag with every step. My family's responsible for the creation of this fantastical Morphia storage container, owns the largest stake in it, and I know almost nothing about it. Of course, he believes I'm a spoiled rich girl who didn't think to do any research.

I follow Ivander and cross onto the ship. When we emerge into the grand atrium, a surge of magic warms my skin. As we pass over the threshold, colors become more vibrant, and I feel like I'm floating rather than walking on the floor.

It's the same feeling I had when I was a child, but I'm seeing it again with new eyes. The vast atrium holds two winding marble staircases and a floating cloud-lift between. A wide expanse of floor flows like cerulean seawater beneath our feet. Each time my boot hits the floor, it creates an illusion of ripples reverberating with the pressure of our footsteps.

Overhead, there's the characteristic black ceiling with twinkling stars suspended in the air beneath it. Glowing illusory animals walk leisurely about the atrium—elephants, horses, and leopards. Even with the night sky darkening the room, golden lanterns with ethereal silver light and a massive, gleaming indigo chandelier keep the area bright and inviting.

Still, I sense an electric current of tension among the remaining staff members pushing mops around the illusion floor. There's something eerie about how fast the guests have fled to their rooms. The hair on the back of my neck stands on end, and I jump when Ivander clears his throat. "Let's go. We'll be some of the last ones tonight, seeing as it took you so long to find me."

An illusion of a tiger's silhouette outlined in shimmering orange stars runs past me and locks its jaws around a pillar. Sentient towel animals run across the atrium carrying toiletries on their backs to the guest rooms above. A towel animal of a dragon breathes a puff of fire before taking flight to bring an extra blanket to an upstairs room.

Morphia is the magic of alteration. We morph what already exists. But we're limited in what we can create in Tamarynth, where there's no raw Morphia and the magic is restrained to what each Morphic can create with their personal gift. Here, Morphic power is enhanced by the sheer proximity to the extracted Morphia. The floating stars, illusion creatures, and towel animals moving on their own wouldn't be possible back home. The luminous jars of raw Morphia kept aboard make the magic stronger, much like it was centuries ago when raw Morphia thrived in Tamarynth. Now the only place children will see live dragons is aboard this ship.

"What about the 'don't be out after dark' rule?"

Ivander sighs, clearly fighting the urge to roll his eyes. "Mandatory for the guests. Cautionary for the staff. The bosses don't care what happens to us. There will always be more Morphics failing their trials to replace us. Besides, for the bosses to enforce that rule, they would have to risk their own lives in the hallways at night. Not happening."

I'm not easily frightened, but something about this place sends a chill through me. It may be breathtaking and full of magic, but there's a reason we keep raw Morphia locked away on a ship far away from our lands.

Ivander jerks his head toward the staircase. Upon second glance, I notice that the wide staircase spirals directly into a hole in the deck, as if it descends into the watery floor. "The bosses are on deck four and staff are spread over decks three and four. You're on three."

He crosses to the banister and leaps onto the marble stairs without touching the glass railing. Crater marks in the marble make the steps appear like the surface of the moon. He moves with the grace of a butterfly gliding on the wind and reaches his hand out to me.

I ignore his offer and take a tentative step down onto the staircase with my arms by my sides. Although it's a bit disorienting to feel like I'm sinking beneath the floor, I follow him to deck three. Compared to the ethereal light and blanket of magic on the fifth floor, I'm struck by how dim and confining the lower floors feel.

In contrast to the wide-open atrium, these hallways are narrow and lit with rectangular iron lanterns rather than starlight and chandeliers. A bloodred carpet extends the length of the hallway, and Ivander points to doors as we pass. "Laundering service. You'll need to know where that is no matter what your job is. Trust me." We walk a few extra paces, but he keeps glancing behind like something might be following us. "The Morphia steers the ship. No need to worry about us going off course."

As a resurrector, I bridge the gap between worlds, living and dead. I've never feared the dark. It's hard to be afraid of much when you can conjure spirits at four years old. But here, the shadows on the walls make me shiver.

"This is the med-bay. Make sure to file an incident report if any of the guests get hurt when you're in charge. If you don't account for every detail, they'll punish you for it."

As he talks, black spots eat at the edges of my vision. I make myself put one foot in front of the other, although the walls seem closer, and the shadows start to move. Splintering cracks shoot through the walls, and trickles of scarlet blood run from the porthole windows. I swallow hard and reach over my shoulder for an arrow, but then I remember they took my weapons.

The blood flows faster in thick currents of red. Outside, it's as if the sea has turned to blood too. The stomach-dropping thought that we're sinking makes my throat tight, and I can't speak. The instinctual urge to race to a higher deck makes my muscles tense. A low rumble shakes the ground beneath my feet, but someone seizes my arm before I can bolt.

Ivander wrenches me inside a wood-paneled room with a back wall covered in multicolored glowing jars. Once he closes the door behind us, the lightheaded disorientation abates, and I gulp fresh air again. "What was that?" I ask, thankful the sinking feeling is gone.

Ivander shakes his head. "Don't ask. You want to sleep tonight."

"I don't scare easy."

"Good." A low voice from behind startles me, and it takes everything I have not to jump out of my skin. Bad time to act brave.

I turn around to face the man who spoke. He towers over me. As he runs a tanned hand over slick black hair, he takes a step toward me. The skin of his face stretches thin over the sharp bones of his skull, making him look more skeleton than man. I catch the metallic scent of blood like I did in the hallway and notice bloody slits in his lips. Dark, half-moon circles under his eyes make him look older than he probably is.

The man wears a heavy, dark gray coat over his shoulders, obscuring all but his hands from view. His fingertips are bloody and raw, more exposed bone than flesh. I can only assume these physical effects are from being in such close quarters to raw Morphia and handling it for extended periods of time. Father told Eliza and me that many of the bosses were Morphicbound, desperate for access to raw Morphia after losing their own.

While Mother warned me to fear everyone aboard the ship when we stayed, I only saw Father nervous when he talked about the bosses. He warned Eliza and me that the position attracts some of the coldest men and women in Tamarynth. Father helps oversee the recruiting process, and he says they're often former prison guards who are unafraid to carry out harsh punishments if needed and don't mind being at sea for the two-year contract. But they're always ex-Morphics. Bosses also receive a significant sum of gems, but Father says it's the raw Morphia that keeps them returning to the position.

I swallow hard, waiting for someone to speak. "This is Boss Stellan," Ivander says. "He'll be taking some of your Morphia this evening."

I've been so distracted by the wall of glowing jars I didn't notice the metal reclining chairs at the left side of the room. Beside each chair, there's a tray with a gray potion and an empty jar beside it. My mouth dries, and I step backward.

"I thought it must be a rumor when I heard a Damarcus was coming to serve aboard." Stellan's dark eyes survey my face. "Yet here you are." Stellan holds up his hand and motions for me to sit in the chair. Every part of me screams not to move, but Ivander hops into the chair next to mine without hesitation. He takes a tiny sip from the gray liquid and holds the empty bottle beneath his eyes. Silvery tears fall into the open jar. He bites his lower lip, but his face relaxes when the tears stop.

Now Ivander's jar glows with light.

Without looking at me, Stellan hands me the potion. It's my turn. I sit in the metal chair, careful of Stellan, and press the odorless potion bottle to my lips. The Damarcus family invented this potion. A potion to extract Morphia. I can't look afraid of the potion my ancestor created. A tiny voice in my head reminds me this same potion drains Morphic abilities too.

As if sensing my hesitation, Ivander says, "It's impossible to give more tears than the small donation jar allows. The process to extract Morphia takes . . . much more."

I take a small sip and icy liquid tickles my tongue. The sensation grows stronger until it feels like tiny pinpricks piercing the inside of my mouth. It has an acidic, sour taste that puckers my lips. When I swallow, the icy stabbing subsides, but my throat burns instead.

Stellan scribbles my name into a journal. "Roe Damarcus," he says as my skin begins to tingle. Then it burns like my throat. My eyes throb, and stinging tears stream from my eyes. I raise my hands to wipe them away but stop myself. My cheeks are white-hot and wet.

"You'll come here every night before sundown to donate your Morphia. If you finish your work after sundown, it is still your responsibility to donate. Even at nightfall. Fresh donations keep the ship strong as a container and provide the magical experience. If you or any staff aboard miss a dose, you forfeit retrial and face immediate extraction."

Ivander's eyes narrow, but he stays silent. I nod with gritted teeth. Stellan continues without regard for my straining muscles and the sheen of sweat on my skin. "The retrials occur quarterly. You will compete with the other staff members for a chance. Guests and bosses vote on which staff member gets a retrial based on your work performance. That means you're going to be a good girl, aren't you?"

The tears stop abruptly, but the stinging doesn't fade as fast. My chances at a retrial are based on a freaking popularity contest. Not only that, but I'll be competing against hundreds of other staff members. I force my lips to move. "How close are we to the next trial?"

Stellan taps a finger to his lips. "A month now. You've been assigned a concierge position. You'll be serving one family for a month-long stay."

Stellan grabs our jars and walks to the back wall. He fits the jars into empty slots, and the air charges with energetic power. He stays staring at the jars with his back turned to us, transfixed, and says, "You may go."

I don't need to be told twice. Without checking to see if Ivander's following, I leap from the metal chair and run for the door. I throw myself into the hallway, trying to get the extraction potion out of my mind and the sour sting out of my mouth.

When I emerge into the hallway, it's like someone has dimmed all the lights and shoved a wasp nest against my ear. An incessant buzzing grows louder, sending sharp stabs of pain through my head. I stumble forward, unsure of which direction I'm supposed to be going. The deck groans beneath my feet in a low rumble. White-hot terror shoots through me as the fear of sinking consumes me again. I look around for Ivander but can't see him.

With another heavy groan, the ship tilts and I fall into the wall. My clothes stick to the paint, but it's not paint. It's hot, thick rivulets of blood and tufts of cobwebs. A scream lodges in my throat, but I can't make a sound. The buzzing is too loud. No one will hear me.

I pull myself from the sticky wall and struggle to stand up straight. If we're sinking, I've got to get to a higher deck. I lurch forward, trying to get my bearings. The stench of blood is so strong I can almost taste it. Nausea creeps up my throat. When I look to the end of the hallway, hoping to see the staircase, my gaze locks on a tall, shadowy, faceless figure. My body trembles, and I have to force myself to keep breathing.

"Slow down. You don't want to wander alone at night."

The sound of Ivander's voice yanks me out of my stupor and cuts off the buzzing in my head. When I turn around to face him, the tense set of his jaw is accusing, as if he thinks I chose to wander off alone in a haunted hallway. I stop and wait for him, dumbfounded by his calm, steady strides. He points down the hallway. "You're all the way on the other end. Follow me."

I look where he's pointing. The shadowy figure is gone, but the cobwebs and blood remain. The groaning of the ship beneath our feet sets my stomach roiling. What did he say again when I asked about the hallways? *You don't want to know.*

As we walk, Ivander talks as if the walls aren't crusted with dried blood and something that might be flesh. As a young girl, I might have loved all this, but that was when I controlled the spooky spider spirits that scared everyone. That was when Father read me creepy stories in the comfort of my four-poster bed, where nothing could touch me.

"You've got a good job," Ivander says, misreading my silent horror for disappointment in my new position. "Hard. Especially with a month-long family." He shakes his head. "But others would beg for your position to stand out for retrial. You could get a bunch of votes by the end." There's bitterness in his tone, as if he already believes I don't deserve it.

"You haven't told me anything about how voting works, so I'm not exactly feeling confident." I try to keep the bite out of my voice, but his scowl tells me I haven't succeeded.

Ivander shoots me a glare but clears his throat. "Bosses and guests vote on which Morphics deserve retrials at the quarterly voting. The nearest one is at the end of the month. Each adult receives a vote, so don't waste your time trying to convince a bunch of kids you're the best staff member. As a concierge, you can receive fifty additional votes if the adult members of your family choose to vote for you, but the families are pretty particular. Most concierges don't earn their family's vote."

I'm beginning to think I should write this down. He continues without asking if I understand. "Bosses vote too. That's why it's so important not to get on their bad sides. Their vote counts for ten extra. There's a mid-cruise vote halfway through the month to entertain guests and allow staff to see their standing. But the only one that counts for retrial is the one at the end of this month." He grimaces. "Guests love gossiping with each other about us. They tend to make a few names popular, and then those few staff members are the only ones getting votes. They will be watching your every move and taking notes on your performance from day one. Each mistake could cost you."

I try to keep my face impassive, but my fingers fidget at my sides. I haven't been properly trained for this position, and I'm going to be judged from the minute I start. I take solace in knowing that the guests' opinions don't officially count until the final vote.

He stops in front of room 306 and opens the door without knocking. "Be quiet. Your bunkmate's sleeping."

We enter a dark room smaller than my bathroom at home. A pair of bunk beds rest against the wall across from the door. There's a closed door to the shared bathroom beside the bunks and a floor-length mirror hanging on the door when Ivander closes it. In the dark, I can't make anything else out.

I stand there and wait for him to leave, not wanting to fall apart in front of him. But he doesn't leave. He stands across from me, a darkened shadow in the tiny room. We're so close I can feel the warmth from his body. I try to steady the rapid beating of my heart. "What's wrong?" he whispers.

I don't know what to say. About my new job. About the bleeding walls. About Boss Stellan. None of it. But everything I've held back today—the anger, the fear—compounds into a ball of rage held back by a whisper.

"What do you mean what's wrong? Everything about this is wrong. None of this is what I thought it would be. It's bad enough having to come here, but now there's almost no chance of me getting a retrial. I may as well have stayed home." The person in the lower bunk rolls over in their sleep, and I lower my voice. "It's not fair."

Ivander's silent for so long, I wonder if he's left the room. Finally, he whispers back in a quieter voice than mine, yet somehow more intense. "No. It's not fair that you got a good job to start. With the bosses kissing your ass because of your great-granddaddy, you'll be out of here in a month. With your Morphia." He scoffs. "Don't tell me it's not fair. I've been here longer than you."

We stay inches away from each other, chests heaving. The knot in my stomach is so tight it takes my breath away. I admire that he had the guts to say it, but that doesn't mean it hurts any less. I wish I were as confident I'd be getting out of here with no repercussions. But I forgot who I was whining to—someone who's been here longer than me. Much longer.

The girl in the lower bunk lights her lantern and interrupts our private corner of darkness.

Ivander holds my gaze with his brown eyes—the intensity in them like burning coals in the lantern light. "Sorry, Alana," he whispers. "Go back to sleep."

The softness of his tone contrasts the dagger-sharp edge he used on me. There's a gentleness when he says her name that I doubt I'll ever get to hear again.

We hold each other's gazes for another long moment.

I'm grateful when he leaves the room without another word to me.

Alana turns back over and pulls a blanket over her head. In the meager light, I climb up to the top bunk and fall onto the thin mattress with a flimsy wool blanket. As I lie there, not thinking about my growling stomach, not undressing, I think about the way he looked when I said it was all unfair.

I'm not sure what I saw in the stern set of his jaw and his tense shoulders. But I know he only saw a spoiled or clueless girl, or both.

I'm less angry than I am afraid he's right.

I do know he knows way more about this place than I do. And he's my competition.

CHAPTER 7

I wake to a girl peering down at me with her lantern raised. I push myself into a sitting position and smack my head on the ceiling. My body already aches, and the new throbbing in my skull doesn't help.

"Are you okay? You've been asleep for a while," the girl says. She wears half of her dark brown hair up while the lower half is left loose, and she's outlined her deep brown eyes with soft black paint.

I realize with an unpleasant lurch in my stomach that she's already dressed in her uniform. "What time is it?" I croak.

"Just before dawn. You'll want to hurry. Breakfast will be over soon." She waves her hand over a cramped wardrobe in the corner of the room. "I laid out your clothes. All you have to do is take a bath before we go."

That's a nice way of telling me I smell. My joints creak as I climb down from the bed and gather my clothes for the bathroom. Exhaustion makes my limbs heavy, but I'm grateful I had no deathmares last night after a full day without using my Morphia. I hold out my hand. "I'm Roe Damarcus. Resurrector."

The girl's eyes widen as she takes my hand. "I've never met a resurrector before. Or a Damarcus." She brushes her hands over a dark blue skirt to smooth the wrinkles. "I'm Alana Reyes. Emotive."

Now that I'm standing in front of her, her beauty is even more apparent. She has long dark brown hair, golden-brown skin, and inviting eyes, but it's her shy smile that makes her glow. Already, her energy makes me feel less tense than Ivander did.

Emotives can manipulate how other people feel emotions. They can't create anger or happiness, but they draw upon people's emotions hidden beneath the surface and enhance or diminish them. I've heard they lose feelings proportionate to the use of their magic. Mother made me visit an emotive healer after Leith died, but she couldn't mask my pain for long.

Alana clears her throat and pats a timepiece on the dresser. "I'd love to talk, but we don't have time."

I run into the bathroom. The tub's so small I have to pull my knees to my chest to wash. There's only one kind of soap. I must have twenty soaps and scented oils in my bathroom at home. After a freezing ten minutes in the tub, I yank a comb through my hair and pull the strands into a quick, messy braid.

Alana has picked an off-white tunic shirt, a black vest, and an indigo skirt with off-white stockings. As I lace black boots, I tell myself I'll wake early enough to pick my own outfit tomorrow. I tuck flyaway hairs behind my ears as I leave the bathroom and stand before the small hanging mirror in our room. The mirror lets out a little cough and I yelp.

"Should have warned you about the mirrors," Alana mutters. "They're chatty. Stand long enough, and you'll get a helpful tip for your future."

"According to today's position of your guardian Rivener, Medryna," the mirror croaks in a rasping voice, "you'll need patience and a winning smile."

"A little vague," I say as I try to get my breath back.

Alana shrugs with a small smile. She dabs crushed black powder into the creases of my eyes and swipes a dash of pink paint onto my lips. "Dress code," she tells me. "Plus, it goes over well with the guests if we're wearing it."

Warning bells sound in my head. Even as a lady of Damarcus Estate, I'd never been required to wear makeup. I nod like I'm not surprised to hear it.

As we walk together through the hallway, Alana points out rooms and the names of people who live there. I'm not really listening, too transfixed by the walls to hear her. Whereas blood and flesh desecrated the walls last night, today they show no abnormalities. They are plain, white walls with iron lanterns.

"We're here," Alana finally says. The sign beside the door reads CREW MESS, but I don't need the sign to know there's food. The smell of bacon makes my mouth water.

When we enter the room, a hush falls over the chattering voices. Although I expected the crew mess to be another small room, it's not. Several long rows of rectangular dining tables with small stools anchored into the floor fill the space. At the front of the room, chefs in white button-down coats restock a buffet line.

The inviting array of food is diminished by the presence of several bosses lining the walls. They wear brown belts that hold daggers, polished short spears, and potion vials. They all wear black gloves, obscuring the grisly, wounded fingers I witnessed last night. All of them have the same gaunt, skeletal faces with bloodstained lips and sunken, bloodshot eyes that remind me of the spirits I call back from the dead. On each of their necks, there's a black tattoo that I assume was once meant to be a constellation but, for most of them, has now morphed into what looks more like a black hole infecting the surrounding skin.

Alana bows her head as we walk past them but relaxes when we move farther away. She wiggles her fingers in a shy wave as she leads me to the front table closest to the buffet. "There's a ton of newbies here today." She sits on one of the stools and pats the empty one next to her. "Whenever we get to port, a load of new Morphics join."

I sit and my face heats under the scrutiny of so many pairs of eyes. The hairs on the back of my neck stand on end. The bosses watch me too. "Then why are they all looking over *here*?"

Alana's lip quirks. "Because you're Roe Damarcus. News traveled fast that the daughter of the only Morphic on the High Council had to join us."

I expect the same judgment I got from Ivander, but she waves her hands in defense. "I'm sorry. I didn't mean for it to come out that way. We don't have any resurrectors on staff either. That might be another reason why they're looking."

Hot shame nibbles at my insides, but I try to ignore it. Being judged for my father's position is one thing, but being judged for resurrection feels like a personal attack. I may as well try to make a friend since everyone else is looking at me like I'm about to raise an army of the dead. "What's your job, then?"

"I'm like you," Alana says, craning her neck to look for someone. "Concierge. I got promoted from deckhand at the beginning of the year. Everyone says I'm getting good with the guests. Maybe I'll actually have a shot for a retrial."

I talk to smother the loud rumbling of my stomach. "How long have you been here?"

Alana blushes and tugs at the ends of her hair. "Only a year. Sorry, I know I shouldn't be complaining until year three. That's what the veterans say, anyway."

I must look surprised because she explains, "I'm only seventeen. I had to come here early because of an incident at my boarding school. I went to Corraine's Boarding School in Kalenar." Her cheeks warm, as if saying the name aloud is too prideful. It's one of the most rigorous boarding schools in Tamarynth, and the teachers are known for having unreasonably high expectations. "I always put so much pressure on myself, but I was doing well. I had a close friend, though, who was struggling and really needed to pass her history course. Her parents threatened to send her to study with her strict aunt in the remote mountains of Illoryan if she didn't bring home perfect marks. Our teacher was known for giving unfairly hard tests."

She bites the ends of her nails before continuing. "My friend was crying during one of the tests, and I knew she wasn't doing well. After she turned it in, I used my Morphia on the teacher to influence her emotions while she was grading." Alana sighs. "Clearly, I shouldn't have."

It's quite the punishment for trying to help someone avoid their parents' wrath. I've heard no one goes to the ship before they're sixteen, but I never considered what it would look like for that grace period to end. I mistakenly thought everyone here would be older, since most are here because they fail their trial just before their nineteenth birthday.

My time at Almanac's Boarding School wasn't as rigorous as Alana's, but it was lonely. I'd have been grateful for a friend like her while I was there. Before I can tell her this, she blows out a puff of breath. "I wish Ivander would hurry up. He always does my nails before work."

My head snaps up. The way she says his name, it sounds like they're friends. I can't help but wonder if he's not eating with her this morning because he knows I'm here. Before I can ask, a commotion near one of the back tables startles us. Bosses descend upon a pair of boys waving their arms emphatically.

Alana sucks in a breath. "Traveston Santos and Jerell Malone. They both had two insufferable families on back-to-back charters. They like to act out the arguments they've had with the families for their friends. You know, do impressions of the guests and things like that. The bosses hate it."

I sneak glances at the back table. One of the bosses with greasy brown hair forces one of the boys' lips open. She pours red liquid down his throat, and he screams. The other boy swallows the same potion, and they're both led away by a pair of bosses.

Alana shakes her head, saying a quick prayer to the Riveners. "The red potion makes your body feel like it's on fire from the inside. I've never experienced it," she adds quickly. "The bosses use raw Morphia from the jars to create potions like an alchemer. Of course, they aren't anywhere close to the strength of a true alchemer's, like your father, but they do create some terrifying concoctions."

"Why do Traveston and Jerell keep doing it, then?" I ask, trying to contain my shock at such a painful punishment for mocking guests.

Alana shrugs. "You've got to let off steam somehow in this place. I guess they decided it was worth the risk."

Someone slams a metal pan of scrambled sea falcon eggs down on the table.

I wrench my head to the right in time to see a short girl wearing a chef's coat staring at us with her arms crossed.

"You know this is a buffet, right? I'm not going to serve you." Her pink-toned skin flushes in the heat of her pan. She seems oblivious to the scene at the back of the room, or maybe she's used to it. Her long, curly blond hair is tied back with a ribbon, but it's threatening to break free.

She raps her nails on the wooden table and narrows bright green eyes at us. "But I've got about five minutes to talk, so spill. Who's the new girl?"

With this declaration, a few others sit down. I figure she knows these staff members well. The blond-haired chef takes a seat, pushing the eggs to the end of the table. Alana reddens when the chef sits but distracts herself by picking at her nails. "Don't overwhelm her. Introduce yourselves first."

The blond girl flicks her thick ponytail over her shoulder and extends her hand to me. Her grip's firm and strong. "Isla Langston. One of the head chefs on board. I'm an enhancer and—"

"And she's never going to get a retrial because she's mean. Doesn't take crap from the guests." A boy with beige skin and midnight hair swept over his forehead cuts her off. "I'm Niko Harada. Also an enhancer, but better at it than Isla."

Isla smacks him from across the table with her egg spoon. "He's a head chef too. The only competent one I work with," she mutters.

Not surprising that they're both chefs. Enhancers manipulate experiences with food and drinks. When I was a guest on the *Celestial*, I had ice cream that transported me to a favorite childhood memory of chasing puppy dog spirits through the gardens with Eliza, before she detested Morphia magic. As Isla and Niko bicker, I can't help but smile. Maybe this place won't be as bad as I first thought. With threads of light beaming through the porthole, it doesn't seem as scary in the daylight.

A girl sits on the stool across from Isla and grabs the chef's hand. She has dark brown eyes and gold paint dusted over her umber cheekbones. Her long braids are arranged in a half updo, and she wears a sparkling red costume and red rhinestone stockings. She squeezes Isla's hand. "You are a volcano when you're stressed." She leans over the tabletop and plants a light kiss on Isla's lips. "But I'll put up with it."

Alana looks away from the two of them. "I'll get us some food. Guests will be waking up soon, and we don't want to be late."

When Alana leaves the table, the girl in the scarlet dance costume extends her hand to me. "Zora Blase. I'm a crafter. I create costumes and set pieces, but I also perform." She taps a finger against the sparkling bodice of her red costume. "This will burst into flames when I'm in the air."

"In the air?" I ask.

Zora laughs. "I perform with the aerial ring, but it gets tricky when I craft. I don't know how much you know about crafters, but we lose our sense of touch when we use our gifts." She pats the bodice once more. "These little flames are going to cost me."

Isla lets out a low whistle. "I wish I had time to watch one of your performances today."

Niko shakes his head with a pointed look at me. "Isla and I won't have much time for socializing. Food preparation is stressful the first days of a new charter."

This group doesn't remind me at all of the scary staff members Mother told me to avoid when I was eight. They also don't seem as annoyed by my presence as Ivander was.

Alana slides a heaping plate over to me as she sits back on the stool. "Here. I wasn't sure what you liked, so I got a lot."

"Thank you." My mouth waters. While the chefs may save the art of presentation for the guests, there's no denying this is the same elite food the ship is known for. The plate's brimming with buttery sea falcon eggs, oat porridge drizzled with spiced honey from Sarryndar, which my mother saves for special occasions, plump sausages, toast slathered in gortha spread made from a rare nut native to the province of Gorthe, breakfast cakes with candied berries and cinnamon cream, and sizzling strips of bacon with a maple glaze.

Before I can shovel the first bite in my mouth, Isla taps her spoon against the side of the metal pan. "Are you just going to assume all of us already know who you are?"

My cheeks flush. "Sorry. I'm Roe Damarcus." I half whisper Damarcus, for some reason devoid of the pride I normally feel when saying my name. "Resurrector."

"Damn," Zora whispers. "What'd you do to get yourself here? I'd think a Damarcus could skip their trial." Zora drops her spoon as she raises a bite of porridge to her mouth. Isla has to grab it as the lack of feeling in Zora's fingers causes her to miss several more times.

Bitterness makes my first bite of eggs taste sour. "I couldn't skip it. I failed like the rest of you."

Alana clears her throat. "She's still adjusting. You all know how hard the first days are."

Niko nods, dark brown eyes warm as he gives me a reassuring smile and takes a sip of juice. He wipes his brow with a towel over the shoulder of his chef's coat. "I'm still adjusting too. This is only my second month. Let me know if you need help."

"Actually," I blurt, sensing Isla and Niko are about to go back to the galley. "I was wondering if you knew anything about the bosses. I saw what happened at the back table." I keep my voice low. "I met Boss Stellan last night, and he seemed . . . odd."

The four staff members exchange looks. Isla leans forward so that her head's bent over mine. In a low, gravelly voice she whispers, "Odd is the understatement of the year. The thing you have to understand is this is not your average job. This is a punishment. We got what we *deserved*."

Niko's dark eyes fall to the table. "I was nervous during my first week, and I burned a guest's dinner. I never do stuff like that at home."

I take a deep breath before asking, "What happened?"

"Boss Charmaine cut off three of my fingers." Niko massages his right hand and shudders. He glances to one of the bosses standing along the wall and lowers his voice to scarcely above a whisper. "She grew them back with Morphia, but it was awful. My fingers didn't feel the same for weeks."

Alana sets down her fork and touches Niko's arm. "It wasn't your fault." She turns to me. "The bosses use the donated Morphia for their own ends sometimes. But non-Morphics using Morphia that way comes at a price. You've seen the way it affects them physically to be Morphic-bound."

My hands curl into fists and fall to my lap. My food lies forgotten. "If the bosses punish people like this, why . . ." It feels treasonous to say aloud, but I force the words out. "Why not bring this to the council?"

Niko nods. "I've been saying for a month that we should revolt."

"Keep your voice down." Isla elbows him in the ribs. "I'll tell you the truth, Roe, though you won't like it. The council won't do anything because we're criminals. We're being rehabilitated before we're deemed fit to return to society. Simple as that. We deserve punishments. Second, any small rebellions aboard are put down. The bosses have raw Morphia and are more than a match for us. Not to mention, rebelling is what almost caused a war centuries ago. Look how that worked out. We all keep the peace, so we have a chance of going home to our families one day."

I'm too stunned to speak. She's right. We deserve to be here in their eyes, and the council doesn't care about what the bosses are doing to those who failed. Rebellions often end in disaster.

Isla clicks her tongue and squeezes Zora's arm before jumping to her feet. "As much as I'd love to stay and chat, I've got to go. Time to start cooking for the people who matter."

Niko pushes his stool out, too, but his fingers worry at the buttons on his coat. "Which restaurant are you at today?"

"Where do you think?" Isla grumbles. "The Harlequin." Her gaze cuts to me and she explains. "Serves upscale dining all day. Wealthier families. Higher expectations. I'll probably see you and Alana there."

She and Niko leave together, discussing the pros and cons of serving well-done cuts of winder meat versus telling the guests to eat their shoes instead. My stomach plummets into my toes at the mention of my job. Up until this sickening moment, I'd managed to shove the idea of serving guests out of my mind.

Alana pushes her plate of food away and glances back toward the door. "I guess Ivander went in early to practice."

Zora takes a sip of the juice Niko left behind. "Crafters can do nails too. I could fix them up for you. Not as good as Ivander can, though." She chuckles. Again, I'm struck by the affection in her tone. I realize Ivander has reserved his bitterness for me, and the feeling is worse than the sour sting from the potion last night.

Alana bows her head. "No, it's okay. Roe and I need to get our jars, anyway."

Zora shrugs and leans over to touch her toes in a folded-over stretching position. As I watch her, a question bubbles to the surface before I can stop it. "Do you work with Ivander? He mentioned being a performer."

Sunbeams from the porthole illuminate the gold dust on her cheekbones. "Yeah, he's a performer, but he could have any job he wants. He's annoyingly good with the guests. Wait until you see him on the silks." She sighs. "Breathtaking."

"If he's so good with the guests, why hasn't he gotten a retrial?" I don't mean for it to come out accusatory, but it does.

She brushes stray crumbs off her costume and stands. "Because every time he gets close, he takes himself out of the running. He's been here a year and a half—since he was seventeen."

"He doesn't like to talk about it," Alana explains, "but he was sent here before his official trial. Like what happened to me."

Zora nods. "He forfeits his chance at a retrial so he can help other Morphics before his final year. I know how it sounds. Trust me, no one wants to be here. But Ivander . . . Ivander's trying to help."

I push my own plate away. A part of me marvels at his desire to help his friends and the other part of me can't believe he'd be stupid enough to risk his own Morphia. There has to be another reason he's still here. Zora's holding something back. But it only reminds me I'm going to have to carve my own way in this place. Ivander may be dedicated to his group of friends, but he made it clear he thinks I already have an edge. And if I get a retrial because of my last name, one of his friends doesn't.

But no one searched for an excuse to leave my table today. No one stopped talking to me when they heard I was a resurrector. Sure, some people stared, but these four treated me like one of them. Although my head's about to burst with new information, I think they've accepted me.

Alana touches my shoulder, and I startle at her kind touch. "We need to go. We can't be late."

But the warm mood fades as I realize I'll still have to watch my own back. Just like I had to fend for myself back in boarding school. Even my friends didn't like to be alone with me because resurrection scared them. And others pretended to like me because of my father but talked behind my back because of my magic. *Witch*, they'd whisper. *Stay away from the Death Witch.*

Zora walks ahead of us, and I follow right on Alana's heels, not wanting to fall behind on my first day. "So how do we make sure to get votes from the guests?"

Alana chuckles and throws open the door to the hallway. "It's our first day of a new charter. We're just trying to survive."

CHAPTER 8

Alana leads me into the storage room after breakfast. I expect rows of empty trunks and cleaning supplies, but the whole room shines with luminescent neon jars. Bosses wearing cloaks and black gloves hand out small jars from the ceiling-high stacks to each staff member. Alana and I join the shuffling line and wait for our jars.

My palms sweat. I wipe them on the fabric of my skirt and whisper to Alana. "I've never worked with raw Morphia before. What are we supposed to do with it?"

"You use it to enhance the guest experience."

As the line thins, we step closer to the bosses. The columns of jars make me wonder about the rest of the ship and how it *enhances* an experience. It feeds on the magic of these jars. It feeds on us. The intrusive image of blood and flesh from last night makes me grateful the magic is contained.

Alana takes a jar from a boss with honeycomb-blond hair twisted into a knot. It's one of the bosses from the mess hall. The jar gleams aqua blue. She clears her throat, lips lifting into a pleasant smile. "Boss Charmaine, this is Roe Damarcus."

The bones of Boss Charmaine's face protrude like Stellan's do. Her pale, peeling skin has deep cracks in it, and the constellation tattoo on her neck has turned blurry and spread so it covers most of her neck. I wonder if that means she's been aboard longer than the others. Boss

Charmaine's bloody mouth remains a tight line as she reaches behind her and pulls a jar from the column. As she plucks one, the other jars fill in the gap without toppling over. "Make magic for your guests today," she says in a flat voice, handing me a glowing violet jar.

The two of us nod to the bosses and duck out of the room without looking back. When the door shuts behind us, I let out a breath. "How exactly am I supposed to do that?"

Alana shrugs. "Open the jar when you want to use it and guide it to enhance what you want. It's more adaptable than your own magic. I use it to make towel animals dance for the children, or I make chocolate volcanoes really erupt. That kind of thing. You aren't limited to resurrection if you have this jar. You can use Morphia any way you want. Non-Morphics are the only ones who face . . . consequences for using it." She must be thinking of Boss Charmaine's cracked skin and her gloved hands.

"You make it sound so easy." I find myself smiling, though. When I was a child here, I had fun with the fantastical elements created by the staff. Mother wrinkled her nose at it like she does all Morphia, but the memories stayed with me. Even on a ship with books that come to life in the library and a weightless game room with illumination pistols shooting concentrated starlight, the staff make the experience. Maybe I can too.

Alana continues, "Just be careful when you use it. Raw Morphia is kind of like lighting a match. A little fire warms your hearth, but too much flame burns your house to the ground. Morphics pay no price for it in its raw form, so it's harder to control than our usual magic. You can make a sea dragon, but your sea dragon may eat someone." She shudders. "That's why it's so important to keep the jars contained aboard. If let go, raw Morphia becomes part of the natural world and creates things that are beyond our control."

"Very comforting," I mutter. I try not to think about the exposed bones of Boss Stellan's fingers caused by dipping his hand into raw Morphia too many times. But that won't happen to me, I remind myself. I'm Morphic, at least for now.

Alana leads me to the marble staircase spiraling through the floors.

"Wait." I stop dead in my tracks. "Where are we going?"

"To the atrium," she answers, brows knitting her forehead into a network of lines. "We have to meet our families."

Sweat gathers on the back of my neck. I feel the same dizziness from when I helped Ivander gather luggage. Alana takes a step toward me and reaches out her hand but stops herself. "Is it okay if I take your hand?"

Warmth surges from my stomach to my chest. Alana's always smiling, but somehow it still feels special when she turns it on me. "No one's ever asked me that before," I mutter.

"I noticed the way you jumped when I touched you earlier today." When my cheeks heat, she says, "We all have something that makes us different. It's nothing to be ashamed of. You should hear all of Isla's food sensitivities."

The way she looks at me, like I'm someone worth putting up with, makes me wish there was a way I could show her how grateful I am. I take her hand. "Yes," I whisper. The pressure of her hand against mine feels so different from the desperate, sweaty grip of those begging me to bring back their family members. It feels nothing like the clammy touch of spirits trying to claw their way back to the living world in my deathmares.

Alana squeezes my hand back. She points up the stairs. "I'll take you to your family. We got the lists last night. I'll help you as much as I can throughout the day. You learn as you go. We help each other."

With the dizziness gone and my heart beating at a normal rate, I hop onto the spiral staircase with Alana close behind. "Does everyone here help each other?"

"No way. We're competing for retrials. Many don't care what they have to do to get one. Our group tries to help each other, though . . . when we can. Ivander's always saying each one of us deserves a shot at that trial."

Except me, it seems. I smother the jealousy that surges beneath my skin. He doesn't know me, so why should he help me? For some reason, his obvious hatred for me still stings.

With nerves jumping like grasshoppers in my gut, I find myself talking more than I would at home. "You and Isla seem close."

Alana stops on the stairs. "What? No. I . . ." She keeps walking but avoids eye contact as we climb. "We used to date but broke up about six months ago. She and Zora are together now, and I'm happy for them. Zora's great but . . ."

"Sometimes you still miss Isla," I finish.

Alana tugs on the ends of her fingers but grins wide before we take the step up into the atrium. The closer we get to deck five, the more I hear voices, laughter, and music. This starts my heart hammering again. I've never served anyone before in my life, unless I count yesterday when I smashed a trunk of precious dinnerware. Every part of my body flushes hot, and I fan myself with my hand.

"Concierge is a great position. Cleaning staff never get votes for retrials." Alana reaches into her pocket and takes out a scroll wrapped with a slim pink ribbon. "Here's your sample itinerary. It lists what a day usually includes. But always listen to your guests. If they want to go to the top deck for lagoon time and you're scheduled for a show, ditch the show."

I gulp hard. What do I remember from my family vacations? Father rarely took advantage of our free admission. We went once a year before Leith died, and I spent one whole day in the library. As I walked through the scenes of horror stories come to life around me, I belonged in the world of spirits and shadows. But meals had been brought to me. No one made me follow my family's schedule.

With trembling fingers, I take the thin scroll from Alana and untie the ribbon. In flowing script, clearly written by Alana, I see the schedule has been broken into manageable pieces. I take a deep breath and throw my shoulders back the way Father would.

I'm not going to walk into the atrium like a scared new hire. The guests are no different from Lysandra's horses. If they sense fear, they'll get skittish too.

"You can do this," Alana whispers as we both step up onto the crowded atrium floor.

A myriad of families dressed in first-day finery speak to uniformed staff members holding drinks and rolled hot towels. Children chase after a shimmering illusion of a bear cub running across the floor. Drinks with fiery red liquid and floating magenta bubbles are carried by staff members on gilded trays. Crafter-made paper napkins shaped like butterflies float into guests' outstretched hands. The same feeling of wonder I had as a child returns to me, and for a moment, I wish the *Celestial* was not the only place where Morphia could run free.

"You'll need your hands for this," Alana says, stuffing her jar of Morphia into the pocket of her skirt.

I shove my Morphia jar into my pocket. I follow her around the edge of the atrium to an offshoot hallway. She points down the hall. "Deck five obviously has the atrium. It also has the Lotus Salon, the library, and supply rooms."

I'm grateful for the recap. I hardly remember all the activities on the ship, much less which decks they're on. Alana's provided a color-coded key in the right-hand corner of the itinerary. Before I can thank her, she whisks me into a supply room where staff members clamor for trays, hot towels, and chocolate-covered strawberries dusted in what looks like powdered starlight. Despite the number of eyes on me, I grab a silver-plated tray and four hot towels as Alana instructs.

There's a cacophony of noise around us. Staff members yell back and forth to each other in frantic tones. "Does anyone have extra heat salves? The Lorensen family is already sunburned . . ."

A staff member grunts back. "They never bring enough of those on board. Don't they realize we can't make apothecary ointments appear out of thin air? Menders can only do so much."

Alana helps me pick a red-orange hibiscus for the center of my tray and small amber gemstones to scatter in a decorative pattern as another staff member jostles my shoulder. "Have you seen a copy of *The Kalenar Timely*?" Her eyes widen as I stammer a quick no. "Mr. Grazielle says he won't leave his room the whole trip if we can't get him a copy."

I'm grateful to leave the chaotic storage room behind. Although the tray only holds towels, a scattering of gems, and a weightless flower, I struggle to navigate the throng of staff and guests. Staff introduce themselves to guests from all over Tamarynth. A woman with brown hair and golden-brown skin introduces herself as Lady Isabella to her staff member. She orders a Sun Drop, the standard drink in Kalenar, though made with glowing golden liquid aboard the ship. Another man wearing iridescent sun protection lotion over fair, freckled skin berates his assigned staff member for dropping his hot towel on the floor. A woman with rich brown skin bestows a Riven Blossom necklace, an ornament more commonly worn in the northern provinces, upon her daughter before following her staff member out of the atrium.

Alana carries her tray with practiced ease and nods across the room to a family with four children hopping on the floor, creating glowing water vibrations each time they jump. "That's my family over there." She nods to a family of four hovering by the staircase. "And that's yours."

The woman holds up a card that reads STALLARD. She places one gloved hand on her hip.

"Just follow your itinerary and try to stay calm," Alana says.

Stay calm. Okay, I can manage that. I bobble my tray and turn over my shoulder, but Alana's already disappeared into the crowd. *Riveners, help me.*

With one hand under the wobbling tray and the other clutching the rim to steady it, I walk to the Stallard family, my legs threatening to give out. The woman drops the sign with a dramatic swoosh when she sees me approaching. "Finally. I was beginning to think you'd fallen over the side."

She wears a midnight-blue, trim-fit gown with an opal-beaded bodice. Black opals are high currency, which tells me she's beyond wealthy and likes people to know it. It's one of the rare dresses that changes color throughout the day according to mood. These kinds of fabrics only work on the ship. Her light brown hair is braided into an intricate crown, and her ivory skin has the washed-out hue of a woman who has been spending too much time inside. A few days ago, she might have belonged among the guests at one of Mother's social gatherings, but today she's my ticket to a retrial.

I drop into a low curtsy before the woman and her husband. The children chatter behind her about the game room and the top-deck lagoon that changes colors. "I'm Roe Damarcus, resurrector."

The woman's mouth parts and her face pales, but she regains control of herself and takes a hot towel from the tray. "*You're* here? A Damarcus . . . I never would have thought. I suppose there are sources of shame in every family." Anger boils in my blood, but the woman continues, oblivious. "Well, Ms. Roe, did you receive any training at all before coming on this ship? The towels won't stay hot if you don't pass them out." Her blue dress slowly transforms into a rich shade of crimson. I'm guessing that's the color of irritation.

The man beside her wears a dark blue coat and vest to match his wife's dress. Although he wears an opal ring, the rest of him looks surprisingly normal. Well-worn boots and too-loose trousers make him look more like a staff member than a guest. The man's dark brown eyes crinkle as he places a hand on the woman's shoulder. "Don't let Asralyn scare you. We haven't done a cruise in a while, and we're a little on edge."

Starting vacation on edge . . . Great.

"I'm Vance Stallard." Vance reaches out his hand, and I let go of the tray long enough to shake it. My arm trembles as I do, and I regain balance before the amber stones slide off.

I call upon the memory of staff members carrying beverages and sputter, "Would you all like something to drink to start your morning?"

Asralyn coughs into an embroidered handkerchief and puts a hand on her daughter's shoulder to stop her chattering. "Darling," she says with a pointed look at me, "we've been here before. Shouldn't you people already *know* our preferences?"

Before I can stammer a response, Vance waves his hand. "No need for drinks. We're already a bit late as it is. So, we'd rather go to breakfast."

"The Harlequin," Asralyn chimes in. "We don't eat that buffet food."

My smiles becoming more forced by the minute, I allow Asralyn to set the name card on my tray, and I hand the tray off to a passing staff member, who I assume keeps the ship clean based on the broom in his other hand.

The little boy squeals as an illusion winder, a shaggy, four-legged beast native to the cliffsides of Windmere, brushes by his leg. His brown bowl cut bobs as he reaches up to stroke the curling gray horns on the creature's head. When his hand goes straight through, he giggles, and his older sister laughs too. Her deep brown hair is braided even more intricately than her mother's and layered with glitter dust.

Asralyn notices me looking and nods to my own hastily plaited braid. "If you want anyone to take you seriously, you'll learn to do your hair properly next time. I've seen children do better."

I'm struck into dumbfounded silence. When I say nothing, Asralyn sighs. "I assume we can't leave this crowded atrium until you know their names. This is Sage. She's nine. And here's—stand still—Ezra. He's six."

This time my smile is real. "Your kids are adorable."

Asralyn takes a step backward as if I've punched her in the face. Her lip curls, and the hem of her dress turns black. "They are not mine." She spits the last word, and the hot fury on her tongue makes my legs turn to jelly.

Vance clears his throat and cuts through the intensely awkward silence. "They're our niece and nephew. Asralyn's sister wanted us to take them. First-timers."

Hot embarrassment makes me wish I could sink into the floor and die. Or maybe resurrect a vengeful spirit to slap Asralyn in the face. I know deep down in the core of my body that she's here to make my life difficult. This woman doesn't care about my retrial or me.

But that doesn't mean the children won't. With instinct moving my arms, I reach into the pocket of my skirt and withdraw the glowing jar of Morphia. "First-timers, huh?" I ask.

When they both nod, jaws slack at the brilliant violet light, I pull aside a staff member carrying a tray of drinks and whisper a request in his ear. I'll risk making us a little late.

Asralyn taps her foot with impatience as we wait. Thank the Riveners it doesn't take him long to return with two bowls of sticky gortha pudding. While made from the same nutlike pod I had at breakfast, this buttery dessert has a special trick that only Morphia can bring to life on board. I just hope it works the same way as it did when I was a child.

I unscrew the lid of the Morphia jar and close my eyes as a wave of light bursts free. I leave the lid off for a flash, then close it, but I connect to the energy the same way I would to the spirit world. I'm careful, like Alana warned me, using just enough to keep control. Then, I take the desserts and kneel before the children.

The energy transfers from me to the puddings, and I experience food the way an enhancer would. I connect to the sticky gortha pod paste and intensify the gooey, syrupy properties of the dessert. When the children each take a bite, their hands and feet become sticky too. What did Father always say? We draw upon what already exists. Intention is important when creating with Morphia. I jerk my head toward the wall. "Try climbing."

Ezra and Sage don't have to be told twice. They run to the atrium wall, stripping off their socks and shoes. With sticky feet and palms, they scramble up the walls like lizards. Children from other families point and yell, "I want to do that!"

I stand and look to Vance and Asralyn. "Follow me. We'll go straight to the Harlequin, and I'll make sure you get a window seat."

Vance winks and makes a sweeping gesture with his arm as if to say *lead the way*. Asralyn's icy eyes narrow, and she grabs the children by their hands, yanking them from the atrium wall. "We're late. Thanks to you. I doubt there'll be a window seat left."

Without another word, she brushes past me. As shame forms a tight ball in my gut, I follow close behind, hoping my ears aren't as red as they feel.

CHAPTER 9

The first day passes in a blur of sweat and close calls. While I'm forgetting my family's drink orders for the third time and carrying heavy trays of winder meat benedicts and omelets stuffed with micora tree root from the banks of Gryndar, I can't help but think of my failed trial.

If only I'd kept calm. I would be training to join the Hawks and putting the finishing touches on my application to university. I'd be sitting in Father's study, breathing in the earthy scent of mushrooms and crushed spider legs while he brews potions and teaches me about his role on the council. I'd be shadowing my father at meetings and helping him choose which Morphic causes to bring to his fellow councilors.

Instead, I help run food and drinks—for multiple courses—to the Stallards' table. Each time I bring the wrong drink or dribble a splash of sauce on the side of the plate, Asralyn's nose wrinkles with disgust. She scribbles notes on my performance to remind me she's keeping track for the end-of-charter voting ceremony.

Despite her distaste, even Asralyn couldn't think of anything to say when we managed to get a coveted table by the window. I'd been begging the hostess to let us into the restaurant, knowing full well we were late, when Chef Isla Langston came out from the kitchen herself to lead us to a window seat.

When I'd gone to the kitchen to ask her why, she'd shrugged with her firecracker smirk, continuing to roll dough for a smoky hearth fruit turnover. "You're Alana's bunk buddy, which makes you one of us now. And maybe I didn't like the smug look on that lady's face."

Deck ten might be my favorite so far. One side of the deck hosts a variety of guest rooms with balconies and a vast ballroom that reminds me too much of home. The green deck takes up the other half along with the restaurant. The Harlequin restaurant sits in an outdoor forest scene with leafy green trees and stone fountains.

My family's window seat rests beside a fountain of a woman with large feathered wings sprouting from the water. Although she's made of stone, she flaps her wings in the spray while the aquamarine gemstones of her eyes follow me. Skilled crafters make wearable wings for guests aboard the ship, but no one's successfully created working ones for use in Tamarynth. I had marveled at her until I glimpsed the gold plaque on her base: OUR GRATITUDE TO THE DAMARCUS FAMILY FOR THEIR GENEROUS INVESTMENT. After that, I tried to look away whenever I got close.

When Asralyn orders a Red Starfall, the cruise's signature cocktail, I'm off to the connected Seeing Stars Bar. The black marble bar is covered in glasses full of red, bloodlike liqueur from the island of Gryndar. I wipe the sweat from my hands before snatching a starlit ice cube. I drop it in tableside, transforming a rolling red sea of liqueur to a glowing white. I have no idea if it's actual starlight, but I'm surprised by how many guests order drinks first thing in the morning.

The best part about this deck, though, are the windows that stretch from floor to ceiling. It gives guests a view of the sparkling cerulean sea, and it makes me feel a little less trapped.

But the tranquility of staring out the windows is shattered by every problem during the day.

Even when I perform the tableside cocktail transformation, much to the children's delight, all Asralyn can talk about is how I didn't put a sparkler on the rim, even though she never mentioned wanting one. Although breakfast takes forever, Vance still wants to see the opening ceremony in Dreamscape Theatre. We've got no time to make it, so I dash us off to deck six only to realize the theater is on deck seven and six holds the gym and shops for souvenirs.

Seeing as we're already here, I'd better use the gift shop to my advantage. We pass by the see-through walls of Starfall Souvenirs, and I make sure to linger there as Vance expresses his disappointment about missing the show. "We'd have made it if we walked there ourselves," he lectures with a pointed look at me. "You are *supposed* to know the ship better than we do. Didn't your great-grandfather oversee the building of this vessel? Not to mention, I *know* your father attends the yearly inspections."

I don't flinch as Asralyn punctuates each of his statements with "She's incompetent, dear. It's not worth it" or "They gave us the defective one." As if I'm some sort of crafter-made object she bought only to realize it was broken. I'm getting used to her dress flushing crimson, and I'm starting to think her wrinkled nose will get stuck that way.

"Auntie, look!" Ezra cries. "The souvenir shop!"

I breathe a silent sigh of relief as the kids, bored with our conversation, press their faces to the glass of the souvenir shop. "Can we go inside?" Sage asks.

Alana did tell me not to say no to the guests. I smile at the kids and gesture for them to lead the way, but Asralyn purses her lips. "I wanted to wait until the last week for them to pick out presents," she snaps. "Now whatever they choose will clutter the room for a month."

Before I forget the manners Mother taught me and spit that I'm sure her attitude is taking up more space than a few toys, Vance places a hand on his wife's arm. "They can have a look around. We missed the show, anyway."

I don't wait for Asralyn's response and follow the kids inside. The souvenirs visible from the hallway glow even more vibrantly once we're inside. Merchandise hangs from the ceiling in spiraling suspended displays adorned with twinkle lights. With souvenirs above, next to, and even below us in see-through compartments in the floor, we're surrounded by merchandise.

Sage runs up to us, clutching a stuffed sea dragon. Its plump body with a long whiplike tail, feathery, soft fins, and small finlike wings resembles a cuddlier version of those found in the lagoon on the top deck. As Sage brushes a hand over the scales, they change from dark green to bright fuchsia and then into deep purple. "Can I get one?" she pleads.

"No," Asralyn snaps. "The scales won't change color once we get off the ship. Put it back."

A staff member with curly red hair and bright green eyes greets Vance and Asralyn with a wide smile. We're some of the only people in the store at this hour—because, of course, there are better activities on day one than the gift shop. The staff member appears thankful for customers. "Is there anything I can help you find?" she asks. "You're smart to come in today. Prices go up later in the cruise."

"Lucky us," Asralyn mutters.

"We're just looking," I hurry to tell her as Ezra almost runs into a hovering display of gemstone jewelry. I snag his arm as the hovering display speeds away from him.

"Actually," Vance says, clearing his throat. "I'm looking for your bathing ointment line. We haven't been able to find Moon Dust in Tamarynth, and I've never found anything that adapts to hair the way yours does."

The staff member leads him to one of the wall displays. "They're specially made aboard. They only last for about a month on land, I'm afraid, but you can purchase a few bottles."

Vance runs a hand through his hair. "Only a month?"

Asralyn gestures to the various paintings on the far-left wall. They're of the *Celestial* sailing against a starlit sky or the top-deck lagoon basking in the afternoon sun. Even in the painting, the lagoon changes colors. "Do you have one of Dreamscape Theatre?"

The staff member's skin flushes red, and she wrings her hands. "That one sold last charter. We weren't able to have a new one made yet."

Asralyn scoffs. "You have crafters aboard, don't you?"

"There was a shortage of paints in our last port stop. They're saving them for the children's paints activities—"

"Did I ask for your excuses?" Asralyn snaps. "I don't see why it would be so hard to make one."

Vance clears his throat. "I'm sure they'll have one made by the end of the month." His weighted tone suggests this is not a request and more of an order. I cringe internally and hope Alana is having a better day than I am.

And the wicked part of me is hoping Ivander's day is going a bit worse.

As the staff member is trying to think of what to say, Ezra runs up to us with a replica of a pistol that shoots concentrated starlight in the game room. "Can I get this?" he yells.

The hem of Asralyn's dress turns black as her patience runs out, and she rips the toy from his arms. Although I'm determined to stay as far out of the way as I can, Asralyn smells my fear and beckons me toward her.

"Since this was your brilliant idea, you can be the one to tell them they're getting nothing until later in the trip."

No way am I doing that. I borrow a trick Leith used to play on me. Instead of telling the kids what they're not getting, I distract them with something more fun. "Who wants to go to the lagoon?" I ask. It takes a little more convincing, but I coax them into spending time on the top deck before lunchtime.

The rest of the day passes the same way.

The kids swim in the lagoon, and I manage to create a mermaid tail for each of them with raw Morphia. I lose a bit of control and the tails propel them much faster through the water than they should, but I pretend the speed was intentional. The kids love it, but Asralyn sneers because she wanted the kids to strengthen their actual swimming skills on this trip. We return to the Harlequin for lunch, and I scarf down a toasted cheese sandwich with Alana in the kitchen. Finally, the kids spend the rest of the day in the game room while Vance and Asralyn enjoy the Endless Night Spa. I don't get a chance to go in, although I'm told it's pitch black inside except for the luminous hot tubs and essential oils that smell like "your most memorable vacation" and "your favorite baked goods."

As the sun sets, I gather the family to head back to their room on deck ten. The highest-paying guests sleep on decks eight to ten while lower-paying guests are on six and seven. The kids begged for room service, so I don't have to deal with the Harlequin again this evening.

When we enter the Stallards' grand suite, my breath hitches. A black chandelier with shining starlight crystals hangs from a ceiling painted to look like the night sky. A massive couch with silver pillows and towel animals sits in front of large sliding glass doors that lead out to an enormous balcony with a hot tub.

The murals change as the kids press their palms to the wall. They shift from swimming sea creatures to unicorns running through the woods to a field of wildflowers. Sage giggles and pulls on her aunt's sleeve. "Can Roe stay with us and play, Auntie?"

Vance sinks into the couch and flips through a book of room service options without looking up, but Asralyn's eyes find me. Her lips turn up as she pets Sage's hair. "No, darling. Roe needs to go see her boss. She didn't do a very good job today."

Vance clears his throat and tucks a rogue curl behind his ear. "We're sorry," he says to me. "But we had to let someone know that this wasn't the service we expected. We paid a lot for this trip."

My heart drops into my stomach. Until now, I'd forgotten about donating my Morphia and seeing the bosses. Panic shapes itself into cold, hard fury in my abdomen. These people had the gall to complain about me.

I'm sorry you paid too many gemstones to be here. This is my life you're messing with. The rage coursing through me threatens to break free in the form of a thousand spirit hands tearing Vance and Asralyn apart.

Stop. Shove it down. I force myself to nod. "I understand," I say, willing my voice not to waver. "I'll do better tomorrow."

Asralyn sits on the couch beside her husband and fans herself with a gloved hand. "Let's hope so. We're here a whole month. I won't put up with your incompetence for that long."

Desperate to get to the door before I cry or scream, I grasp the doorknob with a look back over my shoulder. "Someone will come by for your order soon. Remember not to leave your rooms after dark."

"It's not our first time," Asralyn answers. She plucks off her gloves and tosses them aside. "We know the rules."

The only reply I can manage is, "Good," before I throw myself from the room. Bone-tired and shaking with frustration, I haul myself to deck three. I fidget with the hem of my skirt, dragging my boots on the way to the storage room.

By the time I get there, I'm certain the bosses are going to take turns plunging daggers into my chest. As I wait in line with the other staff members, I can't help but picture a deer punctured with arrows as it tries to outrun its hunters. Just like how the Hawks and I hunted that mender. Did my family ever complain about a guest and send them to the bosses for punishment? The thought disgusts me.

"Are you all right?" Alana asks. She stands with Zora, a few people ahead of me. Judging by the knit of their brows and their wide eyes, I must look worse than I thought.

"Bad day," I croak. Zora exchanges a look with Alana, and they drop their places in line to stand beside me.

Zora wears a black leotard with flowing black trousers, the sheer fabric dappled with rhinestones. "What happened?" she asks, tossing her long braids over her shoulder.

I shrug, folding my arms over my chest. I don't want to talk about how bad today was. Both girls seem to understand I'm in no mood to talk, so they don't pry.

Alana shuffles her feet. "You'll want to prepare yourself. They'll punish you. Maybe with a potion, maybe with the knife." An unsettling silence falls between us. I suppose it's inevitable, but I wish I could turn and run. Alana's head snaps up as if she's remembered something. "When you're done tonight, Ivander wants you to meet him in the theater," she whispers.

This gets my attention. Why would Ivander want to meet with me? He's made it clear I don't deserve any extra help. I lower my voice. "I thought we weren't allowed to be out after dark."

Before Alana can say more, Isla joins us, shuffling between us to choruses of complaints from the back of the line. "Hey," she yells back at them, "I've been standing in front of a hot stove all day. Give me a break." She kisses Zora's cheek and then looks at the three of us with her lips pursed. "Why so silent?"

Zora elbows Isla in the ribs. "Try some tact. Roe's had a rough day."

Isla grimaces. "Oof, yeah, I saw some of that. Heard about it too. Niko said one of your guests made a stink about the color of her shrimp. What a—"

"Language," Alana snaps.

"Sorry. I hope the bosses take it easy on you," Isla mutters. We're two people away from the bosses now, and my palms are sweaty. "I've got something that will cheer you up. One night during this charter, the six of us are gonna hit the bar after the guests have gone to bed. Niko and I have got it all worked out."

One person away from Boss Charmaine now. I gulp and keep my voice low. "After dark? Isn't it dangerous?"

"I warned her we could get caught," Alana whispers, biting her lip. "There are rules for a reason."

"Yeah, I know," Isla says. "But the way I look at it, I'm probably leaving here without my Morphia anyway, so I may as well have some fun."

There's no time to respond. Boss Charmaine extends her hand to me, and we all fall silent. Something tells me she wouldn't approve of secret plans to set up shop behind the highly expensive cruise bar. Her usual gloves are missing, and with a jolt, I notice the tips of her fingers are black from decay. Her fingernails protrude from the dead skin in filed points, as if she shifted them into claws and they never shifted back. Taking deep inhales to keep my hand steady, I give her my Morphia jar and follow her to the chair.

It goes the same as last night. I take the potion. My blood burns, and my Morphia comes out through my tears. The boss takes the jar to the army of other jars but this time, comes back with a knife.

I stiffen, paralyzed with fear. Father's words return to me. Words from when I was young. *The* Celestial *is for bad Morphics, Ro-Ro. Of course it's dangerous for them to work there. It wouldn't be a punishment otherwise. It wouldn't deter them from acting out again.*

Boss Charmaine bends over me as Zora, Alana, and Isla watch. Charmaine presses the cool steel to the tip of my ear. "Few manage to disappoint their guests so thoroughly on the first day. If you're not going to listen, perhaps you don't need your ears at all."

I break out in a cold sweat and scoot as far back in the chair as I can go. Charmaine's face remains impassive, a mask of pressed split lips and blank, sunken blue eyes. "I'm sorry," I whisper. "Please don't . . ."

She holds my head steady with her free hand. She presses my left cheek into the metal chair with her blackened fingers while she slices my ear. Her clawlike nails dig into my cheek, and oozing, dead skin from her raw fingertips sticks to my own skin. I gag from the repulsion.

Hot, stinging pain shoots from my ear across my face. I scrunch my eyes shut, whimpering as blood flows down my neck and saturates my shirt.

As the pain grows, so does my anger.

A pulsating energy builds in my sternum, spiraling out of control until my vision goes fuzzy. I'll make the dead rise up and pull the skin from Boss Charmaine's bones. The longing becomes a desperate, painstaking need. And through the haze of my vision, I catch the edge of a ribbon of silver light bursting from my fingers.

The silver ribbon coalesces to form the spirit of a man I don't recognize. A faceless spirit, content to be my soldier for the night. His mouth's sewn shut, and his neck's scarred from a major wound that might have been a butchered beheading in life.

The other bosses in the room gasp and shout as the man seizes Charmaine by the shoulders. In a blur, he throws her to the ground, and the knife clatters out of her hands. The other bosses rush forward to help, but I pull the spirit back before they can reach her.

Solid. Another solid spirit, capable of real damage. And once again, he *helped* me. Blood gushing from my ear, I slap my hand over the wound and wobble to my feet. Everyone freezes, staring at me with wide eyes and accusatory glares, even the other staff. The bosses draw weapons—more daggers—from beneath their robes.

Although my mouth's dry and I'm dizzy, my voice comes out strong. "If you try to hurt me, I will fight back," I say, knees trembling. "My spirits fight for me."

Part of me thinks the bosses will rush me and drag me off to the cells they keep on the lowest deck, but none of them move. I take full advantage and tear from the room, not looking back to see Alana's face. As I run down the hallway, clutching my bleeding ear, I pray to the Riveners for her to escape unscathed. Isla. Zora. All of them. No one deserves this.

Now that the sun has set, the walls of deck three have changed with the night. Graying and smelling of rot, they appear to close in on me.

But they don't just smell like decay—they've turned from solid walls to a cage of bones with globs of stinking, gelatinous flesh between the rungs. I try to run, but the floor sucks at my feet, threatening to drag me down. Dribbles of blood spatter the carpet, and I'm not certain they're mine anymore. An eerie howl behind me and the sound of gnashing teeth propel me to move faster.

Staff shouldn't have to give Morphia after dark, but the bosses don't care about our well-being. Our lives are unimportant if a guest needs dinner or the ship needs a donation. Our safety is only a priority when it's convenient for them.

For the first time, I'm beginning to understand Ivander's bitterness. He's right to detest the bosses and the way staff are treated. I didn't realize the punishments were this extreme.

I should run to my room, but instead, I throw myself up the stairs, legs burning. When I get to deck seven, I stop long enough to consider which side Dreamscape Theatre is on. Right side. Just as I'm about to move, the stair beneath me cracks, falling away. Heart plummeting with it, I leap forward onto the deck. The deck rumbles beneath me. I have to keep moving. A low growl sounds from the disappearing staircase, and a long, snakelike tentacle shoots out from where the last step gave way. The sticky, dark green appendage drips with steaming slime.

The ooze plops onto the floor and singes a hole through it. Panic drives me forward as I push up onto my feet. My heart slams in my chest as I dodge to the side to avoid the tentacle. It narrowly misses my shoulder and punctures the wall, leaving a smoking crater.

I run, even as the floor beneath me cracks. Something crunches underfoot. I try to keep my gaze trained ahead, but against my better judgment, I look down. Roaches skitter in zigzags beneath my feet. No time to think about it. I'm running, but the ground's splitting open behind me. One step ahead, I bolt from the chasm opening in the floor. The roaches must be running from it too. I catch the edges of leathery, batlike wings as something dives close to my head. I shriek, waving my arms. With a tiny peek out of my half-shut right eye, I see a birdlike body with bat wings and a hooked beak filled with needle-point teeth.

The floor gives another loud groan behind me, but I keep running, swatting the creature from my face.

Suddenly, I pass a girl with a broom in her hand and her eyes squeezed shut. She's frozen, unmoving even with the chaos descending around her. Her fingers grip the broom so tightly that her knuckles have turned white. She mutters under her breath, and even when I yell for her to get out of here, she keeps her eyes shut. Finishing her job tonight is not worth her life.

Despite my better judgment, I skid to a stop in front of her and shake her shoulders. Finally, her eyes fly open. I tug on her arm as the ground rumbles even louder beneath us. "Come on!" I yell. The chasm in the floor continues to advance, but she won't budge. A huge crack opening in the floor knocks us off-balance.

A cold sweat clings to my skin as I realize we must run now or fall to our deaths. I heave at the girl's arm one last time, and this seems to jolt her from her frozen panic. "Run!" I cry, and we both throw ourselves forward. I've lost momentum. It's gaining on us. The girl yelps, and I glance behind me. Her broom's caught on a loose nail. She doesn't have time to drop it before the floor falls out from underneath her.

A silent scream dies in my throat. As I peer over the side to see where she went, a high screech sounds from deep within the ship and I force myself to run faster. With each step, cracks in the floor threaten to bring me to my knees. But I won't let it get me. I propel myself through the gold double doors of what I hope is the theater.

The doors slam behind me, and I lean against them with my chest heaving.

A voice brings me back to solid ground.

"I guess you're learning the hard way," Ivander says, dangling from deep blue silks suspended from the ceiling above the stage. "I told you. You'll want to be careful after dark."

CHAPTER 10

I push hard on the golden handles of the doors to make sure they stay closed. My sweaty palms slip, and I back away, straining to hear noises from the hallway outside.

Ivander chuckles. "It's okay. Doors are barriers. Just like you're safe in your bunk room, you're safe here."

After nothing tries to break through, and no sounds come from the other side, I decide he's right. Whatever was trying to kill me can't reach me if I'm not in a hallway. A bubble of hysterical laughter sneaks past my lips. Something about thinking I'm safe anywhere on this ship after being chased by tentacles and bat-birds seems ridiculous.

The memory of the girl, desperate to finish cleaning before heading for donation, haunts me. I couldn't save her. I didn't try. The guilt weighs heavy, and I can't keep it inside. When I describe what happened to Ivander, his eyes darken.

"You couldn't have helped her. Count yourself lucky you didn't fall too."

Lucky? Maybe he's forgotten he's the one who invited me here. I wouldn't have been in that hallway if I'd gone straight to my room. "Why did you ask me to meet you here?" My voice shakes. "You almost got me killed."

"But you came," he says with a sly smile.

My cheeks heat, and I hope he can't see my face in the dark. He focuses on the strip of silk hanging from the ceiling. He's ignoring me now—actually ignoring me. I want to tell him off, but the fear coiled in my gut freezes my tongue. A shudder racks my shoulders. It could have been me.

With blood staining my shirt, I march down the aisle of the theater. If he's not going to explain himself, I may as well figure out where the best seats are for when I come back with the Stallards. If he's determined to ignore me, I'll ignore him too.

I stride across blue carpeting with silver swirl designs and pass row upon row of royal-blue seats. The stage itself is immense, framed with dark gold architectural filigree and long white candles held by marble statues of witches. Sculpted women with shaggy hair, dark eyes, and creased robes stand in twisted positions at either side of the stage. They each hold a set of candles over their heads. My lip curls, and I'm reminded why "witch" is a disparaging term for Morphics. This is how they imagine our ancestors. It's not lost on me that all the creepy statues are of women.

In the center of an otherwise dark stage, Ivander hangs from bright blue silks. With his long-sleeved midnight-blue shirt glowing, too, he might be floating in the depths of the sea beneath us. I try not to look, but he's harder to ignore than I thought.

Even as he moves, lacing his legs through the silks and bending his back into a deep arch, his eyes stay on me. It's like he's taunting me. After coming close to death tonight, the last thing I want to do is sit still for a performance, but I won't get answers unless I wait. And I can't help my curiosity. I've never seen someone suspended from silks before.

I sink into one of the theater seats to test them out. The seat comes to life beneath me, floating into the air. The whole row of seats floats in the darkened theater, and I swing my legs. I'd forgotten the seats could rise and give audiences a better view of the performers' tricks in the air.

Without warning, his body drops, and I scream. When he catches himself on the silks before hitting the floor, I clap a hand to my mouth. I let my hand fall before he sees and purse my lips into cool disinterest. He pulls himself vertical again and plants his feet on the stage. He grabs hold of the silks, giving them a good tug to test their strength. Then he runs, holding on to the thick strips of fabric and soaring through the air like a bird.

He may only be practicing, but the movement takes my breath away like fleeing from home did, Hawks in pursuit. Although I'd never admit it to him. As he climbs up the silks and transfers into an upside-down arabesque, the roaring of blood in my ears and the urgency I ran into the room with disappear. It's the first truly beautiful thing I've seen on this ship. Something real. No raw Morphia creating animal illusions or chocolate fondues that spout fire. The muscles of Ivander's body ripple with effort, visible even in the feeble spotlight. Despite how much I know I should look away from his powerful form, I can't. He is free in the air, free and beautiful even without magic. He is everything I wouldn't be if I lost my gift. When Eliza gave up her Morphia, she gave up a bit of herself too. I won't let myself become like her.

I force myself to arrange my expression of awe into a grimace as he swings toward me. Ivander clicks his tongue as he registers my annoyance. Finally. "Figured you wouldn't really listen until your heart rate calmed down," he says.

I will my seat to float back down to the floor, and it obeys my command. He doesn't need to know that watching his silks performance didn't exactly slow my heart rate. Once I'm back on solid ground, reality creeps back in. I was one step ahead of the chasm in the floor. Something was chasing me, and I might have been caught if I hadn't run inside the theater. "What was out there?" I finally ask.

"If I knew, I'd tell you. But it changes every night." Ivander lowers himself down the silks, brown eyes locked on me as he descends. "Keeping extracted Morphia aboard comes with a price. The ship isn't as impenetrable as the bosses think. Morphia can create beautiful things, but it can also be very dangerous."

He says it like he thinks I'm responsible for the latest danger. If the extracted Morphia is so dangerous, the bosses should know. I consider not asking at all, but the question comes out before I can stop it. "Why is it only dangerous at night?"

Ivander fixes me with a harsh look that says I should have figured this out on my own. "It's more dangerous at night because that's when every staff member aboard this ship is required to donate their Morphia. As jars of our power are added to the ship, the magic aboard becomes more volatile. We seem to think raw Morphia can be *controlled* as long as we keep it in jars out at sea, but I'm not so sure."

I don't mention that Ivander said *more* dangerous at night. "The floor swallowed that girl," I whisper.

He studies me as if he expects me to argue. But I don't. I won't give him the satisfaction. The bosses don't care what happens to us. I was going to have to learn that one way or another, and I don't think I truly believed it until now. I guess I thought since Father receives regular letters from the bosses and helps oversee the boss selection, things would be different. But I know those letters must leave out the worst of the punishments.

I climb the steps up to the stage, holding my head as high as I can. "Today was horrible. I was horrible." When his feet touch the floor, I speak louder. "You could have prepared me better, as my assigned staff member. Yesterday, you told me nothing. Alana did all the work."

Ivander crosses his bare brown arms over his chest. Silver-blue shimmer dust glistens on his lips and cheeks. My stomach tightens when his lips part. "You were convinced you didn't belong here. I couldn't have done much. Even now, you believe you're different from us."

My breath catches. A throbbing in my ear grows until it threatens to bring me to my knees. It's like he can read my mind. The nasty whispers that remind me I'm here by mistake. I'm not as guilty. I shouldn't have failed.

He arches a brow. "Ah, touched a nerve there, didn't I?" When I don't answer, he drops his arms to his sides and closes the distance between us. I force myself to hold my ground, although I want to shrink away. "You want to know why I brought you here? You need a wake-up call. This place is dangerous. For you. For me. For all of us." He pauses, leveling me with an accusatory glare. "I heard Alana and Isla helped you today. You. A girl who doesn't even think she belongs here."

"I didn't ask them to—"

"I'm not finished." He points to the blood still trickling down my neck. "You're pissing off the bosses, and if you're not careful, you'll drag my friends down with you. And I won't let that happen. I told you the boss votes hold more weight. Their ten extra votes could make the difference for one of my friends. They'll be comparing notes on each of us, trying to catch us doing anything wrong. Anything could knock one of us out of the running, and I won't let it be you."

"I don't want them to get hurt either," I say quietly. He's so close I can practically feel the pulsing of his temple and the strain in his shoulders.

"We all think like you at first. I did," he mutters. "*I'll get my retrial quick because everyone will see it was just a fluke. The judges made a mistake.*" Now that he's down from the silks, he looks smaller but not less sure of himself. "The truth is, we're all a little dangerous here. Just like non-Morphics are. But it's easier to throw us in a prison and take our magic than admit the complexity."

I turn to face downstage, away from him. "My ancestors built this place to keep Morphia contained. It *is* dangerous if we don't keep it in check."

"I can guarantee you that most of the Morphics on this ship don't deserve to have their magic stripped away. And most of them will." His clipped tone bites. "You'll see once you've been here awhile. It took me a month to see it."

It's then that I realize he's not scolding me. He's telling me he believes his friends deserve another chance. Just when I think the weighted silence may sever us both in two, his frame relaxes and he presses his hands together, and a silvery light dances across his fingertips. He reaches out to my bleeding ear.

"Alana mentioned you don't like to be touched," he says hurriedly. Not at all the steadfast, confident tone he uses with the guests or the cold, accusatory tone he used before. "Will you let me help you?"

My chest warms thinking of how kind Alana's been despite the pressure she's under. And he cared enough to listen to her. My brow furrows, but I nod. I won't have him thinking I'm afraid of his Morphia. When his fingers touch the stinging tip of my ear, I don't feel cold and clammy as usual. Instead, I relish the warmth and buzzing energy of the gentle pressure of magic.

He stretches the skin of my ear with his fingers, and the sensation shifts from the sharp stab of pain to a dull tingling. It takes me a moment to realize what he's doing.

He pulls his hands away and says, "Done."

I touch my finger to my ear and feel dried blood but no wound. When I gape back at him, he looks away, almost shy. "How did you . . ." I drop my hands to my sides and try again. "You're not a mender. How did you do that?"

He winces from a deep gash in his pointer finger—the price for using his magic. Blood runs down his hand, and he wraps it with a cloth from his pocket. "Shifters can alter body parts. I've gotten good at growing back the tips of ears. It's one of Charmaine's favorite tactics."

My lips go numb. "She cut off my ear? I thought she nicked it!"

Ivander lets out a quick laugh that lingers like the bubbles of champagne. He stifles the sound the moment he hears the echo, but I don't want him to stop. This is the first time he's laughed for me. "What difference does it make? Either way, it hurts."

Despite myself, I purse my lips to keep from smiling. Ivander reminds me of the books on Morphic gifts Leith used to read aloud that didn't make sense to me until I saw the magic in action.

But I don't have years to waste. The longer it takes for me to earn his trust, the more time he spends thinking I'm stealing his friends' retrials. "You still could have warned me better," I say, indignation returning. "About the hallways, for example."

He reaches out for the silks again. "I did warn you to be careful after dark."

"Yeah, I know this isn't a vacation for us," I snap.

"Do you? You *really* want to know what happened out there? This place"—he gestures wide above his head—"doesn't keep Morphia contained. It keeps it *imprisoned*. Just like it imprisons us." His glinting eyes fall flat. He releases his grip on the silks. "And I would hazard a guess that the raw Morphia on this ship is fighting back."

"Fighting back?" It doesn't make sense to me. Or maybe I don't want it to.

"It's not just the Morphia, though," he says. "The bosses are all non-Morphics, but they exploit the raw Morphia from our jars by using it without restraint. After losing their own Morphia, they'll risk anything to be close to it again. It's changing them."

I know what I can do with a temperamental gift, one I've honed since childhood. I can't imagine it in the hands of a reckless boss with power over others. Even I can't control my magic sometimes. "If it's dangerous, then why does the council keep the *Celestial*?" *Why doesn't Father speak up about this?*

He arches a brow as if he thinks the answer is obvious. "They need us. They need Morphics for their healing, for their craftsmanship, for their militias, but they don't want us unchecked. Don't want us to get too powerful. Making this place has given the high class a vacation and the council access to raw Morphia at will. It keeps us from getting too influential."

It doesn't take a genius to wonder why my father's the only Morphic on the council. My father and I always talked about making things better for Morphics, but he rarely mentioned the ship. If the *Celestial*'s system is broken, that doesn't mean we can't fix it. Father believes in this place for some reason. My great-grandfather invented it for a reason and oversaw its creation. I was proud of this place. Of my family's contribution to stopping the war. The *Celestial* felt like a just punishment—a fair way to achieve retrial.

Now I'm wondering what we've done. If we've not stopped a war, but created one.

"I didn't mean to overwhelm you," he says, the edge finally leaving his voice. "I've been here awhile. I see how things are."

But I'm not upset with him for this. For leaving me to the hallways at night? Yes, I'm angry. For telling me why I don't deserve a retrial like his friends? Annoying, although he may have a point. For telling me the truth about this place? No. It's the most honest anyone's been with me.

He points to stage left. "I laid something out for you." When I don't move, he continues. "The bosses will find a way to punish you if you don't let off steam in the right way. Don't take your frustration out on them, on your family, or in crew mess. Take it out in here."

Still not sure what he's talking about but with my curiosity winning out, I walk to the wings on stage left. I push my way through cables and hanging black curtains to see a costume draped over a prop table. It's a two-piece silver dance costume with dewdrop rhinestones across the bodice. Shifters can alter clothes too, and Ivander's transformed the material so that the rhinestones fall like raindrops. The bottoms are connected to the bodice with a thin strip of sheer, glittering fabric that moves like a waterfall. I'm afraid the material might slip off my body like the liquid it resembles. Where is he going with this?

"It's easier to move in than your uniform," Ivander calls.

I don't know what makes me do it. Maybe I'm invigorated by the idea of ripping off my bloodstained uniform. Maybe it's the idea of sticking it to the bosses in a different way by disobeying the curfew. Maybe I don't want Ivander to think I'm intimidated. Either way, I shrug into the silver costume.

By the time he calls, "You don't have to wear it," I'm already dressed. I unlace my boots and pull my hair free from its bun and walk back onto the stage. When his eyes drop to me on the stage floor and he slides down the silks, I become more aware of my exposed skin. The droplets of rhinestone water cascade along the curves of my body but stay concentrated in the areas I'd want to keep covered.

He cocks his head as I walk toward him. "Your hair's got more red in it than I realized."

It's such an odd thing for him to say. I cross my freckled arms over the thin line of fabric down my abdomen. "Yeah," I mumble to the floor.

Any discomfort I feel falls away as Ivander pulls the silk fabric toward me. He's not staring at me. He's wholly focused on the silks. "This is the only time we don't have to be prisoners. This"—he extends his hand and the silk to me—"helps prevent burnout." He's wrapped his hand in the silks so I don't have to touch the exposed skin of his palm.

I pause, not sure I'm ready to climb an unstable scrap of fabric hanging from the battens. Especially when my spotter has openly admitted that I threaten his friends' chances at life beyond the ship.

"I'm not going to let you fall," he taunts as if he can sense my thoughts, annoyed I would even consider this possibility.

"You better not," I mutter, but I grab his hand. Even through the silk fabric, I feel the warmth of his skin against mine. He pulls me tight against his body. "Is this really necessary?" I mutter. Self-preservation wins over embarrassment as he pulls us both up the silks, and I fasten my arms around his neck. I'm grateful for the fabric of my costume and the silks that mostly separate my skin from his.

The muscles in his body contract with each pull of his arms. The swooping feeling in my stomach reminds me of falling from the roof of my estate when I tied Eliza's embroidered pillowcases to my arms and tried to fly. When we're high enough above the stage that it really does feel like flying, he tilts his chin down to look at me. "Do you trust me?"

My heart slams in my chest, but I keep my voice even. "Why would I? You lured me here to scare me and almost got me killed."

"You're right. Probably should have stayed in your room."

Annoyance makes my panic at being so high in the air dissipate. "But then I wouldn't have had the pleasure of your company."

Ivander stifles what might have been a laugh if he let it go. He reaches to the batten above our heads and unravels another long tongue of blue silk. It occurs to me as he does it that he's hanging on to our silk with one hand. "Careful," I say breathlessly.

He wraps his lower feet in the silks with practiced ease. "Reach out and grab the other set of silks."

"What? No!" No way am I doing this. But his scrutinizing gaze dares me to try, and I don't want to figure out how to get down on my own.

I keep one arm wrapped around his neck and lean back. It takes two tries before I snag them. He's managed to wrap the silks around his abdomen and both feet. "Now, I'll show you how to do a foot lock."

"This high up?" I squeak.

He nods. "And once you're stable, you'll transfer to your own silks."

"No way. What if I fall?"

Ivander flashes a wicked grin. "I'm sure you'll think of something."

Once I get the foot lock down, he shows me splits and arabesques on the silks. Even when practicing simple moves, sweat glistens on my skin and my muscles shake with the strain. I don't do more than watch him with my feet balanced in my silks, but now that I'm suspended in midair, I see why he likes it. Up here we're untouchable, free from the prying eyes of guests and bosses. I can almost forget why I'm here and just have fun.

He's not thinking so much when we're in the air. He talks to me like he might to Alana or Niko. He tries not to get frustrated when I forget moves he taught me five minutes ago. Being here at night feels like a secret. And he's right. The exercise is fun.

I have no idea how long we stay in the air. Finally, he transfers to my silks and helps me slide down. We're both breathing hard, and the effort of holding on to him makes my arms tremble. As we slide in a slow, steady descent, I reach for the core of energy inside me. I want to show him what I can do. I may be a Damarcus, but I deserve my retrial too. Light energy vibrates in my fingers as I pull forth a few spirits.

The spirits of blue butterflies with large wings flutter around our heads. Ivander's eyes dart back and forth as he watches the pattern of their flight. When we touch the ground, he reaches out to stroke one, but his hand goes through it. Not solid, this time.

"I've never seen resurrection," he admits. "It's beautiful." The word slips out, as if he didn't mean to say it. He lets go of me, dropping his arms to his sides fast.

I swallow the lump in my throat. Few people call it beautiful. Not like they actually believe it. Leith did, but even he said I needed to be careful sharing my gift in case I summoned the wrong person and caused trouble. Bringing spirits back from the dead sometimes scares people.

I shake my head. "It may look that way, but my Morphia has changed recently. I'm hurting people."

"That's not what I meant." Ivander pauses. "You're not ashamed of your Morphia."

It's true. I've never been ashamed. Teachers used to punish me for using too much, but Father taught me to hold my head high. Lysandra taught me not to take anyone's shit.

He nods to stage left. "Get your uniform. I'll take you back to your room."

When I gather my clothes and boots and return to the stage, he fixes me with a pointed look. Any softness I saw in him earlier is gone, replaced by his usual scowl. I maintain eye contact despite the way my gaze wanders along his defined collarbone, glistening with sweat.

"Remember what I said. You're always going to get off easier as a Damarcus. Anytime you get in trouble, my friends could end up paying for it."

No argument there. I don't want anyone else paying for my mistakes. "But it's not my fault if the others help me. You may have decided I'm not worth a retrial, but your friends haven't."

Ivander shuts off the spotlight, leaving the silks dangling from the battens. "It's getting late," he says, changing the topic. "I have an early call time."

I follow him off the stage, down the aisle, and to the great double doors of the theater. After an uncomfortable silence, I ask, "What about the ship? What if the floor tries to eat me again?"

"There's a trick I learned from an older staff member when I first joined. If you concentrate on a memory—a strong one—while you're walking at night, you'll have some protection. The ship absorbs our Morphia when it consumes us, so it's always trying to lure us into dangerous parts to keep us from getting back to the safety of our rooms. The memory buys you time. The longer you keep your focus, the better chance you have of finding a room and shutting the door." Seeing my dubious expression, he adds, "Of course, it doesn't always work. Staff members have walked right off balconies before, minds consumed by the ship. Most Morphics do their best to never get caught in the hallways at night and get back to their rooms as soon as they can."

I think back to the girl muttering to herself with her eyes shut. Was she trying to concentrate on a memory? Clearly, a memory isn't always enough. I give him a shaky nod.

I search for a memory to use on the walk back to my room. Not much comes to me.

The only one I can think of is the memory of flying on silks with silvery butterfly spirits fluttering around me. And though I try to banish Ivander from the memory, I can't seem to get him out of my head.

CHAPTER 11

Halfway through my first week, I sit beside Alana, shoveling in spoonfuls of a lukewarm hearth fruit bisque in the break room when Isla walks up to our table, hunched over. Her blond curls stick to the sheen of sweat on her face, and she holds one arm over her stomach.

I drop my spoon and jump to my feet to help her sit on the stool across from Zora. "What's wrong?" I ask. Zora reaches across the table and squeezes Isla's hand but says nothing.

Isla inhales sharply and grits her teeth. Her green eyes slide to mine, but they're scrunched with pain. "This just happens sometimes," she gasps. "I get sharp pains in my abdomen. They come and go. Frustratingly impossible to predict."

Zora rubs her thumb over Isla's hand in a soothing circular motion. Isla's pinched mouth and heavy exhales make me forget I have little time before I have to return to the Stallard family.

A thrill of rage courses through me. If the bosses did this to Isla as punishment, she shouldn't have to work. My mind drifts back to my own punishment from two nights ago. Boss Charmaine hadn't appreciated my little stunt with the spirit during my first punishment, even if I was defending myself. She'd taken her knife and ripped open my forearm. With each slice, she applied more pressure, ignoring my screams. Then, when I was heavy-lidded and slumped from blood loss, she'd taken her jar of raw Morphia and healed the cuts. She'd sewed the skin the way a mender would. Over and over again. Whatever's happened to Isla looks worse.

Ivander walks over with his tray of food and sets it beside me. Although his gaze is trained on Isla, I realize with a jolt that he's sitting next to me. He usually sits beside Niko and avoids eye contact with me altogether. My stomach somersaults, but I don't let it show.

"Should you go to the med-bay?" I ask Isla, concern for her overshadowing my surprise at Ivander's closeness. "It's on this deck, isn't it?"

Isla wipes a curl away from her face and lets out a harsh laugh. "The bosses didn't do this. It's not like that. Menders can't do anything to fix it. Every couple of months, they give me a new diet or breathing exercise to try, but nothing keeps it away forever. Just something I live with."

Alana looks to a clock styled like a compass over the buffet table. "It's time to go."

None of us leave. Alana adds her hand to Zora's atop Isla's. Isla gives her a weak smile. Clenching my own teeth, I steady the rush of hot anger. Isla needs a day off, but I know she's not going to get one. The bosses lining the perimeter of the mess hall can tell she's in pain, but they do nothing to help.

I lean toward Isla. "What causes this? Maybe—"

"Don't," Ivander says with a sharpness that shuts me up fast. "No one knows the cause. Trust me, if there was something Isla could do, she would have tried it already."

I close my mouth, a little embarrassed. Of course, he's right. He must think I'm a spoiled girl who thinks everything can be fixed with Morphia. After watching my sister struggle as a mender for years, I know better than most that that's not true. Isla clutches her lower left side and shuts her eyes. "It's all right," she says. "I asked all those questions at one point." With a heavy breath, she sits up straighter. She tentatively massages the area and opens her eyes. "Comes in waves. Let's hope it calms down before lunch service."

Niko emerges from the galley with a towel over his shoulder and his chef's coat unbuttoned at the neck. He runs a hand through his black hair and squeezes Isla's shoulder. "I'll clean up in here. You go ahead to the Harlequin. Let the others handle the prep. I'll be there as soon as I can."

Isla puts her head in her hands. "Why does this have to happen right now?"

"Let me help you," Ivander says.

Zora shakes her head. "No way. It's too dangerous for you to miss a call time. You remember what happened last time."

Niko gives Isla's shoulder one last squeeze and returns to the galley to clean up from our lunch. Alana stands to help Isla to her feet. Alana's family gets mad if she's late, but that won't stop her from trying to help. Someone clears their throat behind us, and Alana turns to see Boss Balanyr holding his short spear in his rotting skeletal hand. The upper-left side of his head is caved in, as if his skull lost its structure. His split-open lip curls. "Alana Reyes, your family needs you right away. One of the children fell in the game room." His threatening grip on his spear urges Alana to hurry.

She bites her lip and gives Isla an apologetic look. "I'm so sorry. I have to go."

"Don't worry about me," Isla assures her. "Go."

Something doesn't feel right about allowing Isla to walk by herself on trembling legs to the tenth deck. I'm heading to the Harlequin too. The Stallards will be annoyed that I didn't escort them to lunch, but they know the way.

"I'm going with Isla," I announce. Zora exhales gratefully, and Ivander turns in sharp surprise toward me. I bristle at his reaction. Why does he have to question my motivations? I decide I don't care. This is for Isla, not for him. Something tells me either of them would have gone with Isla if missing a show wouldn't get them in serious trouble.

I can't send Isla to struggle through this alone. Not when she helped me on my first day despite knowing almost nothing about me.

As for me, I'll be in minor trouble. My little stunt with the bosses proved one thing. The Damarcus name couldn't save me from my failed trial or the *Celestial*, but it makes the bosses scared to touch me. A sliced ear here and an arm gash there, but they're too nervous to really threaten a Damarcus. My father holds too much power over their positions on future charters.

Ivander was right. They won't jeopardize my chance at a retrial unless they've exhausted every other option.

Isla stands over a sauté pan, frying delicate black murdo fish with one hand on a spatula and another clamped over her abdomen.

Murdo, found off the coast of Sarryndar, are known for their four creepy eyes and jet-black scales that enchant the upper class. I stand beside her, dredging the filets in flour, dipping them into a beaten egg mixture, and rolling them in a blend of breadcrumbs and seasoning that seems as complex as one of Father's potions.

The coating conceals the fragile black meat I spent an hour plucking at with tiny tweezers in order to wrestle out the minuscule bones, inconveniently the same color as the rest of the dark fish. With the chaos of chefs shouting at each other, I feel like I'm back home in our estate's grand kitchen. I used to run between our cooks, snatching fresh hearth fruit pastries from the cooling racks.

Isla talks as she cooks, even with the pain radiating through her gut. "See how they get golden brown and crunchy? That's the color you want. I just enhanced some Kalenar Kurls to let the kids breathe fire after eating them, so I can't taste anything now for about an hour. Could get me into trouble if I'm not careful. This fish costs as much as a yearlong cruise, so the bosses will have your head if you burn through inventory by overcooking it."

I nod but have no intention of taking that spatula.

Isla jerks her head to the other chefs throwing nasty looks in our direction. "They don't like that you're helping me," she mutters. "They think I'll have too good a chance at beating them for a retrial."

"If they're not getting a retrial," I say loudly, "it's because they're gawking at us rather than cooking."

The chefs scramble to look busy, and Isla claps me on the back. "You have a fiery streak, don't you? I knew you did after your spirit attacked Boss Charmaine. I loved seeing the look on her face. Wonder why she hasn't punished you more for it, though?"

Maybe because she's almost as afraid of me as I am of her. My name might be keeping me safe, but I don't want to say that aloud.

Isla nods to a group of boys in chef coats whispering to each other as they prep courses. "You see if those boys can cook like me with a knife in their side. They'd be crying."

I give her a sly smile. "I think you're the one with the fiery streak."

"I've always had to be like this." Isla shrugs. "I grew up with three siblings and parents who had to work all the time. Try taking your little siblings gortha pod hunting near the Gorthe hot springs all by yourself. The extra gemstones for digging up pods weren't worth the headache."

I let out a low whistle. "Eliza and I used to pick the herbs for Father's potions. It was hard enough to avoid the poisonous ones without kids around."

Isla bows her head and shoves the spatula into my hand. "Here. Take this. I've got to go to the restroom." She calls over her shoulder as she runs. "Pity me, and I'll pour boiling water on your foot!"

Now I'm alone at the stove, holding a spatula. Sizzling bubbles of oil leap from the pan, singeing my skin. I can't remember how many times she said to turn them. Frozen with indecision, the charcoal smell of burnt batter makes me want to puke. Before I can decide whether to scrap the filets or try to save them, Niko swoops in.

"Let's not burn down the ship."

He moves the pan off the heat and removes a few coals from inside the stove. "Alana told me to find you," he says, somehow salvaging the murdo. "The Stallards are done with dessert, and unless you get out there soon, they're going to be late for the afternoon show."

Bless Alana for checking on my family too. I rip off the chef's coat to reveal my uniform. I'm about to run back into the restaurant when I skid to a stop. "Will Isla be okay?"

Niko grins. "She's tough. Shouldn't have to be, but she is."

Taking his word for it, I throw myself into the Harlequin's dining room, dodging a colorful archway of flowers. I do my best not to smack into trees with twinkling green leaves and stop in front of Vance and Asralyn with a toothy smile.

Asralyn's nose wrinkles, an expression I'm getting quite used to, and she points a shaking finger to my hair. Sage giggles and points with her pudding spoon. "You have a fishbone in your hair!"

Of course I do. As I pull the ebony bone out, I try to flatten the flyaway hairs the humidity from the kitchen pulled free. Asralyn stands without looking at me, smoothing the folds of her heavy gold dress. She kneels and brushes crumbs off Ezra's vest. Taking her niece's and nephew's hands, she walks past me. "Come along. I'd rather not miss the show."

Vance takes one last bite of a salted honey torte with a candied butterfly still lazily flapping sugar wings and gets to his feet. "I hope you reflect at the end of this week," he tells me. "You'll have three weeks to change our minds about you."

I curtsy to him with a tight-lipped smile. If I were home in Credence, he'd be bowing to me. But maybe I don't want people bowing to me anymore. If my time aboard has taught me anything, it's that I don't want to become like Asralyn. Oblivious to others' pain if it serves me. I can't let them get to me. Not even Asralyn can make me regret helping Isla. Isla got the Stallards into the Harlequin on my first day. She saved me from looking like an absolute fool. Now I'm going to have to save myself.

We take the stairs to Dreamscape Theatre. I grab Sage's and Ezra's hands. Asralyn leads the way, and Vance puts a hand on her upper arm. She shrugs away at his touch and turns a bright, shining smile on the children when we arrive at the open double doors of the theater.

"Look, sweethearts," she purrs, "they haven't started yet. Must be the first event we've been on time for this week."

Ezra jumps up and down with excitement. As we pass over the threshold, I can't help but share his elation. The theater is dark and almost creepy with the witch statues and harsh lines of the gold frame around the stage, but it's like walking into the expanse of night. Millions of shiny, twinkling silver lights dapple the walls, the ceiling, the seats. The stage is set with black silks, a set of trapeze bars, a fiery aerial hoop that I assume is for Zora, and a fine layer of gray mist rolling over the stage floor. A hanging backdrop of luminous constellations makes the stage look like a window into the night sky. A large group of performers stretch and practice acrobatics on the stage before the show begins. With crafters losing their sense of touch for using their Morphia and shifters experiencing physical injury, the performers will have to rotate to keep the show going.

While we wait at the back of a crowded aisle for someone to direct us to open seats, Vance tells me about his work with the infirmaries in the province of Sarryndar. He goes on and on about how ungrateful the menders are who work there and how Illoryan, his home province, has much better medical care. "But of course, Asralyn moved us to Sarryndar for Harrow's Boarding School. She insists it's the best. Wanted the cousins to go there together."

I stop to look at him for a moment. Cousins? Could that mean he and Asralyn have a child together?

I'm saved from answering by a staff member with large glasses and a nasal voice that grates on my nerves. "Sorry, no more seats."

"What?" Panic forms a tight ball in my throat.

The staff member gives me a simpering smirk. "Should have gotten here sooner." Asralyn hmphs behind me and mumbles something suspiciously like "I knew it."

"But we got here early," I plead. "Is there really nothing you can do?"

The staff member looks me up and down. "Haven't you had enough handed to you? A lot of people got here early." At this point, the bosses hate me *more* than the other Morphics and I guess it's rubbing off on some staff members too. I don't even want to think about what punishment waits after this mistake. "Code regulations," he continues. "Imagine if there was a fire. Fire on a ship is bad news. If I overcrowd this theater, there could be a stampede."

Asralyn clicks her tongue from behind me. "Fire is the least of your concerns. If you don't find us a seat, I'll complain to your bosses." Seated guests turn to look at us. When they glimpse me, they whisper to each other. Undoubtedly, the rumor that a Damarcus has to serve on the *Celestial* has spread to the guests.

The staff member bites his lip and pushes his glasses up his nose. "I have to enforce the rules, my lady. Can't cause a panic in a place like this."

"There's only going to be a panic if you don't let us through," she replies evenly. She turns her sharp chin and narrowed eyes on me. "This is your fault—"

"Is there something I can help with?"

I recognize Ivander's smooth, charismatic tone that he uses with the guests immediately. I want to die inside. The last thing I need is for him to see me floundering.

When I turn to look at him, I see that he wears no shirt, only black dancer's trousers and a set of sheer black wings tied to his arms. The defined muscles of his sculpted abdomen draw my gaze. I force myself to focus on his face. His lips are pressed into a tight line. If I didn't know better, I'd say he was trying not to laugh. Great. He finds it hilarious I've made such a mess of this situation.

Despite my better judgment, I've got no other choice but to tell him. "There're no more seats. I got here too late." No use in pretending it wasn't my fault. I'd do it again. Helping Isla was worth any wrath Asralyn might bestow.

"Can't make seats appear," he says to me. "We'll make sure you get front row at the next show."

He turns over his shoulder with a swish of black fabric that moves like shadows. As he walks up the aisle, leaving me alone with the staff member and his code regulations, I mutter, "Thanks for the help."

Ezra tugs on my sleeve. "Do we really have to leave?"

I run a hand through my messy braid. "I'm sorry, but I think so."

The staff member nods and makes an exaggerated wave with his hand toward the double doors. Other guests in the audience are watching now. "How embarrassing," Vance says.

"Roe!" Zora runs down the aisle and pushes past the staff member with a shove of her elbow. Her costume is woven with crafter flame, and it flickers with electric light. The kids gape at her. "What are you doing standing here in the middle of the aisle? The show's about to start." She flashes a dazzling grin and points toward the stage. "Follow me."

"What are you doing?" I ask. The staff member who denied us seats frowns at the flames on Zora's outfit.

"Taking you to the front row. Some seats opened up." She winks. As if in a trance, I follow her to one of the front rows, where empty seats wait for us. "That's not all," she says to my guests. "Thanks to your lovely concierge, we have arranged a very special experience for you. If you're willing, of course, madam," she says with a nod to Asralyn. "You see, I'm set to embark on a dangerous journey through the stars, but I need two brave volunteers to help me."

She makes a show of looking every which way in the theater, ignoring Ezra's and Sage's waving arms.

"Right here!" Sage squeals. "We're right here. We could really go onstage with you?"

"Go onstage?" Zora asks with mock confusion. "You're going to fly onstage." She reaches into the pocket of her pants and withdraws a jar of Morphia.

Vance claps his hands. "Go on, children. This is why we came here. Once-in-a-lifetime experiences. Once-in-a-lifetime *service*," he says with a pointed look at me. "A little taste of magic."

I grab Zora's arm and lower my voice. I try to avoid the tongues of flame in case they're real. "Thank you. But I really don't want you risking anything for me. You don't have to do this."

Her lip curves as she looks at me. "You think this is me? I'm just the messenger. If you want to thank someone for pulling strings, thank Ivander."

My eyes dart to the stage where Ivander's prepping sets and silks. His brown eyes meet mine for a fraction of a second and flit away again.

Zora chuckles and holds out her hands for each of the kids. "He's not so bad once you get to know him," she says to me.

Maybe not, but I don't know him. He's tried to instill in me since day one that I shouldn't be relying on others, yet he's helped me. I don't know what to make of it. Wariness makes me wonder if it's a trick.

The kids jump to take hold of Zora's hands, but Asralyn stiffens. Her wide gray eyes lock on mine while her mouth strains in a grimace. "Is it safe?"

With a start, I realize how much shorter she is than me. She twists a butterfly ring around her pointer finger while she waits for an answer. It takes me a moment to realize she's asking me, not Zora. I lift my chin and say, "I trust Ivander and Zora. They would never put the kids in danger." My eyes drift back to Ivander, but he's back to focusing on the stage.

With a shaky nod, Asralyn takes her seat and smiles to the children. "Go on," she tells them. "Have fun."

Vance, Asralyn, and I settle into our seats as Zora leads the kids to the stage.

While the three of us wait for the show to start, I steal glances at Asralyn. She tugs on the ends of her fingers, eyes following Ezra and Sage like a hawk. I realize she's afraid for them. Before I can ask her anything at all, the lanterns and chandelier lights fade, and the show begins.

CHAPTER 12

With the end of the second full week approaching, the rich upper-class guests are doing what they do best: talking. They whisper behind their hands when staff members walk by, sharing horror stories. I feature in many of them. I'm beginning to wonder if the guests at our Resurrection Balls were just as annoying and I was too distracted by the glamour to care.

"I heard the bosses hate her. This is her first cruise and my goodness, does it show."

Another woman laughs. "She's a resurrector, darling. Goodbye and good riddance."

The guests who recognize me on sight are quick to point me out to those who don't. Seeing as my great-grandfather's idea for the *Celestial* and his role in bringing it to life is important history in every province, having a Damarcus aboard yields ripe gossip. It's entertainment for the guests—the idea of us getting our retrials or not. With preliminary votes coming up, everyone's on edge.

"That's why we need a break," Isla insists. "We can't be worrying about the votes all weekend. I keep trying to set up something fun, but you all keep shooting me down."

Niko narrows his eyes, clearing up the remnants of our lunch. "How about we worry about the mid-cruise ball instead? It's in two days, and I'm still finalizing the menu."

"That's what I'm talking about," Isla says, pushing aside her plate. "You know the bosses won't approve the menu until the last possible moment tomorrow, so why worry now?"

Alana shrugs, taking a bite of grilled vegetables. "Rosemary says she's recommending me to everyone she knows."

Zora snorts. "With the way she talks, I'll bet that's everyone on the ship."

Jealousy singes a hole in my gut, but I make myself squeeze Alana's arm. She's helped me more times than I can count. "I'm glad. There's no one more deserving."

She places her hand over mine and says, "I don't think I'd be getting any votes at all if I had to work for Asralyn."

I push away my sticky gortha pudding and stand, stretching my back. "At this point, I think Asralyn's actively campaigning against me."

Everyone at my table laughs, but it's hard to ignore the staff members at the other tables turning to look at me. By now, my punishments from the bosses are legendary. They may grow each of my appendages back, but that doesn't mean it's painless. The other staff members love watching it too. Most of them thought Roe Damarcus would be the model Morphic prisoner. I couldn't be further from that image.

And the looks on the bosses' faces are worth it. Charmaine, Stellan, Loren, and Balanyr. I've learned their names and the way their brows scrunch when they're frustrated that they can't break me. No matter how many times they punish me with physical pain, I still see the fear in their eyes. The fear, not of whether I'll retaliate, but when. With each punishment they inflict, their fear grows, and not of my father . . . of me.

The positive side is that it means Ivander's been needling me less about getting special treatment.

Despite the punishments, an ember of hope burns within me. It's been building since the end of last week. Even Asralyn can't deny I'm getting better. Fewer dropped trays. More timely arrivals. I may not be getting her vote anytime soon, but there's less flat-out hatred.

As the five of us leave the crew mess, I hurry to get last-minute advice from Alana. The Stallards want to try the flying experience on the top deck today. Guests get to fly over the ship with crafter-made wings. It's an activity the kids have wanted to do since day one, but Asralyn has always said no. Now that she's agreed, I have to make sure nothing goes wrong.

"What do I do if one of them falls in the water?" I ask.

Alana giggles. "Brace yourself for Asralyn's wrath?"

"Not funny. I'm being serious."

We take the stairs to meet our families in their rooms or at an activity. Some staff members don't even get breaks for lunch, but the Stallards like having a break from me.

"I wouldn't worry too much," Alana answers. "They run this experience every day and no one usually gets hurt. Plus, Niko was assigned to bartending duty this afternoon, so you'll have a friendly face nearby."

Zora gives me an encouraging nod before she branches off to start crafting the set pieces for the afternoon show. "You're lucky. I've always wanted to see those wings. The most intricate thing I've crafted were the props for funeral rites back home in Illoryan. Glowing flowers to beckon the Riveners to the deceased or burial markers that change colors on birthdays." Zora touches the vibrant petal of a Riven Blossom hanging from a chain around her neck. She must have made it herself to have a token of home.

I chuckle. "Rather you than me."

Niko lets out a long sigh. "I'd rather be anywhere else too. Food's more my strong suit, and this crowd is really particular about their drinks. Besides, whenever I enhance the drinks, I can't taste anything for the rest of the afternoon."

I take the stairs two at a time, hoping to beat the Stallards to the top deck. My legs burn. Niko tugs at the buttons of his chef's coat with trembling fingers as we walk. It's not fair that he's going to be judged for bartending when he's filling in for someone who got sick. But the bosses wouldn't accept Niko's request to stay in the kitchen.

I reach the top deck and wipe strands of sweaty flyaway hairs from my forehead. Niko gulps as he takes in the Swells & Spirits Bar. "You're going to be okay," I tell him. I use the same firm, confident tone Father used with me when I was worried about Leith going on a hunt. "I've seen you cook. You're incredible."

Niko rubs the back of his neck, and his midnight hair falls in his eyes. "Sure, but this is way different than cooking."

I grin and do an elaborate impression of shaking a cocktail. "If you can't make the best Tide Turner on the ship, then give the guests a show. I know you can do that."

He returns a weak smile. "You're right. That, I'm good at." He inclines his head to me. "I better go, but . . . thanks."

As Niko walks to the bar, I catch the flicker of gemstones in the sunlight. Asralyn wears an amber gown that shimmers in the afternoon sun. Even on the top deck, she chooses a gown. So much for my hopes of beating them up here.

I stride past the pool area and head to the bow of the ship where the flying activities are held. The lagoon changes from bright orange to muted lilac to glowing forest green in the time it takes me to reach my family.

A staff member with long hair tied back with a blue ribbon greets me. "Ah, good. Your concierge has finally arrived. I'm Lira," she says. "I'll be helping your group with the flying experience this afternoon. Looks like we've got clear skies."

When Asralyn makes no comment about me arriving late, the tension in my shoulders lessens. Vance worries at his lip while Asralyn's knuckles turn white as she clings to each of the children's hands.

It's a small group of us here for the flying experience today. Thanks to the heat, most guests are in the pool or lagoon. Niko's going to have his hands full at the bar, pushing out Tide Turners with orange-salt rims that emit their own sea breeze. Beside my family are three girls a few years older than I am. They chatter in high-pitched giggles to each other and wear much more appropriate crafter-made swim clothes.

Lira reaches into a large case at her feet and removes several sets of wings. They resemble flexible bat wings with intricate boning but have sparse feathering and straps that I assume attach to the shoulder, elbows, and wrists of each arm. She fumbles the wings and drops a pair of them. Her face flushes bright red as she scrambles to pick them up and misses a few times. Her sense of touch must be wavering. I cringe and hope the Stallards don't say anything. The wings bring back the memory of the bat-bird from the hallway in my first week. My mouth dries, and I try to pay attention to Lira as she regains her confidence and launches into an enthusiastic explanation of the rules.

"These wings are enhanced with crafter Morphia, which means you'll be able to fly for thirty minutes. There are sensors built into each wing that will chime when you get too far from the ship or when time's up."

Asralyn clears her throat. "What if the kids don't make it back to the ship in time?"

"The wings are pulled back to their creator." She places a hand on her chest. "That's me. They return in thirty minutes whether the kids want to or not. Now, if they manage to get too far from the ship—unlikely, of course—they may drop into the sea. But that's why the wings are made to become flotation devices when they hit the water."

Asralyn pales, and she looks to Vance, who sighs. "It will be fine," he says.

Lira beckons the kids and the three girls forward to pick their wing colors. Ezra chooses red and Sage chooses dark green. The three girls choose black, white, and gold. Lira walks among the group, helping them adjust the wing straps. When the wings are in place, she invites each of the fliers to introduce themselves. Sage and Ezra say their names with pride, but my heart jumps as they speak. I hope it's safe. I've never seen crafters do anything like this in Tamarynth.

A girl with curly brown hair and the gold wings introduces herself as Selene. Her friend with cropped blond hair and a tiny gemstone in her eyebrow announces herself as Taren. The final girl stands with her arms crossed over her chest, and her foot taps fast on the deck. Her chestnut hair falls in her face as she says, "Elayne."

"There's nothing to be nervous about," Lira assures her.

My stomach flips as the five of them shuffle to the deck rail with Lira. Although the rational part of me knows the wings will support them the minute they jump off the side, I can't help the clammy sweat on my skin. It's like watching Ivander on the silks, holding my breath as he drops from the ceiling and catches himself at the last second.

We wait for Lira's signal as she moves down the line to check straps. Asralyn shoves me out of the way to kneel in front of the kids, giving them additional warnings. My shoulder bumps the girl whose body trembles with nerves. "Sorry," she mutters. Elayne, I think.

"Are you okay?" I whisper so that her friends won't overhear.

Elayne bites her lip. "I . . . didn't really want to do this but my friends wanted to. Can't disappoint them." She lets out a fluttery laugh that isn't convincing.

I'd be scared to jump too. Even on a clear day, the smooth-as-glass indigo water of the Rivenwind Sea looks bottomless. The violet mist cloaking the base of the ship is as ominous as it is beautiful. It makes me wonder if any desperate staff members have tried to jump over the side, although we're too far out to sea for them to get anywhere. I've gotten somewhat comfortable with the heights of the silks thanks to Ivander, but I can't imagine pitching myself off a moving cruise ship. "Lira's right," I tell her. "It's a clear day. And crafters are some of the most skilled Morphics."

It's true, although Lira's operating off a limited sense of touch. I'd be surprised if she can feel anything at all.

"I guess," Elayne says as Selene and Taren let out a cheer of excitement when Lira tells us it's time to jump. Sage and Ezra leap with no hesitation. Their aunt's worries dissolve from their shoulders like melting snow. Then the two young women jump, calling for Elayne to stop being such a baby.

"Hey," I tell her before she works up the courage to jump. Elayne turns over her shoulder to look at me. "You won't fall," I say. "I can catch you if anything happens."

I can't tell if she believes me, but she must trust me enough, because she leaps over the side. The wings carry her into the air. The hum of resurrection surges beneath my skin. I'm holding back the power less often lately.

I won't let Sage or Ezra fall, not from the ship my family created. Standing beside Asralyn and Vance at the railing, I watch with intense focus. The wings cast large shadows over the sea, and the kids pump their arms to soar higher into the air. After a few tense minutes, Asralyn and Vance relax beside me. Even Elayne shouts with excitement.

Vance pats his wife's shoulder. "I'm going to get a drink from the bar." When I move to get the drinks, he holds up his hand. "No, you stay put. Watch the kids and keep Asralyn company."

I throw a glance over my shoulder. Niko's surrounded by a large crowd at the bar and—

Ivander's with him. He must have heard about Niko getting moved to Swells & Spirits for the day and stepped in to help between performances. Ivander catches my eye from across the deck and busies himself with the drinks again. He's in constant motion, arm muscles tensing as he scoops ice and stirs cocktails. He tries a spoonful of the cocktails before handing them off to the guests since Niko cannot taste them himself.

Niko mixes a drink called the Nocturne, named after Nashorne's most well-known celebration where all lights in the city go out and the only illumination comes from elaborate fireworks. The drink glass holds a pitch-black, smoking liquid interrupted by bursts of vibrant colored lights exploding from the top. While Niko enhances the cocktail with magic, Ivander gives a female guest a dazzling smile, and I feel a surprising stab of jealousy.

Niko's still a newer staff member, which means his retrial chances are low, but that doesn't mean he should tank his shot at a job he's not prepared for. Guests who take repeat cruises might remember. Again, Ivander is going out of his way to help his friends. But the longer I watch, the more guests crowd the bar and exchange easy banter with Ivander. Every guest walks away from him with a twinkle in their eyes, and a part of me wonders if Ivander's garnering their goodwill for more than just a retrial.

I still meet him in the theater a few nights a week to practice on the silks. Whether it's helping me blow off steam or not, he constantly reminds me, despite my unwillingness to listen, "You have a lot of pent-up power inside you. Focus your anger, your energy, in here, and you won't let it out on them." I could be wrong, but taking punishments from the bosses has earned some respect from Ivander. He's telling me I'm a liability less and less.

And after he helped me get seats before the show, I'm less bitter toward him. Even if most nights in the theater end with us arguing over something as complex as the value of the council or as simple as the fastest shortcut to the theater, I almost enjoy it.

Fingernails dig into my skin as someone seizes my forearm.

"What's wrong?" I ask.

Asralyn points at the water that was clear as glass minutes ago. The deep indigo has shifted to dark midnight. Small whitecaps form as the water turns choppy.

I call for Lira's attention, but the wind picks up, and my words are lost. Sage and Ezra cry out as a gust of wind billows against their wings and sends them spiraling through the air. This doesn't make sense. The weather's behaving as if we're sailing through a storm, but the sky's still clear and the sun's shining. Staff members scurry across the deck to tie down chairs and secure loose equipment. They try to corral guests away from the railing, but the choppy waves are making some of the guests seasick.

"Do something!" Asralyn bellows to me. Her eyes glisten. While a deck chair flies behind me and a woman splatters the deck with vomit, Lira yells for the fliers to head back to the ship. Even if they heard her, the wind is too strong to let them obey.

Other guests scream when they see the fliers turn over in the air. I think of how scared Elayne was to fly, and I still have the imprints of Asralyn's nails in my arm.

Without a second to think, I raise my arms and connect to the realm beyond life. The silvery tether pulls taut as I resurrect spirits on instinct alone.

The spirits of two men, a woman, a tiger, and a stallion burst free. I don't have time to care who they are. Spirits aren't of this plane and can float through the air like clouds, but I need to make them solid enough for the kids to land on.

The spirits feed on my desperate energy and know where I want them to go. Now I have to hope they'll agree to help. The ship pitches with the choppy motion of the water. I regain my footing as the spirits surge forward. One man refuses to move, and I send him back to the spirit world. I draw upon the realm again and bring forth a spirit that resembles the bat-bird from the ship. Somehow I'm pulling spirits from several hundreds—if not thousands—of years ago, when Morphia roamed free.

"How can I help?" Ivander's beside me. His voice breaks through my concentration.

"Take care of them." It's all I can manage, and I hope he understands. Asralyn and Vance can't distract me.

Ivander speaks in a soothing register to Asralyn. It's the same low voice he uses when Zora's nervous about a performance or Isla's in pain. Although his words aren't for me, they calm the rapid beating of my heart. He takes care of the other guests, not just Asralyn and Vance.

As a crowd forms around us to watch, they fire off questions I don't have time to listen to or answer. A man with sandy hair runs his sun-tanned hands over a necklace of shells and stones, a good-luck token made from materials found in the swamps of Gorthe. I try to block out the sharp clinking as he rubs the necklace between his fingers. "Ignore them," Ivander whispers. "You focus on getting the others down."

"My part's a lot harder than yours," I mutter under my breath.

Ivander's brows raise. "Would you like to trade?" Even in a dangerous situation, he won't let go of the chance to act superior.

I allow myself a quick glance at the mob of guests and the puke spattering the deck. "Would you shut up and let me concentrate?"

"Only if you promise to work faster," he replies easily.

We work together for the next few minutes. In fact, it reminds me a bit of a performance. Ivander's in charge of the front of house, placating the guests and addressing their fears. I'm working behind the scenes to fix the actual problem.

It doesn't take long once I've got the spirits underneath the fliers. Ezra falls onto the back of the tiger spirit and hangs on. Each of the spirits may be solid, but my haste to raise them from the dead has left them more corpse-like than whole. The tiger's fur covers its back, but rib bones protrude from decaying skin on its abdomen. I'm glad Ezra can't see its face from this angle because the skin appears to be sliding off the skull. But I don't need them to look pretty. I just need them to carry the guests to the ship.

Another wind gust threatens to pull Sage farther away from the ship, but the feathered creature soars beneath her. She whoops as the bat-bird surges forward. For her and Ezra, this is all part of the activity.

But the university-aged girls realize the danger, and when one of the human spirits grips Elayne tight, she screams as she sees that half his head is caved in.

Eventually, my spirits maneuver all five of the fliers back to the ship as I tug the tether that connects us. It doesn't take me long to reel them back in. Spirits are used to the currents of the afterlife, which are much more intense than wind. Elayne lets out a sob the moment her feet touch the deck.

Sage and Ezra exclaim that they want to do it again.

Some of the guests clap, but most just whisper. Most of them have never seen resurrection before, and I didn't have time to make the spirits look alive and whole.

With the wind still high and the ship rocky, I urge the Stallards to head inside. I expect Asralyn to yell at me, but she remains tight-lipped and silent. I make sure to check on Elayne before I go. Her eyes are wide as she looks at me, and her chestnut hair whips in the breeze. "Was that . . . supposed to happen?"

Luckily, I don't have time to answer before her friends descend on her with adrenaline-fueled laughter. I back away with my gut swirling. Whatever just happened could have left someone hurt, or worse.

Ivander follows me as I lead my family to the crowd of guests trying to exit the deck. A few staff members help the seasick passengers exit first. When I catch Ivander's eye, he looks away. "What?" I demand, nerves frayed.

He clears his throat. "Your Morphia saved their lives."

I'm tongue-tied by the respect in his voice. Any pride I might have felt diminishes when I think of the danger the fliers were in, and all from the jars of Morphia stored below.

He must notice my shakiness because he asks, "Are you okay?"

My knees may be wobbling, but this isn't my first day. I can't faint this time. I give him a brief nod and join the crowd of guests pushing their way to the stairs leading to the lower decks. I try to keep it light even while my hands tremble. "Like you said, you had the harder job. I'll take saving lives over dodging puke any day."

I sneak a glance at the floorboards and imagine a monster clawing its way through the gaps in the wood. It's not just the hallways anymore. Nowhere is safe.

CHAPTER 13

As the five of us head to see the bosses that evening, I explain to Alana, Zora, and Isla what we witnessed on the top deck.

Isla lets out a whistle. "I'd rather eat hot dung than jump off this ship with a pair of craft-project wings strapped to my arms."

Zora nudges her shoulder. "Those wings are well-made. They kept them in the air even with the wind, didn't they?"

"But there shouldn't have been any wind," I say. They may be used to these anomalies, but I'm not. "There wasn't a cloud in the sky."

The lines move fast tonight. The bosses must be overwhelmed with preparations for the mid-cruise ball. Preparations that continue regardless of the events of today.

"Don't worry about what you can't change," Isla says. "We'll get to have fun tomorrow night. Top deck party, remember?"

Alana groans. "That's a bad idea. What if the bosses—"

"Shhh," Isla hisses. "The bosses don't care as long as we do our jobs at the ball." After a pause, she adds, "But I still don't want them to know about it, so hush."

"You're still planning it after what happened?" I ask.

Isla shrugs. "Everything here is a risk. May as well take one that involves Lixor." Isla mimes taking a deep drink from her imaginary glass, earning an exasperated look from Zora.

The closer I get to the front of the line, the more I wonder if I'll get a free pass today. After all, I did save some guests' lives.

But when Boss Stellan beckons me forward, I know that's wishful thinking. I hand him my empty jar of Morphia and climb into the chair. It's the same thing every night. I wait, and they figure out some new way to punish me.

Tonight, he doesn't take out a knife.

He kneels beside my chair as I donate Morphia. His dark hair falls in his shadow-rimmed eyes. When he smiles at me, the hairs on the back of my neck stand on end. The longer I look at him, the more his eyes sink into his face. The more his gleaming white teeth look like rows upon rows of fangs resting in bloody gums. Blood trickles from his eyes and nose, but he doesn't seem to notice.

I swallow hard, resisting the urge to jump out of my chair and run. "Is there something I can do for you?"

Stellan brushes his hand across his mouth, wiping the blood from his lips before it can fall. The exposed bone of his fingers gets caught in the open wound on his face. I swallow hard to keep from gagging. "We've had trouble with you. You fight back. We've received multiple complaints about your work." He shrugs. "You don't respond to punishments, so we've decided to use something you will respond to."

I push myself into an upright seated position. I can't take much more stress today. Stellan leans even closer, hot breath steaming my cheek.

He reaches into his pocket and removes a potion in a crusted brown jar. It looks nothing like the jars of glowing Morphia, and my mouth dries when he holds it out to me. "Drink."

It's not an invitation. It's a command. Careful to avoid contact with his rotting fingers, I take it without thinking but pause. It smells like rotting fish on the lakeshore. One withering look from Stellan warns me to drink before he forces it down my throat.

It doesn't taste as bad as it smells, but the liquid is thick and strangely hot. I gag but force myself to swallow. For a moment, nothing happens. I wring my hands in my lap, waiting for intense pain.

I feel nothing until the scene changes.

I'm no longer sitting in a metal chair in the storage room. I'm running in a snowy forest, boots sinking into the icy drifts. My breath comes in ragged gasps under a wave of fear so intense it threatens to bring me to my knees. A voice in my head tells me I must keep moving.

Hot blood drips onto the snow in the forest around me. I press my fingers to my abdomen. Sticky and wet. A shot of pain runs through me as I cover the wound, but it's not my hand. It's my brother's.

A ragged scream tears through my trembling lips. I'm not sure how, but I know I'm feeling what Leith felt when he died. His fear. His pain. I turn, narrowly avoiding a tree in my way. My heart's beating so hard I think it might burst, but I don't stop. I can't stop. My fingers explore the flesh of my abdomen and massage the frayed skin. Tender to the touch. Shirt drenched in red, copper-smelling blood.

The urge to glance behind me dies under the horrible fear of whatever I'll see. Darkness cloaks my surroundings, making every tree look like a shadowy person reaching out to grab me. Every branch tugging at my clothes slows me down. The rhythmic crunch of boots stamping through snow confirms I'm not alone. I'm being stalked.

My head spins from blood loss. There's a sound from behind me. Something like the creak of a bowstring. White-hot pain shoots through my lower back, and I fall. Darkness edges my vision. I'm scared. So scared . . . So alone . . .

The experience dissolves, and I'm back in the chair.

My chest heaves, and I glance wildly around. My hands grip the metal armrests, knuckles white. Tears wet my cheeks. I can't speak. It's not real. Nothing I saw was real. We never knew how Leith died. I couldn't resurrect him and give myself or my family that closure.

There's no way Stellan could have known, but not knowing what's actually true is harder. It means that fear might have been real.

With blood roaring in my ears, I climb out of the chair, shaking.

Stellan laughs, a sound like the scratch of talons against wood. "You're free to go."

I don't look at anyone and fold my arms tight over my chest. I keep my head down and run from the room.

With no good memories to keep me company, I call out to my brother. Tears stream down my face as I run through hallways that morph into a sticky swamp bog. The walls are overgrown with vines and palm fronds, and yellow-green grasses sprout from the floor with thick snakes slithering through them, flicking forked tongues. I hop over them, grateful for my uniform boots. A snake with a triangle-shaped head lunges for my calf, and I dodge out of the way only to learn my foot's stuck.

Mud sucks at my boots, black and tar-like. Panic tightens my chest, and I twist in the shoe, ejecting my foot as the snake misses my pantleg by a hair length. I don't have time to grab my shoe. The snap of jaws behind me reminds me of the scaled beasts with long jaws and sharp teeth I saw on a family trip to the province of Gorthe. They're getting closer.

Speeding up, I leap to the stairs. One flight. Two flights. All the while, calling out to Leith. I search for the connection I have to the spirit world, yearning for his smile, his laugh.

I end up at the theater without realizing it. When I throw open the double doors, it's eerily quiet. I'm used to Ivander beating me here, but I appreciate the time to remove my remaining boot and walk barefoot to the stage in silence.

I sit on the stage and recline so I'm lying on my back, gazing up at the battens and border curtains overhead. With slow, deep breaths, I try to calm myself. It takes several minutes for my heart to slow and the tears on my cheeks to dry. I sit up with a shaky breath but freeze as I realize I'm not alone. There are three people sitting in the audience. They must have seen me come in, but I sprint to the side of the stage anyway and peer out from behind the wings. Every time Ivander and I have come here, we've been alone.

Now that I'm safe behind the curtains, I can get a closer look. The four people are about my age. Two of them lean back with their legs propped on the seats in front of them. A girl paces down the row of seats. She's wearing a deep blue skirt with a black button-up blouse. Luckily, they're just staff members. Their voices echo in the theater. They don't bother trying to keep quiet.

"I'm so over this," one of the seated staff members groans. Dark hair falls in his face, but he pushes it back to reveal a flesh-eaten hole in the side of his cheek, as if someone poured an acidic potion onto his bare skin. I clamp a hand over my mouth to muffle my gasp.

The girl pacing shakes her head. "Charmaine is such a bitch. She should never have touched you."

"She's jealous," one of the other boys says. "What? It's true. One of the older staff members told me. Said she used to be a crafter. She was one of the best a decade ago and was all set to get her own stall in the Kalenar Crafter Fair once she passed her trial. Only, she didn't pass. Whatever she crafted killed one of the judges. Her Morphia was extracted on the spot. But she missed Morphia so much, she applied for every charter until Lord Damarcus finally approved her to join the *Celestial*."

I suck in a sharp breath.

"Why doesn't she leave already?" another staff member in the seats asks. "She's worked here long enough she could get a job as a prison guard or oversee Morphia experimentation projects or something."

"You've seen what it does to them." The boy grimaces. "Once you're Morphicbound, you don't want to leave. Haven't you heard the saying among the bosses? *You always find your way back.*"

The boy with the hole in his cheek sighs. "Sometimes I wonder what would happen if we took all those raw Morphia jars and dumped them over the side into the sea."

The girl stops pacing and turns to look at him. "Are you kidding? Tamarynth would be overrun by creatures we haven't seen for almost a thousand years."

The girl might have said more, but she freezes. I hear the swoosh of double doors opening and the sound of running feet. Ivander sprints past them and leaps onto the stage. He must not have seen the group either. I hold my breath, waiting for the girl to react. But she doesn't. Not to Ivander. She gasps, face turning purple. Her friends ask her what's wrong. She can't answer and claws at her throat. The girl collapses to her knees, making horrible choking noises.

Ivander's asking me what's wrong and why I'm hiding in the wings, but I cannot take my eyes off the girl as her friends try to help her. "Must have been that potion the bosses made her drink," one of them cries desperately. "Hurry! Get a mender!"

I try to run forward to help, but Ivander holds me in place. As I fight his too-tight grip, the truth barrels into me, and I go rigid in his arms.

Ivander would be racing for a mender if this were real. The sinking realization that no one in Tamarynth will care feels worse than the pull of spirits as they try to claw their way back to the living plane.

Ivander's shouting at me now, trying to get my attention. When he forces me to meet his intense brown eyes, my mind clears. This time, when I look again into the theater seats, they're empty. We're alone in here.

Ivander lets out a slow breath. "You scared me there for a second," he says in a gruff tone, as if it pains him to admit it. He sits on the stage and pats the spot beside him. I join him there and wait for the questions, but none come. We sit in the silent dark. He stays close to me but without touching. I won't say it aloud, but it's reassuring to have him here.

Something has shifted between us since the day he helped my family get seats before his performance. At least, it did for me. But lately, he doesn't just lecture me on how to stay out of trouble or to keep from dragging others down with me. I can't tell what it is, but I know he's confiding in me more. Maybe because he doesn't want to burden his friends. I talk to him because I know he'll be honest with me. He has been from day one—even when I didn't want to hear it. I want more answers tonight, but that means trusting him enough to let my guard down more, even if he decides not to let down his.

I take a deep, shaky breath. "Those bosses . . . are monsters." I brush the tears away before they fall. I don't want to cry in front of him. "I've screwed up. I came here to prove my Morphia isn't dangerous, but I've been acting dangerous." As I think of how Boss Charmaine killed a judge at her trial, I whisper, "I'm a monster too. I've hurt people with my Morphia. At my trial, I could have killed someone. If Father hadn't stepped in at the Resurrection Ball, I might have hurt someone there too. But sometimes it feels good. It felt good to use my spirits to attack the judge at my trial. Just like it did to hurt Boss Charmaine."

I can't tell him what I saw in the boss's illusion. I don't want to relive it. Ivander stretches his feet out in front of him, pointing his toes. Today he's given himself blue nails, a tattoo of an owl in flight in the center of his chest, visible from the opening in his deep maroon performance shirt, and an array of gold earrings. His fingers are wrapped with colorful mender bandages to ease the pain of the breaks from using his Morphia. It's easier to watch the tensing of his muscles than to wonder what he'll say. It's easier to watch his jaw clench as he studies me. My face heats. I've been staring too long.

Ivander takes time to respond. He doesn't rush into reassurance. "It feels good to hurt those who deserve it. Does that make it right?" He shrugs. "I don't know."

The soft spotlight above our heads throws a beam of faded light across his face. "We learn when we're young how to use words to hurt each other, and sometimes it feels good. But we also learn to use them to help." He peers at me with narrowed brown eyes, as if waiting for me to stop him. "Morphia's the same, but no one's teaching us how to be careful with it. They're taking it from us like we're inherently dangerous."

After a pause, he stands. He regards me from this higher position, and I force myself not to shrink under his scrutiny.

"You helped Isla in the kitchen. You didn't have to. Niko told me you gave him some advice for the bar. People don't do that on this ship."

"You do. Your friends do," I point out. I stand to be eye level with him. If he's going to start this shit again, I'm walking out. I've been doing the best I can to follow the rules, his rules, and not get anyone else in trouble. So far, it's only been me taking the punishments.

"That's not what I mean. You're not . . ." He shakes his head, as if nothing he's saying is coming out right. "You're not what I was expecting."

With a name like Damarcus, I have an estate to go home to, a father on the council, and a direct tie to the *Celestial* itself. I should be insufferable and entitled at the least. Maybe I am, if you listen to Eliza. "Maybe spoiled doesn't have to be separate from kind."

Ivander begins pacing, not looking at me as he speaks. His words come out choppy and fast like he's been holding them back for a while. "I've been thinking about the *Celestial*. I've been here almost two years and have seen it at its worst. Containing Morphia to keep it from contaminating Tamarynth doesn't work. Whatever happened on the top deck this afternoon proved that—stormy seas with no storm to show for it. This ship's killed people before, and the guests are still treating it like a toy. And Morphics have their magic stripped away for no reason."

I've been thinking the same without allowing myself to sink into my skepticism. I wait for him to go on.

"They used to call us witches and burn us at the stake, but that wasn't profitable. Non-Morphics needed what we could do, so they tried to control it. They started taking Morphia at the first sign of trouble. Forcing the *good* ones to work for them. Your great-grandfather helped us survive, but we need to do more than that."

His words punch me in the gut. I've been proud to have the Damarcus name, but now I'm wondering if we've done anyone any good at all.

"What if you could speak to your ancestors, the ones who started this place, try to figure out what they wanted for it? Maybe we could get Tamarynth back to their vision."

I shake my head. "It doesn't work like that. Trust me, I wish it did." Images of battered bodies and all-consuming darkness flash through my mind. "Every time I try to bring back my own family, the deathmares are unbearable. I've tried to resurrect my brother . . ."

I stop myself. Talking about Leith feels too personal, but that doesn't mean I can't give him something. Ivander's always given me honesty, and now he's waiting to see what I'll do with it. I can't turn away. "I can try again. To talk to one of my ancestors."

As much as my promise is to Ivander, it's also for me.

I'm starting to feel like my father didn't tell me everything about the first war.

It's hard to envision what they must have wanted all those years ago. I imagine non-Morphics and Morphics turning on each other. Family members against family members. Morphics trying to take power and non-Morphics wanting to keep them from it. My ancestors must have been desperate to stop the war. The trials, the extraction potion, and the ship were born of desperation. I'd always respected my great-grandfather for wanting to showcase the beauty of Morphia on the ship while locking away the dangerous parts of it.

Maybe he didn't care as long as his family escaped unscathed. But maybe he was naive to think a cage would fix everything.

CHAPTER 14

The Lotus Salon is still teeming with guests and staff when I leave. Shifters grow and shrink elaborately decorated nails, change hair colors to blinding neon hues, and add luminescent glitter dust to ball gowns to make them glow, but that only keeps the children entertained for so long. After spending an eternity helping Asralyn and the kids find gowns and suits for tomorrow night's mid-cruise ball, Asralyn dismisses me to take the kids back to their room. In her eyes, I'm still incompetent, incapable of keeping the children from knocking over racks of bejeweled shoes.

I steer Sage and Ezra into the hallway. As we trek to deck ten, I shake off my bad mood with Asralyn and refocus on the kids. "Sage, I heard you've been working on a painting with one of the crafters. How's it—"

"I'm painting a waterfall!" she cuts in with an excited squeal. "When I use the paints Maren gives me, the water moves!"

I'm not surprised. Maren is one of the best crafters on the ship, and I'm sure Sage's waterfall painting is like looking through a window.

Sage skips ahead of me, hopping onto the stairs for the tenth deck. "But Aunt Asry says my paints won't move once we get off the cruise. Isn't that sad?"

Ezra jogs to catch up with the two of us on his short legs. "What about you?" I ask him. "What kind of dessert are you going to order in the room tonight?"

"The *Celestial* Chocolate Volcano!" He throws his hands in the air like an explosion.

Isla uses signature spiced chocolates from the province of Nashorne to create hyperrealistic cityscapes beneath a volcano. It's flavored with various fruit purees and warm spices and, when tempered correctly, the entire dessert appears to be made of shimmering glass. Of course, she also uses her skills as an enhancer to make hot fudge explode out of the top like lava, transforming the entire piece into decadent chocolate chaos. She may lose her taste for a short time in return, but she says the kids' excitement is worth it.

When we arrive in front of the room, both kids beg me to stay. If only they were the ones I needed to impress. After a brief knock on the door, I shake my head. "Not tonight, but I'll help you get ready for the ball tomorrow."

Vance opens the door and smiles down at the kids. "Where's your aunt?"

"Salon," they both answer in unison.

"Ah, yes, I was warned it might take her forever to decide on something to wear. Come on in. I'm going to order dinner."

The kids run inside, but Vance holds the door open and stares at me. I shift under his gaze. Before I can ask if there's something he needs, he puts his hands into the pockets of his loose-fitting night trousers and coughs.

"I wanted to let you know about tomorrow night," he says, staring at the floor. "We'll be voting at the ball. Of course, you know that. I just wanted you to know . . . we won't be voting for you." He pushes a pair of reading glasses up the bridge of his nose. "I didn't want it to come as a shock."

Trust me, it doesn't. Even after saving Sage and Ezra, I'm better known for forgetting their drink orders and arriving late for my shifts. Using the fake smile I've been perfecting for the past two weeks, I give him my best impression of a dutiful concierge. "It's all right. I'm hoping to turn things around. Maybe I'll have your support in two weeks."

He offers a wan smile in return. "Asralyn and I know the ball happens at night. We want to make sure the ship is safe."

I don't think any part of this ship is safe, but that's not the answer the bosses want me to give. They want me to lie. Crafters and illusives will be stationed in the hallways, making them appear "safe" and normal-looking. Staff members will be stationed at all doors that lead outside to stop guests from wandering off, but I'm not sure it's enough to counteract the Morphia fighting back.

"It's safe." I take a step closer to him. "But I wouldn't let the kids wander off on their own. If you need to go in the hallways for any reason, go together. And make sure there's a staff member with you."

Vance nods to me and gives me a real smile this time. In a way, it reminds me of Father's smile when he's been mixing potions all day and can't stop staring at portraits of Leith. It's a sad, tired smile. Before I can offer to do anything more, Vance shuts the door in my face.

Without another moment to dwell on Vance's expression, I race from deck ten to deck three. I take the stairs two at a time, slowing only when I'm passing a guest. By the time I throw open the door to my bunk, Alana's waiting for me. I can't help my excited grin as I shut the door behind me. We get one night of freedom before the mid-cruise ball tomorrow.

As a lady of Credence, I've been to many parties, socials, and soirees, but I've never been to a staff deck party before. Alana's laid out outfits for both of us on the bottom bunk.

"How'd you get out early?" I tear my hair free of its bun and unbutton my uniform.

"Rosemary and Duncan said I'd done such a fine job that I could have the rest of the day off." She whirls around with her hands in the air. "I swear, Roe. I think I'm going to get my trial this time."

"You better," I say, snatching clothes from the bed. Most are pieces from dance costumes, but they're radiant. I grab a black dress embroidered with green vines that snake down the bodice and bloom into full black roses on the skirt. Based on the craftsmanship, I'm guessing Zora sent them.

"Dramatic, much?" Alana laughs. "These are good enough for Kalenar's Crafter Fair back home. You should see it. Crafters and non-Morphics spend the year making clothes to sell. I'd save up for months. The weeks of the annual fair are practically a holiday in our province."

I smile. "Maybe we can go together one day."

Alana grins back as she pulls on a long-sleeved, high-necked blue top with a black skirt. Her arms are covered by blue lace butterflies with fluttering wings. She paints on a dark maroon lip in front of the mirror. As I struggle to get into my own top, she helps me and guides my arm through the hole. We're both laughing by the time she finally gets me in it.

Once I'm dressed, I rip a brush through my long hair, struggling to tame the frizz. Our tiny bottle of soap isn't helping my hair maintain its usual shine. Even with a bit of frizz and dark circles under my eyes, I can't help relishing how nice it feels to dress up again. But there are other parts I don't miss, like dancing with arrogant boys like Reginald or the expectations of perfection at every social event.

I rim my hazel eyes in soft black and paint my lips with the same dark maroon as Alana's, and I don't even mind the untamed mass of hair down my back. With so much pale, freckled skin exposed, I should feel uncomfortable, but I don't.

Alana's mouth droops as she looks at me. With a jolt, I realize what she's done. "You gave me confidence."

"It was already in you. I just brought out more of it." She lets her dark hair free of its braid and it cascades down her back in thick waves. "I hate when people feel bad about themselves. My mom used to tell my sister and me we were beautiful no matter what. Not enough people feel that way." She tucks a strand of hair behind her ear. "Tonight, I will not look at Isla. I will focus on anyone else."

"That's the spirit," I say. "What actually happened between you and Isla?"

Alana turns an hourglass over as we wait for it to get dark and the top deck to clear of day guests. She sits on the bottom bunk with her legs crossed. She rubs her hands up and down her thighs. "I don't just bring emotions out. I also sense them easier than other people. That's how I know what feelings to enhance." Her brow furrows. "I sensed when Isla's feelings started to go away. They got dimmer and dimmer until I confronted her. I didn't try to work it out."

I sit on the bunk beside her, creasing the fabric of her perfectly made bed.

She sighs. "Sometimes I wish I didn't have this gift at all."

I may not be an emotive, but the wave of relief coming from her—from saying it out loud—is tangible. The mix of fear, sadness, and regret for something she cannot control makes me realize there's nothing I can say. I've felt it too. When Lysandra cries as I fail to bring back her son and when Mother cringes telling her friends what kind of Morphic I am.

I take her hands, squeezing them. "Don't feel ashamed of being an emotive. What you do is beautiful." I drop her hands quickly, before my own become cold and clammy.

"You know, I thought you would be stuck-up." She shrugs. "I was kind of nervous to share my bunk with a lady of Credence."

"And I was nervous to share a bunk with the best concierge on the *Celestial*."

Her cheeks redden, but she shakes it off and grabs a slip of paper from the dresser. "I almost forgot. Someone left you a note under the door. I saw it early this afternoon."

I unfold the note and read the elegant script twice in my head.

> *The nightmares aren't real. You're not the monster.*
> *Monsters don't worry about what they are.*
> *Ivander*

Warmth spreads through my core before I can smother it. Alana watches me with a sly smile. "Who sent it?"

Heat creeps into my cheeks, and I turn my face from her. Of course, he's jaw-dropping on the silks and charming with the guests, but that's not the side he shares with me. I won't let myself think about his brown eyes flecked with gold and the gentle cadence of his voice as he confides in me. He's not what I'm on the *Celestial* for.

I shove the feelings down. Emotives are too adept at reading emotions. I sit in silence with Alana, waiting for the moment our guests fall asleep. Then we can go upstairs to a party, and I can forget it all.

CHAPTER 15

A mass of staff members gathers on the top deck of the *Celestial* for our own unofficial party.

Some Morphics flip into the circular pool while others sit on the side with their feet dangling as they sip drinks. In the center of the deck, bartenders serve the crowd. We've created a makeshift dance floor beside the bar, but many ignore it in favor of the lagoon perimeter around the ship. Staff float in bioluminescent water that changes from orange to purple and back to blue with small, scaly sea dragons popping their noses up, ready to be ridden.

Tonight, we're the guests, and no one can tell us we don't belong up here.

The sound of violins and cellos reverberate across the deck, matching time with the angelic voice of one of Ivander's fellow performers. Illusives work their magic to muffle the perception of sound for any bosses who wander too close to the top deck. They expend so much energy that they have to float in the pool in tubes or sit on the deck to recover.

Alana and I jump up and down on the dance floor, spilling our drinks. I sip on a Kally Tonic in a tall glass. Its fruity bubbles float out of the drink and pop around my head, filling the air with a floral fragrance. Alana's Kalenar Sun Drop emits its own light. Isla pulls Zora onto the floor with a powerful tug. Zora wears a long, flowing white skirt with a floral top and her Riven Blossom necklace. "Watch it," she grumbles, saving her drink.

"Come on," Isla yells back, blond curls bouncing in the night breeze. She wears a deep plum pantsuit with bronze fastenings. "Who knows how long we have before Ivander tells us it's time to go to bed."

Ivander presses his lips together as he watches us dance. His eyes drift to each member of our group and linger on me. I catch him staring, and he looks away. He clings to the bar, keeping a watchful eye over the crowd. Over all of us. Niko stands beside him, effortlessly handsome with his black hair styled and a midnight-blue vest over his off-white tunic shirt. He wears formal black trousers that might have been snagged from the *Celestial*'s upscale lost and found.

It's clear from his tugging on Ivander's arm that he's trying to get him on the dance floor, but Ivander sits, immobile, on the barstool. He wears the same black button-down and navy pants he wore on the first day I met him.

His gaze shifts from one end of the deck to the other, surveying the scene. He fought Isla on this idea until the sun went down. "If the bosses find out, there's no telling what they'll do to us. They can't take our Morphia without reason," he'd said. "So don't give them one."

As I dance with the girls, I feel like one of them. They laugh with me and share retellings of my greatest exploits with the bosses.

Isla erupts into peals of laughter. "Remember? Hold on, I can't breathe." She takes a breath. "Remember when Roe's spirit decked Charmaine?"

We all laugh, even Alana. Zora nods to my drink. "You need a refill. Go tell Ivander the staring is creepy."

I stride toward the bar with my drink cradled in one hand. Pushing through dancers, I stop next to Ivander and take the empty seat on his other side, earning an encouraging nod from Niko. "You glad you're not the one mixing drinks tonight?" I ask him.

"Definitely," Niko says. "I vastly prefer drinking them." He squints at the dance floor. "I think Isla's calling for me." He pats Ivander's shoulder and disappears into the crowd, ducking out of Ivander's wild grab to keep him in his seat.

Giddiness from the dancing and the Lixor in my drink makes me bold. "Are you going to sit here all night?" I ask. "If you want me to go—"

"No," Ivander blurts, hands curling into fists in his lap. "I don't. I'm just worried I won't be able to focus."

My eyebrows arch as he avoids my eyes. "Am I really so distracting?"

He snorts under his breath. "You have no idea."

This sends an electric jolt through my sternum that ends in my toes. I can tell he's surprised he said it too. I place my drink on the bar and push it aside, now fully engrossed in this conversation. "Why are you here, then?"

"I'm keeping an eye out for the bosses. None of us get retrials if we're dead."

I want to laugh it off, but the furrow of his brow warns me he's serious. His hunched shoulders and fidgeting fingers remind me he's worried about us. All of us. Even me. He could leave this ship anytime he wants with the goodwill he garners from guests, but he doesn't.

"When did I become one of the people you watch out for?" Although my tone is light, both of us know I'm not joking. He bites his lip, flustered.

His eyes take me apart, as if he's trying to determine which version of Roe I truly am. The spoiled lady of Credence who believes she deserves her retrial more than anyone else, or the girl who helps her friends and saves guests who would run from her spirits given the chance. Then the sharp cut of his jaw relaxes and his brow softens, decision made. He nods to the bow of the ship where it's empty. "Will you walk with me?"

I hesitate but allow him to lead me to the bow of the ship. I know I'm safe with him. For better or worse, he's one of the most protective people I've ever met. Even if his protectiveness pushes me away. Maybe I understand it more now, seeing how dangerous it can be aboard.

We're alone here at the bow, surrounded by the night sky and a blanket of stars. The rolling lavender mist, rippling over midnight waves around the ship, glows silver in the darkness. I lean my bare back against the cool railing with my head turned toward Ivander.

I nod to the stars overhead. Their brilliant white light allows us to see in the dark. "Back home in Credence, I used to spend nights in the woods with my brother. The stars looked like this between gaps in the trees." I try to remember Leith's easy smile, not the fact that he's nothing more than a memory. In the chaos of the past two weeks, I haven't had much time to think about him. Even after all this time, I feel guilty when I forget to think of him.

I fight to keep my breaths even. Maybe I shouldn't risk sharing this with Ivander. Even if we both make it off this ship with our lives and our Morphia, will I ever see him again? After this, he might not want to socialize with a Damarcus.

He runs a hand over his hair and drags it down his angular face. "You're brave, Rosaline. I've wanted to tell you that for over a week now." The way he says my name sends a shiver down my spine. Clear and intentional. Strong. My heartbeat thuds in my throat. "You're not afraid of the bosses, of the *Celestial*." He chuckles. "Not even of Asralyn."

I snort. "Trust me, I'm scared all the time."

"I know." He bites his lip, as if he's not articulating properly. "I know you may be scared, but you face things head-on. You adapt. I'm guessing you didn't come here with your family's support either."

I've never considered myself brave. Not brave like Leith, sacrificing his life to serve the Hawks, or even brave like Eliza, always willing to speak her mind. But maybe he's right. I don't know whether to be proud or scared of how far I'd go to get my retrial. For a moment, I think about Father and Mother, even Eliza, and it makes my throat tight. I swallow hard.

"What about you?" I ask. "Was it hard for you to leave your family?"

Ivander opens his mouth several times only to shut it.

Maybe I've pushed too hard and asked for too much. I wait for the walls to come back, blocking me out again. His brow furrows. Maybe I shouldn't have asked here. It might not be right to talk about in the middle of a deck party.

"Sorry. You don't have to say anything to me you don't want to."

He doesn't leave, though, and regards me with scrutinizing eyes that flash. "Who said I didn't want to?"

Despite the yelling and splashing of bodies catapulting into pool water in the distance, it feels like the two of us are all alone out here on the water.

He blows out a long breath, picking at one of his silver nails. "I—sometimes I feel like I have to take care of the others. Like they're my responsibility." He runs a hand through his hair, biceps straining in the moonlight. "With you, I never feel like that. I *know* you can handle yourself. But I feel a lot of pressure to stay strong for them. I guess I want you to know that I'm not strong. I . . . deserve to be here."

The word *deserve* makes my shoulders tighten, but I wait for him to continue.

"My family and I lived in the province of Aryndar. Close to the capital." His eyes dash to mine, then down to the deck. "My mother was a renowned theater performer and needed to live close to perform for the spokesperson at Alexandrite Estate. It was Malyk then too. He had her perform regularly."

Ivander's mother must have been even more talented than her son to perform at Alexandrite. Every five years, the council votes on one member to be the spokesperson for decisions. Father's been after the appointment for years, but Spokesman Malyk has had it for decades.

Ivander grips the railing, taking a long breath of salty air. "I would go with her a lot because Father runs a market stall in Aryndar. He couldn't watch me while he was handling customers. As I got older, Mother wanted me to come with her to learn. She thought I'd follow in her footsteps onstage, but my mother wasn't just a performer. She was a Morphic."

He leans with his forearms resting on the railing. He emphasized the word *was*. My heart sinks with the realization that she's either dead or without her magic.

"She was a time winder. She could add an hour to her day or take one away. She'd use it to make a performance feel shorter. People would see her performing plays or singing songs, but she could skip to the end. Sometimes she'd add an hour to the end of the day when she was spending time with me."

Time winders may not be as rare as resurrectors or alchemers, but they aren't as common as crafters or shifters. "Don't time winders have trouble staying in the present?"

"Most rarely use their gifts because they see flashes of the future each time they do. Mother told me she never saw what she wanted. It's like seeing your future actions with no context." He grimaces. "It was a tricky gift, but she still didn't deserve to have it taken."

"Does she miss it?"

"Every day." He hangs his head and folds his arms tight over his chest. "It was my fault. All of it."

Without knowing what else to do, I place my hand next to his on the railing. I wonder if he's told anyone else this story. I wish he knew how much it means to me that he's trusted me enough to tell it.

He gazes out over the water. "My grandfather was very sick at the time, and it was beyond the menders' skill to heal him. I'd overheard some of Malyk's servants talking about how Alexandrite received rare potions from an alchemer once a month. I assumed Malyk would have healing potions the rest of the realm couldn't access. So the next time Mother went to perform, I disguised myself during her performance. I shifted my clothing to resemble a guard's uniform and snuck to Malyk's personal stores. But they caught me. Spokesman Malyk took my chance at a trial away and gave me the same choice he gave you. Work sentence on the ship, or they'd take my Morphia then and there."

He slides down the railing and sits on the deck with his legs out in front of him. He points and flexes his toes, like he's remembering that fateful performance all these years later.

I slide down next to him. "It was a mistake."

"That's not all," he whispers. "Malyk was furious. Enraged that this could happen at his own estate. He blamed my parents and had his guards administer the extraction potion to my mother right on the spot."

He bites his lip. "Later, my father told me Grandfather's sickness was incurable. I stole for nothing. Even after that, Mother begged me not to go. Told me it was dangerous and that I'd never get a retrial. My grandfather was the only one who told me to go. He thought I had to try to get my Morphia back. He said it was the most important thing I could do for my family after what happened. Keep my Morphia for my mother, who couldn't. He told me Mother and Father were strong, and they'd be okay without me. I got the letter telling me my grandfather died while at a port stop between charters." His voice chokes on the memory. "Before

I left, he said that if I'm ever in a position to help someone else, take a chance on them. We get when we give."

"That's what you do," I say. "You help your friends." I pause, not sure if he wants me to say it. "You've helped me."

"When I met you, I swore I wouldn't," Ivander admits with a grin. "You make it pretty difficult when you pick fights with the bosses every night." His smile shifts into a sigh. "When I first boarded this ship, I swore I'd get off with my Morphia as fast as I could. But then I met Isla and Alana. Then Zora and Niko. I started to realize I wasn't the only Morphic aboard who deserved to keep my Morphia. If I could help them get their retrials . . . maybe I could make up for costing my mother hers."

Ivander grits his teeth. "You think I'm doing all this to help my friends, but I'm just trying to find a way to face myself again. When I talk to the guests, I'm always thinking how I can use those connections when I get out of here. I'm not this selfless hero the others think I am."

The waves of guilt emanating from him are so strong I want to pull him out myself. "You should get to think of yourself." After a pause, I add, "It may not be worth much coming from me, but I believe your mother will forgive you regardless of what happens here."

His eyes meet mine, as if my words let him come up for air. "It's worth more than you know." The intensity in his gaze raises the temperature of the crisp night air around us.

"Why did you help me?" I ask. My eyes drift down to his mouth, and I wonder what it would be like to kiss him. Or if it would even be worth it if we leave this ship and never speak again.

He exhales, dipping his head close to me. "Because you cared about Isla. You didn't just help her in the kitchen at your own expense. You really cared about her." He smirks. "I'm not expecting you to give up your retrial for any of my friends, but maybe you're not *stealing* it from them either."

That was what he accused me of when I first met him. He may now believe I care for his friends and the other Morphics aboard this ship, but only I know the real reason behind the fear stirring in my gut. The shame and doubt swirling in my abdomen, pushing bile into the back of my throat. Everything he's told me about his mother, the guilt he feels—the punishment from Spokesman Malyk—reminds me of my father.

Father must have known how Morphics are treated throughout the province, Morphics guilty of nothing more than being eighteen and imperfect. In Ivander's case, when he first boarded the ship, being even younger. And Father must know how dangerous it is aboard the *Celestial* for us Morphics too. Yet now that I'm here, I'm realizing Ivander's story—and my similar fate and choice—aren't uncommon. My whole body bristles with anger. I need to get off this ship and demand answers from my father. How could he let this entire punishment system continue when Morphics are sent here for frivolous reasons fueled by fear and hate?

What if my family and the council are part of the problem? I dare myself to think it, to relish in the nakedness of admitting my own place in a broken world. In a surge of desperation, I close my eyes and search for the connection to my ancestors. Anyone who's willing to speak to me, to come forward and tell me the truth of what they envisioned for the trials—for the *Celestial*. They wanted to help people like me, like Ivander, like my father. Where did it all go wrong?

"You're trying to summon, aren't you?" Ivander asks. "It's not working, is it?"

"What gave you that idea?" My eyes are squeezed shut, but I hear his snort.

"Because you look murderous."

He's right. The moment between us—if there was one—is gone as my attention turns from his eyes, his mouth, back to my Morphia. I'm frustrated at a lot of things I can't control or change right now. I sigh, shoulders softening, and open my eyes. It seems I can't change anything tonight. I'm stuck in more ways than one. Even my past life was never something I could control. The parties, the gossip, dancing with Reginald. Maybe it's time to take control and dance with someone who understands me.

"Are you ready to dance?" I ask.

Ivander's cheeks flush, and he pulls his knees tight to his chest. "No."

I stand, pulling us both to our feet. The quiet lullaby of a slow violin medley wafts to us from the center of the deck. "Are you kidding me? You're the best performer on this ship. You're really not going to dance?"

"I usually have choreography," he mutters. "Rehearsals. Pre-written steps."

"Oh, please. You're such a perfectionist." I drag him across the deck back toward the dance floor. He begs me to let him go back to the bar, but he doesn't pull away even though he's got the strength.

Alana waves to me from the middle of a dense circle of dancers. She's with Niko, who's put an arm around her waist. Zora and Isla have disappeared, most likely into a couple of inflatable tubes on the lagoon. If there's one thing I know how to do, it's dance at fancy parties after the lords and ladies have gone to bed. Then it's just people my age and province-dwellers with little status and a much better idea of how to let go.

I pull us onto the dance floor and try to get him to sway with me to the sounds of the violin. "How can you dance when everyone's watching?" he bends down to say in my ear.

An unbidden wave of heat prickles along my skin at how close his mouth is to my cheek. *So the performer gets stage fright offstage.* "Pretend you're onstage. You can criticize my foot placement to make it feel more real for you."

"Very funny."

I twirl myself under his arm, pressing close to his chest. He may be all sure of himself with the guests, but around me, he's shy. There's something frustratingly attractive about that. The truth is, once he finds the courage to dance with me, he's much better than he knows. The muscles of his arms and the effortless flexibility of his legs and spine outpace my stiffer movements I learned from formal dancing at our estate's balls. He whirls me around the dance floor and makes it feel like we're flying.

For a moment, I swear we are.

Until I hear the screams.

Ivander's arms fall from the small of my back as we turn. Panicked shouts come from the lagoon on the port side of the ship. The crowd of staff members on the dance floor rush to the lagoon as the violin screeches to a stop. The people in the pool come up for air. Alana and Niko fight through the crowd to get to Ivander and me.

"What's going on?" Alana asks.

The lagoon forms a circular perimeter around the ship, set into the deck, so we're looking down into the water. People leap from it. Farther down the lagoon, I see Isla's wet blond curls as she throws herself onto the deck. Alana and I push to the front, hearts hammering.

The bioluminescent aqua water has turned a dark scarlet.

As people climb out of the lagoon, they drip bloody water onto the deck. A girl I recognize as the crafter, Maren, spits out a mouthful of red. "I felt something under the water. Something big."

A boy with shaggy brown hair is pulled from the lagoon, and he stumbles onto the deck, clutching his right arm. I put a hand over my mouth. A chunk of flesh is missing from his forearm. He struggles to cover the mangled flesh, but the jagged edges fall through his fingers. His stilted movements and stunned expression suggest he's in shock. We watch in horror as a mass of torn tissue slides out of his grip. Blood gushes onto the floorboards, pouring like rain as people shriek.

I glimpse a large, blue-gray dorsal fin breaching the lagoon water close to the stern of the ship. A gaping maw breaks the surface. It's an endless chasm of jagged teeth around a pulsating throat. Flesh is stuck between the larger teeth. Its roar is a high-pitched screech that rings in my ears before it dives, disappearing into the calm, dark waters. Panicked whispers run through the crowd. This shouldn't keep happening on deck. It's the hallways that have the threatening creatures spontaneously created by raw Morphia, the hallways that are dangerous.

We hear a loud, intentional cough behind us.

Ivander takes in a sharp breath as we turn around, facing the sliding glass doors that lead out onto the top deck.

Boss Charmaine stands in the doorway, wearing a silk dressing gown with her blond hair tied up in a severe knot. "What's going on here?"

CHAPTER 16

No one sleeps. We're ordered to work on preparations for the mid-cruise ball while the bosses interrogate every one of us. While we move marble tables and glittering chairs in the Moondust Ballroom, the bosses take us one at a time into a small room to find out who was behind our party and the bloody lagoon. They wanted to punish us all, but whatever torture they had in mind would've put too many of us out of commission for the guests' big event. Now, their efforts are focused on finding one person to blame.

I move a long banquet table with Alana as the sun peeks over the horizon. We work in silence while Isla mutters to herself. She can't focus on the menu for tonight because she's too worried about what the bosses will do. She clutches the lower left side of her abdomen with quivering fingers. "It's my fault," she whispers to me. "The party was my idea."

Niko grabs Isla by the shoulders and tries to steer her back toward the banquet kitchens. When she won't budge, he bows his head and whispers, "It doesn't matter. We all agreed. No one person gets blamed if we all take the fall."

Boss Charmaine emerges from the silver doors of the ballroom with her gloved hands clasped in front of her. Everyone's already spooked by the creature in the lagoon, terrified to talk because they're afraid of whatever torturous punishments await them. And for what? For throwing a party that breaks the rules when the real danger is the ship itself. A ship that's only getting more violent.

Now Isla bends over with her hands on her knees. Her eyes scrunch shut. Fury prickles down my arms, but I know it's nothing compared to the sharp stabbing in Isla's side that will only worsen with stress. Although the bosses made Ivander leave long ago for the theater to practice his performances for the ball, I can't stop thinking about what he told me.

He feels responsible. For us. For his mother losing her Morphia. Yet I didn't come here to help anyone but myself. I came here to get *my* retrial. But that can't be all that matters anymore. The attack in the lagoon comes back to me. Retrials don't matter if we can't even make it off the ship alive.

When Boss Charmaine weaves between the staff members, searching for her next victim, I abandon the chair I was moving and walk over to her. Ignoring Alana's pleas for me to come back, I stop in front of the boss with my hands curled into fists at my sides.

The staff members hauling furniture around the ballroom freeze, watching me. Boss Charmaine tilts her chin down to glare at me. Her stare is somewhat glassy when she looks at me. "You've got a lot of nerve, girl."

"Guests will be waking up soon to a bloody lagoon," I reply, keeping my voice steady. "I think you want to hear what I have to say."

Charmaine's cracked lips purse, and her eyes scan the room, sensing the large number of witnesses. She must decide it's not worth fighting with me here because she turns over her shoulder and motions for me to follow. We descend the stairs to deck two, and she leads me to the Morphia storage room and closes the door behind us.

Though my nerves are heightened, I try to remember what Ivander said last night. They can't take our Morphia away without a cause. If they did, there'd be a riot. Charmaine sits in a plain wooden chair and doesn't offer me a seat.

"Do you have something to confess?" she asks, pulling a knife out from under her cloak. She's trying to scare me, but all it does is make me angry.

"I know you're upset about the party. We shouldn't have held it, but not for the reasons you think."

Charmaine raises a brow. I get the sense that she's enjoying this.

Keeping my face impassive, I try not to fidget as I talk. All Mother's training on how to be a lady comes back to me, and for once I'm thankful for it. "It's dangerous to be in the hallways at night. I knew that rule when I was a guest here. But tonight, we weren't in the hallways when a staff member was bitten and the water turned to blood. We weren't in the hallways when clear skies and calm waters turned windy and rough. We were out on the deck. The Morphia on this ship's getting out of control." I fight the urge to tell her that the bosses are out of control too. "A guest will get hurt next."

Charmaine leans forward in her chair. "This may come as a surprise to you, Ms. Damarcus, but you don't run this ship. I'm not interested in your opinions about its safety."

"It's not an opinion." I unclench my hands. "It's what I've seen with my own eyes."

She sighs, taking a Morphia container off the stack and lifting the lid. Removing her glove, she dips her wounded, grisly fingers into the jar. Her furrowed brow relaxes when her skin makes contact with the glowing substance. She uses the raw Morphia like a shifter would, allowing the luminous energy to deepen the gold in her hair and style it into a flawless fishtail braid. She's using it, wasting it on something frivolous right in front of me.

She flashes me a damn-the-consequences smile. "If you have no information about who's responsible for last night's breach of conduct, then you go back to work."

The tongue Leith always told me would get me into trouble moves faster than my mind. "It was me. The party was my idea."

She stops, her hand frozen on the jar of Morphia. She shakes her head, knowing full well I'm lying, but realizing she can't prove it. She stands, wagging her skeletal finger in my face. "Then it's time for you to finally take your job seriously." She grips my upper arm hard. "If one thing goes wrong for you at the mid-cruise ball, you *and* your friends will never get retrials. I'll make sure they all pay for your mistakes."

When I escort the Stallards to deck ten just before midnight, we enter a space entirely transformed into a glamorous soiree.

The Moondust Ballroom is set to look like a forest bathed in moonlight. Overhead, an enormous round light fixture bathes the room in a silver glow. Arbors of green leafy vines twinkle as if stars have fallen from the sky, and color-changing footprints appear with each guest's steps on the shiny black dance floor. Waiters weave through the guests with small plates piled high with smoked murdo crisps, boiled sea falcon eggs topped with glowing caviar, and small bowls of ravioli with a gortha pod butter sauce. The bar's crowded with staff members, also in formalwear, getting drinks for their impatient guests. The walls made of windows overlook a calm, cerulean sea glimmering with the reflection of stars.

Although the guests are discouraged from wandering to the top deck tonight, they wouldn't see the bloody lagoon if they did. After a thorough cleaning, it returned to normal, much as the hallways do during the day. But my stomach still turns when guests swim in it. Sage and Ezra almost plummeted into an angry sea while the sun was high and shining. The dangers are growing, and next time, I might not be able to stop it.

Asralyn's mouth drops open at the elegant decorations. She folds her hands over the small waist of her strapless gown. The sweetheart neckline of it is a deep blue, the color of it fading along the length of the full skirt until it's completely gone at the white hemline. Her soft brown hair is in an elegant updo with gold ribbon wound through the strands. Even I have to admit she looks lovely.

Vance wears a blue vest with a matte silver overcoat and sleek black trousers. He kneels to lecture the children about the importance of good behavior during this especially fancy occasion. Sage tugs on a lock of pink hair with a moving butterfly clip in it, desperate to escape.

I take a few steps from the Stallards and push to the front of the bar. If I've learned anything about Asralyn, it's that she doesn't like to ask for good service. Having worked closely with the family for two weeks, I know their drink orders by heart. "Bring them as soon as you can," I tell Lorrence, an enhancer who works magic with the drinks.

"We're all out of star cubes for the Red Starfall," Lorrence whispers.

"The party just started," I whisper back with a note of panic. The stupid drink won't glow without them.

Lorrence raises his hands in defeat. "I'm as unhappy about it as you. Lady Kato requested a bucket of them, and we couldn't refuse her. I'll see what I can do."

I massage the bridge of my nose. "Have someone check the seventh deck supply rooms. Sometimes Rayna likes to stash them on seven for the spa." This can't happen tonight. I can't afford any mistakes. Not when Boss Charmaine is watching everything I do. Not when my friends could be punished for my choices.

When I return to Vance and Asralyn, they fix me with suspicious glares. "Where did you disappear to?" Asralyn asks.

"I placed your drink orders," I reply smoothly. All I can do is hope they turn out correct.

Vance coughs. "We didn't give you our drink orders."

I tick the drinks off on my fingers. "You prefer an Illoryan whiskey, neat. I got you a double. Asralyn prefers a Red Starfall with a decorative sparkler. She says a signature drink must be the best, and without the sparkler, she may as well be back home at her estate." I kneel in front of the kids, touching each of their noses with the tip of my finger. "You," I say to Ezra, "always get a chocolate malt with a fun straw. And you," I say to Sage, "are wise beyond your years. You get ice water with the ice shaped like unicorns." I stand. "Now, if you'll all follow me, I believe there's a surprise for the children with the performers."

A waiter eventually brings the drinks on a heavy tray laden with other orders, and I breathe a sigh of relief. Asralyn's drink is correct, at least it appears to be, sparkling away over an angry red sea of Lixor. My blood freezes as she drops in the star ice cube with silver tongs, waiting for the signature white glow to overtake the glass before taking a cautionary sip. Her lips purse, and her brows raise slightly. She's shocked I got it right.

I lead the way to the performers suspended from silks rigged from the ceiling over a small makeshift stage. The performers clump together, playing violins, a cello, a viola, and a piano. Zora sings a melodic, melancholy tune that for some reason reminds me of what happened last night. My heart sinks at the thought that no matter how beautiful this deck may look tonight, it's still capable of violence.

When I see Ivander dangling from a black silk, back arched and toes pointed, I inhale a sharp breath. Now I'm even more aware of the risky gown I've chosen. My dress is a sleek, silver gown with a cinched waist and an open back. Long white plates of metal crisscross over my back, meant to resemble bone. Zora crafted it for me, using her Morphia to make my dress look like one of my spirits—wispy and silver.

It's a statement, one not meant for the bosses or the guests. This one's for me, a daring silhouette that embraces the dangerous beauty of my Morphia. The Stallards gather around the performers, and this affords me a moment to speak with Ivander as he descends the silks.

"Tired yet?" I keep my voice steady despite the aggravating heat beneath my skin. The prickle of frustration I usually feel around him has become a deep, steadier warmth in my core. After his confession last night about his family, it's hard to look at him the same way. Damn him for making me care. He's found a new family here, a purpose, and like his silks, he manages it all with grace. There's no one to ease the burdens he puts on himself.

"Not in the slightest," he answers, eyes sweeping over the silver fabric hugging my frame. "Turn. I want to see the whole thing."

I do a little spin, revealing the bone clasps against my shoulder blades. "What do you think?"

His lips lift, and he motions to the black silk suspended from the ceiling. "I believe we both chose similar themes for this evening. Watch the performance, and you'll see."

I swallow hard, now captivated by *his* outfit. He wears a deep green vest that reveals his sculpted arms and high-waisted black pants. "What's the theme?"

He turns back to the silks, grabbing a handful of the fabric in his outstretched hand. "Rebellion," he whispers.

My arms shiver with a new chill as I walk back to my family. I point up at Ivander and urge the children to watch, but I watch just as closely.

Sage and Ezra tilt their heads up to the ceiling, transfixed by Ivander spinning in the air. As he spins, Ivander calls down to them. "Young Ezra, what would you like to see flying through the sky?"

Ezra scrunches his nose and bellows, "A dragon!"

Many families are watching now, pointing up at Ivander. They're all smiling—even Asralyn cracks a grin. Ivander's body begins to change, and I finally witness the full power of his shifter magic.

A scale pattern forms over his brown skin, and his fingernails extend into claws. Spikes protrude from his arched spine, and his warm irises glow gold. When he growls, his parted lips reveal teeth sharpened into points.

Then there's a faint cracking sound overhead as the bones in his bare feet snap. A couple of his toes jut at odd angles, and he grimaces, gritting his pointed teeth.

With this extreme transformation, he pays the price for it, although the guests don't notice.

My stomach turns. He shouldn't hurt himself for their entertainment. Though his muscles tighten with pain, he holds himself vertical in midair. The silks on either side of his arms could be the wings of a dragon.

Ezra and Sage clap. I'm so mesmerized, I hardly notice Zora and a few other crafters spinning in hoops of fire at the base of the silks. Not until Sage tugs on my arm, pointing. "Look! They're on fire."

The hoops spin with blinding speed, sending sparks into the air. Zora's slender body spins with the hoop, somehow avoiding the spitting embers. With a jolt, I realize the scene the crafters and Ivander are creating. To the children, he's a dragon flying through the sky, breathing fire down below.

But to the bosses watching from the perimeter of the ballroom, he's a witch suspended above a lit pyre. My father's words from long ago come back to me. *They used to call us witches. They used to burn us at the stake.*

When the crafters stop spinning, Ivander's scales smooth out and his spikes retract. The crowd erupts into applause. Zora gifts each of the children a glowing flower that hums a song when watered.

Sage and Ezra run to show Asralyn their flowers, but I'm only watching Ivander, shaking my head. He descends the silks and cocks his head at me, as if he can't understand what's wrong. Through clenched teeth, I whisper, "Last night, you were the one saying we needed to be careful."

He grins. "Someone reminded me there are more important things."

I'm about to fire back a response when someone taps me on the shoulder. I turn and come face-to-face with Asralyn. Her stormy, blue-gray eyes narrow, and I drop into a low curtsy. "What can I do for you, Lady Stallard?"

She takes a slow sip of her cocktail and inclines her head in a stiff nod to me. "I wanted to say that your improvements have not gone unnoticed."

Warmth rises in my chest. Pressing my lips together to avoid smiling too widely, I give her another curtsy. She waves her hand and indicates the overflowing basket of parchment slips closest to the refreshment table. Guests write names on slips of paper and put their staff member votes in the basket.

"Don't get excited. We voted for Alana, like everyone else with some sense aboard this ship. But I don't see why you couldn't climb the ranks before the final week."

"Thank you," I say.

Asralyn's lip curls. "We'll be on the dance floor if you need us. Please stop hovering."

"Of course." Another semi-awkward curtsy. As she disappears onto the dance floor, some of the anxiety I've felt all night begins to unwind. I flush hot, overcome by a rush of belief in myself, in change.

Turning back to Ivander, I throw up my hands, drunk on the possibility of making things better. "Asralyn told me I did well. I never thought that could happen."

"That makes two of us."

"Shut up." I'd like to knee him in the shin, but this doesn't feel like messing around in the theater together anymore. I can't let this moment go. I lean close to him, lowering my voice. "Think about it. If we had more retrials, and if the bosses stopped abusing our Morphia, this ship could really help people. It wouldn't be dangerous, or a punishment. Once I get my retrial, I'll tell Father things need to change—"

I feel another tap on my shoulder. I swear if it's Asralyn again . . .

But it's not.

When I turn, I see the thick golden hair and broad shoulders of Grayson Caddel.

CHAPTER 17

"**G**ray!" I exclaim, throwing my arms around his neck.

I forget there are hundreds of guests and the bosses watching us tonight. He towers over me but not in the intimidating way Father does. Even if Gray doesn't have Jasper's easygoing smile, seeing him in his indigo vest and long black overcoat with the hawk pin fastened to his chest makes me feel like I'm home again. After a stuffy pause, his muscular arms envelop me, and I inhale the scent of pine trees and salt. I'm still Leith's little sister, even if Leith isn't around anymore.

From the silks, Ivander watches Gray warily. My brow furrows until my gaze returns to the hawk pendant on his coat, and I step back from him. "What are you doing here?" I ask.

"I finally convinced my parents to bring me. We boarded at one of the port stops a few days ago. We're only here for a two-week cruise." Gray runs a hand through his hair, separating the golden strands with his fingers. "I came here for you. I had to make sure you were okay." His voice lowers. "And there are things you should know now that you're aboard."

I open my mouth to ask what he means, but he stops me with a curt shake of his head. "Not here. Not when so many are watching and listening."

"How did you convince your parents?" I ask.

"My parents agreed it was the proper way to celebrate my promotion. I'm captain of the Hawks now."

Although I'm surprised Father didn't tell me he planned to promote Gray, I ignore the sting. Just another thing Father didn't share with me. "That's incredible. I'm sure your parents are proud." There's something off about the already stiff set of his jaw. "You do want to be captain, right?"

Without answering, he takes my hand and leads me out onto the dance floor. Gray ignores my protests, and I have to hope none of the bosses can see us. We're caught between staff members and guests alike. I am shielded by the opulence of our guests. A woman with deep brown skin wears a large gown with glowing lavender Riven Blossom petals woven into the full skirt. A man who witnessed the flight activity disaster avoids my gaze as he swings his partner around and dips him. The man's coat fans out in what look like brilliant red wings. I glimpse Zora sneaking a quick dance with Isla while Isla tries to run back to the kitchen.

After a long pause, Gray answers, "Of course. It's just . . . a lot of responsibility."

There was a time when Gray's brow was unlined, and his words were carefree. His soft green eyes and freckled skin remind me of summer days the three of us used to spend outside in the glades of Carodmoor Forest in Credence. We'd bring a picnic lunch so heavy that Gray and Leith had to carry it together. They'd tell me to look for flowers in the woods and make out while I was gone. At least, that's what Leith insisted they were doing. Gray would roll his eyes and tell me they were only talking. When I'd bring them the flowers, Gray would make me a flower crown with wire from the picnic basket.

As we sway together, I want to ask him if he remembers days like those, too, but I don't. Something's shifted. The last time I saw him, I was fleeing my own home on horseback. Now, I'm dodging a guest swinging under her partner's arm. "It's so good to see you."

Gray hangs his head. "I would have been here sooner, but I thought it might not be the best idea to distract you in your first two weeks. The news from Tamarynth is . . . concerning." His lips press in a tight line. "I never wanted you here. Morphics die here."

"It's okay," I stammer, surprised. Anxiety makes my limbs tingle. I don't know what news he brought me, but it worries me that he came all the way here. Gray was always higher strung than my brother but not like this. I want to put him at ease. "Really, I think I'm getting the hang of being a staff member now."

Gray lets out a long breath, and his eyes hold mine like he wants to say more. "I promise I'll explain everything when I can, but for now, be careful." His voice lowers to a whisper. "Please don't give them a reason to hurt you." He spins me around fast as his parents come into view.

I'm not sure what he's talking about, and dread hardens into frustration. With bosses and his parents around, who knows when he'll be able to pull me aside and explain what's going on in Tamarynth. Turning to fire off a slew of questions, I find that he's rejoined the crowd. His golden hair bobs as he reunites with his parents, no doubt getting in trouble with them for speaking to me. My hands shake at my sides. Gray never needed an excuse to talk to me before. He was proud to be seen with Lady Roe Damarcus. Not anymore. Now I'm a social pariah. A prisoner of the same ship he vacations aboard.

Tears sting the corners of my eyes, but I blink hard to clear them. The reminder of home was wonderful for a moment, and now it's exactly what I don't want. I stalk to the banquet table, wiping my cheeks. If he's going to give me cryptic warnings and then run off to his parents, I'm not going to spend another moment thinking about him.

That's a lie. I do think about him. About home. About Father.

Everything's not as it seems. No kidding. I knew next to nothing when I came here. But even if he's stopped believing I have any chance at surviving long enough for my retrial, I haven't.

The banquet table is on the far side of the room, close to the doors that lead to the hallways and upper-class rooms. It's weighed down with meats, cheeses, and vegetables, but the showstoppers are clearly the dishes you can only find aboard the *Celestial*: Ranzin roast stews, featuring its namesake spice blend that's legendary among the upper class, served in golden goblets. Roasted hearth fruits stuffed with goat cheese and herbs, flaky pastries lathered with Sarryndarian spiced honey, and chocolates that bloom into delicate flowers when touched all perch on gilded plates. Kalenar Kurls, an upscale play on the province's popular street food, feature the finest beef skewered on daggers designed to cook the meat to the guest's desired temperature when grasped by the hilt. The chefs have outdone themselves tonight.

I wonder if Isla or Niko have gotten votes like Alana has. It occurs to me that Alana may be the only one from our group to get a retrial at the end of this month. Even if Ivander refuses his nomination, it doesn't mean he can give it to one of us. The thought ruins my appetite, and I retreat from the table to the long windows overlooking the dark indigo sea.

The inky, blackish-blue depths lap calmly beneath me. The reflections of stars twinkle in the water, giving it the luminescent quality so commonly found aboard the *Celestial*. The sensation of floating over a tranquil, moving world makes me think of the spirits in the after.

What does it feel like for them in the world between life and the beyond? There are rules in resurrection. Spirits can give no specific information about the after—the world beyond. When I access the spirit plane, I see no more than the spirits themselves and the energies willing to accompany me back to Tamarynth. Riveners are the ones leading spirits back and forth between the spirit realm and the after.

There's beauty in that unknown for me. That there's a world beyond the spiritual plane even I can't touch. I used to envision Leith as an explorer of the after, on an adventure so exciting he couldn't come back to me for a visit. It made it easier to accept when I'd try to conjure him and get no response.

I'm planning to check on Asralyn and Vance when a boss I don't recognize bumps my shoulder. At first, he must think I'm a guest because his lips form an apologetic smile, and he hands me a drink. Surprised, I take it from him and sip the midnight-blue liquid. It's sweet upon first taste but fades to a note of bitterness. I wait for some magical enhancement, but nothing happens. The boss's face twists into a disapproving scowl as he realizes I'm not a guest. "If you're just going to stand around and drink, you can check the deck for guests. Make sure no one's wandering."

"I'm supposed to be with my family—"

"I don't want to hear your excuses. Go, now." The boss slurps a spoonful of ranzin roast from a gold goblet, then snatches the drink back with his free hand.

Muttering under my breath, I inch toward the doors leading out of the ballroom. With his eyes still on me, I commit to making one quick sweep around the perimeter before I go back and find the Stallards. I can't risk being away from them for too long.

I push open the doors and edge outside. There's open space here in front of the hallways that lead to the guest rooms. The farther I get from the ballroom, the more goose bumps gather on my arms. No one's supposed to leave the ballroom and bar area unsupervised. If guests want to go back to their rooms for any reason, they must be accompanied by a staff member. Luckily, I see no one in my quick pass.

I'm about to head back when I hear a heavy sob from a hallway leading to the guest rooms. My better judgment begs me to return to the ballroom and forget about the sound, but I don't listen. Heels clicking against the black marble floor, I walk to the mouth of the hallway. My footprints leave a vibrant violet imprint in the floor.

A sharp sob sounds again, and I whirl around. I find a girl crouched on the floor near a hallway. As far as I know, we're reasonably safe in the pocket of space between the hallway and the ballroom, but I'm eager to get her back inside.

"Hey," I whisper. When the girl lifts her head, I recognize her coarse chestnut hair and the freckles across her nose. "Elayne? What are you doing out here?" I glance to the nearby hallway. We don't have time to talk, not here. I wonder where her two friends are, the girls from the flying experience. "Let's get you inside."

Elayne shakes her head and pulls her knees tight to her chest. The poufy skirt of her topaz dress forms a defensive cloud of fabric around her thin frame.

"Please. It's not safe to be in the hallways at night. You know that." When she doesn't move, I kneel on the ground beside her, although it's difficult in my constraining silver dress. "Hey, I didn't save you from falling into the sea to watch you get eaten by a hallway."

Her face blanches, and she hugs her knees even tighter.

I swallow and tuck a strand of hair behind my ear. "Kidding. Where are your friends?"

Her body shakes. I may need to call for help. She points with a trembling hand to the hallway, the one leading to the guest rooms. "I was just trying to explore the ship a little. I hate fancy parties." She pauses, quivering fingers pulling at a loose bead on her bodice. "But that hallway smelled like rotting corpses and . . . the walls were covered in blood, I think."

This is bad. She shouldn't have gone by herself. Where were the illusives who were supposed to make that hallway appear normal? They must have had to rotate after expending so much energy. Elayne was probably walking as they changed shifts. "Well, you're out of there now. If you need to leave the ballroom again, make sure a staff member's with you. They can make it . . . manageable."

Elayne pinches her arm, as if to wake herself from a nightmare. "A creature with black wings sat at the end of the hallway and kept coaxing me toward him. I wanted to get closer. I don't know why. He gave me something to drink and then I ended up here."

Panic rises in the back of my throat. "Let me take you to the medbay."

Elayne's eyes meet mine. They're wide and green, glistening with tears. She opens her mouth to answer, but her body goes rigid. The shaking stops, and her crouched body jolts into an immobile, stiff position. Unable to stay sitting up, she falls over. I try to catch her, but she's too heavy. As she lies in a rigid fetal position, blood begins to run from her eyes, ears, and mouth. Tears sting my eyes. I can't breathe. It feels too much like my deathmare.

No. I already saved this girl once. I won't let her get hurt again.

With a trembling hand, I reach out and seize Elayne's stiff fingers, the only comfort I can give her now. My muscles twitch with adrenaline. I tilt my head up and scream.

CHAPTER 18

"**H**elp! Somebody help us!"

I don't care that my voice echoes off the walls. The violin and cello music shrieks to a stop in the nearby ballroom. I crouch over Elayne's chest and try to see if it's still rising and falling. The blood running from her mouth forms a tiny pool of scarlet on the floor.

"We need a mender!"

Guests and staff flood through the doors leading out of the ballroom. Many still clutch drinks and plates of food. Ladies mutter behind their gloved hands and pull children behind them. I force myself to focus on Elayne again. The sight of her rigid body, pale and stiff, prompts bile in the back of my throat. I've always loved scary stories, but only when they stayed stories.

Two staff members crouch next to me, trying to pull me away from Elayne, but I hang on to her. Ivander kneels beside me. "There's nothing you can do for her," he murmurs.

No.

I wrench my arm from his grip. "What about the menders?"

A different hand grabs my wrist, and Alana peers down at me, brown eyes soft as she, too, tries to pull me away. Her elegant gown of blue tulle and sparkling diamond droplets reddens with blood as she kneels beside me. "She's not breathing, Roe."

No. She can't be dead.

Despite their insistence that Elayne is beyond help, a mender joins me by her side. I think his name is Cassius. I've seen him help guests with seasickness. He gently nudges me out of the way. "I will try," he assures me. "But I think she's too far gone."

He touches his fingertips to Elayne's throat, tracing a path down to her sternum and to her stomach. He lets out a frustrated breath. Blood runs from his nose as he attempts to heal her—the price he has to pay for being a mender. When my sister was a mender, she used to hate when she couldn't help. Watching Cassius's futile attempts to save a life makes me empathize with Eliza in a way I never have before. I'd always thought Eliza would regret giving up her Morphia, but this helplessness must be soul-crushing. Cassius hangs his head, clearly feeling that same despair now.

"What's going on here?" Boss Charmaine demands.

Boss Balanyr stands beside her with his arms crossed and his bushy brown beard scrunched with disapproval. Guests shy away from the bosses and pull their children close. They know the bosses are necessary to keep Morphics in line, but it doesn't mean they want to be near them. Fresh fear stabs my chest. Alana pulls me to my feet.

My lip trembles as I answer, "I don't know. I think she wandered off into one of the hallways alone. She mentioned some sort of creature—"

"Enough." Balanyr cuts me off. The guests shift on their feet. Some of them stand on their tiptoes to peer down the hallway behind Elayne's body. Asralyn's in the crowd. Her face drains of color.

"Roe Damarcus was alone with this girl when she died." Charmaine looks me right in the eyes as her lip curls into a snarl. She motions to the body on the ground and the bloodstains on the front of my dress. "In such suspicious circumstances, we need proof of what truly happened."

Sweat beads along the back of my neck. My hands ball into fists. I swallow hard, only now realizing how bad this must look. "I found her sitting against the wall. She was terrified. And then . . . she fell over."

Ivander tenses next to me. "Roe didn't do this. The staff may not be to blame."

A guest near the front of the crowd, clutching her champagne glass to her chest, asks, "If it's not one of the staff, who could've done this?"

Balanyr faces the crowd with his gloved hands outstretched in a gesture of calm. His dark blue cloak fans out behind him like a set of wings, making me think about the "creature" Elayne saw in the hallway. "If Roe is telling the truth, she should have nothing to fear. She's a resurrector. She'll bring her spirit back so the poor girl can tell us how she died."

Boss Charmaine steers two women toward the girl's body. Selene and Taren. The two girls clutch each other, holding back sobs as they step forward. "Elayne's our friend. We just graduated university together." Selene's voice breaks, and she collapses into Charmaine's arms.

"There, there," Charmaine answers, voice devoid of emotion. Alana rushes over to the two girls, helping to balance the overwhelming grief with warm memories of Elayne.

My brow creases, and familiar dread stirs in my stomach. I'm used to people watching when I conjure spirits, but it's on my terms, not someone else's. For parties, not for proving my own innocence. The people of Credence understand that my abilities aren't always predictable.

"It doesn't work like that," I croak. Clearing my throat, I try again. "I can only summon spirits who want to come back. Sometimes they don't feel like talking about their deaths when they're newly deceased."

Charmaine clicks her tongue. "I knew there would be some excuse. Some reason as to why she can't possibly bring back this girl's spirit."

Balanyr nods. "It sounds like Roe doesn't want any of us to know how she died."

Panic chokes me. I don't have a choice. I raise my shaking hands over Elayne's body, remembering Boss Charmaine's threat. I need this to work. She won't hesitate to take my Morphia. Or my friends'. One mistake. That's what she threatened. And here I am with the worst mistake possible: A guest's death, and I'm in the wrong place at the wrong time.

"I'll— I'll try." My quivering fingers search for the connection to Elayne's spirit. I squeeze my eyes shut, reaching out to the spirit world, straining with every bit of effort I can muster. My core tightens and my palms heat, but nothing comes to me.

A hand on my arm steadies me, and my body relaxes. I open my eyes to see Ivander's fingers resting on my forearm. I'm surprised that the pressure of his touch is grounding, pulling me from the depths of panic.

Deep breath in. Deep breath out. This time, I reach for her without straining. The pulses of energy in each spirit rush to me, eager to visit the mortal world. Then, just as I'm reaching out for her, it's like someone slams a porthole shut.

There's an impermeable block between me and Elayne.

I reach out again, but once more, a door slams in my face. My arms tremble. This is the same block I run into when trying to summon family members. What good is it being a witch of the dead if I can't save myself from being burned at the stake?

When I open my eyes, everyone's staring at me. No one moves or speaks. Blood roars in my ears, and I fight the urge to throw up. Balanyr placates the crowd with a flourish of his hand. "Don't worry. We'll get this all under control."

He fixes the staff members with a menacing, beady-eyed glare. "Take the guests back inside to enjoy the ball. Escort those who wish to leave back to their rooms one by one." He pulls Ivander aside. "Make sure an illusive is in each of the hallways."

Ivander stares at Balanyr, chin up, angular jaw set. "What are you going to do with Roe?"

Boss Charmaine places a hand on me, gripping my exposed shoulder with her glove. The pressure of her touch makes my skin crawl. Her grip tightens. "We're going to extract her Morphia." She strokes Ivander's cheek with her finger, keeping her other hand clamped on me. "And if you try to stop us, we'll take yours too."

CHAPTER 19

A cell door slams shut behind me, rattling iron bars.

It's much rockier in the brig than anywhere else on the ship. My stomach roils with it. Panic has me in a chokehold. I press myself against the bars. "Please," I say, voice unsteady and weak. "You have to believe me. I didn't hurt anyone."

Boss Charmaine kicks at me with her boot, forcing me to step back. "Then why didn't you let us ask the girl how she died?" She crouches in front of the bars. The end of her nose grazes the iron as she bends closer. "In the end, all Morphics are dangerous." She sounds like she's telling herself as much as she's telling me.

My hands tremble as I grip the bars. "I swear. I'm telling the truth. I don't know why I couldn't reach her." Why I could never reach Leith.

On the way to the cells, we passed the Morphia extraction room. The idea of my cell sharing a wall with the extraction room makes my eyes sting with tears. Even when I failed my trial, I knew I had another option. The *Celestial* gave me a chance. Now I have nothing left. Nothing but the death of a young girl that I couldn't prevent.

Charmaine pats the ends of my knuckles poking through the bars. She flashes a simpering smile with cracked, bloody lips. "I bet you're wishing you were better behaved now."

She looks at me with hate and jealousy. This is what she wants. Power over me, power over what she couldn't have.

She made a promise and she delivered. This has to be one of my deathmares. I've been showing off, using resurrection the way Eliza dabs perfume. I thought my power belonged to me. But now, I realize it never did. It was a loan, something I was never guaranteed to keep.

When I was young and worried about my future trial, Leith used to try to reassure me. He'd say, *You don't take a Morphic's magic just because you don't like the Morphic.*

I always thought that was a bit odd considering he took plenty of Morphics to Malachite Prison, but now, it gives me strength. The strength to lash out and grab the clasp of Charmaine's cloak, pulling her closer to the bars. Boss Balanyr lunges toward me, but I'm not trying to hurt her. I only want them to listen.

"Punish me," I say. "Any way you want. But don't take my Morphia." I release Charmaine's cloak, and she shoots to her feet, stumbling backward. "Don't hurt my friends."

I feel more like I'm begging Father to let me back into his study after I'd broken his favorite potion jar than making a deal with my prison guards, but I don't care how it sounds. I'll do what they want.

Charmaine looks to Balanyr without meeting my eyes. "I'll get the potion. Stay here and watch her."

Tears stream down my face now. I feel like I'm going to throw up and pass out at the same time. I keep one hand on the bars to hold myself upright and hold my other hand out in front of me, palm up, straining my fingers.

Balanyr takes a step back.

I'm not trying to hurt him, but he doesn't know that. He has to see I'm not what he thinks. I don't even have to close my eyes, my desperation is so strong. Silver beams of light burst from my outstretched fingertips.

When I enter the spirit world, I'm floating in a gray-blue ether. As I come across translucent silver spirits and their glowing auras of energy, I invite them back to Tamarynth. A brief reprieve from their onward journey in the eternal world.

I call upon the spirits of kittens. Fluffy little gray balls of fur pounce at my feet. Because they lack strength, they don't appear solid. Bright see-through kittens paw at the flowers I resurrect next. Wispy red roses and luminous white chrysanthemums spring from my palm and drop to the floor at my feet. I resurrect butterflies then, blue, orange, white, yellow, and red. They fly around my head, flexing their wings in the living plane once more.

The tears dripping from my face fall through the translucent wings when they fly beneath my chin. "See." My hand trembles as one kitten sneaks through the gap in the bars. The kitten purrs and rubs against Balanyr's large brown boot. "Beautiful." Ivander said so. I know so.

My shoulders hunch when Charmaine comes back to the cell. The spirits flicker as fear diminishes my control.

An odd sense of calm drifts over me as Charmaine's boots trudge closer. If showing them the beauty won't work, I'll try another tactic. I don't care if I have to jump over the side of this ship into the open ocean. I don't care if I have to kill her. The realization scares me, but it also makes me proud. I can be as cold as my corpses if I have to protect my magic.

I won't let her take this from me.

Charmaine shakes the potion in front of me and unlocks the cell door. "There's no one to vouch for you, Lady Damarcus. The situation is too suspicious to go unpunished."

The entry door to the prison flies open, and two people burst inside. I can't see around Balanyr and Charmaine, but my heart leaps at the voice.

"How do you know she has no one to vouch for her?"

Asralyn.

Asralyn's heels click against the ground as she steps into the jail, following Ivander. Her brown hair has fallen from her elegantly styled updo. Ivander steps aside as Asralyn approaches the bosses, arms crossed. Charmaine and Balanyr exchange a look and paint on closed-lipped smiles.

Asralyn taps the toe of her crystal heel against the floor. "I noticed my concierge had left us alone for far too long." She narrows her eyes at me. "So I checked outside the ballroom. When I saw her with that young woman, I became concerned. Vance and I have had a hard enough time getting her to attend to us, much less another guest." She digs her nails into her arms. "But I overheard them. I heard the truth. The girl said she saw the hallways . . . change. A dark creature gave her a drink. Roe did nothing but try to help her."

A heavy, weighted silence follows that makes me feel like I'm being lifted off the ground and crushed all at once. I hold my breath, waiting for my bosses and now judges to speak. When they say nothing, Lady Stallard lifts her chin and throws her shoulders back, much the same way I was taught to do as a young lady of Credence.

At this slight change in stance, Balanyr and Charmaine clear their throats. Even Charmaine, teeth clenched with rage, can't deny a high-paying upper-class guest. Charmaine and I are oddly enough in the same position there. With a stiff nod to Asralyn, Charmaine opens the door to my cell.

I don't wait for it to swing all the way open before scrambling out from behind the bars. My chest heaves, and I wipe the back of my hand across tearstained cheeks.

"Are you sure," Charmaine asks in a low rumble, "that you want this girl to continue as your concierge?"

Asralyn nods. "Now, if you'd excuse us, I'd like to enjoy the rest of my night. This was supposed to be my vacation."

Ivander says nothing. He must have shown her the way, but that still doesn't explain why she helped me. Asralyn's been open in her contempt for my work as a concierge. She's never shown any signs of caring whether I get my retrial or not. I can't read the expression on her face, but I follow without question.

"Lady Damarcus," Charmaine says. I turn over my shoulder. "Remember what we spoke about earlier." She won't let me forget her threats to me or my friends.

Without a word, I follow Asralyn and Ivander out of the jail and into the hallway of deck one. The three of us are silent as Ivander leads us to an illusive stationed outside the brig. She uses her Morphia to make the hallways tame, like in the daytime. It depletes her energy to get us all the way to deck ten. By the time we're outside Asralyn's room, Ivander has to help the illusive stand. The walls are starting to crack, revealing rotting wood crawling with maggots and roaches the size of my fist. I pray to the Riveners that nothing will attack us on the walk back to the staff bunks.

Asralyn says nothing about the cracks. She simply opens the door to her room and holds out her hand. "In," she says to me.

I look over my shoulder at Ivander and the illusive, trying to decide if I should obey her. Asralyn rolls her eyes. "I saved your magic, and now you're not going to listen to me?"

Good point. I get one last glimpse of Ivander's eyes, full of anger, but I'm not sure it's directed at me. Will the bosses decide to punish my friends instead of me? Did I put Alana in danger of losing her retrial? I follow Asralyn into her room, and as the door shuts behind me, the dam holding back my emotions threatens to burst.

The chandelier in the center of the sitting room burns with the final flickers of candlelight. The children and Vance must have already gone to bed. With the dying candles and moon as our only light, it's more creepy than beautiful.

Asralyn walks to the settee and takes a seat, gown fanning out around her. She drags fingers through her hair. It falls in loose curls around her shoulders, and she nods to the spot next to her. "Sit. That's not a request."

Hesitantly, I navigate to the back of the room and sit, careful not to get too close to Asralyn. From here, we can look out through the sliding glass doors to the open sea. There's something soothing about the rhythmic midnight waves reflecting moonlight in the stillness after everyone's gone to bed.

Asralyn stays silent for so long that I'm not sure if I should leave. I trace my finger over the silver fabric of my dress. A light breeze whooshes against the sliding glass door, and Asralyn sucks in a sharp breath.

"It's okay," I tell her. "It's only the wind."

She clasps her hands tightly together, closing her eyes. She opens them again. "I'm always jumpy at night." Her voice is lower than a whisper as she stares out to sea. "Most nights I stay out here until I fall asleep." She kicks off her heels and sits with her feet on the settee. In the dark, she's much less commanding. "I know you didn't kill that poor girl."

My foot taps against the floor, bouncing my knee up and down. I get the sense she's confiding in me, and I'm not sure what to do. Eliza was always much better at listening to people's concerns and helping them. My Morphia always seems to bring people tears that I don't know what to do with. Leith was the one who taught me the importance of feeling *with* someone and not for someone. But every time I tried, I always felt like a pretender. As if everything I said came out hollow and fake like the corpses I dragged back to life. Father told me it was better not to feel too much at all as a resurrector. I'm not sure he was right.

I clear my throat. "You believe me?"

Asralyn shakes her head, brows pinched like her lips. "I didn't want to come back here. Not after what happened. My sister made me. She said what happened was an accident. She even sent her own children with me to prove how much she believed that."

I stay facing the window, although every part of me wants to look at Asralyn's face. "What happened last time?"

Asralyn exhales a slow, shaky breath. She unclasps her fingers and tugs on one of her large sun earrings. "Vance and I came for a vacation four years ago. We came with our daughter . . . Karynna." She pauses on the name. It's the same way people speak the names they want me to summon. "We were only here for a week cruise. It was the second-to-last day—we were even close to port. Our concierge took Karynna to the game room. She spent so much time there with the shooting lights and weightlessness."

Despite my inner voice screaming a warning, I shift and place my hand over Asralyn's. If I can't feel with her, maybe she'll feel me. She'll know I care. Asralyn chokes on a sob when my hand clasps over hers.

"Karynna used to wear her hair in these beautiful braids—like Sage wears now." Her gaze shifts and cuts into me. "Not messy like yours. Hers were perfect. She was so proud she could do them herself." Her eyes go vacant as she fixates on a vivid memory I cannot see. "She waved at me before she left. Her beautiful hair was braided into a crown she made. Not a single hair out of place. That was the last time I saw her. She died in the game room. No one knows how. Some of the children who saw what happened said she got sucked into the walls and was spat back out." Her shoulders shake. "Like the ship was eating her."

I shudder, reminded of what I've seen on the *Celestial* at night. Even so, none of this is supposed to be a threat during the day, or even outside the hallways.

Elayne's story and Gray's warning from the ball . . . I can't help but wonder if there's more reason to be afraid. Asralyn squeezes my fingers and lets go. She swallows her tears and refocuses on the water. "I've missed her every day since, and I've blamed this ship. Vance and I sent complaints to the bosses. Even to the council. Everyone told us the same thing, including my sister. It was only a terrible accident."

Throat thick and tight, I nod. Asralyn's felt guilty and probably a little crazy for the past four years. Maybe I can show her she's not alone. "I don't think it was an accident," I finally say.

Asralyn's head falls, and she clutches her chest. With a shuddering breath, she turns to look me in the eye. "It's the Morphia. Being contained—imprisoned like this. This ship feeds on us. The bosses don't care."

A rush of warmth floods my chest. Not only did she save me, but she has trusted me with this story about her daughter. Karynna Stallard. Although I think the same about the ship, there's nothing the two of us can do about it. Not tonight, anyway.

I reach my hand back out to Asralyn, palm up. "I can try to bring back her spirit. You could see her one last time. Maybe even ask her what happened."

Asralyn pulls her hands back. "No." After a tense silence, she runs her fingers over her face, stretching the skin under her eyes. "Since I met you, that's all I've thought about. But I can't do it. It would be too hard to see her again."

I've known the pain of waiting for a spirit to come and seeing nothing at all. Asralyn sits up straight and fixes me with a narrow-eyed stare. "Don't tempt me again." She sighs and motions to the door. "Now go. We can manage alone for the rest of the night."

I hurry to my feet. Despite my eagerness to leave the room, I can't help but think of Asralyn sitting alone in the dark with the last of the candles dying, gazing out at the sea. As I open the door, I turn back over my shoulder. "Asralyn." When she looks up, tears glistening on her cheeks, I give her a weak smile. "Thank you."

CHAPTER 20

It takes extra time to find my room as I'm reeling from the events of tonight. When I reach deck two, the hallway is pitch black. I stumble on something hard and slippery. The smell of putrid rot makes my mouth water, and I swallow to keep from gagging. I know without looking down what I'm walking on. As a resurrector, the feeling is too familiar. Morbid curiosity draws my eyes to the fleshy bodies covering the floor. My chest tightens at the sheer number of corpses in varying stages of decomposition. They can't be fresh kills, but they could be victims from the past. Real or not, I'm disgusted.

My heel slices through black, decaying skin and I yank it out, covered in slimy entrails. There are so many bodies, I can't see the carpeted floor. I stagger and bite my lip to keep from screaming. I slip on bloody flesh and use the wall to steady myself. The corpses' faces are frozen in screams, teeth rotting, maggots wriggling in their wounds.

Now I look down with intention. I'm careful of where I step and try to pick the more solid bodies to step upon. It's like a terrible rendition of a childhood game. Death does not scare me, but the sight of these bodies fills me with more determination than ever. Is this the *Celestial* showing me its body count? Perhaps it's showing all the Morphics and non-Morphics it has consumed, feeding on blood and magic.

Something large and hairy skitters by my feet. Now spiders the size of dinner plates emerge from the gaps between corpses. The sound of spindly legs hitting flesh grows louder as a few spiders multiplies into twenty.

Although I try to focus on a memory like Ivander told me to do, nothing comes to me. The walls, floor, and ceiling spin like a black vortex. Walking faster, heels puncturing rotting flesh, I count the numbers on the doors. The closer I get to my room, the more the hallway spins. It's like I've fallen inside a tornado. A booming knock comes from inside the walls. Someone—or something—is trying to claw its way free. The knocking gets faster. Harder. Closer.

Head aching with the reverberating echo, I finally find the brass handle to my room and throw myself through the door. When I stumble inside, I almost collide with someone.

"What's going on?" Alana should be asleep by now. It doesn't take me long to realize she's not the only one awake. Niko sits on the floor by the bathroom. Alana has her knees tucked under her chin on her bottom bunk while Isla and Zora crowd together on my top bunk. Ivander leans against the chest of drawers in front of me.

"Easy, there," Niko says, still wearing his formalwear vest and long coat from the mid-cruise ball. "There's not enough room for you to faint."

Isla reaches beside her for a tray packed with leftover flaky pastries with fruit fillings and chocolate-dipped strawberries. She brandishes the tray, offering me a dessert. "Thank goodness you're here. I was so nervous." She massages the lower side of her abdomen, tension causing her body to spasm again.

Still in shock, my eyes fly from the pastry tray to Alana, to Niko, and back to Ivander. "What are you all doing here?"

Alana guides me to sit beside her on the bottom bunk. "We figured after what happened, you wouldn't want to be alone."

I blink hard to clear my distorted, watery vision. The weight of the past two days threatens to flatten me, but each one of my friends have come to make sure I was okay. Each of them stayed, despite their own fears and the late hour. Even though it's their own lives to lose in the hallways.

"You don't think I killed that girl?"

"None of us do." Ivander answers without hesitation.

Isla leans down from the upper bunk, now covered in crumbs from a sugar-dusted pastry. "Don't be silly. Have a hearth fruit tart." She shoves a tart into my outstretched hand.

I smother my surprise at how quickly she answers, as if no part of her suspects I had anything to do with Elayne's death. I hadn't realized how much I needed that reassurance. Relief eases the tension in my shoulders.

Niko laughs, but Zora smacks her girlfriend's arm. "By the Riveners! Have some tact. She may not want to eat after what she's been through."

The truth is, I'm starving. I scarf down the flaky pastry. The red hearth fruit bursts in my mouth, its signature smoky flavor balanced by sweetness. I notice an icy taste as I lick the sugar dust off each of my fingers. Like fresh snow in the morning after one of Credence's winter storms. Isla must have enhanced the flavor with memories.

"Good, huh?" Isla asks, flipping her golden ringlets over her shoulder. "My dishes went quick tonight."

Niko leans forward on his knees, craning his neck up at Isla. "Excuse me? People were getting seconds from my trays."

Zora flexes her feet and points the ends of her toes. "What about Ivander's performance tonight?" She raises a brow at him. Ivander shrugs. "Don't act innocent," she says. "I saw what you did."

Ivander holds out his hands in surrender. The soft light of my room's lantern bathes his angular cheekbones and maroon-painted nails. I can't help returning to the memory of him dangling from the silks, illuminated with a backdrop of scorching flames. It was a risk none of us expected him to take. I certainly hadn't after his constant lectures to me about rule-following.

"Maybe I'm tired of the way things are." Ivander draws in a long breath. "When I first got here, I started to realize I had a way of charming the guests. The longer I stayed aboard, the more guests recognized me and sought me out. The more they trusted me. I thought I could use my connections to influence changes for myself and my family once I made it off the ship. But Roe's started to make me think we should fight back now."

I choke on powdered sugar stuck in my throat. Me? For the life of me, I can't figure out how I've inspired anyone to make any kind of change. Every time I stand up to the bosses, something bad happens. I'm not a great act to follow. And I know I'm not the act Ivander wants his friends to follow.

"Yeah, he means you," Isla says, reading my face. "Don't look so surprised."

Niko gives me a pointed look. "None of us think you hurt that girl, but we need to know who did."

"It might have been the ship," Alana whispers. "But what if it was one of the bosses?"

Silence falls over us at the possibility. The air gets heavier with the weight of the accusation. We're all tense, like we can imagine a boss's footsteps pounding down the hall just because we dared to say it. I wouldn't put it past any of the bosses, but figuring out which one was responsible will take time. Time we don't have. And the longer it takes, the more people will get hurt. If I can get a letter to Father telling him Charmaine killed a staff member years ago, he wouldn't allow her to work here again, but it doesn't help us now. And deep inside, I know my letter wouldn't make it off this ship.

I turn to Alana. "What was it like for you when you found out you'd have to come here?" These people have become important to me. Have helped me see the truth. The answer, the power to change this ship, is with them.

Her brows lift in surprise. I imagine she's hidden the memory far away. She smooths the front of her dress and bites her lip. "It was the only time I'd ever done anything wrong in school. My parents were shocked when they heard I'd used my Morphia on a teacher, but they understood more when they found out why. I'd written them letters about how unforgiving Vivienne's parents could be. Vivienne was crying on the way to the test and asked me if I could help her out. Maybe she only meant she wanted to copy my paper. I don't know anymore." She blinks hard a few times. "My teacher was Madam Harroway, I'll never forget. She was so strict and rarely gave second chances. I should have guessed I wouldn't get away with it."

Her eyes squeeze shut. "I brought out her feelings of happiness and even a tinge of pleasant surprise. While she was grading the test, she marked more questions right than she should have."

I pull my knees tight to my chest. Picturing sensitive Alana about to have her life upended because of an attempt to help her friend makes me want to curl inward.

Her voice shakes as she continues. "One of my classmates ratted me out. That was fine. I deserved it. But then Madam Harroway told me to go see the dean. The worst part was, I couldn't feel anything. Even when I walked into the room and he had me sit in one of those enormous armchairs. Even when he explained to me I'd been called out for reckless and dangerous behavior. Even when he said my trial would never happen and that I'd be going straight to the *Celestial*. I felt nothing. I'd used so much of my power on Madam Harroway, my own feelings were gone."

Isla scoffs, pounding the wall with her curled fist. "That's messed up. I can't imagine the damage it does to hear something like that when you're incapable of feeling anything about it."

Zora murmurs her assent. "You couldn't properly agree to the terms either. Not before your emotions returned."

Alana hangs her head, tracing the lines in her palm with her fingernail. "I went home and told my parents and it all hit me. I cried the rest of the night when I realized I'd thrown away my chance. I didn't think I'd ever get a retrial. I had other professors who vouched for me, but it wasn't enough. Vivienne felt so guilty and tried to speak up, but Madam Harroway was determined to punish me."

I take Alana's hand in mine, and she releases a slow exhale. Mother always said the Morphics aboard were hardly a step above criminals. How wrong she was. How wrong I was. The crestfallen disappointment in Father's eyes and Eliza's smirk flood my memory. A sharp pang shoots through my chest, like I've shot myself with my own arrow.

Niko scoots out from his spot by the bathroom door. "It's not just you, Lana. Try screwing up in front of your entire family. I'm talking about parents, grandparents, aunts, uncles, cousins. They were so excited because I was supposed to become this great chef in Nashorne. I already had jobs lined up afterward."

Ivander reaches out and squeezes Niko's shoulder. They stay like that, drawing support from one another until Niko clears his throat.

"My specialty is enhancing foods with experiences. I made a drink that gave the judges the feeling of jumping into a river and moving with the current. Everyone loved it. After that, I made a dish that was meant to taste like sunlight on your skin. It did, but it also gave the judges third-degree burns. Menders had to come fix their mouths. It was horrible."

"You didn't do it on purpose," Isla calls down from the top bunk. "And you haven't done anything like it since."

He lets out a dull laugh. "Yeah, I know. I have someone test all the food I make before it goes out now."

Isla laughs, throwing her head back. "I wasn't even a chef before all this. Not like Niko. I had picky little sisters who wouldn't eat much. So I'd enhance their food for them. I don't even like food half the time. It's a guessing game to figure out which foods won't hurt my stomach. Sometimes I wish I didn't have to eat at all. My entire future rides on my performance at a job I'm not even qualified for." Isla snorts. "At my trial, I enhanced a simple toasted cheese sandwich because I wasn't taking any chances. But one of those snobby judges said something rude, and my toasted cheese sealed her mouth shut for an hour. My little sisters couldn't stop laughing until they realized I'd failed."

Zora twists a bronze ring on her finger. Tiny tongues of flame twine around the band. She must have crafted it herself. "No one came to my trial. Everyone was so sure I would pass that they didn't bother. After I failed, guards took me straight to the port. I had to leave a note for my family." She swipes a finger under her moist eyes. "I created a cloak that could acclimate to temperatures. If you were hot, it would blow a cool breeze. That kind of thing. But I was so nervous I lost control. The damn thing started choking one of the judges."

Ivander slides down and sits next to Niko. He raises his hand in the air, and Zora throws a chocolate-coated strawberry to him. He catches it, scrapes the chocolate off to our horror, then pops it in his mouth. For some reason, this breaks the tension in the room, and we all laugh. "What?" he asks. "I don't like sweets."

"Monster," Isla murmurs in mock horror.

The silver shimmer dust on Ivander's collarbones, left over from his performance, makes him look like one of my spirits on a visit to this plane of existence. I can't look away. I've felt his muscles contract against my skin, felt the heat of his breath as we spun together on a strip of silk. What is he thinking when he looks at me? After seeing him through the bars of a cell, I don't know anymore. Despite what he admitted a few minutes ago, I've caused more trouble than I'm probably worth. But the glint in his eyes goes beyond curiosity or frustration. It might be respect.

"My older sister passed her trial many years ago now," Ivander says. "She's a mender. Served two years in an infirmary in Sarryndar working with the best physicians. She loved it so much. But she chose to move herself and her family home after Mother lost her Morphia because of me. My sister's kids are young, and they're having to watch my mother struggle to find another job. My little nephew is non-Morphic, but my niece was born a shifter like me. Now my niece asks if her Morphia's going to be taken away too."

Ivander shakes his head as if to rid himself of the memory. "I wonder all the time what could have happened if I hadn't gone to Alexandrite Estate with Mother that day. But I'm going to make things right. The more connections I make with the guests, the more influence and trust I'll have off this ship too. I could make things better for my niece one day."

I lean forward, elbows on my knees and chin propped on my clasped knuckles. Knowing how much Ivander dedicates himself to helping others, even at risk to himself, I imagine he always had a plan for the day after he passed his trial. "What do you plan to do?" I ask.

His long lashes flick up as his gaze meets mine. "I wanted to create a place—a school—where Morphics can train to use their abilities. A place where young Morphics can make their mistakes in a controlled environment. They can learn to keep calm in high-stress situations." He takes a breath. "And when I get out of here, I want you to help me build it."

They're all looking at me now. A hot flush rises in my cheeks. What's he talking about? The idea has never occurred to me before. Before the *Celestial*, I had thought Morphics could only learn through trial and error. If you messed up one time, that was enough to be punished. Now

I know how wrong I was. Anyone can make mistakes. But the idea seems impossible. Most schools receive hefty donations from powerful, mostly non-Morphic families. Like the families on the council. They've been teaching the same way for centuries—maybe more.

"I'm not a professor. That's my mother. She teaches at the University of Credence." I let out a half-hearted chuckle. "Trust me, you wouldn't want me teaching students."

Ivander rolls his eyes and his smirk sets me on fire. The belief he has in me warms me from the inside. His lips press into a serious line. "I want your help in a different way. We've all seen the way things are here—brutal, unfair. I—we," he says, indicating our other friends and himself, "are going to help you get your trial in two weeks."

I hold my breath. Where is this going? "Why?"

"Well, for one thing, we like you." Before I can point out he said *we*, he adds, "For another, you could help us change things. Once you pass, we hope you'll go home and use your influence to talk to Lord Damarcus. I know you wanted to start training with the Hawks, but what if you campaign for the council instead? Then you could advocate for us. Advocate for real change. I still have work to do here. I can still help others get their retrials while I try to secure the favor of guests who might support my school. But you could change things now."

He wants to help me. After all the times he warned me I needed to do this on my own and not interfere with anyone else's chances, he believes in me so much he's willing to throw all that away. With my head spinning and my fingertips tingling with nerves, I dare myself to consider the future. I've always dreamed of joining the Hawks, but am I really of the most use there? Maybe Father's dream for me to learn from him and eventually take his seat on the council makes more sense for me now.

Niko nods and gestures to the small room. "Talk to him about getting us some upgrades. Seriously. Pay us for our work here. It should be a job, not a prison."

"Don't forget the bosses," Zora adds. "They need to stop using the raw Morphia. It's damaging them, and their sick punishments are damaging us."

Alana bounces on her seat next to me. "They should raise the age for trials and offer more retrials aboard the *Celestial*." She runs a finger over her lips, deep in thought. "And maybe . . . maybe if someone fails their retrial, they could go back to Ivander's school."

It means the first arrow in our quiver won't be to take someone's Morphia. It will be to help them.

Isla clears her throat. "I don't want to be that person, but do you all really think this is going to work? I mean, I'm all for helping Roe get a retrial. But . . ." Her face flushes. "I want mine too. What if the council doesn't listen to her after everything we go through?"

It's a lot to ask anyone to forget about their own retrials for me, even if I do have the best chance of changing things because of my father's position. "Then I make them listen. My father could start withholding potions from the apothecaries. I could even dredge up spirits who might have secrets the council members don't want out."

Ivander raises an eyebrow. "Blackmail would be our last resort."

Isla worries at her bottom lip. "We're taking a big risk here."

I nod to her. I've valued her honesty from the start. I can't imagine her without it.

Niko drums his fingers on his knee. "If we don't, nothing changes. The reality is most of us won't leave with our Morphia anyway."

Another nagging doubt seeps into my mind. "What about the ship? Whether bosses abuse it or not, keeping Morphia contained aboard is making it dangerous. We still don't know how Elayne died."

The room grows quiet until Ivander clears his throat. "I don't think we should contain it at all. Raw Morphia has made this ship like a living monster that feeds on us. It's greedy. We've only made it this long because the ship's absorbing the raw Morphia donated each night, so it doesn't need to consume us all. But the more power the bosses extract from us, the more it craves. You've seen the attacks increasing. My grandfather thought we should release raw Morphia in Tamarynth. He said it's more natural that way." Although I'm shocked Ivander said it aloud, the staff member from my deathmare had wondered the same. "Not saying we'd introduce that idea right away. It's sort of a multitiered plan."

Niko nods slowly. "In Nashorne, many in our province still respect the origin of Morphia in Tamarynth. After all, it was raw Morphia that brought people of all backgrounds to this realm almost five hundred years ago. Daring families came from other lands to attempt to live in this uncharted realm for the gifts raw magic would bring. But the Morphia proved more dangerous than they anticipated and most of the native plants, animals, and objects were destroyed. The magic slowly died out over time. But there are those who believe it should still be here. In Nashorne, we honor the creatures of old with decorative statues." Niko's fingers drift to a bronze bangle engraved with a dragon Zora made for him for the ball. It's clear Ivander wasn't the only one with rebellion on his mind.

The gravity of what they're suggesting weighs on my shoulders like Leith's heavy Hawk coat that I tried on as a little girl. Despite the giddy, lightheaded wonder of realizing we might have the power to make a real difference here, I can't help the nerves twisting my gut. If I agree to talk to my father, I'll be openly defying everything my family set out to build. I'm waving a huge red flag in his face that says I think I know better than my ancestors, than the council, than him.

If only I could talk to a Damarcus. I'd take any old Damarcus spirit at this point. But that's not an option. Right now, my friends are waiting for my answer.

I take a deep breath and sit up. This doesn't seem like the kind of commitment that can be made slouching on Alana's bottom bunk. I stare straight into Ivander's eyes, holding his gaze. "When I pass my retrial, I'll do everything I can to make changes to the *Celestial*, the trials, and how Morphics are treated in Tamarynth. No more extractions." I take a breath. "If we Morphics ever *decide* to be dangerous, it'll be on our terms."

Niko whoops and Zora and Isla hang down from the top bunk to pat my shoulders. Alana squeezes my hand, and I squeeze back. Ivander raises a plain strawberry in my honor. "To Lady Damarcus."

"To Lady Damarcus," my friends echo.

I try to relax my face and look confident, but Ivander must read the uncertainty in my expression. He pushes off the wall and steps toward me. Strawberry juice stains his lips bright red. His eyes bore into mine, and I have to crane my neck to look up at him. The others are quiet as they watch the two of us, holding their breath. I can't blame them. I'm holding mine too.

"Will you come with me?" he asks.

His voice is low, and I swipe my tongue over my lips as I prepare to answer. He follows the movement, gaze dropping to my mouth. Now my breath is firmly lodged in my throat, but I realize he doesn't want an answer. He wants me to trust him. I look to Alana, waiting for her to warn me against going out again tonight.

"I'll keep the light burning until you get back," she says, a small smile on her lips. No one admonishes us or warns us to stay inside. It's as if they know how badly I need this after everything that happened tonight.

With a flicker of hope nestled in my chest, I follow him.

Without a word to me, Ivander strides down the aisle and climbs the steps to the stage. Now that I'm here, watching his muscular form in the stage lights, the hesitation creeps back in. The lights illuminate his deep emerald vest and long black pants threaded with shining green light, as if he sewed glowing strands into the fabric. Ivander pulls on the silks and turns his face toward me, full lips pursed and angular jaw set as he waits for me to decide. Decide if I'm ready to act on this changing current between us.

The first thing I do is rip off my heels and throw them behind me. Ivander laughs and points to the side of the stage. "I didn't set anything out, but there should be options for you."

With each step I take, I become more certain. Tonight is my escape. It's my reminder that I can find something beautiful hidden in this disaster of a night. The belief we have in each other, in our friends, is enough. I choose a dance costume that fades from the deep purple of amethyst to light purple droplets cascading down my shoulder blades. Its V-neck bodice is dappled with deep purple stones that might be actual amethyst—not highly expensive but heavy all the same. The waist cinches in, but it's flexible as I move. With my bare legs exposed, my skin prickles.

When I emerge from the wings, twisting part of my hair into a crown braid on my head, Ivander stops moving on his midnight-blue silks. I watch his chest rise and fall faster. Watch his lips move with words he does not speak aloud. Neither of us knows how we got here. We've each taken down pieces of the barrier between us, and tonight is our sign to let it crumble.

Ivander clears his throat. "I—I'm supposed to teach you how to impress your family." He coughs and tries again. "I want to make it certain you'll get a retrial."

I take slow steps as I approach him. "You're supposed to teach me?" I chuckle. "You mean the famous Ivander's skill with the guests can be taught?"

Ivander swallows hard. "Well, yes." He busies himself with tugging on my set of silks, tonight a rich aquamarine. "I can show you the shortcuts that ensure you'll arrive everywhere before the Stallards."

I take a fistful of the silks from him. "Is that all?"

Ivander pauses, taking in my bare shoulders and determinedly looking away from my cleavage. "You take every opportunity to make them feel special. Secure them a table right beside the pool. A dessert that's just been invented. A unique experience from your Morphia that they cannot get elsewhere. Any mistake becomes an opportunity to make up for it. Make whatever they asked for vanish from their mind in favor of what you provide next."

"Vanish from their mind?" I ask breathlessly. We're so close to each other now, and I can't decide if I want to feel his skin on mine. "How would you suggest I make that happen?"

My skin tingles all over, and my abdomen heats. Ivander leans into me with one hand on his set of silks. He's careful not to touch my skin, but with the closeness of his body to mine, I can imagine the contact. Now I'm the one blushing as he toys with me. "Hmmm," he murmurs. "Perhaps an example would help. What would you do to distract me?"

My heart gallops in my chest. He offers a sly smile but does not wait for my answer. He lifts his arms over his head and pulls himself up on the silks. He wraps his foot and takes a step after each pull. He's taught me this basic climb and I mirror him, careful to keep the fabric from bunching beneath me. My muscles tremble less than they used to, but it still takes effort. We're high in the air together and I'm breathless, but I'm not sure it's only from the physical exertion.

There's something so freeing about being up here, suspended on a strip of fabric, when it feels like the rest of the ship is crumbling beneath us. I couldn't save Elayne and I almost lost my magic, but here, I'm free.

Ivander wraps each of his legs twice and settles into a double foot lock. It takes me a few tries of holding myself up while my legs flap wildly before settling into the double foot lock myself. Ivander sinks into a perfect split in the air. I bite my lip, knowing the pain I'd be in if I tried that. "Show-off," I mutter as sweat slides down my back.

Ivander laughs. I'm struck by its ease. I don't often hear it from him. This is the first night in this room that he hasn't spent a second scolding me.

Ivander rises from the split and stands in the air, facing me. Sweat glistens on his chest. The laugh lines fade, and his expression turns serious. "I saw your face after the ball. How afraid you were when I brought Asralyn to the brig. The fear in your eyes—I never want to see it again."

My cheeks warm, and I busy myself by looking down to ensure my feet are wrapped correctly. "It's just a lot of pressure. Ever since I was a little girl, I had the special Morphia. The kind no one else had. I was teased. People were scared of me. But I think I dealt with that by reveling in it. I chose to love being the rare resurrector."

Ivander lets go of the silks with one hand and trails his fingers down my silks until his hand rests over mine. He's careful to keep a layer of silk between our skin. "It is not a crime to come to love your armor."

It's then that I decide I no longer want the thin layer of fabric between us. I crave touch in a way I never have before. My fingers slip over the edges of the fabric and caress the bare skin of his hand. It's soft and warm against my cold fingertips. An electric current of energy passes between us, and I want more. Using both my feet to balance, I let go of the silks and reach out with both arms. His brow furrows as he watches me start to lean toward him.

"You'll fall," he warns.

"Not if you catch me." My stomach swoops as I keep leaning forward and feel myself falling. It occurs to me in a harsh dose of reality that I could send us both tumbling to the stage floor, but somehow, I know we won't. His strong arms grab both of mine and wrap them around his neck. Both of our feet are still secured in our own silks, but with my arms around him, we're pressed against each other. My exposed skin tingles as our bodies meet. The sensation of electric heat shoots through my abdomen and into my extremities. I feel it everywhere.

I gasp, overwhelmed by the feeling of skin against mine and not wanting to scream. He feels nothing like the hands reaching for me in deathmares. He's so alive and unapologetically real.

"Are you all right?" he asks.

"Yes," I breathe against his neck.

He spins us gently, curving his body slightly against mine to get us moving. We're laughing as we swing back and forth. Him, a graceful bird, and me, a swaying stone just happy to be close to him.

As we touch down onto the stage floor, his head dips close to mine. "I couldn't save my mother, but I can help you and Alana. It will be the two of you this time. I can feel it."

The warmth of his breath heats my neck, but somehow, I shiver. "You should save yourself too," I whisper back.

"I am." His lips pull into a sly grin. "The guests will remember me when I leave here. Do you realize how many prominent citizens of Aryndar know my name now? I'm getting closer to the board members for Aryndar's schools with every few charters. Maybe one more year, and I can give Adrionna the chance I didn't have. She'll be taught to use her shifter magic safely."

His niece. He's fighting for himself and his family every day. "You could have done this without me," I tell him.

He tilts my chin up and his eyes hold mine. "Perhaps, but I prefer doing it with you."

I don't want this to end. I wish we could stay here in our cocoon of freedom and joy. But I made a promise in my bunk room to work harder than I ever have before to earn a chance to save more than just myself. And I intend to keep that promise.

CHAPTER 21

A new week brings the results of the mid-cruise voting. Today's results allow us to see where we stand before the official vote next week. Staff members can't seem to talk about anything else and the wealthy cruise guests wield their opinions like weapons.

Alana Reyes, emotive, sits in slot one for a retrial. Taurean Darell, crafter, rests comfortably in slot two. He runs games on the top deck in the mornings and afternoons. His wide grin and cheerful attitude never slip, even in the sweltering heat. It may be easing into fall back home, but the sun shines on the deck every day aboard. Every sailing has perfect weather for the guests to go swimming, but the staff end up hot and miserable. Taurean is so good, you'd think he enjoys it. Ivander Harpyrian, shifter, sits in slot three. The guests agree he would be higher if they knew he'd accept the trial, but they're aware of his reputation for relinquishing his slot.

Despite the mid-cruise votes, anything can change. Votes from a concierge's family are worth fifty extra, so I need to win over Asralyn. In the upper class, once a few names gain traction, all the votes go the same way.

Niko and Isla have helped me by creating unique desserts and signature dishes for the Stallards. Niko comes to the table and grills winder steaks made from the shaggy beasts in Windmere that scale mountainsides and are legendary for meat that melts in your mouth. Our table definitely gets some jealous looks for that one. He even includes a show with fire in the shape of dragons for the kids. Isla's sorbet, made from the sweet kibli fruit native to Illoryan, is the ice to Niko's fire with snowflakes of sugar falling over the top and chocolate characters ice-skating on the surface.

The biggest improvement in my day has been Ivander's decision to work by my side. When he decides to help, he jumps in headfirst.

Even if he sometimes skips rehearsals to help me make magic for guests, no one would know from watching his performances. He's been spreading rumors that the night of the mid-cruise ball was a misunderstanding and I was a key figure in making sure no one else got hurt. Ivander's dedication to gaining the guests' trust means his words spread like wildfire among them.

The two of us stand on the top deck with the Stallards in the sticky heat. I've set Vance and Asralyn a picnic lunch. Knowing of Asralyn's safety concerns now, I've given her a table with a full view of the pool.

"Look out for Ezra," I tell Sage as both kids run for the pool. The water changes color from clear blue to deep violet to shimmering silver as they swim. I look to Asralyn, and she gives me a stiff nod back. Ivander and I watch the kids dive for luminescent seahorses with tiny wings that Ivander created from his Morphia jar. We toss in toys like a miniature dolphin that lets the kids hang on to her dorsal fin for rides and a ball that sings songs as it zips in and out of the water.

We've been working so hard the past week that I haven't had time to consider what's happening between us. At some point he decided I was worth more than my name. I guess I've started to realize it too. I understand now where his protectiveness comes from. I'm used to staying guarded too. That's how people are most comfortable around me and my Morphia. But there's something different about Ivander.

I can be honest with him because I know he's honest with me.

Always.

We both push further and take more risks than anyone else. The more he takes risks for me, the more I understand what he's willing to put on the line for others. Since he set foot on this ship, he's thought more about his friends' retrials and his family's future than his own, and now I might be one of those friends—perhaps more. There's a cloying sense of guilt at the idea of allowing him to help me get mine, but I know why I'm doing it. I'm more determined to get home than ever.

After making sure the Stallards are comfortable, Ivander and I make our way to the lagoon. A stack of translucent, inflatable tubes forms a tower next to the steps leading into the lazy river. We each grab a tube and offer them to the guests lining up for their turns. Our fingertips brush every so often, and my cheeks heat.

Taurean sees us and steps aside, running a hand through the curls of his dark hair. "Shift change, huh?" He bends into a small bow. "Lady Damarcus, you're the highlight of the afternoon. The guests love you."

I roll my eyes. "The guests love *you*. They tolerate me."

Ivander and I have been hosting this activity for the past week. Guests line up to float around the ship in inflatable tubes or on the backs of small sea dragons, but there's a twist. I allow them to float with a lost friend or family member—sometimes even a historical figure they're curious about. I can't do it for all the guests, but I do enough to make an impression.

The deathmares are horrible. I wake from them screaming with Alana peering over me most nights. I tell myself the sleepless nights will be worth it when I get my retrial. The waking deathmares leave me confused and panicked. Just yesterday, I witnessed a staff member jump over the side of the ship and into the sea below, only to realize it was a deathmare. A mere memory from the past. It still left me feeling sick and unable to focus.

"Mr. Baronster," I say to a man wearing a billowy tunic shirt and flexible, crafter-made water pants. I recognize him from Credence. Like Father, I have an uncanny ability to remember the names and faces of most of the families in our province.

"I didn't realize you were on this cruise."

Mr. Baronster shuffles his bare feet. "I'm only here for a week this time." His eyes dart to the deck. He can't look me in the eye now that I'm here. My ears burn when I realize how I must look to him. A far cry from the girl dressed in a heavy gown, standing on the dais of her father's ballroom, winning respect from the crowd. I tuck a loose strand of dark auburn hair behind my ear.

Ivander clears his throat, sensing the awkwardness and, as usual, smooths it over. "Would you like to see someone, Mr. Baronster? You're the first guest today."

Mr. Baronster stands straighter. "I just lost my Great-Aunt Emalda, but I don't really want to see her." He gulps, twisting the unity ring on his finger. "Actually, I lost my hound dog last winter. Dane went everywhere with me. I'd like to see him again."

I hand Mr. Baronster the inflated tube after he shakes his head at the sea dragon and try to ignore the way he recoils when my hand brushes his. I want to scream at him that I'm the same person. But I've gotten much better at hiding what's going on inside my head over the last three weeks. The truth is, I'm not sure he would have respected me back home either. The guests at Father's balls jumped in line for my gift, but they wanted a performance. They still regarded me like a theater spectacle. They weren't really there for me.

As Ivander and I both force smiles, we help Mr. Baronster into his tube on the water. I reach out and work to keep my voice steady as he recoils once more. "It works best if you take my hand."

He inhales a deep breath and grabs my hand. Inwardly, I cringe at the sensation of his flesh against mine. I close my eyes. This is why Eliza gave up her Morphia. She didn't want anyone to be afraid of her. She wanted to trust the interactions she had with people. No one pretends to put up with her anymore just to access her powers of healing. This is why Leith joined the Hawks. To put the dangerous Morphics in prison so they didn't make people more afraid of the so-called less dangerous Morphics like me.

Well, look at me now, Leith. Maybe you'd be afraid of me too.

With my eyes closed, I enter the spiritual plane. Dane's spirit comes to me easily, annoyingly easier than a human spirit. He bounds over, black ears flopping. The ends of my fingers tingle as Dane's spirit splashes into the water beside Mr. Baronster. The intensity of the emotions stirring inside me are so strong that Dane doesn't just look solid.

He is solid.

He licks his master's face and paddles beside him. Exercising my resurrection every day has made me strong enough to hold the connection for an entire trip around the lagoon. I maintain the connection while Ivander continues to help guests into their tubes or onto the backs of scaly sea dragons. "If you're waiting for a resurrection, step to the side. Roe will help you as soon as she can."

Ivander's chatting pleasantly with a few guests when two men wearing flexible compression bodysuits approach me. The swimsuits are flecked with iridescent scales, created by a crafter to adjust to temperature underwater. They push past the guests waiting in line and stop so close to me that their breath singes my skin. I will myself not to step back as they tower over me, crossing their burly arms.

"Pretty girl, isn't she?" the man asks his friend. "Too bad she likes to play with our dead."

The other man tilts my chin up and leans down so that his nose is a hair from mine. There's a rule against touching staff members, but guests break it often. I've heard of young women staffers having to evade advances by male guests. I recoil as his fingers move from my chin to stroke my cheek. "Is that what you were doing at the party? Playing with death? Maybe you won't find it so funny a game when you get off this ship and find out the world isn't kind to you without Daddy's protection."

Although ship rules say guests can't touch staff without their consent, that never stops men like this. I swat his hand from my chin without holding back. I relish his look of shock.

Ivander places a firm hand on the man's shoulder. With surprising strength for someone more slender than the two men, he forces the man back. "You can't skip the line, sir." His voice, an octave lower than usual, holds a note of warning. "I'm going to have to ask both of you to go to the back of the line."

His dark eyes pass to me, and his gaze urges me to act like nothing unusual is happening. I beckon a young girl forward and help her climb the steps to sit atop a snakelike, green-scaled dragon with feathery, finned wings.

The burning hatred in the men's eyes makes my hands tremble as I hold the slippery dragon steady. I dare a quick glance behind me to see if they've taken Ivander's advice. The two men have turned their fiery glares on Ivander, but he doesn't move. If he's afraid, his body doesn't betray it. If anything, the tension in his neck and the set of his jaw screams fury.

"This place used to keep you Morphics in check. Not anymore." One of the men spits at Ivander's feet. Ivander only raises a brow, but I can see spikes beginning to pierce through the exposed back of his staff swim uniform. When Ivander shows no sign of backing down, the men mutter something foul but leave the deck.

After a pause, Ivander claps his hands together. "Well, that was a free show, ladies and gentlemen. I'll be here all night."

The guests waiting by the lagoon laugh. I turn back to my little guest, grateful for Ivander's uncanny ability to shift the mood of a group. I try to focus on the connection with the spirit of a young girl's mother, but my hands shake and ball into fists. I struggle to maintain the connection. Anger seizes my concentration. Is this what Father's reputation has shielded me from?

A tap on my arm makes me jump. I whirl around, afraid one of the men has come back.

But it's Gray. He's still wearing his stiff overcoat and black boots, even on the top deck. His mouth is set in a grim line, and his hands dart into his pockets. Ivander's eyes pass over the hawk pin on his lapel, but he says nothing.

Gray glances down at the pin but hurriedly redirects his gaze to me. "I need to talk to you." The words come out choppy and fast. I'm reminded of his warning at the mid-cruise ball.

I look to Ivander, hoping that this counts as protocol for not refusing a guest's request. "Are you okay?" he asks. When I nod, he says, "Go on. I'll hold the line until you get back."

I follow Gray to the bar in the center of the upper deck. He weaves through the crowd of guests in their swim clothes, but he's easy to track in his heavy coat. He leads me to the circular tables beside the bar. He chooses one surrounded by empty tables and motions for me to sit.

The moment we're seated, he leans across the table, voice hushed. "I'm going to talk fast, and I can't stay long. My parents don't know I'm here."

"Gray, what's going on?" My heart thuds in my chest.

He lets out a heavy breath. "I know you didn't hurt that girl at the ball. I know you, and you wouldn't do that. I think someone wanted you framed. I wasn't sure, but with the fires at Alexandrite Estate and rumors of your father's assignment—"

My blood runs cold. This is more than me being in the wrong place at the wrong time. "What fire? What assignment?"

"There's been growing tension between Morphics and non-Morphics back home while you've been gone. Morphics are demanding more seats on the council. They set fires as protest at Alexandrite Estate to put pressure on Spokesman Malyk and the council. That mender we tracked in the woods was a vocal opponent of the mandatory infirmary service for Morphics. When we picked him up, it caused an uproar."

Gray and Jasper used to think this all the time. They'd say tensions were rising again—that there might be another war brewing between the Morphics and non-Morphics. Eliza and I never believed it. Our family stopped the conflict centuries ago. As children, we couldn't believe families would turn on each other again.

"There's more." I watch his face tense.

"There are other rumors Spokesman Malyk may be encouraging your father to develop a potion that could eliminate Morphia before it appears in children. No more extraction, and supposedly safe to give to anyone. Something that would simply make it disappear."

My heart drops into my stomach. Father never mentioned anything about an assignment from the council. Nothing out of the ordinary. But if the last few weeks have shown me anything, it's that my father decides when he wants to share information with me. I pivot to my more immediate concern. "Why would they frame me?"

"That's the thing. I don't know. You don't go far beyond your family's estate, but I do. There's cruel talk about Morphics. Saying shifters use their disguises to steal and to trick people. Illusives play with our minds. You play with the dead." He waves his hands, seeing my face. "I don't believe those things. But go in any tavern and you'll hear that the only Morphics we really need to keep around are menders and crafters.

I suspected that many would not want you leaving this ship with your Morphia, but after the ball, there's no mistaking it. I don't know if this was personal against you or against your Morphia, but you have to know that someone doesn't just want to prevent your retrial." He pauses, letting his words sink in.

"Someone is willing to do anything to take your magic."

CHAPTER 22

Even if I'm being framed for murder, I can't miss my shift.

With the day of voting drawing nearer and Gray's warning weighing heavy on my mind, I feel more nervous than ever. Vance tells me I've gone above and beyond since the ball, but it doesn't matter what he thinks if Asralyn's not on board.

After another long day, Asralyn has ordered me to get Vance and the children set up with dinner in their room, then to join her in the Endless Night Spa once I'm finished.

I'm in need of a spa evening, sure, but this isn't what I'd had in mind.

Palms sweaty, I grasp a brass handle and push open the door to a private spa room. Instantly, the warm, comforting smell of hearth fruit turnovers and cinnamon greets me. I remove my boots and stockings. The cool black marble tiles are smooth beneath my bare feet.

I don't see Asralyn yet, but the room is nearly as dark as the rest of the spa—with shiny, floor-to-ceiling black tiles. Embedded in the ceiling are tiny dots of silver starlight, offering a whisper of light in the darkness. A thin layer of fog wafts from the pool, taking shapes like my spirits. It shifts into flowers, dissolves into running horses, then dissolves again into the hummingbirds that visit our gardens at home. A staff member emerges from a closed door and hands me a silky, midnight-blue robe and water clothes.

"She's waiting in the pool," they tell me. The pool's hidden by a wall of black stone, so I strip off my sweaty uniform when the staff member leaves and shrug into the flexible, blue-scaled material that covers my chest, torso, and pelvis. I wrap myself in the satin robe, chilled by the faint breeze in the room.

I step out from behind the wall and approach the rectangular spa pool set into the floor. Lit from the bottom by white lights, under a black ceiling with a glowing star pattern, it's like I've entered another galaxy. Water dribbles from an elegant fountain at the back of the pool. The only outside light peeks through curtains over a set of floor-to-ceiling windows overlooking the sea.

Asralyn's drawn the shades to keep the room dark. I barely glimpse the shadow of her sitting on the submerged steps by the fountain. Her light brown hair's braided in a crown to keep it dry. I'm reminded of the crown she said her daughter wore. How many hours did it take Asralyn to teach her to do her own hair?

Her pursed lips and relaxed posture make it impossible to guess her mood. Nerves prickle in my stomach. "Let your hair down, Roe," she says, voice softer than usual. "You have such beautiful hair."

As I take my hair out of its tight bun and comb my fingers through it, I remember Isla's warning from breakfast a few days ago: *Never go off alone with a guest again.* She has a point after what happened at the ball. With trepidation making my legs stiff and heavy, I descend the steps and wade into the warm pool. Isla can smack me over the head with a spatula later. Asralyn's in control of my votes.

She clears her throat. "The spa wasn't taking any more appointments for the day. Too close to sundown. But that darling friend of yours—Zora, I believe—she overheard me talking about wanting to come after her performance and convinced them to keep it open."

My lips tug at the thought of Zora bolting in full costume down the hallways to beg the spa not to close. All to give me a chance at impressing Asralyn.

"I'm glad you got some time to relax." I let my guard down a little and smile. "Seems like this isn't much of a vacation for you."

Asralyn sighs, trailing her hand along the gush of bubbles flowing from the side of the pool. "No, it's not. It's more of an exposure, really.

My sister thought it would be good for me to come back here in real life. Not just in my nightmares."

I know nightmares. Every night I've been waking from deathmares in a cold sweat, gritting my teeth, tears streaming down my face. Long, dark red streaks trail down my arms from where I've dug my nails into my skin. I'm glad Asralyn can't see the evidence in the dark now. I feel the pain of all the death I conjure like it's mine.

I think of the first time I went into Leith's room after his death. It was harder than going to the funeral. Some days I can go in and sit on his bed without crying. Others, I can't. The ups and downs of grief never stop. I used to want to punch the people telling me it'd get better with time. For me, it never did. Some days are just as raw and painful as the first.

Father used to say, *Don't be angry with the people trying to help you. They don't know what to say because there's nothing that can be said. Nothing eases our pain. Be angry with the ones who find it easier to turn away and hide.*

He was right. The awkward conversations were better than facing the friends and family who never reached out. The ones who avoided Leith's name in conversation like a disease. Like they do my Morphia.

"How old was Karynna?" I ask. Asralyn's lips part as her eyes lift from the water to find me. I wonder how long it's been since she's heard her daughter's name said aloud.

She coughs. "She was eight. I think she and Sage would have loved being here together. My sister doesn't like to talk about her. She doesn't want to make her own children sad."

I wade closer to sit beside her on the steps. "Not talking about something doesn't mean it didn't happen."

She nods, silent in her grief. "I'm sorry," she finally gasps. "I met someone from your province at dinner last night. She told me your brother died when you were young." She shakes her head. "If I had known, I wouldn't have told you about Karynna. Not that way. I would have asked if you were ready to hear something like that."

The lump rises in my throat again, and I have a harder time shoving it down. I'm not used to Asralyn's armored composure slipping. Her gentle tone threatens to break me. I reach under the water and grab her hand. "My brother's name is Leith. He—he looked after me."

She squeezes my fingers, studying the sheet of water coming out of the pool's fountain. "Karynna was Morphic. She was able to make her father and me see things that weren't there."

"An illusive," I murmur. I don't know why I never expected Asralyn and Vance to have had a Morphic child. But it can happen in any family. Why not them?

"She was a little like you, I think. She wanted to use it all the time, even when we told her no. She didn't understand why other people didn't like it sometimes, and she'd get so tired afterward. Sometimes she'd sleep for hours or have trouble standing after a big illusion." She lets go of my hand. "Vance and I didn't know how to teach her. We thought going on the *Celestial* would show her what happens to Morphics who . . ."

She doesn't finish, but it's not hard to guess what she's thinking. It's the same way I used to think. Dangerous Morphics. Morphics who wielded their abilities without regard for consequences. "I bet that didn't work," I say.

Asralyn laughs a short, bitter laugh. "Of course not. She didn't see how bad it was for the staff. She only saw this place as a fantastical playground. Until . . ."

Until that all changed. After a prolonged silence, I sniff the air. "Is that why you chose this scent?" I'd noticed it was an odd choice for the spa where guests usually go for botanicals.

"We used to make hearth fruit turnovers. Back home in Sarryndar, we had hearth trees." The smile fades from her lips. "I had them cut down after she died."

Abruptly, Asralyn climbs out of the pool. She dons her robe and opens the curtains, revealing the setting sun over the blue sea. "I notice you're no longer working alone. You've been excellent. No one can argue that." She turns, staring at me with her stormy eyes as she drips water onto the black tile. "But I'm not sure if it's you I have to thank or your friends."

Blood pounding in my ears, I swallow hard. I rise from the water.

"It's me. I wanted to be better. My friends help here and there, but we all help each other."

Asralyn shrugs. "I've seen how hard you're trying. How much you care about Sage and Ezra. Maybe even about me." She grabs a towel and pats her arms dry. "Our family will vote for you, Roe. I don't know if it will be enough to counteract the boss votes. But that's my decision."

My face flushes, but before I can thank her, she holds up her hand. "The sun will be going down soon. I can make it back to my room alone." She smiles. "You don't want to be late for the bosses tonight."

Although she doesn't want me to thank her, I climb out of the pool and walk to her. She touches my cheek with her fingers. "Be careful, Roe. Survive."

I clasp my hand over hers, pressing her fingers tighter to my cheek, like maybe her daughter would have.

We stay there, standing in silence, outlined by the light of the setting sun over the sea.

CHAPTER 23

The bosses take their time siphoning my Morphia that evening. Although I've been doing a much better job as a concierge, none of them seem to care. The days run together. The punishments don't stop, and I do my best to seem unfazed. Even if I'm screaming on the inside.

I sit in the reclining chair with my fingertips pressed into the cool metal armrests. Boss Charmaine brings me a glass of smoking liquid after I donate. She shoves it into my hand and tells me to drink the chunky brown sludge. My nose wrinkles. I grew up with an alchemer father. No way am I going to drink something that smells this rancid.

She leans down so her hollowed eyes are level with mine. Her voice lowers an octave. "Drink."

Alana, who stands a few people in line behind me, shakes her head. I can't tell if she's trying to warn me against drinking it or telling me not to cross Charmaine. Either way, it reminds me who holds the power here. It might not matter who the guests vote for if I can't scrape together a single boss vote at the end of the month.

Pinching my nostrils shut, I chug the smoking potion. It's oddly tasteless on my tongue. I wait, legs twitching with nerves. I'm reminded of what Asralyn said to me before I left the spa this afternoon. *Be careful, Roe. Survive.* If only she knew how few choices I have.

Then the room dims into a hazy blur. Not this again.

The glowing jars of Morphia fade until the vibrant colors of the storage room disappear in favor of a dining room. A black chandelier hangs from the ceiling over a dark wood table set with elegant silverware and ruby-red plates. The familiar floors and stained-glass windows fill me with a confusing mix of comfort and unease. This is our family dining room back home at the estate. As soon as I recognize it, I see Father, Mother, and Eliza sitting at the table. Mother pours Father a glass of wine, and my heart lifts to see them.

Until I hear what they're saying.

"Don't take it to heart, Cyrion," Mother says, taking Father's hand. "He can't understand the pain this has caused our family."

"It's not just what he said, Addy. It's how he said it." Father slams his fork down on the plate so hard it cracks. Eliza jumps in her seat. "He said he'll never trust our family again."

Eliza folds her arms over her chest. "That's not fair. She doesn't speak for our whole family."

"Hush," Mother snaps. "But you're right. Roe is a small part of this family. The rest of us have proven we're upstanding members of society. Your family, Cyrion, especially."

Father puts his head in his hands. "It doesn't matter. It will never matter."

Silence falls over the table until Mother clears her throat. "If she loses her Morphia, no one will talk anymore. As long as she comes back like the rest of us." A jolt runs down my spine. "I mean, non-Morphic . . . She'll be accepted again. No one will be afraid."

Father nods slowly, brows knitted together. "Yes. I believe, over time, the Damarcus name could recover."

As quickly as the image appeared, it evaporates. My home disappears, and my family dissolves into a cloud of smoke. I jolt back into the room with the bosses and the line of staff members craning their necks to see what happened.

I jump up from my chair even though my head spins and my knees threaten to buckle. "What did you do to me?" I yell. "Was that real?"

When Charmaine says nothing, I step closer. Her face doesn't change, save for the torn corner of her mouth that turns up in a sly smile. Tears threaten at the corners of my eyes, and rage pulses in my temples. I push down the urge to slap her, or worse. Like it or not, I need her.

I force myself to move. With long strides, I lunge for the door. If she's not going to tell me the truth, then I'm not going to stay. If I stay here any longer, I'll do something I regret.

The faster I walk, the more my chest hurts. I dig my fingernails into my palms so hard they leave marks. My breath heaves. It can't be real. Father would never say those things about me. Our place in society was never more important than I was.

With night descending on the *Celestial*, I try to focus on a memory to keep the hallways tame. To keep the ship from consuming me. As I run up the stairs, hardly aware of where I'm running to, I start to focus on something else—someone else.

Ivander. Knowing he's waiting for me in Dreamscape Theatre eases the ache in my chest. When did the dread turn to anticipation? My body warms, tingling with the desire to see him on the silks. The memories of us come fast and vivid, and I cling to them in these volatile hallways.

His hand on the small of my back as I try a new skill on the silks. Him flying through the air, catching himself at the last second and glancing my way just to see if I'm watching. The glint in his eye when he secured front-row seats for the Stallards after I thought I was the last person he'd help. Him believing in me enough to skip rehearsals, all to give me a chance at more votes. His bare skin touching mine when I decided to finally let him in.

When I push open the double doors to the theater, I find Ivander already in flight. His legs are wrapped inside the wide strips of scarlet silks, and he lets go with his arms, hanging upside down. Reaching out with his hands, he seizes the silks, twisting his body in the fabric. It's like watching a bird diving for a fish in the sea. He drops, allowing his body to plummet toward the ground. My heart drops with him, but I'm not surprised when he catches himself.

I can't help the pins and needles prickling in my hands and feet. The swirling of white-hot yearning in my stomach. I've never felt this before. This intense, all-consuming sensation of desire for something, someone solid. After the boss's cruel illusion, I need something real.

"Ivander." My voice breaks on his name. Our diminishing time together aboard weighs heavy on my shoulders. The stress of bending over backward for guests, minding the bosses, and the raw horror of seeing this ship hurt people, kill people . . . Our time together has built a wall around us. A wall I hope won't crumble when we leave this ship. If we make it off at all.

A small part of me doesn't want to leave in case I never see him again. Maybe that's why he sticks around too. Even though we're prisoners on the ship, the daily routine is a measure of comfort as opposed to the uncertainty of life off the ship. It's the only guaranteed way he knows he'll be able to see the friends he's made each day.

Ivander drops to the stage, arms stretched over his head as he keeps hold of the crimson silks hanging from the battens. "Three more nights," he calls to me. "Unless a drink order takes you out of the running."

I mount the stage, taking the steps two at a time, mouth open in mock offense. "Hush. It was one wrong order. I told Isla not to tell you."

He chuckles, shaking his head.

I cross to the wings of the stage, where he lays out a new costume for me each night. The costume I have tonight is a maroon-and-gold scaled bodice and tight-fitting maroon shorts. I slip on the accompanying golden feathered wings that hang from my arms and attach to the bodice. A bird of fire.

As I walk back onstage, I'm lost in his words. Only three more nights. I want more from Ivander, but I'm afraid to puncture the trust we've built together. Neither of us wants to go back to the way things were when I first boarded. But if Ivander's taught me anything, it's the necessity of trusting myself in freefall.

Leap of faith.

"You never finished telling me what happened after Malyk caught you stealing for your grandfather," I say, joining him back onstage.

There's a pause as Ivander senses my shift in mood. No more playing around. I exhale, realizing he wants to tell me but can't figure out how. He clears his throat. "No one dared argue with Malyk. My mother cried—begged him to reconsider. He didn't. It was horrible."

I grimace, imagining how desperate she must have felt. I remember how desperate I felt in the ship's prison. Not even my father would dare argue with a spokesman.

"My father tried to stop them from taking her Morphia. Malyk's guards stabbed him, but luckily, he recovered." His leaden tone is heavy with guilt. "It's not as unusual as you think. The worst part was having to tell my sister what happened. What I did."

Barefoot, I cross closer to him. Emboldened by his openness with me, I reach to touch his cheek. "I'm sorry."

His brow furrows. "I know you don't like to be touched. All of us try to be mindful of it. But the night they tried to take your Morphia, you touched me."

I take his hand and squeeze. "It's easier when I choose it."

His lips lift, and he steps closer to me. So close I can feel the heat from his body. "It's better this way. Like I've earned you," he says.

I let out a heavy breath. "Back home, nobody listened. Mother didn't understand my deathmares. She doesn't know what it's like to feel the dead's fingers clawing at my skin, trying to use me to visit the living plane. Most of the time when someone touches me, they want something from me." My shoulders stiffen when I speak of Mother. I can't think about what I saw back in the extraction room. I won't let that illusion ruin what is real right in front of me.

"Everyone has something that bothers them." He shrugs. "I'm afraid of the open ocean."

"What?" I'm unable to contain a smile despite the tension in the air. "You're kidding."

He tugs on the silk, blushing as he pretends to test its strength. "I was terrified my first night on this ship. But I didn't have a choice."

"You never seem scared."

"*You* never seem scared," he says. "I felt selfish coming here. I was scared of everything. My grandfather was the only one who thought I should go. He said it was brave."

Ivander lets go of the silk, standing with his hands by his sides, crimson pooling around him like a cloak of blood. "Sometimes I wonder if the real reason I keep pushing off my retrial is because I'm scared to go home and find things worse than when I left them. What if after every connection I've made, nothing changes?"

I reach out again, and this time, I touch his bare arm. The warmth of his skin makes my heart flutter. "It's okay to have two reasons for doing things. It doesn't mean one's worth more than the other." I rub my finger up and down his skin. There's an ink tattoo of a rose losing a flower petal on his arm. One he doesn't normally wear. "I thought I wanted to join the Hawks to protect my province. But I think it was more to prove to myself that I wasn't like the dangerous Morphics they hunt. I wanted to feel closer to Leith."

I'm surprised at the words tumbling out of me. There's a powerful release in letting go of my fears with only Ivander to hear them. "If they take my Morphia, I wouldn't be me anymore. I'd lose any chance I have at seeing my brother again."

I know it sounds silly. I've never succeeded in raising his spirit before. But losing my Morphia ensures I will never see him again.

Ivander regards me with the scrutinizing eyes I remember from when we first met. He squeezes my hand. "You may not be able to raise your brother's spirit, but trust me, Roe. Your Morphia is not the only thing that makes you who you are."

I shiver at his words.

Ivander steps closer to me. "Is it okay if I—"

I nod, pulling him closer to me. His fingers trail up my forearms with gentle pressure. The way he touches me makes my whole body burn, like I really am a bird on fire. It's a delicious, dizzying heat. Being with him feels good in a different way from summoning spirits.

As we stand close, a hair length apart, his hand curls around the silk above his head. On second glance, it's not a silk, but a coil of rope. His other arm wraps around my waist. "Do you trust me?"

"Yes," I whisper.

A sandbag falls, and we shoot into the air together.

My breath leaves me as I clamp my arms around his neck. "I've got you," he murmurs. The fluttering nerves in my stomach fly away. I laugh as we soar around the stage. It's a far cry from when I thought he would let me fall on my ass my first time in this theater.

When he eases us downward, I relax my grip. The bottoms of my feet tingle as we land. I stumble, but he grabs my arm, steadying me.

"Are you okay?" He looks down at me with his head cocked.

"I . . . I can't even describe how I'm feeling right now." I collapse on the stage, heart thumping with too many emotions to name.

Sitting, I wrap my arms around my knees. "After my brother died, I guess I sort of closed myself off." Ivander sits on the stage across from me. "I didn't want to get close to anyone. The person I loved more than anything left me. I couldn't go through that again." He says nothing, but his deep brown eyes absorb the energy from mine. Flecks of sadness, fear, and regret reflect back to me. "I didn't really think anyone could love me. I decided a long time ago to like scary things because I thought I was one of them."

His lips purse. "Just because you think something about yourself doesn't make it true. For what it's worth, I'm not afraid of you." He smirks. "For you? All the time."

I open my mouth to say something back. Something that will make him understand the acceptance and sincerity he's given to me. But instead, I blurt out the words that have been clamoring to escape since Gray spoke to me. The ones I haven't wanted to tell Ivander or anyone because it might make them true.

"I think someone's framing me for murder." If he's afraid of me getting hurt, he should know. He should hear it from me. "My friend, Gray, the Hawk, thinks someone tried to pin that girl's death on me at the ball."

Ivander's lips part in silent shock. "Why would someone do that?"

I shake my head. "I don't know." The words stick in my throat, but I push them out. "It sounds like someone doesn't want me to keep my Morphia."

"It sounds like murder," he says bitterly. "Do you think it could be one of the bosses?"

"Keep your voice low. Anyone could be listening," I whisper. "I wouldn't put it past Charmaine. But it seems like a lot of work just because she doesn't like me."

"Who else?" he asks. "It's strange you couldn't summon that girl after she died. How often does that happen?"

"Not often." He's right. Occasionally, some spirits don't feel like coming back to the physical plane of existence. Most don't mind, as long as I keep them here for a short time. "Maybe I was nervous. My emotions affect my abilities."

But I have no idea who would frame me.

Ivander clears his throat. "Is there any chance your Hawk friend might have an ulterior motive telling you this?" My cheeks flush, and Ivander raises his hands in defense. "I had to ask. We don't know who we can trust right now."

The memory of Gray kneeling in front of me, eyes red-rimmed and lip trembling, floods back to me. On the day of Leith's funeral, Gray had taken me aside. Right after Eliza. His eyes, caught between the deep sage of moss and the bright green of the fields we used to lie in on hot summer days, had locked with mine. "I will protect you, Roe. Just as I'll protect your sister. He'd want—" His voice broke on the words. "He'd want me to look after you."

Gray never wavered in his promise. When we came home from boarding school over the summers, he scolded neighbor boys who'd left dead rats outside my door at school. I hadn't needed much defending. I'd brought back the rat spirits to nip at the boys' heels. But what I appreciated most was the time Gray took to talk to me. He rarely let me feel lonely for long, even if he'd grown distant and stiff with his own grief over the years.

Ivander doesn't know him like I do. "I trust him. He came here to protect me. He's not trying to hurt me."

I raise my hands over my lap with my palms facing the ceiling. If I try again, Elayne might be more willing to talk. I have to remember that she was murdered moments before I tried last. She might not have wanted to be questioned while crossing over to the spiritual plane.

Ivander nods, but he eyes my hovering palms. "What are you doing?"

"Summoning." Squeezing my eyes shut, I let out a long, slow breath through O-shaped lips. I try to calm myself, breathing deep into my belly. One breath in and a long breath out. If Elayne's going to come to me, I need to relax.

I find myself walking through a grayish-blue, foggy expanse of space. Glowing silver spirits pass by me, flooding the spirit plane. Some look dazed, coming to the in-between from the world beyond. I wish I could ask them what adventures they've been on, but I suppose I'll have to wait to die to find out.

"Elayne," I whisper, my voice echoing. I picture the girl I remember and reach out to her. Straining and searching for the vibrating pulse of energy that connects me to her spirit.

As I walk, feet gliding with each step, I slam into what feels like a solid wall.

It knocks the wind out of me. I cough and splutter. The realm grows dark around me, and then suddenly I'm back, sitting on the stage with Ivander. The room spins before I'm able to focus on his face.

"What happened?" he asks, leaning forward to steady me with his hand. The pressure of his fingers against my shoulder grounds me.

"I don't know. Some kind of block."

"Like what happens with your brother's spirit?"

"No. With Leith, I feel nothing. It's like I'm blocked from the moment I start. This . . . this is different."

Gritting my teeth and setting my jaw, I raise my palms again. This time, resolve hardens like a stone in my gut. I lock my arms in place. If I can't summon Elayne, I'll try someone else. My great-great-grandmother. The only woman in Damarcus family history to be an alchemer.

If I'm trying something that usually fails, I may as well try her. Something innate, a feeling I don't know how to explain, calls to her. It's as if some unconscious part of me knows she'll tell me the truth. Truths maybe even Father kept from me about our family.

"What is the true Damarcus family legacy?" I whisper.

My fingers tremble with the strain, and I slam into the wall again. This time, my vision goes dark fast, and I can't breathe. When my eyes fly open and I'm back on the stage, I choke. Ivander lunges toward me, clapping me on the back. I remember to breathe again.

Ivander's widened eyes shut as he sinks back into a sitting position. "Don't scare me like that," he says.

"Wasn't my fault," I gasp. We sit in silence until I get my breath back. The ends of my fingers tingle from the effort of trying to summon. I brush them against my thighs, trying to rid myself of the tangible feeling of failure.

Ivander taps a finger against his cheek. With each thoughtful tap of his finger, the nail color changes. Blue, green, purple, red, pink. With each color change, the skin of his lips opens up. Blood dots his mouth, and I put a hand on his arm to stop him.

Without acknowledging me, he lets his hand fall away from his face. "This can't be a coincidence. Someone's trying to keep you in the dark."

Panic rises in the back of my throat at the thought that someone could affect my own Morphia like that. But Ivander seizes my hands and squeezes my tingling fingers, sending a rush of warmth up my arms. He waits, making sure the contact is all right with me. I smile and squeeze back. "What if it's not just my family members and Elayne? What if I'm not able to summon anyone anymore?"

"Then try," he says, voice low. "We need to practice for your retrial, anyway. You need to stay calm while summoning."

He's right. But my frustration is making it harder. I need a strong emotional connection. Something real. I close my eyes once more and reach for the spirit world. I become weightless and let go of the tether that keeps us in one world, bridging the gap between life and the spirits. "Who do you want to see?"

Ivander coughs in surprise. "Me? I— What are you doing?"

Without being fully aware of it, I reach out my hand. "It's easier when I can connect the spirit to someone here."

After a heavy silence, he takes my hand and the connection builds instantly. I wonder what the connection might feel like if our lips touched. The silver tendrils of light spring from my fingers before he finishes saying the name. "My grandfather."

A man with warm brown skin and a graying beard holds his hand out to Ivander. I've seen spirits come back looking the way they did on the day of death and others come back looking the way their family best remembers them. Some come through wispy and weak, but Ivander's grandfather appears strong and commanding, even in the tunic shirt and trousers he must have died in.

Tears form in the corners of Ivander's eyes. "Could have dressed up a little, Grandpa."

His grandfather throws his head back and laughs. "Why should I try?" he asks in a throaty rasp. "We both know you're going to look much better than me." He nods to Ivander's sapphire-blue vest and shimmering pants. "Tell me I'm wrong."

Ivander reaches out for his grandfather, and I close my eyes again. Strengthening the connection, I tug at the silver light connecting him to this world. *Give me a little more.* I feel a surge of energy and open my eyes to see Ivander throwing his arms around his now-solid grandfather. The two cling to each other. Ivander's grandfather folds him into his chest, whispering into the thick curls of his hair.

"I'm so sorry I wasn't there," Ivander says. "I should have given up my Morphia for more time with you."

The man releases his grip on his grandson and holds him at arm's length. "Don't you dare. This is where you needed to be." He turns to me. "Take notes, girl. My Ivander's going to change the world. He wants to open the first school to train Morphics. I know he'll do it too."

Ivander looks bashful, which is a first experience for me. The strength of this connection makes my arms quiver. I'm going to have the worst deathmares of my life if I don't cut off soon. "I can't hold much longer," I say.

He wraps his arms around his grandfather one last time. "I wasn't ready to lose you." His voice trembles. "I sometimes think I shouldn't have come here at all."

"You don't know what happened after you left, child, but I do. Your mother and father were so proud you took one last chance to save your Morphia." His grandfather pats his back, already fading into a wispy mirage as the connection dies. "Your mother regretted every day not telling you how proud she was, even though she was terrified for you. Adrionna was proud of her shifter uncle. She believed you'd come home as Professor Ivander. Don't give up on yourself because none of us ever have . . ."

When he disappears, Ivander sinks to his knees. With the connection severed, the warmth is gone. Cold steals over my lips, and I shiver.

Ivander hangs his head. The stage is wet from his falling tears. "Thank you," he whispers.

Although he's the one crying, I can't help the wetness on my cheeks. The connection I felt to his grandfather was stronger than any spirit I've ever raised.

The more someone believes in me, the stronger I become.

Ivander traces over the rose tattoo on his arm with his finger. "My grandfather knew I loved being in front of people. Performing for them. He told me I'd make a good teacher. He taught in one of the boarding schools in Aryndar, and he said teaching children was the same as performing." He imitates his grandpa's rasp. "You have to get up there and make them excited about learning."

"He sounds like a good man," I say. I know how important it is to have family members who believe in you. I also know how hard it is to lose them. "And he's right. You'll make a wonderful teacher."

But I can't help the rising tide of frustration. A block is preventing me from seeing Elayne or my family members, but no one else?

Ivander reads me easier than I would like. "This is good news. You can still summon. We'll figure the rest out." He takes my hand. "Your gift is beautiful, Roe. I've spent my time on this ship trying to get my friends retrials. I'll be damned if I can't make that happen for you."

I lean forward and press my forehead to his, even though I'd like to do more. But he's just seen his dead grandfather. I'll settle for the feeling of his skin warming mine. "When I go home, I'll fight for you too. All of you."

"I know you will." His lips are mere inches from mine. He inhales a sharp breath, and I hold mine, waiting. But he must also decide it's not the right time because he pulls away and sits back. "What am I going to do without an unforgiving rehearsal schedule and four performances a day?"

I pretend to think about it. "Visiting Credence would be a start. Damarcus Estate has a lovely theater you might enjoy."

"Is that an invitation?"

I intertwine my fingers with his. "Yes." Because I have to believe we'll get off this ship. Alive, and with our Morphia. No matter the horrors we have to face to make that happen.

But for tonight, we're safe. We're a pair of stubborn witches, proud of our magic, ignoring the chaos waiting for us beyond the safety of the theater's walls.

CHAPTER 24

The morning the guests finish voting is the same day the month-long cruise ends and the guests disembark. I avoid the atrium, not wanting to watch as the votes are cast.

Alana has explained to me how it works. Adults write the three names they're voting for on parchment and drop them into a basket. Bosses are the only people allowed to count the votes. They set up clear cylindrical jars to represent each of the leading staff members with the most votes. The jars are made by crafters to calculate the number magically, a way to keep the bosses honest.

They use stones to represent the votes. She reminds me fifty additional votes are added for concierges if their assigned family votes for them and ten additional if a boss votes for them. Guests pass through the atrium throughout the morning to see which staff members are pulling ahead.

Despite many of the guests lamenting that it's their last day on the *Celestial*, they're buzzing about how lucky and exciting it is to be here to witness one of the quarterly retrials. Not that any of them stay for the retrials. Once the families know who wins, they depart the ship like nothing's happened. Our Morphia, which fueled their entire cruise experience, can't follow them home, so why would they care to see who gets to keep their magic? Their lives don't change at all.

Alana and I agreed that watching the vote is torture. That's why I've taken Sage and Ezra to the game room for illumination tag. Inside, a maze of stairs, tunnels, upper levels, and lower levels are pitch black except for the neon paint on the walls and floor. Overhead, blue stars illuminate the ceiling, and a brilliant white moon sets an ethereal glow. At random intervals throughout the game, anyone inside floats into the air.

The kids wear luminous vests and squeal with delight as they shoot concentrated starlight at each other. The beams sparkle like clusters of melted diamonds from the barrels of toy pistols.

"Got you!" Ezra exclaims, pumping his fist as he shoots a beam of starlight at my vest. There's a vibrating noise as my vest registers the impact.

"Not so fast!" Alana comes up behind Ezra and sends a beam into his vest at close range.

"No fair," he yells and throws himself through a tunnel to get away. The four children from Alana's family run on the upper level, screaming as they shoot us from overhead.

"Got you, Lana!"

Alana clutches her chest and falls dramatically to her knees. As she falls, the room becomes weightless again, and the kids giggle as we all lift into the air. I paddle with my arms and grab Alana's hand to keep her from floating away from me. The end of her braid trails like a tail behind her. We watch her kids take turns spinning each other in the air. "This is the best behaved your kids have been the whole trip," I say.

Alana glances both ways, but this might be the only room bosses don't lurk in. They don't like losing their footing every few minutes. "They're better when they get to run around—or float around. Their parents make them sit in three-hour meals twice a day. I wouldn't be well behaved either."

A couple of kids zoom past us as they activate thrusters on their vests. "Are you nervous about retrials today?" Alana asks.

"Not yet," I whisper back. In truth, I haven't had time to be nervous. I've been too busy attempting to be the perfect concierge to worry about getting enough votes for a trial. Although my sleep is plagued with deathmares from using my Morphia, the shitty dreams will be worth it. I'm used to them, anyway. It's harder knowing everyone's counting on me. If I don't get home and make changes fast, most of the staff members I've met here will lose their Morphia as their time on the ship runs out.

As the gravity returns, we float along with the children to the floor. I'm grateful for the solid ground beneath my feet. Once we touch down, Alana points toward the entrance of the game room. With a jolt, I see Asralyn hovering in the entryway, wringing her hands.

Vance and Asralyn have never come in the game room before. My heart drops. "I'll be right back," I mutter, making my way toward the entrance. After removing my goggles and holstering my starlight pistol, I stop in front of Asralyn. Her seafoam-green gown darkens to a forest green as she shifts from foot to foot. She twists an opal ring on her finger.

"What are you doing here?" I ask, lowering my voice.

Asralyn worries at her bottom lip. She continues to fidget with the opal ring, twisting it around and around again. "I— I swore I'd never step foot in this room, but I kept picturing it. Some gory scene with Karynna on the floor . . ."

I touch her shoulder. "You don't have to go any further if you don't want to."

She lifts her chin in the way that used to make my blood boil. Now I see the quiet strength in her jaw and hardened eyes. She folds her arms over her beaded bodice and nods, allowing me to guide her farther into the game room. "The emotive healer I talk to back home said this would be a good exercise for me. She thought if I could go inside and keep my anxiety down, it could be healing. It might stop my imagination from running wild." We walk arm in arm through the maze of silver starlight and glowing, colorful walls. Kids laugh and shriek as they pass. "But it doesn't seem right that they still let kids play in here."

"Alana told me nothing bad has happened here since. The bosses checked it again and again." I shake my head. "No one really knows what happened."

Just as no one knows what happened to Elayne. Although I can't explain now, I wish I could tell Asralyn she's right. As far as I'm concerned, no one should come back on this ship until we can make it safe. She's right to be afraid of this place. But that's not what she needs right now. She's trying to heal from the nightmare she keeps replaying in her head—not reality. And I know all about nightmares. Instead, I try to think of the good Karynna experienced in this room. Her joy at shooting starlight and darting through tunnels before joining her friends in the air.

Asralyn tilts her head back to look up at the star-studded ceiling. "I never realized how beautiful it was in here." Her eyes slide over the glowing blue paint on the walls and the silver stars above. "I never pictured it like this."

Then a child shoots a star beam into her dress. With no vest, there's no vibration or twinkling sound, but the child shouts, "Gotcha!"

Asralyn clutches her chest and gasps. A tear streams down her face, but then she's laughing.

It doesn't take long to corral her niece and nephew. Other parents duck their heads in and yell for their kids. Staff members take children by the hand and help them hang up their vests and goggles. My hands shake as I hang up Ezra's and Sage's vests. The nerves are starting to creep back in as I realize we're all about to head to the atrium.

I lead the family, almost mechanically, from the game room. We descend the stairs without speaking and make our way to deck five. Sage and Ezra skip ahead of me, shouting about how I'm going to get my retrial the second their feet hit the atrium floor. Vibrations in the illusion of puddled water reverberate from their small feet. A blue illusion of a penguin waddles across the floor, entertaining families who are already waiting. It almost helps distract me, too, as I've never seen a penguin in real life; they're all on an island north of Tamarynth.

The atrium is just as packed as it was on my first day. Staff who know their names aren't getting chosen unload luggage from the ship. Most of them will be loading new luggage in the afternoon as new guests arrive. No rest. No chance at a break. It feels like I'm in one of my deathmares. I don't want to turn around and do this all over again. I can't.

We find Vance in the crowd after pushing our way through groups of people. I was too overwhelmed on my first day to take it all in, but the sheer number of staff hits me now—concierges, chefs, performers, deckhands, housekeeping, hosts, waiters, and many more.

Alana guides her children behind me as she searches for their parents.

She carries a four-year-old boy on her hip without breaking a sweat. It makes me wonder if her sister is younger than her. I've never asked, and yet our time together on the *Celestial* is almost up, if our plan works. This can't be the last time I see her.

We find a spot near the vote counters, but I'm not tall enough to see over the shoulders of the guests standing in front of us, who are a few very tall men. "Good thing most of them won't leave this ship with magic," one man says.

"True, but you can't argue with how great this place is. I'm thinking of taking the kids again next month. It's a good lesson for them in what can happen if we let these Morphics go unchecked," the other guest says, jerking a finger toward a staff member.

My nostrils flare as it takes everything in me not to march over to the two men and show them what an *unchecked* Morphic looks like. These guests may decide our fates, but they do not know us.

Vance bends down to me. "Looks like they're counting the last ballots."

My mouth dry, I try to thank him, but nothing comes out. "It's tight right now," Asralyn says, gripping Vance's arm. "But they haven't put in the concierge family votes yet. At least, I think they haven't."

I crane my neck and stand on my tiptoes to look for anyone else I recognize. Ivander and Zora are nowhere to be found. I'm guessing they must be in the middle of their final show for the guests who don't care about the retrial votes. I glimpse Niko and Isla hovering by the marble staircases, whispering to each other. Neither of them are in the running.

I force myself to croak out words. "Whose names are on the jars?"

This is it.

Vance is the only one tall enough in our party to see everything that's happening. "Alana. Taurean. Those are all expected." He cocks his head to the side. "Looks like Ivander's name has been scratched. I guess he already told the bosses he wants to pull out. If I were him, I wouldn't gamble with something like this."

I smile, knowing Ivander's not going to let anyone drag him to that retrial over his friends. My smile falters when Vance speaks again. "Wait, there's another name there. Ambriel. Mender. Oh, I think she's the one who works in the med-bay. I've heard she's great with kids."

Blood pounds in my ears. We weren't counting on anyone else. No one who would be strong competition, anyway. It's odd, hoping against hope that someone else's dream will crash and burn to make mine come true—

"Your name, of course," Vance adds.

My stomach flips, but for once, in a good way, like I'm back on the silks with Ivander. We did it. The first step of many, but we did it.

Asralyn snatches my hand, excited like me but not quite for the same reason. We both hold our breath as Boss Stellan adds a few stones to each jar. It's getting close now. The murmuring in the crowd dulls to a charged silence. Each boss gets an extra ten votes to give to a staff member, and I'm surprised to see that at least one of them must have voted for me.

Boss Balanyr counts out a large pile of stones. A rush of nerves flutter in my stomach. Those must be the family votes for Alana or me.

Boss Stellan taps the glass of Taurean's jar, and his voice booms throughout the atrium. "Taurean, crafter. You have received your retrial."

The crowd cheers. Taurean jumps up and down, knees pulled high to his chest. I can't help but smile. He pushes his way through the crowd and shakes Boss Stellan's hand. Taurean waves to the crowd. That's the first slot gone. There are two more.

"You may proceed to deck three for your trial. The judges will be waiting for you."

Taurean wipes sweaty palms on his uniform trousers, proceeding to the staircase.

Boss Balanyr adds the large pile of stones to one of the jars, and Vance seizes my arm.

"That's your jar!" he bellows.

I freeze. Boss Balanyr compares the level of stones in the jars. Charmaine walks over from where she's been leaning against the wall, studying the proceedings. She whispers fiercely in Balanyr's ear, but he shrugs.

"Rosaline, resurrector. You have received your retrial."

A wave of applause rushes over me. Asralyn wraps me in a tight hug. Tears stream down her cheeks as the kids cheer. Before I know it, I'm being hoisted off my feet. Niko lifts me into the air while Zora and Ivander fight through the crowd to reach me. They're still dressed in elaborate costumes, but they clap as they get close. Isla smacks Niko's arm. "Don't grab people," she says.

Niko's shoulders dip as he deflates, setting me down. "But it's a special moment."

"I don't care—"

I wave my arms at Isla, laughing now. "It's okay. I can't believe it!"

Our unbridled excitement infects other staff members. They're probably just marveling at how a girl so hated by the bosses with undoubtedly the creepiest gift on the ship could have made it this far. And the truth is, I couldn't have. Not without Ivander, Zora, Isla, Niko, Alana . . . I've got the second retrial slot. There's one more open.

I turn in time to hear Boss Charmaine call over the roaring crowd. "Ambriel, mender. You have received your retrial."

Ambriel rushes forward to shake Charmaine's hand, tears wetting her cheeks. That's the last slot. Taken. My friends and I fall silent as we look around for Alana. "What?" Isla shouts. She puts a hand to her mouth as Zora grabs her arm.

Niko shakes his head, looking to Ivander for an explanation. "What happened? She was in the lead. Everyone knew it."

Ivander's mouth hangs open. I can't make eye contact with him. Of course Ambriel deserves it, too, but Alana was a sure thing. Everyone's been talking about her for weeks.

The rest of the time goes by in slow motion. I tear myself away from my friends and make myself move toward the Stallard family. I don't expect the lump that rises in my throat as I stand before them. At the beginning of the cruise, that feeling was for an entirely different reason.

Sage and Ezra grab on to my legs. "Will we see you next time?"

"Of course," I choke out, although one look from Asralyn tells me the truth. There won't be a next time. She's certain of the danger aboard now.

Vance extends his hand to me. "Thank you for helping our family." He swallows hard, pushing the frames of his rectangular glasses up his nose. "Your father should be proud of you."

Unable to speak, I shake his hand. It's funny that I can't think of one moment I'm particularly proud of as a concierge. It's a collection of little moments that has made me feel responsible for this family. Knowing what happened to their daughter makes me wonder if the entire Damarcus family is to blame. We didn't take the time to learn what life was really like on the *Celestial*. We didn't stop to ask if it was fair, if it was dangerous.

Asralyn presses a slip of paper into my hand. "I've written where you can find us in Sarryndar," she says. "You must write and tell us what happens with your trial. Good or bad."

I let out a heavy exhale. The atrium's starting to empty as families depart the ship. Those staying for additional weeks leave for another deck, on to the next activity.

My body trembles, but I take Asralyn's hand and kiss her opal ring. I can't forgive everything she put me through, but I understand her better now. "You were not an easy first guest." I straighten and smile. "But it was worth it. I'm glad to have met your family."

I curtsy to the four of them and cross to the spiral staircase. Although Ezra and Sage call out to me, I don't look back. I blink back the tears threatening to fall. Curling my hands into fists, I force them to stop shaking.

With surprise, I realize that some of the staff are crying and hugging each other. Many of them have reached the end of their four-year work sentence. When they depart the ship, they'll be directed by armed soldiers to a Morphia extraction zone in Windmere.

The thought makes the joy and adrenaline from getting my retrial vanish. If I fail my retrial, I don't get four years to prove myself. One retrial. Maybe I should have waited a year, delayed my trial like Ivander.

But I can't allow myself to think about failing—not this time. There are no heavy, expensive gowns or important family members to hide behind. My friends helped get me this far. But now, I must walk into my retrial alone.

I must leave with my Morphia if I want to have any chance of saving their magic too.

CHAPTER 25

I thought I'd be alone with the judges and two other contestants, but when I get to deck three and reach the end of the hallway, a crowd is waiting outside a large wooden door.

Taurean and Ambriel eat oozing slices of spiced honey torte on silver plates with forks from the Harlequin. Their friends surround them.

Mine wait for me too. Even Ivander is here.

Without thinking, I run to them. I stop short as I get to Ivander, not sure if I'm planning to hug him or kiss him.

He lifts me gently by my waist, spinning us with his graceful dancer's body. Giddy excitement swirls in my gut and I laugh.

As he sets me down, I realize he's wearing a deep brown overcoat and a black vest with gold buttons. His flowing trousers are decorated with swirling silver embroidery I'm guessing he added himself.

"Someone dressed up." I enjoy his sheepish look. I long to know what he'd do if I kissed him, here and now, in front of all our friends. He'd probably die. I don't want to ruin this victory with a kiss that would inevitably come with questions. Like, what if I don't succeed? Would he kiss me off the ship, or would our connection end here? Still, that glint in his eye makes me wonder if he wants me too.

"Our next performance isn't until later tonight. And I figured this was a special occasion." His lips pull into a sly smile. "I owe the rich girl

I met at port an apology. She may have been trying to steal my friends' retrials, but I helped her do it."

In spite of myself, I grin. "That girl needed to be brought down a few pegs. She needs no apology. She's grateful."

Then my face falls. The next performance. Even if I pass my retrial, nothing will change immediately. I won't see Ivander again. The disappointment I feel reflects in his gaze. He'll spend every night alone in the theater again. A pang of jealousy shoots through me at the thought of him taking on another reluctant trainee in my place.

Niko puts his arm around my shoulders and holds up a piece of flaky biscuit crust smothered in a fluffy spiced honey mousse and a lopsided mountain of cream. "Doesn't look pretty but tastes amazing." He closes his eyes, taking a bite of the decadent dessert. "When it's not for the guests, we don't have to worry about presentation."

"What happened to Alana?" I ask before all the other voices threaten to drown me out.

Niko's arm falls from my shoulders, and his mouth tightens around the edges. At the sound of her name, Alana turns to face me. She's been standing with Isla and Zora, congratulating Taurean and Ambriel. Her eyes are puffy and bloodshot.

Isla mutters something that sounds like "bullshit," but Alana stops her. She squeezes both my hands in hers. "The votes were close." She shrugs. "I made a couple mistakes at dinner one night that must have affected my family more than they said. They mentioned it to a couple other guests who changed their votes."

Rage and sadness melds into one inside me. It's not fair. When I open my mouth to say I'm sorry, Alana cuts me off. "That's not all. My family still swore they'd vote for me. Last night, they told me after I put the kids to bed. Just last night." She exhales a shaky breath. "But I asked Lady Rosemary after they read the votes, and she said they forgot. They *forgot* to vote."

Isla curses them under her breath as anger hardens in my gut. Alana forces a tight smile. "I'm lucky because I'll get another chance. I just really thought it was my turn."

A wild impulse urges me to give up my trial. Give it to Alana.

"They won't allow you to give it to me," she says, knowing exactly what I'm thinking after our weeks of being bunkmates. Weeks of being friends. "Besides, I want you to change things for all of us. Not for me. You can't do anything if you're stuck on this ship."

"That's why you have to pass," Isla insists, setting her drink on a nearby bench. "This place is a nightmare for someone like me, but so many of us didn't get a choice. The pain I get is excruciating, and I never know when it's going to happen. The bosses don't care, but they don't care about anyone."

Zora places an empathetic hand on Isla's shoulder. "We're counting on you so other Morphics don't have to go through this."

The large door finally swings open. The gathered staff go silent.

Ivander's fingertips touch the ends of mine, and a nervous thrill shoots through my gut. "They're allowing us to go in with you. Do you want us to?"

All I manage is a quick nod. I expect the nerves to get worse until they set my body on fire, but they dissipate as I walk forward into the retrial room. Alana's brought a black cloak with silver fastenings to throw over my shoulders. I guess she thought I might feel more comfortable standing in a cloak than in my uniform, and I admit, it's nice to have the weight. I follow Taurean and Ambriel to the center of the room and pull my hair out of its bun. Messy auburn waves fall over my shoulders. It all felt so different last time. This time, I'm numb.

The room is much smaller than the one I used for my first trial. Porthole windows on the starboard side offer a peek at the blue water outside. On the port side, we see land. Our friends cluster on the starboard side, beneath the portholes. There are no seats and no decorations. In the back corner of the room, there's a reclining metal chair and a potion.

I feel nothing when I see it. I can't allow myself to consider the possibility of extraction.

Taurean shifts from foot to foot beside me. He's changed into a ruddy brown overcoat and a worn matching vest. A wolf pin is tacked to the outside of his coat. He must have been a member of Tamarynth's army before coming here. It's hard to imagine outgoing Taurean as a soldier. Ambriel picks at her nails as she waits for the judges to speak.

"Rosaline Damarcus." One of the judges with curly black hair and bright red lips wrenches my attention forward.

I force myself to face the judges' table. It's just a wooden table bolted into the floor. I don't recognize any of the judges. Falling back on years of training, I dip into a low curtsy.

"Lady Rosaline Damarcus, you will be going first."

My chest clenches as Taurean and Ambriel scoot to the side to stand with the other viewers. They let out tiny exhales of relief. I straighten, rolling my shoulders. The judges will see no fear from me.

"This is your one and only retrial. You won this opportunity due to your performance, as recognized by our guests and your superiors. Please understand that if you pass your retrial, you will be permitted to keep your Morphic gift of resurrection indefinitely, provided you avoid criminal activity." The judge pauses, losing her place in her journal and finding it again. "If you fail your retrial today, you will be permitted no more chances to keep your Morphia. The extraction will take place immediately. Are you ready?"

Time stands still. The nerves I felt at my last trial have transformed into unshakable determination. Having my friends with me makes me forget I'm in a retrial, and it's like we're back in mess at lunch. When I glance to Ivander, his expression is calm. There's no doubt in his eyes. I might know less about the Damarcus name than I thought I did, but I know more about myself. "Yes, I'm ready."

A murmur of cautious excitement runs through the room. The four judges set their writing quills on the table and lean back in their chairs. For a moment, I wonder if they're waiting for me to start. Not knowing what they expect me to do, I close my eyes and reach for my connection to the spirit world.

Palms tingling, I take long, slow breaths. I can't let the raw thrill of summoning overtake me. I've practiced with Ivander. I wait for one of the judges to call out a name. A friend. A family member. Maybe one of our council members from a few centuries ago. I wait for their instruction, building the silver tether between myself and the spirits.

But nothing happens. All I hear is the shuffling of boots scuffing against the floor. A chill crawls up the back of my neck. It's been too long. Too still and quiet. My eyes fly open, and my breath lodges in my throat.

The judges are out of their seats. It takes me a minute to find them. I look to my right and see the four judges, along with a few of the bosses I recognize: Charmaine, Loren, and Balanyr, standing with the viewers. There are other bosses I had limited interaction with as well.

But what really catches my attention are the long-handled knives.

The four judges and army of bosses hold blades against Taurean's throat, and Ambriel's. And each of my friends'.

With my breath rattling in my chest, I force myself to stay put. Alana cries out as Charmaine yanks her head back farther and presses her knife harder against the sensitive skin of her neck. Taurean elbows his captor in the nose, but his captor slices his cheek. Blood spatters the floor.

This isn't real.

I force myself to stay calm. This is how I lost control last time. I allowed an illusive to trick me. But what do they want me to do? Trials are high-stress situations where the Morphic uses their magic to help or protect. I flex my fingers, trying to determine how I could disarm the bosses without hurting them. Perhaps they're challenging me to protect my people without drawing blood.

"This is real!" Alana yells, but Charmaine clamps a hand over her mouth. I can't let the illusion win this time, even if the dread in my chest is crushing.

I didn't even get this far last time. Maybe my friends being in on it is part of the temptation to break. One of the judges, a muscular man with a thick, vein-popping neck, drags Ivander away from the group. His grip is tight on Ivander's shoulders, and I grimace at the fear in Ivander's eyes. Ivander struggles, twisting and turning his body to break free.

The judge pulls Ivander to the back corner of the room. To the extraction chair.

Ivander shouts, spitting and clawing at his captor. I hear the sickening crack of bones as Ivander pays the price to shift his nails into claws. He tears into the judge's arm, ripping his flesh open with his right hand. The wet tear of splitting flesh and the gush of copper-scented blood make my stomach clench. The judge screams, slamming his body into

Ivander. Ivander stumbles backward, bracing himself against the metal chair.

"Roe!" he screams. He reaches inside the pocket of his coat but comes out with nothing as the judge straps his arms down. "Run!"

Despite the panic clawing at my throat, I don't move. This isn't real.

Ivander strains against the confinement, but he can't break free. The judge reaches for the cloudy gray, odorless potion.

It can't be real.

But what if it is?

Once the judge secures Ivander in place, he grasps the potion and squeezes Ivander's cheeks to force his mouth open. Alana screams as Niko yells, "Roe, help him!"

That's when I decide it doesn't matter what's real.

The slim chance any of this could be reality makes me raise my arms. It's a freeing, adrenaline-filled realization that I don't care what the judges think of me. If they're afraid of me. I know it in my core now, in the sudden, bone-chilling way you realize someone's lying. Whether it's part of my trial or not, it's not an illusion. They'll hurt my friends just to push me to the edge.

And if I don't stop that judge now, he's going to extract Ivander's Morphia.

When I summon, I don't think about it. I don't concentrate on the spirit world. I'm not searching desperately for a connection to a willing spirit. It's easy, like turning the pages of a book or letting an arrow fly. Like breathing, it comes to me without thinking.

Spirits burst from my palm in gaseous plumes of silver mist.

With great, heaving breaths, I summon the dead.

The silvery spirits form solid corpses. I don't have time to make them look pleasant and cheerful for the witnesses. They're not even fully formed. As the dead rise, so do I. My feet float from the ground as I hover in the air, drifting above the floor.

Half-formed humans stagger forward, their bloated bodies black with decomposition. Gaping wounds reveal exposed bones, and wriggling maggots nibble at the frayed edges of their skin. Flesh slides off their skeletons each time they take a step. Their faces are frozen in screams or slack-jawed from lost muscle.

It's not just people taking shape. I conjure wolves with torn ears, emaciated limbs, and snarling skulls with hollow eye sockets. Ravens with feathered bodies and wings made of bone. Skeletal snakes with patches of flaking scales and bloodred eyes.

For a moment, I marvel at how much easier it is to conjure corpses than fully formed spirits. Maybe, while I've been spending so much time trying to make spirits look pleasing to the living, I forgot the beauty and power of death.

I've lost track of how many spirits I've brought back—five, ten, twenty. And they're all fighting for me. The human spirits lunge at the judges and bosses imprisoning my friends. They don't fight like humans, relying instead on otherworldly speed and strength. They rip the knives from the bosses' hands and float into the air to aim kicks at their heads. I don't control the actions of the spirits, but they feed on my intentions. Because my blood is boiling, some of the human spirits don't simply knock the bosses into unconsciousness. One spirit bites into a boss's neck using the exposed bone of his jaw and rotting teeth. The boss, whose name I'm not sure of, lets out a gurgling scream as blood fills his mouth.

A wolf pounces on the judge holding the extraction potion, ripping into the corded muscle of his flesh. The judge screams and tries to pull away, but the wolf holds fast. The screams aren't only coming from the bosses and judges now. I recognize Ambriel's high-pitched yelp, and one of her friends begs me to stop. With the adrenaline still running hot in my veins, I'm not sure if I can.

A raven dives for Charmaine's eyes, scratching at her closed eyelids with long talons. She bats at the bird with wild swats as she runs from the room with her eyes squeezed shut. A wave of satisfaction crashes over me as I think of myself running through the hallway at night, waving my arms at the bat-bird diving for my head.

The uninjured bosses let go of the staff and run from the room, dodging blood spatter and wolves snapping at their heels. I force my mind to calm. As I relax, my spirits also calm. The corpse-like human spirits form a defensive wall in front of the Morphics, defending them from any boss who decides to come close. But I'm reluctant to shed any more blood. Two of the judges lie dead on the floor, but the other two throw themselves through the exit door as wolf spirits chase after them. I let them go, now more aware that my friends are watching, powerless to stop me. But maybe they don't want me to stop.

With my adrenaline waning, my spirits flicker, growing less solid with every passing moment. The dead bodies on the floor jostle me out of my head. Two dead. No, four. Fear makes me pause. Fear of myself and my own power. I'm what they should be afraid of. The Morphic who can't keep her anger—her fear—in check.

No. Not anymore.

I look for what's important. My friends. Niko helps Ivander out of the metal chair, severing his bonds with a knife. Where did Niko get a knife? He must have stolen one from a boss. Ambriel tends to Taurean's bleeding cheek, swiping her hand over the gash with practiced ease. A thin trail of blood leaks out of her nose as she works, and I'm reminded of Eliza. Ambriel's eyes dart to me, and then she hurriedly looks away. I see the flash of fear in her eyes. Although I may have saved us from forced extraction, it has come at a price. The blood on the floor and the bodies drained of life make my stomach turn.

Alana closes her eyes, and I know she's trying to help us all calm down. My breath comes out in ragged gasps, but it slows to deep inhales and steady exhales. Alana's expression smooths into a blank stare as the rest of us relax. It's only when my body calms completely that the fear of myself subsides. I don't regret what I've done, not fully. The reality of what happened settles in my chest.

This wasn't a trial. This was an extraction. For all of us.

CHAPTER 26

The room spins, and I fall to my knees. Taurean gingerly touches the mended cut on his face. "Shit," he mutters.

"What do we do now?" Niko asks, voice higher than usual. He and Ivander sit on the floor beside the shattered potion bottle and the judge's limp body.

I can't make myself move. My knees ache from slamming into the floor. Confusion and fear muddy my mind.

Isla crosses to the door. She opens it a tiny crack as Zora begs for her to keep it closed. "I don't see anyone," Isla whispers.

"Yet," Niko says. "They'll bring backup to deal with us. More bosses."

Ambriel's jaw clenches as she holds her friend's hand. Her friend is crying and refuses to look at me. "Why would the other bosses come for us? They're the ones who broke the rules." She trails off, turning an ashen gray as she looks at the blood-drenched floor.

Ivander pushes himself up and stands. He reaches into the folds of his long coat and pulls out a knife. The silver hilt is embossed with a twisting smoke design. As he grips it tight in his clenched hand, he says, "The bosses aren't playing by the rules anymore."

Clearly, this has never happened before. I'm not the only one in the dark on this. It needles at me that the judges appeared to be in on the forced extraction too. I pull my cloak tighter around me. "Where'd you get the knife?"

Niko unveils a belt tucked beneath his chef's coat. Knives hang from each of the loops. He hands them out. "I served in Tamarynth's army for about six months before I came here. They give each of us one when we start training. They're cheap and simple, but effective."

Ivander crosses to me and helps me to my feet. The weight of his palms against mine provides a rich comfort I never thought I could experience from someone else's touch. He hands a blade to me. "A few charters ago, Niko and I snuck out during a port stop. We smuggled knives onto the ship. They're the only weapons that are easily concealed." He shows me his knife, the one with engravings on the hilt. "I buried mine at port when I first came here. Thought I might need it at some point."

I can't tear my gaze from the knife. This disaster has been building for a long time. Father never told me how bad the relationships between Morphics and non-Morphics had become. Eliza and I were mostly confined to the estate. We rarely traveled to the other provinces, and we'd been only once to Alexandrite Estate.

The blade weighs heavy in my hand, and I turn to face the other staff members. The acrid smell of blood singes my nostrils. I try not to look at the mangled corpses on the ground.

"We need to figure out what's really going on here. The extractions. Elayne's death," I say. "All of it."

"The only way we can do that is by getting you off this ship and back home," Ivander says.

Although part of me is stunned to hear our plan spoken aloud, in front of others, I know he's right. Father has the answers, and I no longer have the luxury of waiting on his timetable to give them. It doesn't matter that I'm afraid of what he'll tell me. "How will we sneak off the ship?"

"It's simple enough." Alana smooths her rumpled skirt with fidgeting fingers. Her own emotions are starting to return after calming ours. "You have cloaks. And knives if anyone tries to stop you. The bosses will be in a panic, anyway."

"Which makes them more dangerous." Isla steps through a smear of blood to get to me. "Whatever they planned in here—"

"It's obvious what they planned in here," Taurean mutters, shaking his head. "No, I worked my ass off for this. This retrial was supposed to be my ticket home. Whatever's going on here . . . It's not right. My friends and I are getting off this ship too. Now. Not later."

Maybe he's right. We need to get as many staff members off this ship as we can before the bosses hurt anyone else. I can't hide in here and pretend anyone is going to fix this for us. We've been so determined to keep our plan a secret, we were keeping it secret from the wrong people. Morphics can be our strength in numbers.

Taurean and his friends don't wait for a debate. He nods to us, knife clenched in his hand, and leaves the room with his friends. Ambriel bites her lip, teary, as she looks at me. "He's right. I've been here nearly four years. I hope you can change things, but I can't wait for you."

She and her friends leave the room, shutting the door with a resounding thud behind them. I'm losing time to come up with a plan. Niko claps Ivander on the back and tucks his knife back inside his chef's coat. "It's settled then. Ivander, you'll go with Roe. She needs your help getting off the ship."

"Alana should come with us too," I add, surprised at the steady sound of my own voice. "We may need an emotive." We might need her to calm people down if tempers flare. I hate doubting my own father, but knowing there's so much he didn't tell me makes me less confident in how he'll react.

The truth is, I want to take all of them with me. We all need to get off the *Celestial*. "Zora and I will stay," Isla says. "Niko too. We'll help as many Morphics off the ship as we can. We'll warn everyone we can not to board."

My fingers twitch at my sides. Even with a knife in my hand, I don't feel prepared to defend myself against the bosses. They still have all our raw Morphia at their disposal, and they're clearly not afraid to wield it. I don't like the idea of anyone staying behind, even if they're trying to help. "What if the bosses try to hurt you?"

Zora puts a hand on her hip. "Then we'll take a page out of your book and fight back."

Ivander's eyes slide over the dead bodies on the ground. "Please be careful. It doesn't matter if Roe changes anything if you're not here to see it."

Isla bites her lip. "Only if you promise to make it out too."

Ivander folds Isla into a tight hug. He and Zora do a quick handshake they no doubt spend more time rehearsing than their dance numbers.

Niko wraps him in an embrace but lets go quickly. "We don't have time. I'm not going to let any of us get killed because we were busy saying goodbye."

As the words leave his mouth, the large door creaks, and we all jump. My heart leaps into my throat, and I whirl around with my knife in front of me.

Gray bursts into the room with a resounding bang. He wears a long maroon coat with intricate bronze fastenings and polished brown boots with gold buckles. He's the picture of a captain, but he shuts the door fast behind him like he has something to hide.

Ivander lifts his knife and points it in Gray's direction. Niko backs him up, with Zora close behind. The way they hold those knives makes me wonder if it's not the first time they've had to use them.

"What do you want?" Zora snarls, lip curling.

"I want to help you." Gray nods to me. "But we need to leave now."

His face, paler than usual, dares us to challenge him. He opens his mouth to say more but closes it again and turns, gripping the iron doorknob. He wrenches the door open. "If you want to get off this ship, we go now."

In a matter of seconds, I have to decide if I trust the man I've known for most of my life. My gut tells me he wouldn't hurt me any more than Leith would have. I give a silent nod of reassurance to the others.

"This is it, then," Ivander murmurs.

We stand in silence together, but the moment doesn't last long.

Ivander lowers his knife and grabs my hand, pulling me from the room. Alana follows close on my heels. When I turn back over my shoulder to make sure Isla, Niko, and Zora are following, Alana shakes her head at me.

"Don't look back," she whispers, a mantra for herself as much as me. "They have their own plan now."

She's right. But what's *our* plan? Nerves make my palm sweaty in

Ivander's. Gray stays close to the wall, motioning for us to follow. Instinctively, we stay quiet.

As midday approaches, most staff members and bosses will be on the upper decks. Most are running activities or helping new guests load onto the ship. However we plan on getting off this ship will attract immediate attention. They'll try to stop us.

When Gray stops in front of the staircase, he turns back around. Ivander's hand hovers over the slit in his coat, ready to seize his knife again, but Gray only puts a finger to his lips. "Be silent. If anyone asks you anything, don't answer. I'm going to try to get us out of here without arousing suspicion."

Ivander raises a brow. "How do you plan on doing that?"

"Never mind how I plan to do it," Gray mutters. "I'll explain once we get you out of here, but it's chaos up there right now, and I don't have time to field questions."

He bounds up the spiral staircase, taking them two at a time.

Ivander looks to me for a decision and I nod to him. Even after everything that has happened today, I trust Gray because I know Leith would have.

We follow close behind him on the stairs. By the time we get to deck five, we're panting.

Gray pauses, steadies his breathing, and walks onto deck five like he owns the *Celestial* itself.

Ivander, Alana, and I exchange nervous glances but fall into step behind him.

Gray's right about one thing. Amid the masses of guests clinking glasses with dazzling fire sparklers sticking out the tops, bosses stalk around, ripping staff members from the atrium. Staff members, looking confused, follow as the grips tighten around their arms. My mouth dries, and I try not to think about what the bosses might be doing to them. They're hunting for someone. For us.

All we can do now is hope Niko, Isla, and Zora are able to get as many Morphics as they can off the ship and to safety. It's a hollow dream. Which province is safe for runaway Morphics? But I can't think about that right now or I'll shut down.

An illusion of a white Thoroughbred horse gallops around the atrium, entertaining the guests. But then a scream sounds from a hallway leading to the Lotus Salon. Guests' heads snap up as several staff members halt.

"Don't stop," Ivander whispers. Keeping my gaze trained on Gray's back, I follow the bobbing of his broad shoulders as he strides across the atrium. We're near the gangway leading off the cruise ship now. It's the same platform staff members use to load luggage on board.

I'm so focused on the light filtering through the exit and the idea of solid ground under my feet for the first time in a month that I don't realize when Gray stops. Ivander throws out his arm to keep me from crashing into him. Alana grips my shoulders from behind to steady me. When I see the man who's stopped us, I let the curtains of my hair fall around my face.

Ivander tenses beside me. His clawlike nail grazes my back. He's ready for a fight, not just with his knife.

Boss Stellan holds up his hand to Gray, arching a brow as he looks over our small group. "Isn't this an odd companionship?" he asks, passing a gloved finger under his chin as he pretends to think. "I can't figure out why three staff members would need the captain of the elite Hawk hunters to help with luggage."

Gray clears his throat, green eyes hard as he stares at Stellan. With his hand hovering over whatever weapon resides under his coat and his jaw set in a firm grimace, I'm reminded of why my father made him captain. "These Morphics no longer get to carry bags," he says, voice low and calm. "I've been ordered to take them to Malachite Prison."

Stellan pauses, brown eyes sliding over the three of us. His gaze lingers on me, and I resist the urge to scratch my skin that's now flushed hot and itchy. He knows something's off. He glances over our heads at the chaos descending over the atrium. Guests are starting to get upset that their staff members are disappearing, either taken by bosses or escaping on their own. Stellan's eyes return to us, and there's an odd flicker in them as he steps aside. "Then by all means, take them."

Gray doesn't acknowledge the change of heart. He walks straight toward the platform leading from the *Celestial* to solid ground. As we pass Stellan, holding our breath, his hand flies out and seizes Alana's shoulder.

Alana lets out a small shriek, but Stellan lets go as quickly as he grabbed her. He locks eyes with Gray again. "Don't stop until you're where you need to go."

We don't wait to hear more. I pull my cloak tighter as we follow Gray off the ship. A pile of forgotten luggage rests on the grass. Most of the staff members have disappeared from the port. Whoever was checking Morphics in for their first cruise is nowhere to be found. "Everyone knows something's wrong," Ivander whispers.

Alana exhales a harsh breath. Her face goes blank as she says in a flat tone, "There's plenty of fear. I feel it everywhere."

"Might be us," I mutter.

But that's not true. Not entirely. I'm afraid, of course. For Isla, Niko, and Zora. For every Morphic still aboard the *Celestial*. For any unknowing guests caught in the crossfire. But I'm also filled with a lung-crushing exhilaration because I know Alana and Ivander are free.

As Gray leads us to a Windmere stable, we keep our heads down and our steps quick. I inhale the earthy smell of soil beneath my feet, and I revel in the peaceful scent of it. After a month aboard the *Celestial*, I'm back on Tamarynth soil. Alana's been aboard for months, and Ivander . . . almost two years. Despite knowing we're far from safe, I feel freer than I have since the day I failed my trial.

Then Ivander places a hand on my arm, drawing my attention. He nods back in the direction we came. All I see are a few bosses unloading heavy crates from the ship. Another man takes the crates and loads them into a carriage waiting not far from the platform.

I can't see what's inside the crates, but I don't need to. My throat tightens.

The bottom left side door of the carriage is emblazoned with the small silver sigil: A potion bottle with a thin wisp of smoke twisting around the body of the bottle, like a noose.

The Damarcus family sigil.

CHAPTER 27

Five hours later, we're deep in Carodmoor Forest, approaching the unofficial border between Windmere and Credence, my home province.

The sun set hours ago, and Alana exhales gratefully when Gray slows his gallop. "Can we stop for the night?" she asks, shifting in her saddle.

An excellent horseman like all Hawks, Gray weaves through the trees on his stallion like he's riding a shadow. "Not yet. There's no telling who might be after us now."

Ivander clicks his tongue, and his red mare canters to match pace with Gray's dark bay. "We need a break, at least."

"Some of us haven't sat a horse in a while, Gray." I pull back gently on the reins and slow my horse to a stop. If I leave the choice to Gray, he'll have us riding until we reach Damarcus Estate. It's not fair to ask Ivander and Alana—who've been on a ship for months—to ride for two days straight without rest. With the dark pressing in on us, I can't see Gray's expression, but the thud of his boots hitting dirt reassures me he's agreed to stop.

Swinging my leg over the side of the saddle, I hop down from my mare and lead her to the slow dribble of a stream nearby. Leaves crunch underfoot as I crouch. I dip my hands into the water and sigh.

Alana joins me, plunging her whole face into the stream. She emerges, smiling wide. "This beats our tub on the ship, doesn't it?"

I grip fistfuls of mud in my hands and allow them to slip through my fingers. I missed the feeling of solid earth under my feet and soil in my palms. And I was only gone for a month compared to the others.

Gray gathers wood and twigs to start a fire, making a pile by Ivander's feet. "I can help," Ivander offers, but Gray shakes his head.

"Don't worry about it. You three rest." Gray drops a fresh branch onto the pile, glancing at Ivander and Alana. "Although, you two aren't crafters, by any chance?"

They shake their heads, and he sighs, trekking farther into the forest in search of firewood. If we had a crafter with us, they could start a fire in no time by fashioning a match from a dry piece of wood. They might only lose their sense of touch in a couple of fingers.

As it stands, the three of us aren't that useful in the middle of the woods. There's a chance Ivander could shift our clothes for better camouflage, but the expenditure of energy and accompanying pain wouldn't be worth it.

As we huddle close to the pile of sticks, Ivander's shoulder brushes mine, and Alana crouches on my other side, face glistening with water from the stream. "He *can* start a fire, right?" she asks, pulling her knees close to her chest.

I nod. Gray's spent plenty of nights in the forest with the Hawks. The thought makes the hair on my arms stand on end. Why would he give up everything he's worked for to break the law and help us escape the *Celestial*? I know what he felt for Leith was real, but it was real seven years ago. Is keeping a promise to protect me worth losing his position in the Hawks, maybe even his freedom? I see my own uneasiness in Ivander's tense shoulders and Alana's darting eyes.

With the thought fresh in my mind, I think about the other parts of today that didn't make sense. "Where did you learn to use a knife?" I ask Ivander.

I've trained with a bow and pistol since I was old enough to run around outside. Crafter-made bows and arrows are expensive, and pistols are even more so. They were all as much a part of my training and Eliza's as playing the piano or learning how to waltz. But knives are desperate weapons. They require getting intimately close to the danger you're fighting. For someone with a knife, it's not a matter of winning a competition or elevating their social standing. It's a matter of survival.

Ivander pulls out his long knife. Even in the dark, the swirling pattern of symbols and lines etched into the hilt draws my eye. He hands it to me, fingers passing over mine as our hands touch. My skin tingles from the quick contact, the warmth from him richer than any fire we could have lit.

"I learned from the other kids when we'd go in a group to Aryndar's markets. There were a couple of Morphic kids in our group, and a few of them had been jumped before. It wasn't something Morphics talked about often, but many of us knew there were people who might try to kidnap us, or worse. I always thought my Morphia would be enough to fight them off, but then Adrionna started coming with me when I got older, and I knew I had to carry a knife every time. I couldn't take chances." He turns the blade over in his hands, letting it glint in the moonlight beaming through the trees.

Alana leans toward us. "Roe doesn't know what it's like. She grew up as a lady of Damarcus Estate, remember?" She nudges me—playful, not judgmental.

She's right, but maybe I wasn't as immune as I thought. Father used to be very careful about locking all the doors to our estate at night, then checking the entrances multiple times. He'd always bark at Eliza and me if we left our windows open. At boarding school, I'd been bullied because my gift scared people. I'd glimpsed a letter Mother wrote to the school asking how they could ensure my safety. I hadn't thought the reason I'd started training with weapons so early might be because my parents were afraid.

Ivander adds, "There are always people out to kill Morphics. Sometimes to sell them for illegal extraction. People take the raw Morphia and use it themselves, or smuggle it all the way to Gryndar. Forced extraction is illegal, but no one's looking out for people like us."

Just like on the *Celestial*. It's another way greedy people abuse Morphics and their magic. As far as I knew, the only raw Morphia was aboard the *Celestial*. Throat tight, I admit to myself that illegal extractions of Morphia are probably more common than I realized. I can add it to the long list of things I had no idea were happening.

"Of course, there are always people—assassins—who like to kill Morphics for no reason at all."

I know what he means, but there is a reason. Hatred. Jealousy. Both. If I hadn't been born a Damarcus, resurrection might have gotten me killed. "Have you ever had to use it?" I ask, nodding to Ivander's knife. "To defend yourself?"

He tucks the knife back in its hiding place within his coat. "More than I wish I had," he says as Gray returns with branches in his arms.

Kneeling on the other side of the wood pile across from us, Gray reaches into the deep pockets of his coat and pulls out a chunk of flint and some dry kindling. He manages to light the fire and points to the stream. "That water should be safe enough to drink. The Hawks have camped here before."

From his other pocket, he takes out a few pieces of hard bread and a handful of jerky. I'm not sure if the meat's squirrel or deer, but the three of us scarf it down. Although I nearly break my teeth on the bread crust, I don't complain.

Ivander sits up straighter, inclining his head to Gray as the flickering firelight illuminates his face. "So why does Roe trust you so much?"

Gray is caught off guard by the question but answers despite the catch in his throat. "I was in love with her brother before he died. He was a Hawk too. I became close with his whole family."

Ivander nods and the tension in his shoulders releases. He looks almost relieved at the mention of my brother.

"Where'd you get the food?" Alana asks. "I'm guessing it didn't come from the *Celestial*."

If she's like me, she's already missing Isla's cooking.

Gray pokes the fire with a stick. "Bought the food in the port market. I told my parents I'd be gone for a while. Then I went back to the ship and came to get you." He throws the stick into the fire, and a swarm of embers leap into the air. "Hawks always carry a fire starter, but they wouldn't let me on board with mine. That reminds me." He reaches across his horse to a bow and quiver of arrows attached to his saddle. "Here. They keep personal items locked away beside the extraction room."

It takes me a moment to recognize the white bow and quiver of arrows as the ones I left at port before sailing. I grasp them with tears in my eyes.

When my fingers clasp the smooth wood, indecision forms an odd lump in my throat. Something about holding this expensive childhood birthday present no longer feels right when I'm sitting beside Morphics who've used knives to defend themselves. I set it on the ground.

A question for Gray lurks on my tongue, like the creature hungry for blood in the ship's lagoon, but I'm too nervous to let it rise to the surface. The crackling fire before us almost makes me feel like I could be back home in Father's study, but that peaceful illusion is slipping away.

I dig my fingernails into my knees. Memories of Father aren't warm anymore. "I know there's a lot you weren't telling me back on the ship. Can you tell me now?"

A weighted silence hangs heavy and threatening between us and Gray. Like a vat of hot oil threatening to tip over. I pull in toward myself tighter, not wanting to touch anyone as I wait.

Gray lets out a shaky breath and looks over the tongues of flame to meet my eyes. "Yes," he says slowly. "I think it's time."

Alana leans forward, and Ivander shifts beside me, but neither speaks. They wait, as expectant and fidgety as I am.

"I need you to know that everything I didn't tell you was because I thought I was keeping you safe. You were so young when your brother died." Gray struggles to say the words.

My heartbeat is thunderous. I strain to hear him over the pulsing in my temples.

"Leith and I were always part of the Hawks. That part's true. But we weren't capturing Morphics to put them behind bars, when we could help it." His eyes drop to the fire as the words come faster. "We were trying to help them escape. Jasper, Leith, and I—there were others too—we knew most of the Morphics taken to Malachite weren't dangerous. Some were. Some always will be, but most were like the three of you."

My stomach rolls, and I struggle not to pitch forward. "Did my father know what you were doing?"

Gray shakes his head. He snaps a branch in half. "Leith tried to talk to him about the Hawks. How he felt like it was hurting people more than helping them. We even told him Ruefold, the prison for non-Morphics"—he adds this for Alana and Ivander's benefit—"is much less crowded than Malachite. It never seemed like people came out of Malachite. They won't even let Hawks inside. No one knows how bad it is in there."

Although my tongue feels like cotton, I force myself to speak. "What did he say?"

"You have to understand, Roe. Your father's place on the council is precarious. If the council had a unanimous vote, they could oust him. He doesn't speak against the way things are done unless it's absolutely necessary. I imagine it's why he's tried to keep you in the dark for so long. The Damarcus name and his family's legacy keep him afloat. He wouldn't do or say anything to jeopardize that just because Leith and I told him to."

Ivander sits up straighter, brows lifting as he takes in Gray with new eyes. "But you and Roe's brother helped Morphics escape anyway. How did you hide it?"

The corner of Gray's mouth lifts. "We'd swayed enough Hawks to join us. We could make it look like they got away during hunts. Or like they slipped the cuffs on the way to prison. Leith was good at distracting the captain. It didn't always work, but we got enough away to keep trying."

My head spins, and my vision blurs. I might be physically sick. All my life I've been proud of my brother for being part of the Hawks. I wanted to join because he believed in their cause. The *real* cause.

It's all a lie. "What happened to Leith? Did you lie about that too?"

Gray's shoulders dip as he runs a hand through his hair. It's gotten longer, falling into his eyes. He's stopped cutting it to fit Hawk protocol. "I haven't told you everything about the day he disappeared. I still remember the light snow on the ground and the gray sky in the morning. I don't know how to describe it, but the day felt off. Like my body knew something was wrong before my mind did."

Whenever people talk about Leith—those who loved him and still do—it feels like he's here for a moment. When people talk about the dead, those who've passed live again in the space of a few words. But this, with Gray, is different somehow. Instead, it feels like I'm watching Leith die all over again. Like the illusion the bosses punished me with back on board.

"We were helping a Morphic escape that day. A crafter. She'd made a sign that would attach to the inside of a front door. It could tell a family who was waiting on the other side. Vendors, family members, thieves. The family who bought it accused her of lying to them when it didn't reveal the thief coming to rob their home."

"But crafter-made objects don't always work. It's not easy to craft. Crafters make mistakes just like any non-Morphic inventor would," Alana says, frustration in her voice. "Non-Morphics gamble on our magic but get mad when it doesn't work."

Gray holds up his finger. "The sign was working. Halfway. The problem was, the thief was a family member. The sign couldn't list both associations. Not that it mattered. The Hawks had to hunt her anyway. But we were going to save her, and our efforts were going well. At first. I was distracting the captain, and Leith was helping the girl escape . . . But then Jasper and I couldn't find him. We looked everywhere. All night. Into the next morning. He just disappeared."

I know the rest of the story. The part Gray doesn't have to say aloud but does anyway. He tells Ivander and Alana how he and the rest of the Hawks returned the next morning to give my father the news. Father fell to his knees. Mother screamed. Eliza and I hardly understood. Even Eliza, being older, still expected him to walk through the door.

Father ordered the Hawks to search again for the crafter girl and for Leith. He went with them, hunting everywhere. After they couldn't find him on the second day, he sent a report to the council, explaining the situation. He left out the part about any Morphic being involved.

I understand that detail now. There was no proof the crafter girl harmed Leith, so Father hadn't wanted public perception to turn on Morphics. But I know Mother did. Especially when they eventually found blood in the woods and a mender identified it as Leith's.

We knew then he hadn't disappeared. He was dead.

Still, even with the blood, it took another year for me to accept he was dead and not missing. Another year of the Hawks searching. A year of sending troops to search Carodmoor Forest. A year of the mender telling me the amount of blood he found was too much to be a good sign.

Gray looks right at me when he says the words I haven't allowed myself to think for all these years. "But we never found his body, Roe. A year of the most highly trained hunters searching, and we never found anything more than blood." He grits his teeth. "All I know is no one's allowed in Malachite Prison, and I'm not obeying any more orders until I have answers."

The gravity of his words pulls at my own whisper of suspicion. I haven't dared to wonder—couldn't let myself. When I was younger, anytime I said it aloud, Lysandra begged me to stop. Mother told me not to pursue it. But sitting here with Alana and Ivander, on the run from the *Celestial*—the legend my own family helped build—Gray's words puncture me like one of my arrows. My brother's been dead for seven years. I've known this truth for almost half my life. But I'm unlearning a lot of truths lately.

What if the reason I can't summon my brother is because he's not really dead?

CHAPTER 28

I fall asleep with my forehead pressed to my knees. The deathmare comes fast, like it always does. But somehow, this deathmare is worse than any of the others.

Bones cracked at odd angles. Faces contorted in screams.

The mangled bodies of my friends lying at my feet.

Ivander's legs jut out, broken in multiple places. Before I can try to help, my consciousness drowns inside each of them. I jump from body to body, feeling the pain of each of their deaths. It's my turn to scream. The muscles in my broken limbs stiffen with pain. *Wake up. Wake up. Wake up.* Jaw-clenching, fiery-hot pain subsides into the cold numbness of blood loss. The precursor to death.

"Roe?"

The pressure of fingers digging into my shoulder forces my eyes open. Ivander shakes me awake. He's alive.

I uncurl from my slumped position. My fingernails are raw and bloody, and my neck stings. Gingerly, I touch the scratches on my throat.

Ivander watches me. His eyes dart to my neck but don't linger there. "It was just a nightmare," he whispers.

I don't answer. I swallow hard and glance around our makeshift campsite. Alana's curled in a tight, sleeping ball while Gray keeps watch. The weight of yesterday settles on my shoulders, heavy and tense. It's too overwhelming to handle. I grit my teeth to keep the tears from my eyes.

Ivander stands and motions for me to follow him. He doesn't wait for me, which makes me curious enough to pull myself together. Gray glances up when I stand and mouths "hurry back" before returning his attention to the trees. I tiptoe away from the campsite after Ivander, grateful to see his legs are working just fine. He's okay.

"Where are we going?" I whisper. He strides over fallen branches and weaves among trees, stepping over mud and kicking rocks out of the way. He walks faster, and I'm forced to keep up with him at a jog. Flyaway hairs stick to my forehead and sweat collects on the back of my neck.

Finally, he stops in a clearing and turns over his shoulder to look at me.

"Barely a day off the ship and you're training me again?" I ask.

"I thought it might help get you out of your head. Moving always does for me."

I suppress a smile. "You're going to have to help me find a way to control my emotions that doesn't involve physical activity."

He cocks his head. "Why? If you need to move, move. Shouldn't bother anyone else." He bends down and unlaces his boots, removing his shoes and socks. He stands barefoot in the moist earth, like we're back on the *Celestial*'s stage.

He's right. With sweat on my skin and my muscles stretched from exertion, I feel better. I feel alive. "It might bother my fellow council members one day."

He crosses his arms. "Who cares? You won't stay quiet to make them like you. You won't do things like your father did. You won't stay silent to make sure you keep your place." He steps toward me. "You're going to be impossible to ignore."

"My brother used to tell me I was good at that." I grin. "I'm very distracting."

"Trust me," he says in a low voice. "You are."

The crisp early morning air raises the hairs on my arms, but I'm not sure it's the chill that's responsible for the shiver running down my spine. I don't look away from his face as I bend down and remove my own boots. The soil squishes between my toes. After a month on the sea, standing in dirt is better than any luxury spa.

I close the distance between us, feeling my core heat up the nearer I get to him. "I'm sorry," I whisper. "For what you had to go through growing up in Aryndar."

Ivander comes even closer, and now I can feel the heat from his skin. "I'm sorry anyone ever said your gift wasn't valuable. When you brought back my grandfather . . . Resurrection is one of the most beautiful things I've ever seen." He clears his throat. "I longed for the nights you came into the theater. Even if it was just to argue with you." There's a twinkle in his eye as he breathes in deep. "You were so strong. I didn't feel like I had to hide from you."

"I'm glad you didn't." The indent of his collarbone makes my heart somersault. My fingertips tingle; I want to touch him. To get as close to him as I was on the silks. I swipe my tongue over my bottom lip. Ivander's eyes follow the movement. "I never told you what I thought about in the hallways," I say, breathless. "Who I thought about."

My chest rises and falls faster than it should, like I'm high up on the silks for the first time again. We've been pressed tightly against each other in the air, but this feels different.

"Can I touch you?" he whispers.

"I hoped you'd ask." I nod, but I move first and press my lips to the crook of his neck. He tenses at my touch but relaxes when my hands slide over his shoulders to his back. His hands slip down my shoulder blades as he draws me closer. I raise my chin to meet his gaze. His lips part as he waits for me to move. My fingers curl into the muscles of his back, and I stand on my toes to press my mouth to his.

The smooth pressure of his lips sends a shiver down my spine, and I try to remember to breathe. My stomach flutters as I grow bolder, matching the rhythm of his lips. When we're this close to each other, the warmth of his body envelops me. I can't get close enough.

He kisses me back, harder than I expect. His arms fold farther around me, gentle at first, then tighter, and end up on my hips. He pulls me to him. The smells of the sage he burns in his room and the roses he receives at the end of performances still cling to his skin. The tight curls of his hair tickle my fingers as I bury my hands in them.

Just as the morning sun filters through the trees, he pulls back from me slow and careful, as if he doesn't want to stop. His chest rises and falls with rapid breaths. I've never seen *him* out of breath. I try to keep him close to me, but the stern set of his jaw reminds me we have to get back to camp.

"I wish we could stay here," I admit. The taste of salt lingers on my tongue.

"Me too," he says. "But because of us, the *Celestial* is a day away from destroying itself, and there's so much we don't know."

Not to mention those crates we saw with my family sigil being loaded off the ship. My answers aren't here with Ivander. They're at home.

"Roe!" Gray's unmistakable call interrupts our oasis. He must have come looking for me when I took too long. Damn his excellent tracking skills.

Ivander's lips curve, sensing my thoughts. "We better get going."

When Gray finds us, he lets out an exasperated huff and tells us it's time to go. By the time we get back to camp, Alana's already stamped out the flames and scattered the remains of our wood pile. She gives me a small, knowing smile when Ivander isn't looking but hurries to mount her horse. Gray unties his stallion's bridle from the tree trunk.

I know Carodmoor Forest about as well as Gray does. We're still one and a half days' ride from the estate. "We need to move faster," I say once I realize.

"You're right." Ivander adjusts his horse's saddle. His eye contact sends a flush of heat through my body as I remember the pressure of his lips against mine. "I've been thinking. There are costs to using Morphia. No magic comes without a price. But what if that's just another excuse to keep Morphics from pushing ourselves?"

I ignore Gray's impatient cough urging us to hurry up with the saddles. "There *is* a price for using our magic." We all pay it. All except alchemers.

"But what if we're so afraid of the consequences that we don't push as far as we can? Why are we so afraid?"

I snort as I swing up onto my horse. "Well, for one thing I'm afraid of experiencing death every night and seeing it when I'm awake. For another, your gift actually breaks your bones."

Ivander shrugs, keeping his feet on the ground. "The bones don't stay broken for long."

Something about the gravity of his tone keeps me from firing back a retort. Especially because I'm starting to wonder if he has a point. The deathmares aren't real. They feel real, but they don't permanently injure me or anyone else. They've always felt like a check on my power. Like a stomachache after too much of Isla's rich, sticky gortha pudding. And the deaths I witness while awake are nothing more than events of the past. It's almost as if my gift wants to show me the truth of how spirits died. Perhaps it only bothered me because it never showed me Leith.

When I was a child, I never thought about the consequences. I conjured spirits with reckless abandon. I don't really remember the deathmares, but maybe that's because I don't remember them being awful. I even used to enjoy the time I spent walking through them at night. Like my own dreams were a performance. I even found it interesting to exist in a waking deathmare. I'd witness a death and marvel at how a life could be snuffed out so quickly. It made me more appreciative of my own. True, I hated the feeling of spirit hands against my skin, but some touch is pleasant to me now. What if I stopped being afraid of what I see when I go to sleep? What if I learned from the deaths I witness?

Ivander must sense the change in me, in my posture, in the shift of my shoulders. When he realizes my guard's come down, he says, "I think you're stronger when you use your Morphia without thinking. Your body remembers. Of all of us here, your power is the most limitless. How might you get us home?"

Perhaps my price is as natural as paying with sore legs and heaving lungs after running too far. Perhaps it's as natural as burning eyes after staying awake through the night reading. When did I become so scared of those dreams that they turned into nightmares? So scared of myself?

Maybe I can forget my limits again.

I don't know why I never thought of it before. I pat my mare's flank and drop her lead. Resurrection isn't anything to fear. It's nothing more than what most magic is. A gift. The real danger is in what I do with it.

Alana urges her horse over to the two of us. "What's going on?"

"We have to keep moving," Gray says, but even he lacks his usual commanding edge. He knows I've got an idea and won't let it go.

When my eyes shut, I find I don't have to reach for the spiritual plane. It comes to me as easily as breathing. With an inhale, I connect to the silver tether. I pass into the plane, bare feet propelling me through the gray-blue expanse of space.

Spirits fly by, glowing orbs of silver light that take shape as I get closer. That's when I feel them. Two horses. One black with white hooves, and another with a red coat and a white star across his long face.

I bring their spirits back, fully formed and solid.

When my eyes open, the spirit horses paw at the ground and snort. It's as if they're trying to tell me to hurry up. They'll carry us faster than any living, mortal mount. Faster than crafter-made carriages.

The living horses rear back, skittish upon smelling deceased horses who look no different than they do. "We'll have to share," I say as my only explanation in response to Alana and Gray's bewildered expressions. Ivander beams as he looks at me.

We're close enough to Lysandra's horse farm; I know she'll find the steeds we're being forced to leave behind. We don't have time to do more than transition from the horses to the two spirits, but at least we don't need bridles or saddles. They know where to go because I do. Ivander and I take the black horse while Gray and Alana take the red one. "I should be able to keep them solid long enough to get us home."

"Get us as close as you can." Gray shakes his head, a half smile dimpling his right cheek. "If only Leith could see his little sister now."

Without warning, the horses gallop forward, gliding over the forest floor like inflatable tubes skimming the surface of the top-deck lagoon. Their legs pump with the movement of galloping, but their hooves don't touch the ground. They glide so fast my stomach dips like I'm swinging on silks again.

By the time we ride over the pebble-streaked pathway that cuts through the rolling green hills of Damarcus Estate, the spirit horses retain almost none of their original form. Their legs are white bone with hunks of bloody flesh still clinging to their ribs. The bones of their faces are visible, but thin stretches of skin hold round eyeballs in place. I doubt the guests on the *Celestial* would appreciate this show. I almost laugh, thinking how Asralyn would react.

Surrounded by its manicured green lawn, the grayish-brown stone exterior of my family's estate is more imposing than I remember. Sharp triangular turrets jut into the sky. Moss and thick greenery crawl up the sides of the home, shrouding the thin rectangular windows in a casing of nature. The greenery grows dense on the exterior, the leaves changing from green to red-orange from left to right. The front porch of the estate is solid stone. An untamed growth of flowers and herbs sprouts all the way around the perimeter of the mansion. Father plucks his ingredients from that wild garden in the mornings.

Home.

I cannot imagine what Alana and Ivander must be thinking.

Father always said, *When they come to my home, they expect witches. I give it to them.*

Although I'm used to the harsh angles of the turrets and the great stone walls, I'm unnerved by how quiet it is. There's no one gardening outside or picking herbs for the apothecaries across the province. Father usually has an array of visitors, and there are no carriages winding up the path as we approach.

The stables off to the side, beside my room's window, are empty of people. Even the green fields are empty of neighbors who sometimes come to train with our supply of weapons. The sky's devoid of letter-carrying ravens, and the road's lacking its human courier counterparts.

"Something's wrong," Gray murmurs. Someone should have seen us approaching the estate. Mother should be running out of the house, with Eliza close on her heels.

I didn't think we'd be able to walk right through the front door. Even Father, rattled by the reports of a girl's death on the *Celestial*, should be storming out. Knowing that the ship must currently be drowning in chaos makes this quiet feel not only eerie but insulting. How dare this place be so serene and undisturbed?

As I vault myself from the spirit horse, boots slamming into the ground, the others follow suit. Their feet have just touched the ground when I finally let go of the horse spirits and allow them to return to the spirit world.

I run up the walkway and take the stairs two at a time. Ivander tries to slow me with a warning, but I ignore him. Nothing frightens me now. The only thing I'm afraid of is going another moment without the truth. I grip the wrought-iron doorknob in two hands, wrenching at it with a mighty tug. I expect the door to be locked, but it swings wide open, sending me stumbling backward into Gray. The heavy door slows before it hits the stone wall beside it, and the four of us take the opportunity to file into the entryway.

Alana treads on my cloak, murmuring a quick apology. Ivander shoves one hand into the seam of his coat, most likely gripping the hilt of his knife. Gray is stiff and quiet beside me.

The massive black chandelier hangs overhead, every candle lit. The dark wooden floors with ancient maroon rugs groan under our feet. The walls are obscured by generations of family portraits hanging in golden frames. The great brown staircase twists to the top floor. Beside us, a marble statue of a serpent, fangs exposed, curls around a flower.

Everything looks the same.

The only sounds are the creaking of wood under our feet and the hiss of our breaths. I don't see any servants passing to the kitchens with silver trays in their arms.

Then Alana seizes my arm, and it takes me a moment to realize why.

My father, Lord Cyrion Damarcus, descends the steps of the staircase with a pistol on his belt and a potion bottle in his hands.

I'd be scared if this weren't a regular occurrence. Father doesn't make deliveries without some way to defend himself. There are thieves and travelers who wouldn't hesitate to steal an alchemer's elixir in order to sell it.

But it's the way his brows lift and his mouth presses into a line when he sees me that makes me pause. I can't tell if he's angry or even surprised to see me here. His brown eyes dart from me to Gray, and then to Ivander and Alana behind me.

He continues to descend the steps, shining black boots thudding against the rug. His grip tightens around the potion bottle when he reaches the ground floor and sees the dried blood on my cloak.

Stroking the end of his black beard, he stops to lean against the banister.

The four of us stand frozen, waiting for him to speak. Gray inclines his head, but I offer nothing more than stony silence. I know I ran away despite his warnings not to go, but I thought he'd have something to say. After a month, I thought he'd at least ask me what happened.

Ask if I'm okay.

The mistrust, anger, and hurt I've been suppressing since my first night aboard the *Celestial* bubble to the surface. If he's not going to talk, then I will.

"I guess one of us should start with the truth," I say. I didn't realize how angry I was until I got here. He doesn't care if I've passed my retrial. His mind's far away, not on me. "The *Celestial* is not what you think. Right now, the bosses are extracting Morphic magic. For nothing. For themselves. They're hurting people. And the ship's killing guests and staff—all on its own."

"Your family's plan to contain Morphia isn't working anymore." Gray finishes for me when my voice breaks.

When Father told me not to go, I thought he was embarrassed. I thought he wanted to spare me the disappointment of failing another trial.

But the horror was so much worse. The bleeding hallways. The cracked walls threatening to swallow me whole at night. The bosses and their brutal punishments. The Morphics aboard aren't criminals like I thought. I think of Elayne and Karynna and who knows how many others who have been killed aboard.

I never expected the ship would want to feed on my Morphia like a monster. Did Father?

Father massages the bridge of his nose. When he answers, his voice is heavy and sad.

"I know," he admits, straightening. "It didn't go as it was supposed to. Especially not for you." The lines around his eyes soften, and he gives me a sad smile. "You weren't ever supposed to leave the ship with your Morphia."

CHAPTER 29

I take a lurching step forward, not even sure what I'm planning to do. Ivander grabs my arm just as Alana shrieks.

Bodies race from the hallways off the main staircase and entryway. Men and women, maybe seven of them, rush past my father and toward us. I don't recognize any of them, but their tunics and trousers are frayed and dirty. Their lips are cracked and their hair is brittle and half-washed. I can't imagine any of these people are guests.

Ivander draws his knife just as Gray draws his own. I fumble inside my coat for the dagger Ivander gave me. My fingers close around the hilt as Alana screams again. This time it's a raw, unrestrained, gasping scream that rattles my core. She falls to her knees, hitting the wood floor with a thunk.

Her voice cuts off. I look over my shoulder at her, watching her face go blank. She must have tried to alter their emotions. Her hands shake, but her lips move as she tries to speak. "In pain . . ." she gasps. "Don't hurt them."

I don't know if she's talking to us or the group of people rushing us, but I don't have time to figure it out. At first, I assumed they weren't armed, but now I see they're better armed than we are. They have pistols on their belts, ready to use if their bare fists aren't enough.

Ivander shouts, ducking between me and a shifter woman's claws. Her exposed skin has transformed into some type of armor, and lethal spikes protrude from her joints, her entire body a weapon. The resounding crack of her bones as she shifts echoes through the entry room. Ivander can't seem to puncture her armored skin with his knife, and with Alana on her knees and more of these raging Morphics racing toward us, it's clear we aren't going to escape. How do we protect ourselves if we can't hurt them?

Ivander finally draws blood from one of the girl's nostrils, and she howls in pain.

A man swings his fist at Ivander, but Ivander ducks easily, spine as flexible as water. He whirls behind the man and lands a kick squarely between his kidneys. But there are too many of them, and Alana's warning flashes in my mind.

Gray drops his knife, perhaps unwilling to use a blade against flesh.

Why isn't he fighting? With a sense of foreboding crawling up my spine, I turn my palms face up, willing a spirit to come to our aid. The silvery tendrils of glowing mist spring from my fingertips as a low voice rumbles, "Don't let her summon!"

Cuffs clamp around my wrists, the engraved symbols blocking my gift like a physical wall.

We're overrun. There must be ten of them now. Two women haul Alana to her feet. Alana blinks hard, regaining the panic she lost from her Morphia. "What . . . What's going on?"

"Stay calm," Ivander cautions. He doesn't struggle against his own cuffs and the men holding him in place. The trembling of his fingers is the only thing that gives away his fear.

With all four of us cuffed now, held by men and women who smell of damp earth and soiled clothes, I stand rigid and powerless. My father looks back at me, hands jammed into the pockets of his oversized coat.

Despite my repulsion at the sticky, lukewarm skin touching mine, I stop struggling. This man holding me captive and taking my only ability to defend myself is still my father. I want to understand him. So, I wait. We're at his mercy, even if we don't know why. Gray shifts beside me. Three men hold him in place, but he isn't going anywhere either. Right now, we all want answers more than freedom.

Father sighs. "I knew this day would come," he says, voice barely above a whisper. "But it's so much harder than I thought it would be. So much harder."

I take a deep breath. "Why don't you start with the biggest lie you told me?"

The corner of his mouth lifts. Maybe Eliza could stand here with her lips pressed in a tight frown, but that's not me. She was always good at holding her ground with our parents, composed and regal. But I fight even when I have nothing but words to fight with.

Father inclines his head to me. He holds up his hand and motions for one of our captors to step forward. He whispers in the man's ear, and the man retreats down the hall in the direction of Father's study.

I exchange a look with Ivander, unease pulling my gaze to his. His eyes reflect the same cautious curiosity in mine. The man returns with Father's cauldron, fire-building materials, and bottles of ingredients clutched in his arms. The smell of ground herbs, earthy insects, and pungent liquids singes my nostrils. "I can show you," Father says. "It would be best for you to see the truth. Then, you'll understand why."

He drags a nearby chair in front of us and positions himself before the cauldron. I used to sit in that chair on rainy days and watch through the window as Hawks trekked through the mud. The memory feels so far away now.

The man who carried the materials builds a small, contained fire beneath the cauldron. My eyes burn when I think of how many times I've watched my father work with complete trust and admiration. Fear holds me tighter than my captors as I wait for his next words. "I think I'll begin with the lie I've been telling the longest. You deserve to hear the truth before you see it." Father draws a breath but meets my eyes as he continues, "What you know about our family—what the world knows—most of it's a lie. The *Celestial* cruise ship had a purpose, just not the one we shared with Tamarynth at the time."

Father's eyes drop from mine and fall to his potion. He sprinkles herbs, thyme and sage, into the base liquid. He pours a vial of deep purple liquid into the cauldron and stirs with his hand. He clears his throat as steam rises. "We Morphics were never going to win the war the first time. The conflict brewing between Morphics and non-Morphics was too great. Two centuries ago, they'd killed too many of us. We didn't have the numbers nor a unifying leader to overcome that. So, my great-grandfather put a stop to it."

So far, the story sounds the same. Mostly. A Damarcus put a stop to the war, but I always thought it was because he didn't want it. Not because the Morphics couldn't win. It's like someone's pressed a cube of ice to the back of my neck, letting the freezing trail of water slide down my spine. But I continue to hold my head high. Just the way I've been taught.

Father continues but dumps crushed bone into the cauldron as he speaks. There's something ominous about the off-white powder as it plinks into the boiling liquid. "He came up with an idea that allowed his home realm of Tamarynth to keep Morphics for society's use but didn't let us get too powerful. The council saw his invention of the trials and the work sentence on the *Celestial* as the perfect way to keep Morphics in line. The ship he funded would entertain people with magic and keep Morphia contained, away from the land of Tamarynth. After all, what harm is a keg of magic floating on the sea?"

He chuckles without true mirth. His eyes dart to mine and away again, as if he wants to gauge my reaction but is too afraid of what he'll find. "Spokesman Armeris knew he needed menders and crafters. Even saw uses for emotives and enhancers. The council especially saw the need for alchemers—the need to keep them close."

"We know this. So what was the real purpose for it?" Gray asks, voice low and cold.

Gray never talks to Father this way. Father's brows raise, but he inclines his head. He continues to stir the boiling potion, faster now. "The *Celestial* wasn't supposed to contain Morphia and Morphics forever. Only for a time. Only until someone from our family—a Morphic—was strong enough to use it."

Use it? I've never heard anything about *using* the ship. If my great-grandfather didn't want Morphia contained, what was he storing it for?

Father motions with his free hand to me. "Our ancestor decided we would play their game for a time, until we were ready to wage our own war. One we would be certain to win. This time, we would have an army and so much Morphia at our disposal that we couldn't lose. That ship is a powder keg ready to explode."

My head's spinning. "You *want* a war. Our family legacy is creating some massive weapon for a war we only pretended to stop? I thought we wanted peace."

Father shakes his head, anger in his voice for the first time. "This wasn't peace, Roe."

Ivander clears his throat, voice placatingly calm. "You mentioned an army. What army?"

My father's black brows knit together as he stirs. He plucks a few loose strands from his own hair and sprinkles them into the liquid. "Malachite Prison has become more than a holding cell for Morphics. It's become my army. When the Hawks deliver Morphic prisoners, I keep them there. They'll be my soldiers—my generals—for the next war. My ancestors continued this tradition for centuries, waiting for enough time to pass, for a Damarcus strong enough to use that army to come along. Regrettably, too many died waiting for that fateful day. I'm not going to wait any longer."

Gray throws himself against the men holding him in place. He strains against his cuffs, gritting his teeth hard as he tries to get to Lord Damarcus. I've never seen Gray this temple-throbbing, red-faced angry. "You didn't forbid Hawks from entering for their own safety. You're using the prisoners. Hurting them."

Lord Damarcus shakes his head fiercely. "No, none of them are hurt. I use a potion to keep them . . . calm. In a sort of trance."

That's when I realize who our attackers are. The ragged people holding us in place are prisoners, *Morphic* prisoners. Their glassy-eyed stares and mindless obedience . . . Father's potion. I wonder if that's the potion he's brewing now, one he intends to use on us.

"You're using them without giving them a choice," Ivander says, coming to the same conclusion. "How does that make you better than anyone else on the council?"

Lord Damarcus flexes the fingers of his free hand, examining a black opal ring on his pinky finger. It's an heirloom from one of his grandparents. I was always proud to see him wear it. Proud of our legacy. Every day since I arrived at the *Celestial* has chipped away at that pride, leaving nothing more than a bitter taste in my mouth.

"Yes," Father admits, then goes on without answering the second question. "But it will be worth it when the world looks different. Morphics should be the highest in society. We should make the council." A tear trickles down his cheek, and he lets it fall into the potion. He blinks several times and more fall. I've rarely seen my father's tears, but seeing them now disgusts me. As if hearing the thoughts in my mind, his eyes flick to me. He holds my gaze. "Making that happen became more important than anything. Than anyone."

Than me. He doesn't say it, but I know he's thinking it.

"I believed in this enough to make my son part of it."

Father pauses, and every nerve in my body tingles like my skin's on fire. He can't mean—

"Leith's going to be my general."

CHAPTER 30

My vision blurs and my lungs constrict. I can't breathe, can't think. The dizzying realization threatens to bring me to my knees.

Alana's gasp is the only sound, and the room stays like that, still and silent, until Gray growls low in his throat. He stands straight-backed while the three men hold him in place, but the venom in his tone is unmistakable. "No," he whispers, voice low. "You made all of us think he was dead. Your own daughters." His voice rises a degree. "He loved them more than anything, and you lied to all of us so that you could make him a pawn in your war."

"Not a pawn," Lord Damarcus answers. "A leader. If I could have told any of you, I would have. Please, believe me. This legacy has been entrusted to the alchemers since the first war. I was doing this for you and Roe. For all others like you. Like us."

My body shakes, and I can't stop trembling. Leith. My big brother is alive? It was all just another lie. Another lie I don't know how to process. I feel like I'm floating, rising above the scene as I look down, like a spectator of my own life.

"Rosaline." Ivander's voice is soft behind me. Ivander fixes people. He doesn't like to watch them break. But I don't know how to hold it together. Not when this building rage is the only thing keeping me standing.

Lord Damarcus motions to one of our captors. "Bring four goblets. Quickly," he commands. Without hesitation, the man releases his hold on Alana and heads in the direction of the kitchens. My mind's still spinning when he returns with four silver goblets that once held hot hearth fruit cider in the wintertime.

He dips each of the goblets into his steaming potion. My hands clench, and I strain against the cuffs around my wrists. I won't drink anything he gives me.

"What is that?" Gray asks, voice unsteady. Before Lord Damarcus answers, one of Gray's captors walks forward and takes the full goblet. Although Gray struggles, the man holding him in place yanks his head backward. The man with the goblet forces the liquid into Gray's mouth and covers his mouth until he swallows.

"I'm sorry," Lord Damarcus says as the captors continue down the line, pouring the potion down Alana's and Ivander's throats. "I need you to see. It will help you truly understand." He swallows hard. He has the gall to look ashamed. "Then you'll see what I sacrificed. You deserve the truth now."

"Roe . . ." Alana begins, sensing the anger nibbling at my thin threads of self-control.

I ignore her, straining against my captors so that Lord Damarcus has no choice but to look at me. Making my brother lead an army against his will became more important than our family. More important than Lysandra losing her child.

"You're above nothing," I spit. "If you're willing to lie about Leith. To me, to Eliza, to Lysandra. Then you'll lie about anything." A thrill of heat runs through me, cutting straight to my core. "I don't recognize you anymore."

The memories rewrite themselves. The soft smiles he shared at the dinner table. The immaculate waistcoats I never see him without. The casual warmth of spending a morning with him in his study, volunteering to catch the rats he needs for his next potion. I recognize nothing. This is the punctured image of a man I know I've lost.

Lord Damarcus shakes his head, and the lines in his forehead crease. One of my captors tips my head back. I writhe back and forth to escape her grip, but she pulls my hair until tears sting the corners of my eyes. She moves as if to yank my mouth open, but I don't let her. I drink from the goblet held out to me without fighting. There's no sense in fighting when the others have already drunk. The potion smells like Father—incense, sage, smoke, and the pages of an old book. My tongue burns with the taste of strong ginger and cinnamon from his favorite tea.

"It allows me to show you my memories. No matter how much they pain you, you deserve them. I hope in seeing them you realize my actions were only because I saw them as entirely necessary." Black spots eat at the corners of my vision. Lord Damarcus fades from view, and the pressure of my captors' grips releases.

The world goes black and then blinks back into light. I'm standing in the study. It's clear I'm seeing through Lord Damarcus's eyes and not my own, as I appear to be in a secret meeting. Lord Trevor, a man who helps Father with the affairs of Credence, Boss Balanyr, Boss Charmaine, and a woman wearing an expensive dress whose name I don't know gather around Lord Damarcus's cauldron.

I dip my hand into the boiling indigo liquid, then withdraw it, letting the liquid fall through my fingers. It's strange seeing through his eyes while feeling my own hot rush of betrayal. I knew he oversaw the selection of bosses, but what's he doing holding a meeting in our home with two of the worst of them? That indigo potion looks too familiar . . .

"Will she suspect anything?" Lord Trevor asks, wringing his hands.

I feel my head shake. It's strange, like an out-of-body experience. Sort of like how my movements feel in the spiritual plane. "It's the same potion she takes every night at dinner. She won't question it."

The corner of Boss Charmaine's mouth lifts. "What does she think it's for?"

A muscle in my—Lord Damarcus's—jaw twitches, but his voice comes out calm when he answers. "Her nerves. I've told her it calms her and helps her summon."

Boss Balanyr leans against the bookcase and runs a skeletal hand crusted over with blood through his beard. "But what will it do on the night of the ball?"

This must be the day before the Resurrection Ball, when Mother,

Eliza, and I had gone out to retrieve our gowns from the tailor. Lord Damarcus sighs and stirs the potion with a large ladle. "The one she drinks at dinner prevents her from summoning family members. But this one will have the added benefit of making her summoning less controlled."

The horror cuts through the scene and into me. The potion I consume every night is worse than poison. It has prevented me from raising my family members' spirits all my life. An ability I thought was beyond my reach was nothing more than another of Lord Damarcus's lies.

"If she loses control at the ball, she'll be much less sure of herself when she goes to her trial. She'll drink one more dose at dinner the night before to make sure," Lord Damarcus continues in a flat, emotionless tone.

Charmaine clicks her tongue. "When she fails, what if she chooses to board the ship? She might be so desperate for her precious magic that she—"

"She won't." Lord Damarcus cuts her off. "I will do all in my power to make sure she does not leave her trial with her Morphia."

Lord Trevor wipes his glasses with a handkerchief and bites his lip. A flare of anger dulls to a murmur of sadness as I look at a man who used to bring me new books to read each time he visited our estate. "Perhaps she could be made to listen. Her resurrection might one day make her as useful as your son."

My head shakes fast. "She could resurrect her great-aunt's spirit. She was the only female alchemer in the family. Even in her own day, she spoke out against the family and began to learn of the ship's true purpose."

Trevor clears his throat. "But if Roe agreed to the cause, why not let her keep her magic?"

"You don't know my daughter," Lord Damarcus rumbles. "You cannot control her. Even potions like these won't work forever. And if she ever decides she does not agree with the cause once we've let her keep the dead at her disposal, it could result in utter disaster. It is a terrible price, but I will pay it."

You mean I will pay it. My mind races with yet another betrayal. Boss Balanyr taps his heavy boot against the wood floor. "What if you cannot prevent her from boarding the ship?"

I feel my arm move as Lord Damarcus reaches beside the desk and withdraws a crate full of empty potion bottles. "You will take this back to port with you. I will fill these, and all you must do is make sure a small amount is mixed into the extraction potion she drinks each night. I made it so that it would mix imperceptibly into any other liquid. It will stop her from raising spirits of family members."

There must be dozens of bottles. More than enough for a month at sea. He raises two more bottles that have already been filled. One is filled with a bright green potion and another is filled with a thick gray liquid, tar-like in consistency. "These two are for emergencies only. A few drops of the green will prevent her from resurrecting a spirit of your choosing. The gray . . . should only be used if the aim is to kill."

My own blood runs cold. The green potion must have stopped me from raising Elayne. The boss who handed me the drink at the mid-cruise ball must have known I would find her dead. Poor Elayne must have drunk the gray potion while she was in the haunted hallway.

"Take it to port with you," Lord Damarcus commands. "If she fails and manages to board, the ship will leave in a few days. You will have what you need to make sure she does not receive a retrial."

"What if we just took her Morphia while aboard?" Charmaine asks, swiping her tongue over her splitting lips. Her countenance is less skeletal away from the ship.

"You know why," Lord Damarcus states calmly. "If you take Morphia without cause, there will be an uprising. But if she looks at all like she might achieve retrial, you will make something so horrible befall her that no one could argue with her Morphia extraction. Send me word with ravens of any developments should she board."

Boss Balanyr crosses his arms. "And if we do this, we get another three years of time on the ship? The pay too. In advance?"

I feel Lord Damarcus incline his head. Boss Balanyr and Boss Charmaine come around the side of the desk and examine the potion bottles. "As long as we seal it," Charmaine begins. "No one will question what's inside."

Her voice becomes fuzzy, and I blink several times to clear the sudden fog distorting my vision. The scene's dissolving. There's a swooping feeling in my stomach. I can't tell if it's from the potion or from the dizzying, damning realization that my father has been responsible for the flaw in my magic all my life. The potion I drank at dinner every night was a lie. Was it in the honey he drizzled on my toast or in the steaming mugs of cider he shared with me on rainy nights in front of the hearth fire?

Even more disturbing is the knowledge that he was responsible for Elayne's death. That night, a boss must have given her the potion in the hallway. Then, they returned to the party with . . . I'm guessing a hair or some of her blood to mix with the light green potion. I recall the boss I talked to on the night of the ball handing me a drink.

Bile rises in my throat, and I fight the urge to throw up. I've returned to my own body, and my captors still hold tight to my arms. The others are stunned into silence. My knees tremble, and the disorienting return to reality makes me dazed. Lord Damarcus watches us with wary regard. I can't believe he thought this memory would comfort me and help me understand. If anything, it has illuminated a bitter truth. Cyrion Damarcus is terrified of his Morphic daughter and always has been. He doesn't know what I'm capable of anymore, and I certainly don't know him either.

I strain against my captors, wanting to lunge at my father, but I remember they are as much prisoners as the rest of us. Alana shakes her head at me, and I cease struggling despite wanting nothing more than to wrap my fingers around someone's throat. I can't speak. Nothing I could say would be enough.

"You thought if the murder was pinned on Roe, they could take her Morphia," Gray says in a shaky voice. "But you failed."

"You were stopped," Ivander breaks in, "by a non-Morphic woman who saw the good in Roe. By someone who lost her own young daughter to that abomination of a ship years before Roe."

"That was regrettable," Lord Damarcus concedes. "Our ancestors never realized how dangerous containing Morphia would get. But it all became less important. Don't you understand that? The killing. The lies. Everything I've had to do to get here. It's all to win a war we couldn't win before. To make things better."

My knees feel weak again, and I realize the edges of Lord Damarcus are fuzzy. The hair on the back of my neck stands on end. Reality is fading once more, and I have no power to stop it. I cry out, but nothing prevents me from descending into the memory.

Fresh snow on the ground and trees I know as well as the contents of my bedroom. Carodmoor Forest. Shouting in the distance and the far-off galloping of horses over dense snow. One word screamed over and over a great distance away. "Leith!"

My stomach twists. I'm back in Lord Damarcus's body, but my feelings are all my own. Panic rises inside me so quickly that if I were in my own body, I'd lose my balance. I'm seeing the day Leith disappeared.

No.

The day he was captured.

As Lord Damarcus, I stand over my son's body. A crafter-made arrow is lodged in his left leg, turning the snow scarlet. A man at my side crouches next to the wound and looks back up at me. "We have to let him bleed enough that they think he's dead."

"But not enough to kill him," Lord Damarcus says through gritted teeth. "If you kill my son, I will kill you."

Leith tilts his head up to look at Lord Damarcus. It's as if someone has shoved a knife through my chest and twisted. For the first time in almost a decade, those stormy blue eyes meet mine. A lock of dark brown hair falls in his face, and he blows it off with a heavy breath. Even while losing blood, his eyes twinkle. "That's a nifty little potion you gave me, I'll give you that," he admits in the familiar lilting tone that makes my heart ache. "Prevents me from raising my voice and shouting for help. If you need a name for it, I'd go with the Muffler." He opens his mouth and tries to yell, but nothing comes out but a croak.

I crouch to be level with him. The snow crunches beneath Lord Damarcus's boots. "Are you not angry?"

"Beyond angry," Leith replies easily. "But I don't currently know what you want or what you're planning to do with me, so I see the smarter course of action is to stay calm."

The man crouching beside the pool of blood huffs. "We need to move him soon. Those Hawks may find us."

Leith glances down to the arrow poking out of his leg. Despite his blasé tone, his face blanches when he sees the blood. "I'm guessing that's a paralyzing arrow too. Crafter-made." Leith lets out a low whistle. "Not cheap. You went to great lengths to stage my death."

Lord Damarcus's head snaps up, giving me whiplash. "I am going to great lengths for a much larger reason."

Leith's brow furrows. "Whatever it is, it better be the most important thing you've ever done. Because you will ruin my sisters' lives." I've never heard this venom in his voice before.

Leith's eyes cloud and have trouble focusing. He's losing too much blood to stay awake. I reach forward and brush my finger against his cheek. If it were truly my hand, I'd be so grateful to touch him again, but in this body, I'm repulsed.

"I know what you tried to do, son," Lord Damarcus says in a low voice. "You were freeing those Morphics you hunted. So was I, but in a different way. I sought out Morphics who failed their trials or who aged out of the *Celestial*. I smuggled as many as I could to Malachite. Most got to keep their Morphia."

Through gritted teeth, Leith asks, "Why? At what cost?" He lets out a shaky breath. "There's always a price."

I reach into my pocket and withdraw a small potion bottle. I wish I could stop Lord Damarcus's hand, even in the memory. As Lord Damarcus tips it into Leith's parted mouth, his eyes become glassy and unfocused. "Yes," I murmur. "There is."

The scene begins to fade, and this time, I want it to keep going. I've seen him alive and talking. I don't want to lose him again. Lord Damarcus wants me to understand what he sacrificed. He believed in his mission so much that faking my brother's death felt worthwhile. It only makes me hate him.

Alana lets out a small cry of anguish. Gray is so still and silent, it's as if he's frozen. Seeing Leith must have been as shocking for him as it was for me. Without looking, I feel Ivander's eyes on me. I've told him enough about Leith for him to know my world is spinning.

"What about Mother and Eliza?" I ask, voice hoarse. Every part of me wants this to be a nightmare. I want to wake up and go back in time. To when we were a happy family. I remember the nights Lysandra would come have dinner with the five of us. We'd always end up laughing over old stories or games—even Mother. "They're non-Morphics."

Father exhales, as if he's relieved I'm not screaming at him. "Which is why we will not get rid of all of them. But Morphics will have the positions of power. And you, darling. If you can understand, then I won't take anything from you. I'll give you the chance I didn't give you before to keep your magic. You can have a seat on the new council. Right next to me."

I bite my lower lip hard enough to draw blood. I don't believe him. "I came here to ask you to help me. To help make things better for Morphics, but not like this. You don't get to start another war using those you've imprisoned."

Lord Damarcus's expression hardens, a muscle jumping in his cheek. Nostrils flare in his tan face, and it takes everything in me not to recoil on instinct at his authority. "This is how power shifts. It's not pleasant. It's messy." He holds his hand out to me. "I thought you weren't afraid to get your hands dirty."

With his hand extended to me and the pressure of my captors' grips relaxing, I allow myself to wonder if he's right. This is my father, after all. Maybe the price of change must be weighed against the cost of society staying the same. But my mind drifts back to being on the stage with Ivander, conjuring butterflies because I wanted to show him something beautiful. I think of his idea for a school for Morphics—somewhere we could go to learn how to use our gifts. Somewhere that would allow us to make mistakes without punishing us for it. I think of the arrow sticking out of Leith's leg and the potions I drank nightly at dinner. The anger in me intensifies.

There's a new world to build in Tamarynth, but it matters how we do it.

Lord Damarcus's hand falls to his side when I don't accept it.

He sighs. "I knew you couldn't be trusted with this."

Gray shifts on his feet, wary gaze following the potion bottle. "What happens when your soldiers aren't in a trance anymore and don't want to go to war?"

Lord Damarcus pauses, as if it's the first time he's considered that those he's kept confined for so long might not be the obedient soldiers he hoped for. There's the possibility even his son and great general may not be willing to go along with a plan he had no part in creating.

"I hope," Lord Damarcus begins in a low voice, "enough of them will understand why I had to do it. I am acting on my ancestor's wishes. The Damarcus family has always been doing what's best for Morphics."

It's clear to me now. Clearer than I want it to be. My family's great deed, our grand legacy of inventing and investing in the creation of the *Celestial* and the potion to contain Morphia, has been the real threat to Morphics for centuries. That thirst for power is the reason Morphics are failing retrials and suffering on the ship. The reason people are sitting in prison cells, unaware of where they are and why they're there.

How many Morphics boarded the *Celestial* to keep their Morphia and ended up prisoners? How many died in prison for a war that might never come?

I shake my head, heat flaring through my limbs. A muscle twitches near my mouth as I itch to use magic. Anything to escape the hold of my captors. The hold of my father. Alana's words come back to me. *They're in pain. Don't hurt them.*

She must have felt their agony, their misery. I won't hurt them even if I'd give anything to make Lord Damarcus bleed. I don't give a damn about family legacy or responsibility to an ancestor long dead. I care that he lied about Leith and kept him in a prison cell. I care that he tried to extract my Morphia. My father, the person I always knew was proud of me. The only person in my family after Leith to tell me resurrection was a gift, not a curse of nightmares.

Lord Damarcus's brown eyes drop to my flexing fingers. I know what he's wondering. Will crafter cuffs be enough to hold me? He doesn't wait long enough to find out. Motioning for one of Gray's captors to come forward, he withdraws a different potion from the pocket of his waistcoat and passes it to him. "Don't give it to them until I give the command."

When the captor nods and pockets the potion bottle, Lord Damarcus pinches the bridge of his nose again. He looks between me and Gray.

Voice soft, he says, "Take them to Malachite Prison."

CHAPTER 31

I don't know what I expected the most notorious and lethal prison in Tamarynth to look like.

The Hawks deliver Morphic prisoners to Malachite but are never allowed inside. Parents tell children stories about inmates peeking into windows to keep them in bed. Across the provinces, separate divisions of Hawks bring their Morphic prisoners to Credence. I always begged Leith to tell me what it looked like from the outside, and he always found a way to change the subject. As far as I knew, the only people allowed inside were my father, a few of his trusted prison guards, and the prisoners themselves.

It's only after our captors drag us beyond the estate that I realize how close the prison has truly been all this time. During a short carriage ride, we travel past a grove of thick-trunked willow trees, past a black water creek, and arrive at a massive, rectangular expanse of groomed, dead earth.

Colossal stone gargoyles sit at the four corners of the dirt field. There are no carriages hauling prisoners here now. Only the stone gargoyles overgrown with moss and twisting vines interrupt the empty space.

"Where is it?" Alana asks in a trembling voice. After losing her emotions during the attack, she struggles to contain the overwhelming fear now coursing through her. Her teeth chatter, and Ivander reminds her to breathe.

Lord Damarcus has not accompanied us to the prison. All the times he told us he was leaving to deliver a potion to Alexandrite Estate, how often was he coming here?

Gray points to an oval-shaped crater in the center of the dirt field. "Underground."

Only I seem to notice how his finger shakes as he points. Anxiety must be gnawing a hole in his gut. The thought of seeing Leith like our captors, unfocused and unaware, scares me too.

Our captors pause beside one of the gargoyles. As I wonder what we're waiting on, the gargoyle with a square, ghoulish face, curled talons, and large ribbed wings framing its muscular body *moves*.

It stretches its front paws into the dirt, sinking its talons into the dry soil. The gargoyle yawns, revealing pointed teeth on its mossy face. Its eyes glow green as its gaze finds us. Upon scanning our group, it sinks into a low bow, and our captors are allowed to drag us over the perimeter of the dirt field.

Ivander and I lock eyes. No crafter should be able to create such a large, sentient object without the council approving it. But not many council members pay visits to Malachite Prison. Once again, I'm shocked by the depth of my father's deception. It must have taken several crafters to create something so large.

The four of us shuffle our feet as our captors prod us toward the oval-shaped pit. A voice in the back of my head warns me not to go any farther. Not to let myself get dragged into whatever waits beneath the surface.

But I don't have much choice. Even if I managed to break free and make a run for it, one of the captors would catch me. I've tried reaching for my resurrection magic, but it lurks beneath the surface of my skin, unable to emerge within the confines of the cuffs.

Our captors stop at the mouth of the gaping crater in the ground. Alana and I exchange a glance. Her hands tremble against her cuffs. With trepidation, I peer into the hollow abyss. As I look down into the depths, I begin to make out a miniature city in the darkness.

It makes sense, knowing that every province's Morphic prisoners are sent here. Still, I'm unprepared for the sheer size of the underground prison. Two towers of endless cells stand tall in the pit. The only surface connecting the towers to each other is a bridge at the top supported by an iron bar that stretches down to the lowest depths of the prison. The cells have stone floors but are covered on all other sides by a patchwork of bars. Every level has a landing connected by staircases. The landings extend to tunnels carved into the walls of the pit that I assume are used for prison staff and supplies. Guards traverse the staircases with torches in their hands, hauling large potion canisters.

"This can't be real," Ivander whispers beside me.

Given the moans and cries of discomfort, the potion must not be as effective as Lord Damarcus hoped. Our captors push us from the ledge, and I try not to scream. There is only a narrow stone staircase with no railings leading down to the bridge connecting the towers. One misstep, and we fall innumerable stories to our deaths. It's a sickening way to ensure no one can make a quick escape.

After the four of us climb down three or four stories, we make it onto the stable bridge. We are led across to the landing of the uppermost cells in the right tower. For the first time, one of my captors, a woman with cropped, dark hair and dirt smudged into her sunken cheeks, speaks.

"Lord Damarcus keeps us fed and comfortable. We drink our potion in the morning and at night." Her voice has a dull, leaden quality, as if she's reading from a book without comprehending the story. Several low moans erupt from the cells. "Those who don't respond to the potion anymore have their Morphia extracted."

"Then what happens to them?" Gray asks.

The woman doesn't answer, but my stomach flips. If this is how Lord Damarcus treats his future soldiers, what does he have planned for us?

A prison guard approaches us, and a lightning strike of recognition jolts through me. His graying hair and rectangular glasses have been present around our dinner table since I was five years old. He's determined not to look at me and clears his throat as he speaks to our captors. "Take them to the high-security rooms on the lower floor."

"Lord Malechor," I say, desperate to catch his eye, but he walks away without looking at me. The clomp of his boots on the narrow walkway sends sharp pangs of panic through my body. We're not going to get help, so we need ideas.

Our captors, along with several prison guards, lead us down several more flights of narrow staircases. They creak with each step, straining under the force of our weight. The deeper we descend into the prison, the darker and colder it gets. At the bottom level of the tower, we arrive at rooms carved out of stone with bars only in the cell doors.

I am as far from escape as I can get. My chest constricts, tight and painful from the effort of holding back my terror.

Torches are mounted on the tower walls, lighting our way. The prison guards lead the four of us to two separate stone cells. A prison guard unlocks the cells with a large metal key. I note he stores it on a key ring on his belt. Once he swings the cell doors open, our captors shove Ivander and me roughly into one cell, and Gray and Alana into the other.

The bars slam shut behind us. The rattle of them banging shut echoes in the hallway. A guard mutters to another, "Are we giving them a dose?"

Although I can see through the gaps in the bars of the door, I am completely cut off from Gray and Alana by the stone walls on either side. "Not yet. Lord Damarcus wants to make sure he doesn't need them." I exhale gratefully. He must believe we'll come over to his way of thinking. Or he wants to use us as scapegoats for whatever he's planning. Either way, I don't care. I plan never to drink another one of Lord Damarcus's potions again.

There are two beds in this room, about the same size as those on the ship. I've traded one bunk for another. I sink onto one of them and Ivander sits on the bed across from me, its springs creaking. There's a nightstand with a lantern and a few weathered books. We have a small table and chairs, a bucket of water with a bar of soap, and a chest of basic apothecary items. The groaning of the staircases over our heads supplies a constant stream of noise. Between the moaning and thuds of prison guard boots, I can't think.

I put my head in my hands. A body-shaking sob tears through my chest.

I can't hold it back, and this time, I don't try. Tears fall, and my eyes throb, hot and itchy. How did I go from the elation of earning my retrial to sitting here? Put here by my own father. A man I trusted. A man I was proud to call my family. I believed I was part of a long line of alchemers devoted to making Tamarynth better.

"Do you want to talk about it?" Ivander asks softly.

I lift my head, eyes burning and raw. Though my throat is tight, I try to croak out a sound. Nothing comes out. I try again. "Why didn't I see it all sooner? I could have—"

"Could have what? Anticipated your father's betrayal, and what? Killed him? That's not you."

"Maybe it is," I whisper.

"Listen to me," Ivander says. "You're not a killer. You have defended yourself when you needed to. You hurt the people who hurt you. That does not make you your father."

"What if it does?" My shaking subsides, but now the quiet fears have me in a chokehold. These are the fears I only whisper in the dead of night, terrified to make them real. "He believes in what he's doing."

Ivander lets out a dry laugh that vibrates off the stone walls. "Plenty of people believe in what they're doing. Those bosses believed in torturing us. They believed it was worth it so they could use our Morphia. That doesn't make it right." He pauses, unclasping his hands. "I don't think all of them were that way. Stellan . . . I think he let us go."

I hadn't considered that. The thought of it eases the tension in my shoulders. Maybe we weren't the only ones starting to question the way things were running aboard the ship. Now that I think about it, I'm not sure Stellan was there the night of Elayne's murder. He might not have tried to stop it, but maybe he didn't want to be part of it.

I take a breath. "He's lied to me. About my brother. About everything I thought I knew about our family. I should hate him. I think a part of me does. But why . . ."

"Why does it hurt so much to hate him?" Ivander's lips press into a line. "Because he's still your father. The one you remember."

I swallow hard. My mind's still spinning. Every nerve ending in my body senses more than it should. In the span of less than a day, I've been cut down and scattered to the wind. My father was my compass, and I've lost my sense of direction. This will break me.

"Why are you okay right now?" I don't mean for my voice to come out so defensive. I don't have the right to be angry that he's not as defeated and hurt as I am. He didn't know my father before today.

Ivander sits up and leans his back against the stone wall. "Maybe this whole thing has just made me believe in us more. In you." He motions to the spot next to me on the bed. "Is it okay if I sit next to you?"

"Yes," I say, watching him in the lantern light. Soft brown eyes and strong jaw made gold by the fire. When he sits beside me, the warmth of his body calms me. His voice lowers, a deep rumbling as he leans closer. "And is it okay if I touch you?"

I nod, the rush of his heat near my body making it hard to speak. I shudder as he lifts his arms over me, his cuffs settling at the back of my neck. The firm embrace, the pressure of his arms around me, pieces me back together. Somehow, I can breathe again. Finally, the touch of skin against mine is a welcome balm for my frayed nerves rather than the source of my discomfort.

It feels like how it did when Leith believed in me. I remember the warmth well, and now I'm desperate to absorb the faith Ivander has in me.

He lifts his arms, and I bow my head, for once missing the contact of another. We are only parted for a moment, as he then takes my face in his hands, tracing a finger down my freckled cheek. His hand falls to my hair, tugging gently on a strand, but I stay still. He leans over and leaves a kiss on my neck. The pressure of his lips makes me shiver.

He pulls away, tilting my chin up to him. "You never said we were liars when we told you the truth about the *Celestial*. It takes some Morphics months to see the ship for what it is. You looked at every part of that ship with your eyes wide open. You saw the parts that were scary. Beautiful. Sickening. You allowed yourself to see it. Don't you realize how rare that is?"

I don't know how he can still believe in me after everything that's happened. After all my family has done? His hand drops from my hair and rests on the top of my thigh. Warm, with just enough pressure to know he's there. I expect him to stop, but he keeps going, maybe sensing how close I am to giving up.

"You didn't make excuses for any of it. All you thought about was how it needed to change. You don't care about your family legacy as much as you care about what's happening now. That's how you're different from your father. That's why we all fought for you to get your retrial. Why we're here now."

I don't know if the others even got off the ship alive, but I know I tried to give them their best chance. I squeeze his hand over my thigh.

"The lords and ladies of the provinces don't have the answers. It's not the guests on the *Celestial* who are going to change things. It's you and me. The school I want to build. People like Gray and your brother."

Tears sting my eyes, threatening to spill over again. I want to draw him to me and absorb the hope he has for us, but I don't get the chance.

Someone taps against the bars of our cell.

Those light blue eyes and ringlets of soft brown hair are a surprisingly welcome sight.

Eliza dangles a key between a gap in the bars. "If you want a chance of leaving this place, you don't have time to kiss him."

CHAPTER 32

Eliza slides the key into the lock, looking both ways as she wiggles it around until we hear a click. Her knitted brows soften, and she beckons for us to stand. "Hurry. We can't keep the guards distracted forever."

We? My limbs are stiff and heavy, but I force myself to tiptoe toward the cell door. For once, I'm actually excited to see my stuffy sister. Who's looking . . . not so stuffy. Forgoing her usual dress, Eliza wears a sage-green cloak over brown riding pants and a gray lace-up blouse.

She catches my expression and wrinkles her nose. "What are you looking at?" Without waiting for my answer, she whispers, "Drop that cloak. We don't need you running around in bloodstained clothes, drawing more attention to yourself." She tosses a much smaller key to Ivander. "For the cuffs."

As he works to unlock the cuffs, she reaches into a woven bag over her shoulder. She pulls out another pair of brown riding pants, a plum lace-up blouse, and a brown overcoat.

Once he's free, Ivander helps me with my own cuffs. The moment they slide off my wrists, I feel lighter. "Allow me to introduce my sister," I say with a wave toward Eliza.

As Eliza passes pants, a shirt, and a drab black cloak to Ivander, he extends his hand. "I'm Ivander."

"Don't have time," she answers. "I don't care if you fell in love on the ship of nightmares. Introductions later. Both of you, turn around and strip."

My face heats as I pull off my clothes and wiggle my feet into the riding pants. Questions run through my mind. How did Eliza know I was here? Who else is with her? I shrug into my brown coat and open my mouth.

"Nope," Eliza snaps in her bossy whisper. "Don't have time to answer all your burning questions now. I will, I promise." She looks me in the eyes as she says it. "I'm not going to lie to you like he did." She nods to Ivander and motions over my head. "Grab the lantern. It's dark as pitch down here."

Ivander seizes the lantern as I tie the laces of my boots. We follow Eliza, half crouched and silent, out of the cell in the base of the tower. My heart leaps into my throat, but there's no one here. My sister lets out a heavy breath. "Thank the Riveners," she murmurs. "The potion's working."

"We can't make it all the way to the top level without being seen," Ivander says. "Where are we supposed to go?"

"They keep the weapons in a storage room on this level. It's not usually under heavy guard since no one enters this prison without Father's permission. Besides, he cares more about guarding the prisoners," Eliza answers grudgingly.

And I know he can't possibly have an endless supply of men and women willing to work down in this pit.

Eliza motions for us to follow close behind. We're flanked by iron-barred cells and gray stone walls on either side. The cells are unoccupied, or those inside are fast asleep. The number of sleeping prisoners and guards we pass makes me uneasy. The sounds of our boots hitting the floor echo off the walls, and I hold my breath.

The torches offer meager light as Eliza leads us past the staircase heading to the next tower level. Part of me longs to dash up it, find Leith, and try to get as far as we can, no matter who sees us. I have my Morphia back now. But my need for a real explanation outweighs my desire for escape.

We reach the end of the hallway, and Eliza knocks on a great stone door: three fast, two slow. The vast door with its cracked, mossy stones groans as it opens. The sharp scrape of stone against stone sets my teeth on edge.

Ivander's eyes dart back and forth as he holds the lantern out in front of him. He guards Eliza and me from behind, waiting for an attack that never comes. "Get in. They're not going to bite," she barks.

Torches light the weapons room, which resembles a cave more than anywhere else in the prison. With muddy stone beneath our feet and a dome-shaped interior, it feels like I've crawled into a bear's den. That is, if it weren't for the vast piles of crafter-made bows and arrows, pistols, ceremonial swords, and flexible, crafter-made armor resting on the floor. There are even cylindrical iron bodies that might be projectiles.

"Whoa," Ivander gasps, shutting the door behind us. "How long has he been collecting?"

"For generations, we think," Eliza says, leaning against the moist stone wall. I expect her to recoil from the grimy residue soiling her clothes, but she doesn't flinch.

Father must have crafters working with the weapons to make the arrows fly faster. Smugglers have to be providing Father with the materials for weapons, seeing as he's amassed so many I think he could arm all of Tamarynth's forces.

I've barely stepped into the room, Ivander still behind me, when I see the three people clumped together in the dimly lit space. Alana, Gray, and . . .

It has to be him.

He's tall—as tall as Gray—and older than I remember him, with longer dark hair and a scruffy beard over his warm ivory skin. But that twinkle in his eye and easy, lopsided smile gives him away. He takes a small step toward me.

Leith.

He wobbles a little, and Gray steadies him from behind. "Roe?" my brother asks, voice breaking as he speaks. "You're so much older. You were just a little girl—"

I don't wait for him to finish.

Don't wait for him to tell me it's okay. I don't stop to think if I'm comfortable or not because I know I am.

I run to him and throw my arms around his neck.

"Hey," he croons into my hair. Gray holds on to Leith's shoulders to keep me from knocking him over.

I let go fast, sheepish as I shove my hands into my coat pockets. "Sorry. I didn't mean to hurt you. I just . . . can't believe it."

Leith squeezes my shoulders. "I know. I never thought I'd see you again." His eyes dart back to Gray. "Any of you. It still doesn't feel real."

Ivander holds out his hand to Leith. "I've heard so much about you."

Leith's eyes slide from Ivander's outstretched hand to my face, but he never could resist new people. I can't hide my grin at Ivander's second attempt at introductions. Leith smiles and shakes his hand. After a hasty round of hellos where Ivander and Alana introduce themselves to Leith and Eliza, we all stand in the dark, waiting for someone to speak.

"Anyone care to catch us up?" Ivander finally asks. "How did you get us in here without any of the guards noticing?"

I whirl around to face Eliza. "And how did you find out about Leith?"

My sister crosses her arms. "It was a few nights after you left. I overheard Father talking to one of his prison guards. I heard some things I didn't understand. But the more I listened, the more I learned. Leith was being kept in Malachite Prison." Which is when she learned what we had—that Father was planning to use the imprisoned Morphics for an army in a second war. That the *Celestial* was part of his plan.

"I decided to tell Mother," Eliza admits. "I got worried Father was in trouble. And I was worried about you too." Her eyes narrow. "Don't look so shocked."

Once Mother surprisingly got involved, she and Eliza began to learn as much about the Damarcus family tree as they could. Mother, being an accomplished professor, found pieces of research Father hadn't destroyed. Some of his aunt's old diaries, stashed in the floorboards of their bedroom, mentioned the *Celestial*'s original nefarious purpose. My great-aunt called it *the bomb*, and our family was waiting to light the fuse.

As soon as they gathered enough to realize what Father was planning,

Mother sent Lysandra a letter, and the two began working on a plan to free Leith.

"I know they don't usually get along," Eliza adds. "But Mother knows Leith was always there for us." She elbows our brother in the ribs. Despite the playful nudge, he stumbles into Gray, still unsteady on his legs. Gray grips Leith's shoulders hard to keep him from falling and doesn't let go this time. "She knew how hard it was on Lysandra, losing him."

Mother knew she had to tell her. According to Eliza, Mother and Lysandra developed their plan. They knew Father was using a potion to keep Leith unable to fight back, so Eliza snuck in and replaced his potion with a harmless substitute. "It was really hard, by the way. I had to hire a shifter to change my hair and everything."

After a few days of drinking the substitute, he became more aware. It took Mother a while to get a key, but they freed him. Eliza unveils the key from under her cloak now.

"We weren't exactly sure what Father had planned for you, Roe. But the more Mother found out about our ancestors, the more she began to suspect he was trying to take your Morphia."

"That's not all," Leith adds, glancing down at his worn boots. "You asked how we got here without anyone noticing. It's because we put the guards on this floor to sleep. And the other prisoners." He squeezes his eyes shut and lets out a breath. "I used a potion—"

"You're an alchemer," I exclaim once the realization hits me. I don't mean for my voice to come out as loud as it does. For years, people wondered why Leith wasn't an alchemer. It's almost always passed through male family members. "You're a Morphic."

"Father told me it would be too dangerous to tell anyone. Even you two." Leith frowns. "He and my mother were the only people who knew. I thought it was to protect me. Now I think it was to prevent me from stopping him."

"And me," Gray says, careful to avoid my eyes. "I knew."

"Oh, right," Leith adds pleasantly. "Had to tell Gray. I knew he'd think it was sexy."

Gray's cheeks turn bright red. "Stop."

"You both need to stop," Eliza says, tapping her foot. "That potion won't work forever. You're way out of practice. And you know where we're going."

Ivander clears his throat before Leith can say something else to make steam come out of Gray's ears. "I'm glad we have the truth, but we still need to figure out what to do about it."

"Couldn't agree with you more," Leith says. "Personally, I'd like to climb out of this hole and see the sun. Now that I've got this one back, I'll need to work on my tan."

Gray rolls his eyes. "Why would I care about a tan? I'm the palest person you know."

"It's to make you jealous."

"Hey," Eliza snaps. "They need the rest of the bad news."

My throat tightens. How could this get worse?

"Father's decided it's time to mobilize," she says. "There's a council meeting tonight in Aryndar. Carriages have been bringing jars of Morphia here from the *Celestial* for weeks. He's going to unleash raw Morphia and use it to kill the council members."

Father wouldn't do that. Maybe he'd kill the council members, but he wouldn't hurt innocent people. The voice in my head warns me not to trust lines in the sand. He's already crossed more lines for the sake of the world he's trying to build than I ever thought possible.

If he were to open even ten of those jars in Aryndar, that much raw Morphia would infiltrate the province's landscape, its infrastructure. Magic would produce creatures, objects, and places beyond our understanding and control. Tamarynth would look as dangerous as it once did when Morphia was free and not only coursing through Morphics' veins. If Father unleashed crates of it, the whole of Tamarynth could be affected.

Alana, quiet until now in the corner, is the first of us to speak. She takes a step forward into the light. "How do we stop him?"

Eliza taps the tip of her chin. "He's coming here to gather his army. At least, part of it. He'll need to wake them. Some of them have been taking the potion for so long, they'll go with him no matter what he says."

"Others may fight with us," Leith adds. "I've managed to talk to some of them. Convinced them to stop taking their potion. Spit it into the water bucket, that kind of thing." He shrugs at our collective surprised expressions. "I didn't say I couldn't be a general. I just don't want to be his."

"How will we know when Lord Damarcus is here?" Alana asks, glancing uneasily toward the door.

As if on cue, an echoing trumpet sound wafts down to us from above. The thunderous sound of movement overhead scatters dust from the ceiling.

Eliza looks up, biting her lip. "We'll know."

CHAPTER 33

The trumpet blast and Father's arrival snaps us into a chaotic frenzy of action.

Gray examines weapons, distributing some among the six of us. Eliza slings a quiver of crafter-enhanced arrows over her shoulder and passes one to me.

"This is still your weapon, right?" she asks, a smirk pulling her cheeks tight.

We may bicker like sisters do, but that look she gives me warms my chest. Even with Father failing me, I still have family. Family who'd been fighting for me when I didn't know it.

We hurry to slip on armored vests fashioned out of flexible but impenetrable leather fabric and grab as many weapons as we can fit on our belts without weighing us down.

Leith kneels in front of me. "Boot's untied again," he says. "They gave you shit uniforms on that ship."

"Do you remember when we went?" I ask him as I tie my hair up in a thick bun at the back of my head. "It was only a year or so before you disappeared." I smile. "You couldn't get me to come out of the library."

"I remember," Leith says, finishing with the laces of my boot and standing. "Those books you could walk through gave me the creeps. You remember how the scenes came to life? I never understood how you could choose the horror stories when the killer could be standing right next to you. But that was always you." His brow furrows, and the corners of his mouth turn down. "Honestly, that whole ship gave me the creeps. Even then. It just felt off. You'd have felt it, too, if you were older. I know you would have."

My stomach lurches, and though Eliza's giving us all "hurry up" looks, I can't help but ask. "Why do you think he did it?" My voice breaks. "I thought he loved us."

Leith runs a hand through his hair. "I think he did," he finally says. "Maybe even does. I think he believes he's building us a better future, but he forgets we're here, miserable, now."

Gray taps Leith on the shoulder. "It's time to go. Lord Damarcus will be sending someone to collect weapons for the attack. You know what happens if he finds us here."

Leith nods. "Same thing you were afraid he'd do to us if he found us together in the stables." Gray smacks him and Leith mumbles, "Kidding."

"All right," Eliza says, fidgeting with one of her curls. "We're ready."

Except we're not.

All our plans involve harming prisoners who have had no choice for most of their lives. Many may choose to fight by my father's side. They may desire the world he's trying to build and not mind the brutality needed to form it. But that doesn't change the fact that every one of them is a victim. Every one of them is a prisoner, like Leith was.

On top of that, none of us knows the layout of the prison as well as Father or any of the prison guards. Eliza's explained there are underground stone tunnels that connect to the staircase landings on each tower. We'll need to use them to avoid Father's army on the staircases, but she fails to mention how the six of us are going to actually get out of here alive.

And we must find a way to stop an army from leaving this prison. Who knows how many jars of raw Morphia Lord Damarcus has at his disposal? He's been working on this plan for years while we've been working on ours for minutes.

After coming to a final, shaky agreement, we split into groups: Eliza,

Gray, and Leith; Ivander, Alana, and me. "We'll give you all the time we can, Roe," Leith says. "See you on the other side."

I nod to him because it's all I can do. There's a good chance I won't be able to do this. I've never summoned this many spirits. I've never summoned for *as long* as I'll need to for this makeshift plan of ours to work. And if we're caught, we'll be lucky to leave this prison with our lives. It will all have been for nothing.

Alana, Ivander, and I head out of the weapons room and hug the wall in case any of the prison guards are awake again. We follow close behind Leith, Gray, and Eliza, hearing nothing but the distant beat of boots on landings as guards farther up patrol the cells. Each freestanding tower has landings at each level for guards to traverse, but the only way from one tower to the other is over the bridge at the top of the prison. All other travel must occur on the staircases built into the towers or through the tunnels. With the moonlight shining down from the opening, there's nowhere to hide. Nowhere but the tunnels.

I see why Father liked this design. The prisoners don't have much to keep them hidden from view.

We dash into the first tunnel we come across, holding our breath. "Ow, that's my foot," Alana whispers as we jam ourselves into the tunnel's mouth. We make it inside just as a pair of boots hit the ground floor.

"Sorry," I mutter.

"Don't stop," Ivander whispers. "The guards are coming for the weapons. If they see our cells are empty, they'll check the tunnels."

Leith goes ahead of us through a separate fork in the tunnels. Eliza and Gray go with him as guards. Using the materials Eliza smuggled in, he's going to make a potion that will break the prisoners from their trance. This should give them the choice, albeit a hurried one, to choose between joining my father or fleeing the prison.

My hands tremble at my sides. Most of this plan falls on my shoulders. Mine and Leith's.

"How far do we need to get?" Alana asks as she edges forward, kicking loose rocks with her boots. Even with Ivander's lantern, the winding stone tunnels are nearly too dark to see in. A distinct moldy smell complements the steady plink of water on the dusty floor.

"I'm not sure," I whisper. "Do you feel anyone?"

Alana shuts her eyes, searching for the emotions of anyone nearby. I try to void myself of emotion to help her, but the rhythmic thudding of my heart quickens. She blows out a frustrated breath. "It's hard to tell when you're a nervous wreck beside me."

"What about Ivander?" I mumble. "He's throwing you off too."

"Trust me, it's not him." Alana closes her eyes again but runs into the wall. Ivander steadies her.

"Don't feel bad," he says to me with a teasing grin. "I learned to handle my nerves a long time ago. Can't be much of a performer if you get stage fright."

That doesn't give me much confidence that I should be the one shouldering the bulk of the plan. It certainly seems like Gray or Ivander would be the better choice. But here I am, leading this charge against the man who raised me.

No. The man who lied to me.

The dark tunnel takes a sharp upward left turn. We follow it, lungs heaving as we struggle not to cough from the dust. My eyes water, but I force myself to stay quiet. No one's behind us yet, which means we have to use our advantage and stay hidden as long as we can. We need to make it at least halfway up the pit.

Ivander throws out his arm, stopping Alana dead in her tracks. I run into her back, skidding to a stop. I'm about to ask what's wrong when the sounds of heavy boots hitting the tunnel floor and a man's voice send a thrill of fear through my gut.

Boom. Boom. Boom. The footsteps get closer. Should we go back? But where? Even if we backtrack, he'll catch up to us. Any guard knows the tunnels better than we do.

My mouth is so dry I can't make a sound. It wouldn't matter if I could. I have no ideas. No grand plan. I can't stop the frenzied rattle of adrenaline quaking through my body.

A warm hand wraps around mine, squeezing my fingers tight. Alana grips my hand fiercely in her own. The tension in my hands relaxes. No matter what happens, we're all in this together. I won't leave them, and they won't leave me.

The man's close enough now that he sees the light from Ivander's lantern. It's then that I hear the cracking of bone. Sharp, intense fractures of small bones. Ivander's back stiffens, and I realize he's shifting. His fingernails extend into sharp talons, and his skin transforms into rough, armored scales. He grimaces through the pain, but I remember he told me the pain is not as severe as a typical break.

"Who's there?" the guard calls.

When no one calls back a response, the guard finally rounds the corner, coming face-to-face with our small group.

He doesn't have time to scream before Ivander lunges at him. One of his taloned hands sinks into the man's shoulder and the other clamps tight over his mouth.

Blood blooms from the man's shoulder, and he struggles against Ivander's grip as he unsheathes a dagger at his side. He tries to stab Ivander's upper arm, his abdomen, his thigh, but the knife hits armored scales each time. I realize Ivander's copied the Morphic woman who fought him at my family estate. The man's eyes widen as he realizes he's unable to escape.

As Ivander holds him steady, Alana kicks the man hard in the stomach. Ivander's grip slips, and the man falls to his knees gasping. Alana aims another swift kick to his head, knocking him out. She takes some of the herbs Eliza lent us and shoves them into the unconscious man's mouth. "Should keep him knocked out for a few hours."

Ivander and I both gape at her, surprised she knocked the man out so easily. Alana tucks a strand of hair behind her ear and blushes. "I didn't want him to hurt any of us," she mutters.

There's no way to hide the body, so we have to hope no one comes this way. We continue through the tunnels unobstructed, walking in silence except for the occasional debate over which fork in the tunnels to choose. Each step brings us closer to the reality that any one of us could be the next body lying on the ground.

"Stop here," Alana whispers. "I think . . ." She pauses, listening for footsteps. "We've got to be halfway by now. I'm sensing more feeling."

Even if we're not, we've run out of time. If I don't do my part now, we run the risk of Father taking the army with him before we've had a chance to stop them.

Then staircases groan as people pile onto them.

We halt.

Even in the tunnels, the sound reaches us. Father's letting the prisoners out of their cells. He'll have them on their way to the council meeting once he equips them with weapons and armor. I swallow against the bile rising in my throat.

"You can do this," Alana whispers. Her knitted brows and pinched mouth relax into a dreamy expression of vague calm. As she looks at me with that familiar blank expression, I feel a surge in confidence. Without meaning to, I smile. "That's better," she says in a flat tone, but she squeezes my fingers again.

Ivander puts his hand against my back, fingers tracing a path down my spine. I shiver at the pressure. When I meet his eyes, he winks. "Just close your eyes and pretend we're back in the theater."

I let my eyelids flutter shut and lift my arms as I imagine a bright spotlight and heavy satin curtains. I envision the marble witch statues and stars in the ceiling before I rip a hole right through to the spirit world.

CHAPTER 34

When I tear a hole in the boundary between our world and the spiritual plane, it rips a hole in me.

I grit my teeth so hard I'm afraid they'll shatter. My arms, straining with the tension of summoning a horde of spirits, spasm as I hold them in front of me. The cataclysmic power of what I've done jolts from the bottom of my feet to the top of my skull.

The spiritual plane looks as it always does: peaceful, unobstructed by material objects or structures. The silvery, translucent spirits drift on a nonexistent breeze. Some of them ignore my presence while others immediately notice the gaping hole in the protective veil, a wispy curtain of silver fog that's supposed to separate the living from the dead. They rush forward to investigate, and I struggle to hold them back. While the spiritual plane itself, just beyond the veil, serves as an in-between space between the living world and the world beyond, their curtain is not easily torn. I don't know if it's ever been torn.

This is where the plan gets intense. The tear should allow many spirits to pass through, but only those I allow. Spirits race toward the tear. Their eagerness—their curiosity—becomes mine. I find myself wondering what it would be like to let all the spirits through. Would I have the strength to keep them from overrunning our world?

I can't think like that. *Hold them back.*

Vaguely, I'm aware of Ivander and Alana shouting my name. Asking if I'm okay. I shut them out. I can't return to their world yet. I'm not finished in *mine*.

With a powerful shove of my flexed palm, I push the spirits back. That's when I start to summon the spirits I really need. The ones who hurt the most. The ones who cry out to me, begging for a chance at justice.

The spirits come to me fast and without warning, the way a light rainstorm shifts into a sudden downpour. They rush through the crack in the veil. I expect to struggle with knitting the fabric of the spiritual plane back together, but it's as if the spirits know what's going on and want to help me. I slam the hole shut behind them.

When I open my eyes, every hair on my body stands on end. My fingers sting as I concentrate on the tethers between so many spirits. I've summoned more than I ever have before, but it's not the number of spirits that matters. It's who they are.

I have summoned the spirits of Morphics who died in this prison. The ones who died at my father's hand as they waited for a war that never came. The ones who died because of my grandfather. His grandfather. Those who perished on the ship as it sucked them dry and consumed them.

A voice from below startles me. Ivander's voice. "As the dead rise, so will you."

What I take as encouragement is much more.

I realize I'm suspended in the air, floating with the energy of the spirits. I hear screams from the prison guards before I see them. For I *can* see them now.

I can see everything through my spirits' eyes.

With so many spirits now in the prison, I'm unable to make them all solid. Most are half formed, composed of exposed bone, blackened, decaying flesh, and sunken, bloodshot eyes—if there are any eyes at all. But I want it that way.

I want Father to be terrified of what he's done.

"Can you see him?" Alana whispers.

"Yes," I say, now effortlessly calm. I no longer see Alana; I'm rooted to my spirits' eyes. "He's near the prison entrance. At the top between the two towers."

But Father's prisoners are now spilling out of their cells and onto the walkways. They take stumbling steps on unsteady legs. A few, out of practice, fall right off the side of the walkway, tumbling to their deaths below. I take a breath. They're technically in our way, but they're still entranced and unaware of their surroundings.

I see him. My father controlling his prisoners from the bridge. His bushy brows lift, as if he's surprised at the strength of my power. But the stern set of his jaw reminds me he'll show no mercy.

The spirits wait for my command, hovering in midair. The prison guards lose color in their faces as the spirits descend around them.

Father regains his composure, a flush returning to his cheeks. He licks his lips, then bellows, "Don't let her trick you! They're only spirits. They can't hurt you. She won't be able to use so many at once."

My vision snaps back to the tunnels as someone pulls hard on my calf.

"Can't let you float around up there all day," Leith says. He guides me back down to the tunnel floor. A rush of relief overtakes me as the other half of our group joins us in the tunnel. The spirits will continue to wait for my signal.

Eliza guards one end of the tunnel with her arrow strung while Gray brandishes a pistol at the other. I look Leith up and down, searching for the potion vial. Even with the spirits I've managed to conjure, it won't be enough without him. "Did you do it?" I ask.

He reaches into his coat and pulls out a cylindrical bottle with a wooden stopper. The potion inside is a deep shade of cobalt blue. "If this works, thank Eliza. She's the one who brought the ingredients I needed. Wasn't too hard to mix them together."

"Tell her the problem," Gray growls.

Leith sighs. "He's the *lead with the bad news* type. When I uncork the bottle, the potion comes out like a storm. It spreads and multiplies in the air, but downward, like rain. It should work its way through the prisoners, but we need to find a way to get it to all of them. Someone needs to get to the top of the prison and upend it over them."

"The staircases are too crowded," Gray says. "And the tunnels will be swarmed soon. Even with your spirits giving us backup, we can't get high enough, quick enough."

"Damn," I mutter. Our best chance is to keep using the tunnels to make our way up, but all of us know that's going to be too slow. We need some way to get up there faster. The only thing I can think of is handing the potion off to a spirit, but I'm not sure I trust them to remain solid long enough to carry the bottle.

Ivander clears his throat. "I can do it."

When we turn to face him, he continues.

"I've been a performer since I was a kid. Practically all my skills require upper body strength and balance." He nods to me. "I'll climb. There's a bar that runs all the way up to the base of the bridge between the towers. If your spirits can give me cover, I'll get to the top."

My heart drops at the idea of him making this climb alone, but I force myself to nod.

Eliza smirks, clapping Ivander on the back. "I say give it a try. The rest of us will use the tunnels and meet you at the top as soon as we can."

He straightens and takes the potion bottle from Leith. Leith holds up his finger. "Be careful with it. I don't have enough materials to make more."

Ivander nods and pockets the potion. He flexes his fingers and holds his arms over his head, stretching his shoulder muscles, then bends down to touch his toes. As he bends in half, his fingers unravel his boot laces. He removes both shoes and socks. Leith and Gray raise eyebrows as he stands and flexes his feet.

He shrugs at them. "Better traction."

Panic rises inside me. He's about to scale a slick iron beam, with guards and my father trying to stop him. If he falls, he's dead. There's no net. Nothing to catch him. It's hard to breathe knowing I could lose him.

I stand across from him, aware there's no more time to waste for any goodbyes. But my fingertips brush the sharp edge of his shoulder, and I long to pull him close to me. This boy who became my first window into the truth. My first completely real person, not an illusion or a nightmare, on a ship full of them. We let go of our fears together and trusted each other. Now, I stand up for myself *and* my friends. Maybe I can rewrite my family legacy.

I work hard to keep the tremor out of my voice. "Be careful. Just pretend we're onstage."

He pauses, takes a breath. Then leans down to kiss me. His lips brush against mine. His hands trace from my hips up my abdomen to the slope of my shoulders. Then he pulls back and turns away. Leith and Gray smirk at me, but I don't spare them more than a passing glance before my attention returns to Ivander.

As he heads down the tunnel with all of us watching him leave, he takes one last look back at me and winks.

Before he's out of sight, Gray begins ushering us through the tunnels. He kneels, examining the pattern of footprints and dirt to determine which turns to take. Sometimes he holds up his hand to stop our progress. Other times he signals for Eliza and me to pull back on our bowstrings and loose into the stretch of tunnels ahead.

Eliza's crafted arrows always find their marks, slicing through throats before the prison guards can scream. Mine are less dependable, puncturing shoulders before Gray and Leith run ahead to finish the job. My nerves are getting the best of me. The farther we get, the more stops we make. Guards and prisoners spill through the tunnels, either on their way to get weapons below, or coming up behind us as they try to make their way out of the prison.

Soon, we're forced to guard both sides, and our progress is painfully slow. I can't wait any longer. "Alana," I say in a hurried whisper. "I need to help Ivander. Just keep an eye on me and make sure I don't run into any walls. Eliza, you'll be the only one with the bow for now."

"Fine with me," Eliza shoots back. "You haven't exactly been helping."

I purse my lips at her but concentrate on the spirits tethered to me—connected to my life force. No longer using my own vision, I switch to the spirits in the main area of the prison. I shift from seeing through the eyes of a teen girl spirit at the bottom of the prison, to an older man midway up, to a younger boy drifting by the rightward tower.

As I share consciousness with the teen boy spirit, I'm overwhelmed by his own pain. A performer—like Ivander—killed during a rehearsal on the *Celestial*. Strangled by the hanging curtains themselves, despite the other staff members trying to save him.

I'm sorry, I think to him.

The boy responds by deflecting a stray bullet with his hand. While joined with him, I feel his determination—his anger at my father.

I find Ivander climbing the beam and call on more spirits to form a cocoon of silvery, floating corpses around him. "You're faster than I thought you'd be." My voice comes from the boy spirit, sounding too deep in my ears.

"You're slower than I thought you'd be," Ivander fires back as he pulls himself up and uses his feet to brace himself. "Four guards were shooting at me with pistols before any of your spirits showed up."

He keeps climbing, trying to make it to the bridge without falling. He'll need to pull himself all the way up the support beam, flanked by the two towers of emptying cells and legions of prisoners on the stairs. Blood drips from his right shoulder, but he climbs like a spider, fast yet calculated. Each movement of his limbs pulls him closer to the top. His hands are steady, and only a small muscle beside his eye jumps when his foot slips.

I yell. But he catches himself.

"You screamed," he points out, offended that I thought he might fall.

"You don't have a net," I say. "And pretty far to fall."

I realize he hasn't looked down once. He knows how far he has to fall, and we both know my spirits won't be strong enough to catch him the longer I hold on to them. The longer he climbs, the higher he goes. The only way forward is up.

He's two cells from the bridge now.

Although Lord Damarcus can't see Ivander yet, he notices the clump of spirits rising to the top of the prison, level with where he's standing. He calls on the guards to hurry the prisoners' progress. With a start, I realize some of the prisoners have already traversed the treacherous stone stairs and emerged from the prison. Even if we manage to release Leith's potion, it won't stop all of them.

I remind myself we don't need to stop all of them. Just enough to make Father's mission futile.

Ivander hauls himself past the last cells, panting now. He grits his teeth and makes the transfer from the beam to the edge of the bridge my father stands upon. A surge of elation rises in my chest—until Lord Damarcus slams his boot down on Ivander's fingers.

Ivander shouts and lets go, dangling by one hand. I force my spirits to clump around him, creating a net of death if he falls. But the spirits are only partially solid, and I know they won't be able to stop the momentum and weight of a falling body.

Fingers slipping, Ivander uses his one free hand to reach into the folds of his coat. He can't possibly hold on much longer. Digging in hard with his other hand, using talons now to hold him fast to the bridge, he brings the potion bottle to his lips.

Lord Damarcus stomps hard with his boot again, this time on Ivander's other hand. Ivander cries out in pain, but his taloned grip holds. He clamps down on the cork with his teeth and unstoppers the potion bottle.

The lid comes off.

The potion works exactly as Leith said it would.

Rain falls from Ivander's hand. It starts as a slow trickle that smells of eucalyptus and sage and grows to a heavy downpour. Sheets of rain fall on the scores of prisoners marching from the bottom of the prison to the top.

Without warning, too many things happen at once.

Gray, Leith, Eliza, Alana, and my half-conscious body stumble out of the tunnels and across the walkway at the top of the right tower, rushing to meet my father on the main bridge.

The entranced prisoners stop dead in their tracks, even as guards and Lord Damarcus shout for them to keep walking. Then they're brandishing their weapons at the guards or turning them on my spirits, confused. Lord Damarcus didn't plan to keep the Morphics in a trance forever, but there's no way he's got the time to win over the awakened Morphics he's been keeping prisoner. And he knows it.

Father lunges and wraps his fingers around Ivander's neck.

He rips Ivander from the ledge, tearing his talons as Ivander fights to keep his grip. Ivander stays perfectly still and doesn't try to kick or struggle. Leaving the spirit's view and flashing back to my own, I scream.

JULIA ALEXANDRA

"Don't!" I bellow, but I'm not loud enough to be heard over the downpour of rain and echo of confused prisoners.

With another fierce tug, Father yanks Ivander by the neck, dislodging Ivander's talons.

He plunges soundlessly through the air, too surprised to scream.

CHAPTER 35

P resent in my own body again, I lunge forward, but Gray holds me back.

There's a noise from above. Something drops from the sky, through the prison opening stories above us. Two large, feathered strips of cloth fall fast toward Ivander. Not fast enough. As if driven by instinct, I call on my spirits to help in any way they can. A spirit soars toward Ivander, and then time stands still for everything but the falling objects.

A time winder. It occurs to me I've never seen a spirit wield their Morphic gift before. Ivander reaches up and seizes the crafter-made wings, his fingers moving over straps and buckles as he falls. My heart fills my throat as he tries to secure them in place.

Only when the wings extend and catch him in midair do I breathe. Then he's flying, as calm and elegant as ever.

Typical Ivander.

Time speeds up again, and the time winder spirit dissipates. He pumps his arms, gaining strength and speed. With each stroke, he propels himself higher. Lord Damarcus stares down at him, gaping as Ivander flies back to the top level. Alana and Gray grip my wrists tightly, but out of surprise, not to hold me back.

Suddenly, Isla, Niko, and Zora are climbing down from the crater into the prison, leaping down the narrow stairs until they reach the bridge. Zora watches with pride as Ivander uses her creation to fly.

Lord Damarcus gnashes his teeth, but Isla's undeterred. Though she stands at least two heads shorter than my father, Isla walks boldly up to him, Niko beside her. My two friends share a look and then punch him in the face with more force than I knew they had. He stumbles backward as Isla, Niko, and Zora run to us.

I throw my arms around Zora. "Thank you," I murmur. Ivander's alive because of her.

"How'd you get here?" Alana asks our friends, breathless.

"After we helped as many Morphics off the ship as we could, we took a crafter-made carriage to your estate, Roe," Niko explains. "Didn't leave the ship too long after you did. It was a bloodbath. Bosses got violent, but we fought back. When we got to the estate, your mother told us where to find you."

Zora nods. "Your mother sent out warnings to the council members in Aryndar to evacuate. She doesn't know if the message will reach them in time."

The smell of burning wood singes my nostrils, and I look up. Billowing smoke rises into the sky above. "What happened?" I ask.

"Some of the prisoners were aboveground when we got here," Isla says in a low voice. "They're lighting carriages of raw Morphia on fire."

Lord Damarcus stops dead. He stands unmoving for long enough that I wonder if he's going to pass out.

Gray grabs Isla by the shoulder and turns her to face him. "What?"

"We couldn't stop them all," she insists. "The jars were already melting."

"They've lit a fuse," Leith says. "They've released raw Morphia in Tamarynth."

Lord Damarcus curses, dragging a hand down his face. "They weren't supposed to release it. They should have waited for my command."

Before we can determine exactly how bad that is, the prisoners start moving again.

Many of them are desperate to be free of the prison, but others look to guards for instruction after so long trapped down here. Some have even collected on the bridge near Lord Damarcus, probably out of desperation. They have nowhere else to go. Nowhere they remember, anyway.

Ivander lands beside us, his wings falling from his arms. I want to run to him, but when his feet touch down, my father draws a pistol and a knife.

The group of us huddle toward the edge of the bridge, near the rightward tower. With prisoners below us, clamoring to get out, and prison guards prepared to help Father fight, we don't stand a chance of overcoming his forces. Not without my spirits.

"My army will leave this prison," Lord Damarcus says. "Once the council's gone, it will all be gone. The old way dies, and we remake the world."

I think back to what Father said to me back at our estate, when he was dismantling my world. His family legacy had become more important than anything—more important than us. He had to separate himself from the adoring father who loved his family. He thinks this is the way to protect us.

I have to show him he's wrong. I don't need his protection. Not anymore.

I push my way to the front of the group. Father's eyes soften, and his mouth sags as he shakes his head. "Roe, you don't know what the world is like. You didn't see the homes burning because Malyk thought Morphics were inside, plotting against the council." He drops the pistol to his side. "The menders forced to work in infirmaries. The number of times the council looked the other way when Morphics were killed or kidnapped. We are not as far from Gryndar or Correndra as you think. One alchemer on the council has no chance of changing that."

"You were the one who kept it all from me." I raise my arms, and the spirits form a dense cloud of floating bodies rising from the bottom of the prison to where we stand. "Look around you," I say. "You've killed more Morphics than a war could. All because you were chasing a goal from centuries ago. The *Celestial* wasn't worth it, and a war isn't the answer." I pause. "It's not my answer. Not when this is the price."

Lord Damarcus raises his pistol again. "You think *you* can do better?" I force myself not to step back. If he was going to shoot me, he would have done it already. "I'm sorry, my daughter, but I'm an alchemer. I pay no price."

I can't stop the dull, humorless laugh that rises from the back of my throat. "You have no daughters. No son. No wife. Not after what you've done. Have you not paid?"

Without waiting for his answer, I let loose an expulsion of energy. The spirits, with their misery and agony and wasted lives, advance on Father. They form a thick tornado of silvery corpses, their bones protruding through half-formed skin caked with dried blood left over from old wounds.

Father cries out for his guards and his soldiers to defend him. Confused prisoners race to protect the man they still think is their leader, but they can't get past my friends and siblings. The guards shoot from where they stand, unwilling to get too close to my swirling vortex of spirits. Bullets ricochet off the cyclone.

"Stay back," Gray shouts at us. Leith freezes behind him, unable to tear his eyes away from Father.

Eliza draws an arrow back on her bowstring, aiming for Father. "Don't come any closer, or I will shoot."

"I'm not afraid of you," Lord Damarcus says, swinging his knife at the spirits as they reach out with bony fingers.

He might be talking to the spirits—the deaths he's responsible for—but I wonder if he's talking to us, my siblings. Me. For so long, he wanted me to know the world would think my gift was scary. Unnatural. But it wasn't the world that taught me my magic was the frightening kind.

"You are afraid," I say, walking right through the center of my tornado of spirits. I glide through the dense cloud, untouched. "You were so afraid of me that you tried to take my Morphia. Twice."

With a powerful shove of energy, I knock Lord Damarcus off his feet, and he's sucked into the vortex. I raise my hands over my head, lifting him high from the prison. My friends and I follow. They clamber up the steep stone steps and out of the bottomless pit of Malachite as I drift with the spirits. It's a bit like floating in water, serene and effortless.

Outside, the prisoners waiting beside the large gargoyles back away from the tornado of energy. When I let my father drop to the ground, the pistol and dagger fly from his hands. I look to the weapons, wanting to hurt him, but I feel a hand on my arm.

Alana stands beside me. Ivander, Gray, and Niko cross to the soldiers waiting by the gargoyles to explain and orient them, to give them the choice Lord Damarcus didn't.

"Let me," Alana says. "For a man who's never felt empathy, I'll bring him to his knees."

I nod.

She stares into the distance, unseeing as she concentrates. The lines between her brows disappear, but Father doubles over. His raw, tortured screams make me want to stop her, but I recognize them. They're the screams of Lysandra when she learned Leith had died. The tears streaming down his face are mine the night after I was first tortured by the bosses. His knees hit the ground, and the confusion on his face is the same I'm sure Mother felt learning her husband lost so much of himself to violence and greed.

Lord Damarcus clutches his heart, clawing at his chest. It's the same heartbreak Eliza and I felt when we learned our brother was never coming home. The same pain Leith felt as a prisoner for almost half his life.

A young spirit approaches my father then. Despite the corpse-like appearances of the other dead, she appears whole. Her blue eyes are bright, and her freckled skin reminds me of my own. Her brown hair, arranged in a tightly woven crown from the day she died, barely blows in the wind from my waning tornado.

Father hunches over, breathing hard as raw emotion overtakes him. The small girl bends over and touches his cheek. When her fingers brush his skin, he looks up at her. His mouth goes slack, and it takes me a moment to realize why.

The expanse of space, aboveground over the prison, devoid of trees and obstructions, begins to shift. From the slack jaws and wide eyes around me, I gather everyone else is seeing it too. An illusion takes shape: Burning estates, a leveled forest with animals and trees flattened. The dirt on the ground runs red with blood. I hear the pop of pistol fire and the boom of an explosive weapon. Bodies lie on the battleground, torn apart. Young and old alike.

This young girl's showing a war neither side is winning. A future.

"There is no victor," the spirit girl whispers in an echoing voice all of us hear.

As she walks away, her head turns to me. She's beautiful. Not a single hair out of place in her braids. My breath catches as I look at her.

"Karynna."

With that, I lose my grip on my spirits. Tears stream down my face, and my connection to them falters. Their forms turn hazy until they start to disappear. One by one and then all at once, returning to the spiritual plane and the world beyond it.

Alana lets go, freeing Father from the emotions racking his frame. Isla and Zora help Alana stand. Her legs tremble from the loss of energy. When the scene falls away, Gray lunges forward. He grabs Lord Damarcus from behind, securing his arms in a powerful hold so he can't escape. A Hawk until the end. He's caught the most dangerous Morphic yet.

Suddenly next to me, Ivander puts a hand on my arm as Niko holds two pistols out in front of him, arms shaking. My friends form a defensive circle. Now that the spirits have disappeared, the prisoners could overtake us.

But the prisoners aren't watching us. They're watching Father.

"What do we do now?" Ivander whispers at my ear.

I step forward, approaching my father as Gray holds him in place.

Eliza and Leith stand behind me. Gray pushes his knee into Father's back. Eliza's arrow is aimed at his throat, but Leith's hand grazes my shoulder. "Please," he says.

I don't know what he wants me to do with him, but it's the same desperation I feel. The urge to spare my own flesh and blood. To not end up like him.

"I don't know what the world will do with you," I say to my father. He peers up at me through familiar brown eyes, narrowed at me. "But it won't be by my hand. You will go before the High Council. They will decide your fate." I hold his gaze. "I cannot kill my father."

Father smiles up at me. A pained half smile. For a moment, I see the man who raised me. "One day you'll see this was the only way."

I pause. "I know you have to believe that."

Without another word to him, I nod to Gray. Eliza lowers her bow, but she stares daggers at our father. Leith squeezes my hand. Zora crafts metal from the pistols to fashion cuffs. Ivander and I begin to help the rest of the prisoners pouring out from the underground prison.

Many of the prisoners glare at my father, resenting their imprisonment. Others look reluctant, as if they might have followed my father, had he been free. There's no way of knowing how deeply Father's potion affected them. Even scarier, how deeply his belief affected them too.

Gray's eyes narrow as he locks the cuffs around Father's wrists. "We don't know what the council will do with him. They might pardon him."

It doesn't matter. I won't stop a war by killing my father. Even if the part of me buried deep inside, sometimes hidden even from me, wants to leave his lifeless body on the ground. I won't kill him, but if I let him go and allow his army to follow him, the council won't want to hear my side of things. My province would assume I sympathized with his cause, and I could say goodbye to any chance of sitting on the council myself.

It's time the council had a new Damarcus, anyway.

CHAPTER 36

ONE YEAR LATER

In the early morning hours, Eliza and I take a carriage to Almanac's Boarding School. Dewdrops glitter on the grass, and fog rolls over the hills of Credence. The brisk chill of winter has come early this year. I pull the fur-lined edge of my cloak tighter beneath my chin.

I wear a sapphire-blue dress with a laced silver bodice and a full-bodied skirt. My hair loses some of its auburn shine as the days grow shorter, but my freckles never fade. With trembling fingers, I tug on the pendant of my necklace. Engraved with the Damarcus family sigil—a potion bottle with a wisp of smoke twisting around it—I never take it off. I won't forget the true Damarcus family legacy. I won't brush it away like it never existed.

"Quit fidgeting." Eliza leans forward and smacks my hand. She wears a pale peach dress with rose quartz beaded along the bodice. Her light brown hair is pulled into a tight bun, with curled tendrils hanging beside her face. "He doesn't need to know you're nervous."

How could I not be nervous? So much has changed in the year after I turned my father in to the High Council. The council held a month-long session where they questioned me, my friends, my siblings, prisoners, and of course, my father.

Father didn't lie. He spoke measuredly and never looked at me once. Mother cried through the whole thing.

Most of the prisoners went immediately to physicians and menders and then back to their families, if they could remember them. Families were ordered to keep them homebound until after the trial, and Tamarynth soldiers enforced the rule by patrolling the provinces for any sign of unrest. Those with no relatives went to a boardinghouse—one I now help fund.

The council's still trying to figure out what to do with them. Can the formerly imprisoned Morphics be trusted?

The High Council questioned me individually for days—the interrogations felt endless. They were reluctant to let me take my father's place on the council. Wealthy lords and ladies of Aryndar spoke out against my appointment, but the Morphics in Credence have been writing me letters of support. They want more, and they're not alone. Boss Stellan even came and spoke in my defense and described the deteriorating conditions of the ship. Morphics and their families from every province have been writing letters to the council detailing the ways in which they desire change. I'm finally helping shed light on the crimes, subtle and blatant, committed against Morphics, ones that I didn't see before. Or didn't know to look for. Father hid so much from me.

Eventually, the lords and ladies of Credence voted for my ascension. Tensions have never been higher, and they still need Morphics on their side. It helps many of them knew me personally and respected my Morphia from when I helped them connect to lost family. Now, I think they're even starting to respect my ideas for change.

Of course, this all threw Tamarynth into a new kind of uproar. News of what Lord Damarcus had done traveled fast. His family's plans for the *Celestial*. His treatment of Morphics in Malachite Prison. The Damarcus name became highly unpopular with Morphics and non-Morphics alike. And I agreed with them. I hated the name almost as much as they did, but I didn't let that stop me. With Mother's help, I assumed control of Damarcus Estate. Leith preferred working with the Hawks and needed time to recover from prison. Eliza thought it would send a bad message if we replaced Father with a non-Morphic.

So, there I was. Lady Roe Damarcus of Damarcus Estate, newest member of the council.

I'm terrified a unanimous vote from the council members could force me out, but I'm doing what I can in the meantime.

Now, Morphics caught using their magic in a dangerous way are sent to a school rather than prison. I've advocated for all boarding schools to have a Morphic training program implemented within their regular studies. That has been a headache in itself since the stuffy, rich families who fund the boarding schools are reluctant to have any changes at all. We're working to add more Morphic council members from each of the provinces. That's been a struggle too. I can feel the fear like I'm borrowing Alana's magic.

The fear that Morphics are getting too powerful. The fear that if there is another war, we might win.

I'll do everything I can to ensure peace. Although I wanted to get rid of the trials immediately, fast change is hard, so we've tried our best to repurpose them. Those who fail their trials take remedial courses at the universities. Ivander's been developing the curriculum with my mother's help.

A larger question was what to do with Father. The council didn't have long to decide. After the first two weeks of the trial, Father escaped his imprisonment.

No one knows how he managed it. They suspected me at first, but after numerous individuals corroborated my story of what happened in the prison, the council eased up on me. They realized it would have been easier for my father and me to start a war than for me to turn him in and then help him escape. Rumors say he's hiding out in Carodmoor Forest. Gray and Leith swear that's a lie. They spend almost every day out in those woods training the Hawks. When they're not training, Gray and Leith travel to other provinces, revamping their Hawk programs—

Eliza pinches my forearm, startling me. "We're almost there. Didn't you say you needed to read that letter?"

Of course. The letter from Asralyn. She's tried to send them every two weeks since they started the Morphia Discovery Center. Now that raw Morphia's been released in Tamarynth, the world is changing. Asralyn's helping people become less afraid of the magic. The same way she's had to teach herself. We thought rogue Morphia would be just that—rogue and unpredictable. But instead, with room to breathe, it's just like the Morphics on the ship and in Father's prison.

It's freed.

I unfold the letter, inhaling the rosewater scent of her expensive perfume.

Dear Roe,

I hope you're well. Vance won't talk about anything but the discovery center. What exhibits we'll have and how best to showcase the way Morphia's changing everything. Just yesterday, we found a lemon in the garden that tasted like sunlight. Sunlight! Ezra and Sage were beside themselves. That reminds me, Sage was painting, and her paints started to move. Just like they did on the Celestial. *She was so excited. I'll admit I was a little frightened, but Vance reminded me it would make a good museum piece. I suppose he's right.*

I know it's all conjecture at the moment, but do you know if it's true what they're saying? That with the release of raw Morphia, it could bring spirits into our world too. I think you know why I ask. I don't know if I could handle seeing her and knowing she's not really here.

Every day's a new discovery, it seems.

Speaking of, what are they doing with that damn ship?

My best,
Lady Asralyn Stallard

My cheeks hurt from smiling. I may have lost a father, but with Asralyn checking in on me, I've gained as much as I've lost. I can't answer her question about the spirits. I suppose the changes could affect the spirit world, too, but I haven't felt the same shift there we've felt everywhere else.

Niko's told me stories of hearth fruits he's harvested for his kitchen that transport him into memories. Ivander and Mother talk about students who daydream in class and end up seeing things that aren't there, just as illusives do. Gray reports from the infirmaries, where patients have had their broken bones spontaneously mend.

It's a new world I hope Asralyn's Morphia Discovery Center will help us navigate. She's documenting new appearances of magic and helping non-Morphics navigate the changes in their environment.

As for the *Celestial*, Zora and other crafters have begun repurposing the ship. What started as a project to rehabilitate it shifted when they discovered the Morphia inside had taken over. It seemed the power of the raw Morphia flooding Tamarynth had a startling effect on the ship, starting with the jars on board melting into the floorboards. Once dangerous at night, the ship's now a danger all the time. I voted to destroy the ship. The council voted against me. They want to repurpose it, but I'm unsure what purpose that might be. Isla and Zora moved close by to oversee the process in Windmere Port. "Better to know what's going on than be lied to again," Zora had said.

We bump along cobblestones as we pull between thick willow trees in the shadow of an immense school. With stone walls and sharp turrets, the boarding school resembles a palace. Warm light glows in the windowpanes, and off to the side of the school, a greenhouse lets students out for the day. I don't know if anything I've done has made a difference, but here, as the carriage rolls to a stop in front of Almanac's Boarding School, I know something we've done has been for the better.

Children run outside with books in their hands and smiles on their faces. They point to the carriage and whisper to each other.

Eliza steps out of the carriage just as the school's massive, ivy-covered wooden doors creak open. With my heart fluttering in my chest, I lift my skirts as I step down onto the stony carriage path and tell the driver to wait for us here.

Eliza takes my arm. "Do I need to wipe the drool off your chin?"

Ivander steps out onto the stairs and into the sunlight, brown eyes crinkling at the corners as he smiles.

He wears a deep blue vest with bronze buttons and a long-sleeved black tunic shirt underneath. He has a black coat with intricate braided trim and the same bronze buttons as his vest. The coat is a little too fitted and long in the back for any professor I remember in school, but maybe I would have paid more attention had they all looked like him. He looks every part the professor, which makes me want to do all kinds of things with him.

I grin back. Despite filling his new role as teacher well, he can't help but wear a long, elegant coat more befitting of a performer. Behind him, Alana pushes open the door and runs across the grass to meet us. She throws her arms around Eliza in a tight hug. She stops when she gets to me, bouncing on her heels as she waits.

I nod and hold my arms out to her, and we embrace.

"Niko wanted to see you both, too, but he's busy with the lunch crowd," Alana says. Her dark hair cascades down her shoulders, and she wears a long brown skirt with a maroon vest.

Eliza shivers and points toward the doors as kids brush past us, running back inside the school. "Well, go on. Show us what you've been working on. We're freezing out here."

Although the air's getting brisk, it's not cold. Not yet. Winter is still a month off. I know my sister's desire to get inside stems more from nerves than anything else. After everything that's happened, she's as desperate as I am to believe we've done something worthwhile.

"Right this way, my lady," Ivander says with a flourish and bow. "If it's all the same to you, I'd like to escort Lady Rosaline."

Eliza drops my arm and links her arm with Alana's. "Go ahead."

The way he says my full name makes me shiver as if a wispy spirit touched my skin. The pressure of his arm over mine after writing endless letters and sneaking in weekend visits makes my body heat from the inside out.

As we walk over the cherrywood floors, under massive chandeliers, and past multiple marble staircases, he points out changes as we pass them.

Although Eliza and I both went to school here, most of the wealthy donors were reluctant to embrace our new ideas. They weren't excited about allowing their hallowed halls to include a Morphic education department. They especially didn't like the idea of a "nobody" performer with shifter Morphia and a dance background spearheading the program. However, after a few fancy dinner parties thrown by me, plus Ivander's network of influence he curated with the upper class aboard the ship, the donors allowed a trial run at Almanac's. The council agreed as long as I took responsibility for any negative consequences.

I don't recognize some of the hallways. Decorated with colorful flowers and paintings by the students, it's a far cry from the dusty portraits of old men that adorned the walls before.

"As you know, Ivander and I don't run this place—"

"Yet," Ivander interrupts.

"Yet," Alana concedes. "So, we've had to compromise on a few things. But I think the changes we've made have really helped."

They've revamped the history class to include the true history of the *Celestial* and the Damarcus motivation for stopping the war. My stomach twists as they talk about the class. I'm glad the students are learning the truth, but sometimes I still can't believe it's real.

"We've shut down the extraction room," Ivander says. "Extractions should never be performed at a school, anyway. And it scared the kids to have it there in the first place."

He goes on to explain—for too long, if Alana's and Eliza's glazed expressions are any indication—how he's running the drama program for the kids. He helps with the performances and has even squeezed in an aerial silks class.

"But," Alana says, pushing open the door to what used to be one of the cafeterias, "this is our crowning achievement."

The interior steals my breath away. It's not the stuffy lecture hall I remember eating lunch alone in when I was a kid. There's a stage in one corner with a set of silks hanging from battens and a net to catch kids if they fall. Another corner of the room holds a kitchen set with a wood-burning stove, an ice chest, and more knife sets than Isla would know what to do with. In the center of the room, there's a circle of plush pillows serving as chairs, with incense burners providing a calming ambience.

In another corner of the room there's a wardrobe of materials—I'm assuming for crafters—that students are working with now. On the far-left wall, there's a large chasm of black paint and an hourglass. That section is for the illusives and time winders. The illusives can project their illusions on the black paint while they're starting out, Ivander tells us.

And honestly, I have no idea how you teach a time winder, but I'm sure they're figuring it out.

"We have at least one Morphic with each skill to teach the kids," Alana explains. "Shifters, enhancers, emotives, illusives, time winders, crafters, and menders. The menders mostly learn in the infirmary."

"We haven't had any alchemers yet," Ivander adds. "Or resurrectors. But we'll be ready when we do."

"It's incredible," I whisper, breathless. Eliza grabs my hand in silence. I wonder, if she had a place like this, would she have given up her Morphia?

I swallow the lump in my throat. Ivander takes my hand when Eliza lets go. His gentle touch makes me want to break after holding so much in for the past year. But I don't break. The Lady of Damarcus Estate can't allow herself to crumble.

"It's just like we talked about," he says. "My mother has even agreed to come help with the time winder training." His voice lowers, quieter now than it was before. "She's been wishing she could get her Morphia back. If an alchemer could create a potion to take Morphia, couldn't your brother make a potion to give it back?"

I don't answer at first. Leith's considered it, of course. How could he not? But the danger involved in trying to give someone Morphia makes us pause. Not just the idea of giving it back to someone who lost it, but what happens when non-Morphics decide they want Morphia too?

Leith has no idea what the effects of a potion like that would be, but I don't take away Ivander's hope for his mother. Instead, I squeeze his hand back and look him in the eye, giving him the only truth I've been able to provide lately. "I don't know."

Reluctantly, Ivander lets go of my hand and crosses to the stage. "I want to show you something." He removes his coat and tosses it to the floor. The closer he gets to the stage, the more children make their way over. By the time he takes the stage, a small crowd has formed around Alana, Eliza, and me. They gaze up at Ivander with wide eyes and half-parted lips. Even Niko watches us from the doorway. He holds a tray of candied gortha pods in one hand and waves to me with the other.

Ivander climbs up the silks, pulling himself to the top. He dangles there, muscles rippling in the way that makes my body melt. As I hear the familiar crack of his bones, he grits his teeth. "This trick is not for any of you," he says to the kids.

As the cracking continues, webbed skin sprouts from his arms, changing into a dark bluish-black color. It takes me a moment to realize what he's creating until the skin extends and showcases the thin boning running up and down what is now clearly a wing. Without warning, he drops from the silks.

This time, he doesn't need the silks. He catches himself with shifted wings and soars throughout the classroom.

The kids whoop and exclaim with excitement as he somersaults in the air, landing lightly on the ground.

"You look impressed," Ivander says, stopping in front of me. He breathes hard from the exertion but smiles anyway.

I hurry to close my mouth and shrug. "I've seen it a hundred times, actually."

But even I know this shouldn't be possible—not before raw Morphia was released. The freed Morphia is making us stronger.

"Zora gave me the idea," he says. With the flourishes and showman skills of a born performer, he turns a hand to me. His beaming smile makes the children fall silent. "Now, please welcome our special guest as she takes the stage."

I want to murder him. I've practiced on the silks, but if he thinks I'm getting up there and performing for these kids who've been watching *him* for the past few months, he's going to be disappointed.

But his next words surprise me. "Roe's a resurrector, and she's going to give you a demonstration of what she can do."

My heart drops. I wasn't allowed to do much resurrecting back in school, although that didn't really stop me. "Are you sure?"

"Never been more sure," he answers. As I walk up the stage steps with blood roaring in my ears, he says, "Show them something beautiful."

I take a breath and conjure a spirit. Easily. I give them an animal. A large gray horse with powerful legs and white socks on his feet. Although most of him appears solid and lifelike, patches of skin on his face are missing, revealing exposed bone and chunks of brown, decaying flesh. He snorts, pawing at the ground.

"Whoa!" one boy yells.

"That's scary," a girl screeches, running to the back of the crowd.

But another girl with dark, curly hair and a gap between her front teeth approaches the stage. She reaches up toward the horse's nose as he leans down to sniff her hand. Ivander gives her an encouraging nod. "It's okay, Adri. You can touch her."

This must be his niece. Now I'm even more nervous. I wait for Adrionna to approach and hold my breath. Her fingers graze the bone, and she murmurs, "Cool." My throat tightens as her cheeks dimple. She grins at Ivander. "Can I take one home to show Mother?"

My chest warms as Ivander and I both laugh. Tears threaten at the corners of my eyes. The children are not afraid of me.

I summon again. This time, not being so careful to make the spirit look fully formed. A little bone peeking through here. A little blood there. "Scary isn't always a bad thing," I say.

Resurrection saved my life. What looks like a nightmare to everyone else has been my greatest strength. It only took my friends telling me it was beautiful—showing me that I was good—to help me see I didn't need to be afraid of myself. Now I'm never going back. If Tamarynth decides the Morphics are too terrifying, then I will show them how we're beautiful.

I'll always try for peace, not war, like my father. But if this realm decides Morphics need to burn, then I'll remind them what we can do. I won't hold back. I take Ivander's hand in mine, and his touch anchors me to the future we want to build together. When I meet his fierce brown eyes, the belief he has in me ignites.

I will let the dead rise.

ACKNOWLEDGMENTS

For the readers who disappear into fantasy worlds and choose to escape reality within book pages, thank you for choosing this one. I'm honored you sailed on the *Celestial* with me, and I hope you discovered a new found family within its pages.

Books are a source of magic in a world that at times seems utterly bereft of it. Hold on to them.

First and foremost, I must thank my incomparable agent, Ellen Goff. Ellen, you have been my steadfast guide through this wonderful journey, and I knew you were the one from our first conversation. You've been endlessly understanding and supportive. I cannot wait to see where the sea takes us.

To my incredible editor, Eileen Rothschild, you truly understood this book and loved it as much as I did. I left every conversation with you feeling even more amazed by your endless support for Roe and her journey on the *Celestial*. The faith you put in me gave me faith in myself.

I want to thank my entire Wednesday team for the incredible amount of work you put into getting this book ready for publication. I'm ceaselessly inspired by your efforts. To Char Dreyer, for guiding me through every step of this process and answering all my questions with so much enthusiasm and compassion. To Austin Adams, Brant Janeway, Alyssa Gamello, and Cassie Gutman: You are an extraordinary team. Thank you to Merilee Croft, Jen Edwards, Kerri Resnick, Lena Shekhter, and

ACKNOWLEDGMENTS

Alexis Neuville for all of your hard work. Thank you to the entire HG Literary team for always being there with any support I needed.

To my copyeditor, Michelle Li, your kindness in comments and attention to detail left me in awe. Thank you to Sarah and Bianca for your insightful reflections and care with this story. To Tlotlo Tsamaase, you gave me such thoughtful, detailed, and knowledgeable feedback. I'm truly grateful for your assistance in enhancing Ivander and for your kind words. Your help meant so much to me, and I'm so grateful to have met you.

To Micaela Alcaino: From the initial cover sketches, I knew you would bring the *Celestial* to life in all its majestic beauty. The end result is nothing short of spectacular. You have fulfilled my childhood dream of seeing this gorgeous cover on a shelf and knowing it's mine.

For those who helped this book make it to new countries, thank you. Thank you to the entire team at First Ink for all your hard work. I am so grateful to have such an incredible UK team working with me. To Charlie Castelletti, you truly believed in this book and in me, and for that, you have my endless gratitude. To Emma Jones for taking this book the rest of the way. Thank you to Imogen Bovill and the team at Abner Stein. Thank you to Julia Demchenko and Martyna Kowalewska-Martycz.

To my wondrous writing friends: I always considered myself a solitary writer. I thought my sister would be the only one I could depend on to share this journey. I'm grateful to report that I was very wrong. Samika Parab, you have been an invaluable source of support both as a brilliant writer yourself and as a wonderful person who I connected with instantly. You were the first besides Caitlyn to read MOTC. C. D'Angelo, you truly understand both sides of this journey. I have never met anyone who shares the same passion I have for mental health and for writing books. Shalini Abeysekara, you are genuinely one of the most kindhearted people I've ever met, and our every conversation leaves me feeling uplifted and encouraged. Your debut is a new forever favorite. Thank you Bori Cser and Mikayla Bridges. We are the "Favourites"! Leslie Vedder, Kamilah Cole, and Dana Swift, thank you for your endless support and for writing incredible books I have fallen in love with.

To my incredible street team, you have surpassed my wildest expecta-

ACKNOWLEDGMENTS

tions and shown more love and support for this book than I ever thought possible. To the 2026 Debut Writers' discord, I truly do not know what I would have done without you. To my monthly Wednesday group, I'm so grateful to share the experience of becoming debut authors and navigating the mysterious, wondrous world of publishing together. For every reader, reviewer, book influencer, artist, and creative who shared words or content in support of this book, never underestimate the power of your love for a debut author who never thought she'd get here. I will carry your love with me beyond this book.

Tzeyi Koay, there are no words to describe what your friendship has meant to me, but the word I'll settle on is life-changing. I never knew I could connect with someone so deeply and so quickly and share everything writing and life-related. You are not only a phenomenal writer but a cherished friend. I'm so grateful for you, triplet!

To Alyse Bailey, you were the first to believe in my books outside of my family. I still remember you reading an early draft of *Celestial* and saying, "This is the one!" I'm grateful for all the wonderful feedback you gave me that has not only enhanced my books but shaped me into a stronger, more confident writer.

Thank you to all my friends who have helped me get here. I wish I could include every person who has had an impact on me, but word constraints have always been my downfall. To Eileen Sanchez, who sat next to me in our first graduate school class and became my best friend. Our friendship is eternal. To Ashton Horton, Lauren Saarela, and Alexia McKendrick, for being forever friends. To my Life Journey team, who has cheered me on every step of the way and shared in this process from my first editor meeting to publication. To every teacher who has believed in my writing and encouraged me to dream.

Finally, for my family, thank you. To Granddad, for giving me typewriter Snoopy and showing me you believed in my writing when I didn't know how much you'd noticed. I know you would be so proud of me. To Cindy, who shows me what it is to love everyone and always think of others before yourself. To Grandmama and Granddaddy Mac, for your steadfast love and support. To Tita and Papa, for being my second home and giving me more love than any one person should hope to experience.

ACKNOWLEDGMENTS

To Dad, Bridgette, and Reagan, for supporting me endlessly. Ray, you talked to me about my books as if they were real long before they were.

Dad, you have never missed a chance to tell me how proud you are. I know if I need anything, you are there. Thank you for being the secret captain of the *Celestial*.

Mom, you gave me my love of reading long before I knew how grateful I would be for it. Your love for books became mine. You will always be here for every step, for good.

Above all, I must thank you, Caitlyn. For without you, none of this would have been possible. When I didn't believe, you believed in it for me. When I was afraid no one would like this book, you loved it for me. When I wanted to give up, you told me I would make it one day. Whenever I asked you in a moment of utter despair if I would get an agent and a deal, you said with certainty, "Yes." I will never forget your unwavering certainty. And Caitlyn . . . you were right.

Since we were kids, we played make-believe and lived in the worlds of stories as if they were real. Now, you help me make them a reality. This book could not exist without you. *I* could not exist without you. You are my best friend, and I cannot wait to see where we go from here.

Now, on to the next magical adventure.

ABOUT THE AUTHOR

Shaylene Pase

Julia Alexandra lives in Orlando, Florida, with her best friend, who also happens to be her twin sister. Julia can be found writing fantasy stories with magic, danger and chaotic found families. She is passionate about mental health and is grateful to have writing on her own mental health journey. Julia writes for those who find magical worlds a comforting escape from their own. She enjoys reading, collecting too many stuffed animals, and writing to fantasy orchestral music.

If you enjoyed *Midnight on the Celestial*, why not try these First Ink books . . .

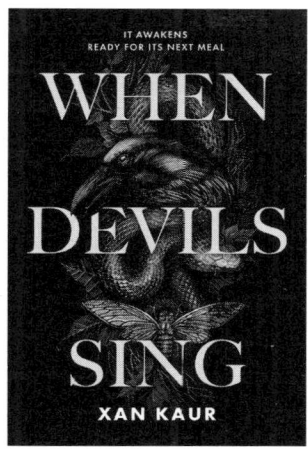

When Devils Sing
Xan Kaur

We Are Hunted
Tomi Oyemakinde

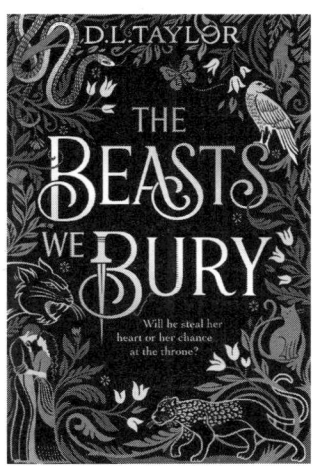

The Beasts We Bury
D. L. Taylor

The Sleepless
Jen Williams

@firstinkbooks